RISE OF THE DEVA'SHI

JENNIFER ALLIS PROVOST

Bellatrix Press

BELLATRIX PRESS

Rise the Deva'shi

Book Three of the Chronicles of Parthalan

By Jennifer Allis Provost

http://authorjenniferallisprovost.com/

Ebook Edition

Copyright © [2017] by [Jennifer Allis Provost]

All rights reserved.

Cover Design by Cover Villain http://covervillain.com/

This book is available in print at most online retailers.

Contents

PROLOGUE

“Tera!”

“Not now, Sasha,” Latera yelled, then she turned back to her other sisters, Elia and Jannei. Latera was certain that whatever Sasha wanted wasn't nearly as important as the daisy chains they were making.

“Tera?”

Latera sighed; if Sasha told their mother that her cries had been ignored, Latera would be punished. She dropped the flowers and followed her sister's voice, and found her at the edge of the pond. Latera sat next to Sasha, and looked at their reflections. All four sisters had the same sky blue eyes, their father's legacy, and the younger three bore his golden curls. Only Latera had red hair, a trait inherited from a grandmother she'd never met.

“Well?” Latera asked. “What's so important?”

“Pretty.” Sasha pointed at the pond.

Latera rolled her eyes. “You called me over to look at water?”

“No. Ripple.”

“Ripples?” Latera peered at the water. The surface was rippling, and before Latera's eyes the gentle ripples formed a whirlpool. But the pond was manmade, fed by no running water.

“No! It's not right,” Latera yelled as she stood and pushed Sasha behind her. Sasha wailed, whether from the push or being denied knowledge of whatever was happening in the pond Latera didn't know.

"Get the guards," Latera shouted, then she glanced at the pond. The swirling water had risen from the pond's surface in a swirling column, and it moved toward the sisters.

"Sasha run," Latera shrieked, then the water had hold of her and she was spinning, screaming. Latera saw the castle guards running toward her, but they were too late.

She was gone.

***

The world was one big bruise.

Latera opened her eyes, and saw that the world wasn't a bruise, but a dark, dank room. She was lying on a dirt floor that stank of rot, and the dampness was seeping through her thin summer dress. As Latera's eyes adjusted, she saw figures crowded around her.

"Do you speak?" asked a woman wearing a shapeless gray cloak.

Latera stood, and proclaimed, "I am Latera, first born of Harold and Ladyslava, heir to the kingdom."

The woman chuckled. "That lineage won't help you here."

Latera looked around the room; it was so dark that she couldn't tell where the shadows ended and the walls began, and everything reeked of smoke and herbs.

"Please, where am I? How did I get here?" Latera asked.

"You're in Parthalan. Your kind calls it Faerie," a male voice rumbled. He stepped forward, and Latera saw that he wore a gray cloak identical to the woman's, the hood pulled low over his face.

"Relle opened the door," he continued. "Apparently her spell was not as strong as she claimed, for it collapsed as soon as you came through."

"And, now you will send me home?" Latera asked.

The man laughed. "Home? Why would we send you home?" He leaned closer, and added, "Once we get that door open again, we'll get your sisters, too."

The shadow people rumbled with laughter, and fear gripped Latera with its icy fingers. She looked around the room and saw a hide-covered door. Latera grabbed a dagger from a nearby bench, clumsily brandishing it as she backed toward the hide.

"You will not harm me," Latera cried, then she bolted out into the night. The man's voice followed her into the night.

"Let her go," he rumbled. "Either we'll find her come first dawn, or she'll die in the forest."

Chapter One

"Will there be women in this village?"

Aeolmar's gaze slid toward Luth. "Missing Innetha already?"

Luth snorted. "Hardly. She refused to become my mate. Again!"

"Of course she said no," said Luth's brother, Bron. "What self-respecting woman would have you?"

Aeolmar almost bit through his tongue; he thought Innetha was many things, but respectable was not one of them.

"*I* hope there will be women," Adhaire said, bringing his horse alongside Luth's. "After I complete my Trial by Stealth, I'll want to celebrate!"

Aeolmar glanced at the young *nuvi*, doubtful of his chances. Adhaire recently won the Trial by Combat for a third time, but had only recently mastered calling fire. Aeolmar assumed it would take Adhaire a few tries to master stealth, as well.

"Have faith," Finlay said, reading Aeolmar's mood as he often did. "Adhaire will be a fine hunter."

"Of course," Aeolmar agreed, unwilling to say more until Adhaire actually failed. Once that happened, he would petition Asherah to have the useless *nuvi* removed from the *sola* and sent far, far away from Teg'urnan.

Not that Aeolmar intended to witness Adhaire's failure himself. Aeolmar had chosen to hold this exercise in a village that was a half day's walk from his birthplace, Savey. Once the Trial was underway, Aeolmar planned to slip away and visit his home. Nothing remained of his childhood home but a charred patch of earth, but it was home nonetheless.

Aeolmar touched the small bump over his heart made by his mother's pendant, secure in a special pocket. For this trip he'd taken the pendant with him, rather than leave it behind in Teg'urnan. He liked having a piece of her with him, and he hoped his mother's spirit rested close to her grave, since he needed her advice now more than ever. He was tired of his life as First Hunter, tired of being alone, of palace life... Gods, he was just tired.

The hunters arrived in the village of Brennus and found the inn. It was overseen by Ingvarr, a man known throughout the west for his hospitality as his mate, Elma, was for her fine cooking. While Finlay spoke to Ingvarr about boarding the horses, Aeolmar investigated the stables. He'd never left Myrnnhe anyplace he wouldn't sleep himself, and needed to see his horse's accommodations for himself.

As Aeolmar approached the stables he spied movement at the far corner; a small form clad in a tunic and leggings, a flash of bright hair. Intrigued, he followed the person toward the back of the yard...and almost bumped into a girl coming the other way. She gasped and dropped the saddle she was carrying, then bent to scoop it up an instant.

"May I pass?" she asked, balancing the saddle on her hip.

Realizing that this girl was the one he'd followed, Aeolmar took a long look at her. Her hair was flame red, bound up in a braid that did a poor job restraining her curls, her eyes were pale blue, and her skin was golden and a bit burnt across her nose and cheeks. What amazed Aeolmar most was her size; she was hardly larger than a child, yet she had a woman's curves. And she held that saddle as if it were weightless.

"May I pass?" she repeated, tapping her foot. Aeolmar stepped aside, then she stalked past him and placed the saddle on the workbench. After watching her for a moment, Aeolmar joined Finlay and the innkeeper.

"Who is that?" Aeolmar asked, indicating the stable.

"My stable girl, Latera," Ingvarr replied. "She has a way with horses, you know. Some of my patrons only stop by for her services."

"We'll need her to accompany us," Aeolmar said. Finlay raised an eyebrow, but Aeolmar ignored him. "If we stable our horses here and walk to the location, it will add days to our journey. I'd prefer to take the horses as far as we may."

"Of course," Ingvarr said, looking at Latera. She saw the innkeeper's gaze, then busied herself with the saddle. "Latera is a willful girl, and may refuse just for the sake of refusing. Let me send my mate to speak with her, my lord."

"No need. I'll ask her myself," Aeolmar said, striding toward the stable. Finlay and Ingvarr followed.

"Do we really need to bring her?" Finlay asked.

"How long do you want to be out here, days from Asherah?" Aeolmar countered. When Finlay grunted, Aeolmar assumed his second agreed. Aeolmar entered the stable and confronted the girl behind the workbench.

"I am Aeolmar, First Hunter of Parthalan," he announced.

"I'm Latera, and I brush the horses," she replied, never looking up from her work.

"Please excuse her, my lord," Ingvarr said. "She's a human who was lost here and is still learning our ways." Ingvarr glared at Latera and added, "She claims she was royalty in her homeland."

Aeolmar looked at Latera, noting her slanted eyes and pointed ears. "Why do you look like one of us if you're human?"

"I didn't always," she replied. "I'm told it's the effect of the realm."

Aeolmar frowned; he had known many humans, and none of them had taken on fae characteristics no matter how long they'd lived in Parthalan. In the midst of wondering who had told Latera such lies, he realized he was still glowering at her. He lightened his expression and continued. "My hunters and I will make camp a short distance from here for two nights. We will need someone to care for our horses. Ingvarr tells me that you have a way with them."

"Hunters or horses?"

His eyes narrowed. "The latter."

"Yes, I do," Latera replied. "Will you stable them here?"

"No. You will travel with us."

Understanding dawned in her pale eyes, and she glanced at Ingvarr. "Won't I get in the way of your hunt?"

"We aren't hunting," Aeolmar replied, "This is a training mission. My hunters have scouted the area, and there are no demons nearby. You won't be in any danger."

Latera was silent for a time. It was an unusual request to take a young woman into the forest with five hunters, but Aeolmar believed it was a necessity. Her presence meant that the hunters wouldn't need to worry about their mounts, and therefore they would get the Trial over with sooner. Then the hunters would return to Teg'urnan, and Latera would again be safe in her stable.

Yes. This is the best way.

"Very well," Latera said. "When do we leave?"

✳✳✳

After she'd packed a few things, Latera joined the hunters in the inn's courtyard, and together they rode into the wood. While the hunters rode warhorses Latera was astride Elma's elderly pony, Petal. Latera didn't know if she envied or hated the hunters.

Aeolmar rode at the front while Latera was at the rear, flanked by Finlay and Adhaire. The *nuvi* regaled Latera with his exploits; Aeolmar noted that he left out that all of his adventures had happened while in training yard. After Adhaire's fifth such tale, Finlay took over and told stories about Queen Asherah. He said that she was called Asherah the Ruthless, and by some the Assassin, and could destroy any demon she faced.

"What of him?" Latera asked, nodding toward Aeolmar.

"Our First Hunter?" Finlay asked. "He's only the most feared warrior in Parthalan. Some say he's even more fearsome that Asherah."

"That's a lie," Aeolmar called over his shoulder. "Asherah is the finest huntress ever to grace Parthalan's soil."

"You think I tell lies about the queen?" Finlay countered.

Aeolmar looked back and saw Finlay smiling, while Latera studied her pommel. "I think you say whatever nonsense comes to mind."

Finlay laughed. "Nonsense, is it? When we return to Teg'urnan I'll throw myself at Asherah's mercy and appeal to her good heart."

Aeolmar suppressed a smile as he faced forward. Though their binding remained secret, all of Parthalan knew how Finlay loved the queen. Few suspected that she loved him in return.

It wasn't long before the hunters found a clearing with room for the horses and tents, and bordered by a stream on the western edge. While Latera saw to the horses and the hunters set up the tents, Adhaire resumed boasting.

"I'm glad we brought the girl," Adhaire said. "After I complete my Trial, I'll take one of the wineskins, and—"

Aeolmar grabbed Adhaire's shirt. "You'll do nothing of the sort," Aeolmar said. "Latera is not a woman to woo. She's here to care for the horses, nothing more. Furthermore, she is under my protection. Understood?"

"Understood," Adhaire croaked, and Aeolmar released him. As the *nuvi* gasped for breath, Finlay took Aeolmar aside.

"Wasn't that a bit harsh?" Finlay whispered. "Latera's a pretty girl. Adhaire merely noticed."

"I promised her she would be safe," Aeolmar replied. "How would you feel if you were a girl surrounded by five men twice your size? I cannot have him making her uncomfortable."

Finlay frowned but didn't argue. A short time later, Adhaire set out into the forest to begin the Trial by Stealth with Luth, Finlay, and Bron following close behind. Aeolmar lingered at the camp, assembling a fire in the center of the clearing.

"You're not part of the game, my lord?" Latera asked. She sat across the fire pit from him, repairing a stirrup.

Aeolmar's mouth quirked. He liked that she was interested. "I'll follow once the fire is set."

"Are you sure you'll find them?"

"Yes, I'll find them," he replied. "Ingvarr said you're a princess?"

"I'm the first born of King Harold and Queen Ladyslava, heir to Gannera," Latera replied. After a moment she added, "My lord."

"How did you come to be in Parthalan?"

"I don't really know. I was with my sisters in the courtyard when a wind rose from a pond and brought me here. That was six winters ago, and I've been here ever since."

Aeolmar blinked. Had she really arrived in Parthalan by way of a magical vortex, or was that another of Ingvarr's tall tales? Instead of questioning her about the vortex, he asked, "Do you like it here?"

"Ingvarr and Elma are good to me." Latera looked up from her work. "Why do they all talk about how scary you are? You don't seem scary to me. My lord."

Aeolmar laughed. "I can be scary, when I need to be."

Latera watched him for a moment. "You should laugh more often. Then no one would be frightened of you." Her cheeks darkened, then she bent to pick at her stitching. Aeolmar whispered the words to call fire, and in another moment, it was crackling away.

"I'll set out now. We'll try to return before dark. Remain close to camp, where it's safe." Latera nodded, then Aeolmar entered the forest. As the trees closed around him he decided to track the hunters instead of visiting his childhood home. He didn't want to stray too far from the camp, or from Latera.

Chapter Two

Latera speaks

I watched Aeolmar disappear among the trees, and wondered what I'd do with myself until the hunters returned. The horses were fed and watered, and the stirrup I'd been repairing was as good as new. A nap sounded like a lovely way to pass the time.

The elder sun had barely moved a hand's width across the sky when I heard shouting. I turned toward the noise and saw Finlay and Bron carrying Aeolmar into the clearing. The First Hunter's head lolled to the side and his leg was a bloody mess.

"What happened?" I demanded.

"Ambush," replied Finlay. They entered the main tent and deposited their leader on the sole table. "You'll see to the wound?" Finlay asked. I nodded, then they were gone.

I looked over Aeolmar, assessing how I could best help him. Not only was he bruised, bleeding, and unconscious, he was covered in sticks and leaves. "And you are the most feared warrior in Parthalan," I said, brushing the detritus from his jerkin. "You look like you fell out of a tree, fool man. Stay on the ground, and leave the trees for the birds."

I cleaned his wounds and bandaged his leg, then I had the brilliant idea of moving him from the hard table to a bedroll... and found that I could barely shift him. Since moving him was like shoving a mountain, I settled for placing rolled blankets under his head and knees. Figuring he'd be hungry when he woke, I started some porridge. I was standing over the pot slicing fruit, and concentrating so intently on not slicing my fingers I almost didn't hear them.

Apparently, it hadn't occurred to these hunters that they could be followed back to our camp. I dropped the fruit and looked for a weapon, my gaze settling on Aeolmar's sword. I grabbed it from its sheath, took a step and almost dropped it. I hadn't realized how much a sword weighed, and the hunters carried them as if they weighed nothing. I'd barely tightened my grip when a twig snapped behind me. I turned around and faced what had to be demons.

I'd heard tales of demons but had never seen one, and here were three, less than twenty paces from me. They stalked the far edge of the clearing, staring me down, then the largest barked orders at the other two. I stood in front of the tent, struggling to keep the sword aloft.

The big one moved forward, and growled, "Step aside."

"Leave here and I'll let you live," I shouted. They laughed.

"I'll enjoy your screams, girl," he said, followed by such crude descriptions of what he was planning to do to me my face heated. That heat burnt away the lingering bits of fear and I rushed him, bringing the sword down on his arm and pushing him into the fire. I stared at the demon's severed arm at my feet, shocked and sickened and utterly amazed. Had I really attacked a demon, and won?

The other two lunged at me, and I tore my gaze from the arm in the dirt as I evaded one and sliced the other's neck open. He gaped as his blood flowed out onto the ground, then I spun again and plunged my sword into the other's chest.

I stood panting over the demons, both of them dead at my hand. I'd never killed anything before, not even a mouse. Ladies in Gannera weren't taught to hunt, and I hadn't been taught to defend myself since as royalty I'd had legions of guards defending me. After my abduction, I hadn't even hunted for food. Instead I scavenged roots and berries to *fill my belly, then I found my way to Brennus, and Elma's kitchen. Give that woman a large enough pot and she could feed all the nine realms.*

Despite my lack of experience, both of the demons were quite dead. My mother would have been horrified. I should have been horrified, but instead I was curious, and leaned in for a closer look. One had scales on its neck and a snakelike tongue, while the other's hands were covered in black fur, like a panther, with claws where its fingers should be. While I scrutinized the bodies, the big one—whom I'd quite forgotten about—grabbed me from behind.

He clapped a great scaly hand over my face, the sick smell of him filling my nose and stinging my eyes. I flailed my sword, but couldn't make contact with the beast. He was grunting in my ear, squeezing my neck and chest with his stump of an arm until black spots danced at the edges of my vision.

The beast stiffened and fell forward, trapping me between him and the ground. His hand moved off of my face, and I took in a great lungful of air, grateful I wasn't dead. Something wet like water but hot like fire soaked through the back of my shirt, and I screamed.

The demon moved off me and I screamed louder, certain that he was about to finish me off. Once free, I scrambled to my knees and nearly jumped out of my skin when a hand touched my shoulder.

"Latera, it's me," Aeolmar said, crouching before me. "It's only me."

My gaze travelled from Aeolmar, to the beast, and back to Aeolmar. "It's dead?"

"It is," he confirmed. "Are you hurt?"

I shook my head, then covered my face with my hands and sobbed. Aeolmar tried lowering my hands, but I was shaking too badly to comply. When that didn't work, he pulled me into his arms.

"I have you," he said, his mouth against my ear. "You're safe. I promise, you're safe." He held me as I bawled into his shoulder, smooth-

ing my hair and rocking me like a baby. Once I'd gotten myself under control I looked up, hardly able to see him through my tears.

"You shouldn't be walking with that wound," I said, humiliated by my tears soaking his shirt.

"You're right," he replied, "but you shouldn't be killing demons." He surveyed the area and demanded, "Who's here with you?"

"No one, my lord," I replied.

He pointed to the two smaller demons. "Then who killed these two?"

"I did, with your sword."

"You cut off the mordeth's arm with my sword?"

"Mordeth?"

"A demon warlord is called a mordeth," he answered, pointing at the largest corpse. I saw a small knife lodged in the base of his skull. Aeolmar yanked the knife free and rolled the corpse onto its back. He went still when he saw its face. "This mordeth is called Mersgoth."

"You know its name?"

"Everyone knows Mersgoth's name," Aeolmar mumbled, his gaze fixed on the corpse. He swayed, and for a moment I feared he'd faint.

"Are you all right?" I asked.

"What? Yes, yes." Aeolmar stared at the demon for another moment, then turned to me. "You cut off Mersgoth's arm?"

"Yes, then I pushed him into the fire." I looked around the clearing, shivering in spite of the warm day. I turned back to the First Hunter. "What if there are more?"

Aeolmar stroked my forehead with his thumb, tucking the stray curls behind my ear. "If there are more you will get behind me, and if I tell you to run, you will run. Do you understand?" he asked. I nodded, not trusting my voice. "I won't let anything hurt you. You have my word.

"Let's get away from the bodies," Aeolmar said, and I realized that I was still clutching him. I forced my hands to let go of his shirt and *got to my feet. Aeolmar followed suit, cursing when he put weight on his injured leg.*

"Let me help you." I ducked under his arm and supported him against his side. "Once we're inside the tent I'll check your wound."

"You not only guard me, but you're my healer as well?"

My cheeks warmed, and I refused to dignify that smirk with a response. As I rewrapped his wound in silence, Aeolmar moved my braid off my neck.

"Quite a lot of blood got on you," he said. He dipped a fresh bandage in the water bowl and cleaned my neck, then rubbed an ointment onto my skin. "The salve won't be much help for the pain, but it will keep you from scarring," he mumbled. After I finished tending his leg, I stood and gathered the soiled bandages, then Aeolmar caught my arm.

"Yes?" I asked over my shoulder.

"I must wash the blood from your back," he said. "Have you another shirt?"

"I can't just wash out this shirt?"

"The blood will eat through the cloth."

"Oh." I looked at Aeolmar, his wide blue eyes and pursed lips telling me he was just as nervous as I was over me possibly not having a shirt. He cleared his throat and dropped his gaze; maybe he was a bit more nervous than me.

"Latera, the shirt you're wearing is about to fall off your body," he said. "If you don't have a spare say as much, and I'll give you mine."

"Of course I have a spare," I grumbled. I located my pack and retrieved my second tunic, then I stomped back into the tent. I stopped before Aeolmar, fresh garment in hand.

"Turn around," he said. I did, and Aeolmar peeled the ruined shirt from my back.

"It really was falling apart," I said, as the bloody flakes settled around my feet.

"*Demon blood is like acid, burns through almost anything it touches. It's why hunters wear leather.*" Once my back was bare I heard water sloshing, then Aeolmar swept the damp rag across my skin. I hissed and pulled away when he touched a tender spot near my neck.

"*Wait,*" he said, a firm hand on my waist. I heard him rustling around, then he spread the burn ointment across my back. It was warm, not hot like the demon's blood, and comforting.

"*That feels good,*" I said, rolling my shoulders.

Aeolmar grunted. "*Be careful how you move for the next few days. Try not to stretch the burn.*" His hands left my back as what was left of my shirt crumbled to the ground. I clutched the clean shirt against my breast, unsure if I should leave the tent or just put it on right there. Gods, I'd never been half-naked with a man before, and the first time just had to be with someone like Aeolmar.

If he found my modesty amusing, he didn't say so. "*I'll give you a moment,*" he said as he left the tent. I'd just gotten my tunic sorted out when he reentered, carrying his sword. He looked from the blade to me and said, "*I believe this sword weighs almost as much as you do. Have you ever wielded one before today?*"

"*No, my lord. I've only ever used this dagger.*" I indicated the knife I'd stolen my first day in Parthalan.

"*I know Ingvarr told you to say 'my lord', but you don't need to call me that. If it wasn't for you I'd be cold and dead and the lord of nothing.*"

He continued, "*In my saddlebags are some rags and cleaning oil. Would you bring them to me?*" I did, and he motioned for me to sit next to him. "*Here, I'll show you how to clean it.*"

I followed his direction, and by the time the others returned Aeolmar's sword gleamed as though newly forged. As I fetched water for hunters and horses alike, I heard Aeolmar tell Finlay that the girl they hired to care for the horses had defended him from a demon attack. Finlay emerged from the tent and ruffled my hair while I fed the horses.

"You killed the demons?" he asked.

"Yes," I replied. "Well, Aeolmar killed the big one. But I got the other two!"

Finlay smiled. "Not bad, little one."

While Finlay and the others took care of the demon's corpses, I busied myself with the horses until the elder sun went to rest. When I returned to the tent it was to ask Aeolmar what was to be done about dinner; I wasn't a very good cook, but these hunters didn't look like they could prepare anything worth eating. Aeolmar listened to my question, and asked one of his own.

"Tell me," he asked, "would you like to be a hunter?"

I stared at him. How could I possibly be a hunter? I was too small, too slow, too weak ... too everything I was, and everything he wasn't. "I don't think I would be a good hunter," I replied.

"Nonsense," he said. "Mersgoth is an old and feared demon. He's destroyed entire contingents of my hunters, and many, many innocents. He gave me this wound today. But you took him down, and two others."

"But you—" I began, but he held up his hand.

"You cut off his arm. You burnt him. And you don't even know how to use a sword." I looked at my feet and said nothing. "Latera, you're brave, and swift, and intelligent. Those are the most important skills for a hunter to possess. I woke as you were fighting the first two, and you were amazing." He grasped my hand and pulled me down beside him. "Come with me to the palace, let me train you. You'll be happy there, much happier than in a stable."

His offer was tempting. I considered my time in Brennus, and how fond I was of Ingvarr and Elma. Life at the inn was hard but good, a stark contrast to my pampered childhood in Gannera. I didn't think I'd be so cared for in this palace, but life there had to be easier than hauling hay and sleeping in a stable.

Aeolmar didn't rush me as I weighed my options. I watched his eyes; they were kind, not in a twinkling way like Ingvarr's but ...different. Deeper. They told me he was faithful, and compassionate, and that he would protect me in this strange land that had just gotten a great deal stranger. I wanted a leader like him, and I knew I would follow him across the plains of hell if only he asked.

"Yes," I replied, "I'll accept your offer and go to this palace. I hope I prove worthy of your faith in me."

Aeolmar smiled. "I think you're worthier than you know."

CHAPTER THREE

The hunters and Latera returned to Brennus the next morning, and met Ingvarr in the common area in front of the inn. The innkeeper watched as they dismounted, his sharp gaze noting how Latera seemed at ease among the men she'd only met the day prior.

"You're back early," Ingvarr said, by way of greeting.

"We were ambushed," Aeolmar began, then he was interrupted as Elma ran out of the inn and caught Latera in her arms.

"I knew I shouldn't have let you go," Elma cried.

"I'm not hurt," Latera insisted, gently untangling herself from Elma. "I promise, I'm all right. Let Aeolmar speak."

"As Latera said, she wasn't injured," Aeolmar said. "In fact, she showed remarkable courage. I'd like your permission to bring her to Asherah's court, so she may become one of us. A hunter."

The innkeeper and his mate stared first at each other and then at the First Hunter, until Ingvarr broke the silence.

"A hunter?" Ingvarr asked. "Why would you want a stable girl for a hunter?"

"As I said, we were ambushed," Aeolmar replied patiently. "I was hit by a spear, then I fell and struck my head. When I woke, Latera was fighting off demons."

"Demons?" Elma squealed. "Are they still out there?"

"They've been dealt with," Aeolmar said.

"You killed them?" she pressed.

"No," Aeolmar replied. "Latera did."

Ingvarr's gaze moved from Aeolmar to Latera. "You killed demons?"

Aeolmar gazed at Latera so intently she blushed. "She did. I owe her my life."

"I always knew you were destined for great things." Elma patted Latera's shoulder, beaming. "I just wish I could have led you to them myself."

"You took me in when I was lost, cared for me when no one else would," Latera told her. "I couldn't have asked for anything more."

***

It didn't take long for Latera to gather her things for her journey to Teg'urnan. After organizing, and then reorganizing, her few possessions, Latera approached Ingvarr and Elma.

"Thank you," she began. "If not for your kindness, I don't know what would have become of me."

"It is us that should be thanking you," Ingvarr replied. "You know a great deal of our patrons only came here for your way with horses."

Latera scuffed the ground with the toe of her boot. "I like the horses."

"And they like you as well," Ingvarr said, then he pressed a gold coin into Latera's hand. "You've earned that, so take it and don't complain. You'll always be welcome here, Latera. Remember that."

"Please don't forget us," Elma said.

"How could I ever forget you?" Latera countered. "You're the best people I've ever met."

Elma stepped back from Latera and handed her a sack. "I've packed you a few loaves of bread and some dried meat, and I filled the water skins. Make sure those men stop well before sun rest so you don't have to eat in the dark."

"I will, Elma. Thank you, for everything."

Latera hugged them once more, then approached the waiting hunters and mounted her horse. Aeolmar had purchased Petal from the innkeepers, and Latera was just as excited about the horse as she was about moving to the palace.

"Ready?" Aeolmar asked.

"I am." Latera rod with the hunters out of Brennus, and never looked back.

***

"I can't believe it took us four days to get here," Latera said, when she and the hunters reached the royal road that led straight to Teg'urnan's gates.

Aeolmar's gaze slid towards Latera. "Did you expect us to fly? Or hire a magic handler to create a portal?"

Latera shuddered. "No, nothing like that. It's just that you can cross all of Gannera in less than three days."

"Parthalan is the largest land in this realm," Aeolmar explained. "Along with the elflands of the north, one can explore for years and years, and still not learn all the land's secrets."

"I think I've had enough of secrets," Latera mumbled, fingering a charred spot on her reins. The second night of their journey, Latera had watched Finlay dump an armload of wood into a makeshift fire pit. He'd whispered a few words and flames burst forth. She'd demanded to know how he did it, and Finlay explained that all hunters are taught to create fire. He'd demonstrated his skill by tossing fireballs about and Latera, heretofore distrustful of magic, watched in rapt attention. She begged him to teach her, which he did during the next day's ride. The lessons were going well, until Latera singed Petal's mane and frightened the poor thing out of her wits. After a stern lecture from the First Hunter, Finlay decided that lessons on fire-starting were better left for less flammable environments.

"You'll get better at calling fire," Aeolmar said. "Once we reach the top of this rise we'll be able to see Teg'urnan."

The hunters crested the hill and Latera saw Teg'urnan for the first time, gleaming like a silver mountain in the afternoon sunlight. The palace at the heart of Parthalan sat atop the Hill of Rahlle, with six gleaming towers stretching toward the clouds, and a high stone wall with a central gate and several watchtowers surrounded the grounds. Above the gates the statues of the stag and doe, representations of Olluhm and Cydia, eternally leapt toward each other. The windows in the towers shimmered like jewels set into stone, sparkling and many-hued. In addition to everything at inside the palace walls, a bustling city was nestled at the base of the hill.

"It's a sight, isn't it?" Aeolmar asked. "I'm sure it's not as amazing to you as it was to me when I first came here. You were born in a castle, but I'm from a village smaller than Brennus."

"Where I was born is a thatched hut compared to Teg'urnan," Latera murmured. She turned to Aeolmar, and asked, "Will I be given a map?"

Aeolmar laughed. "You'll find your way around soon enough. Come, this way."

They passed beneath the gate and to the right, and Latera learned that in addition to the city at the base of the hill, another city existed within the walls. Aeolmar indicated various shops, pubs, and the location of the blacksmith and other trades as they passed. When they had traversed half the circumference of the wall and were directly behind the palace, Latera saw a large arena with a dormitory attached to it.

"This is the *sola*," Aeolmar said, "where you will live with the other *nuvi*—that's what we call those in training."

"Are there a lot of *nuvi*?" Latera asked.

"Yes," he replied, "but not all of them go on to become hunters."

They continued on, and Aeolmar led Latera to the royal stable, which was comprised of spacious stalls on either side of a wide corridor. There were as many grooms as there were horses, and tack hung from the walls in every color and style. Latera remarked to the First Hunter that if the stable in Brennus had been this fine she might not have taken his offer of coming to the palace.

Once the horses were seen to, Aeolmar said," And now, I'll introduce you to the queen."

"What? No," Latera said, shaking her head. "I'm filthy, and not properly dressed."

"You think Asherah will care what you look like?" Aeolmar countered. "Asherah is a warrior herself, as well as Parthalan's first huntress." When Latera's frown deepened, he added, "As First Hunter I can order you to her presence."

"Can you order me to a bath first?"

Aeolmar's temper flared, but he noticed how Latera's nose crinkled and the spots of color that bloomed on her cheeks. Somehow, her flushed cheeks dulled the edges of his anger. "I'm not accustomed to being defied."

"I'm not accustomed to being paraded in front of royalty like a grimy beggar."

"You're not grimy," he said. "You look like a beautiful girl who's been out for a ride, nothing more than that." The spots of red grew bigger and spilled down Latera's neck. "Asherah won't care what you look like. She will only care about what you've accomplished. Of this, I promise you."

Latera's shoulders relaxed. "You're certain?"

"I am."

Aeolmar extended his hand. Reluctantly, Latera took it. As she curled her fingers around his, she asked, "Is it customary for the First Hunter and his *nuvi* to walk hand in hand?"

"Absolutely not. However, I remember how swift you are, and don't want to risk your flight. Not that I couldn't catch you," he added.

Latera snorted. "Doubtful, that."

They entered the palace through the main doors. Aeolmar ignored the stares directed at him and Latera, while she marveled at the beauty of Teg'urnan, from the ornate scrollwork that graced the window frames to the gray stone floor, polished until it sparkled. Colorful tapestries hung along the walls, and Aeolmar pulled Latera to a halt before the largest, which showed Asherah beheading the prior king.

"You see?" Aeolmar asked. "Asherah is a warrior first."

Latera nodded, then she pointed at a second, smaller tapestry that depicted a battle. "That central figure looks like you," she said.

"That's because it is me," Aeolmar replied. "It depicts the Battle of Esguth. Afterward, I was named First Hunter."

Latera studied the tapestry, noting how the image of Aeolmar was surrounded by fallen demons, and how the First Hunter scowled at it. "If you hate it so much, why not take it down?"

"I don't hate it," Aeolmar replied. Latera tugged on his hand, and he realized how hard he was squeezing hers. "Forgive me," he murmured, releasing her. As she shook out her hand, he warned, "Don't run."

"Even if I did, I wouldn't be able to find my way out of this maze," Latera grumbled. With that, Aeolmar led her through a second set of massive doors, and into the presence of the Queen of Parthalan.

Asherah the Ruthless sat on a silver throne set with blue stones, itself atop a dais carpeted in red velvet. Upon seeing Aeolmar and Latera, the queen rose and approached them. Asherah was tall, nearly as tall as Aeolmar, with blond hair so pale it had undertones of blue, and so long it fell past her hips. She had large, dark eyes, pale skin, and ruby red lips. The queen wore a silver and blue gown with a high neck and trailing hem, the diaphanous fabric swirling around her like mist. Latera knelt and bowed her head.

"Rise, child," Asherah said, "I'm not that sort of ruler." As Latera stood, Asherah asked Aeolmar, "Why have you brought me a visitor?"

"My lady, this is Latera," Aeolmar replied. "She's from Brennus, where I hired her to mind the horses while Adhaire completed his Trial by Stealth."

"Have you brought her here to work in the stables?" Asherah asked.

Aeolmar's eyes narrowed, and he continued, "Instead of only minding the horses, Latera killed two demons, and gravely wounded Mersgoth, who is now dead."

"Mersgoth is dead?" Asherah repeated, returning her attention to Latera. "That is no small feat, my dear. Mersgoth has been wreaking havoc in my land for many centuries."

"That is what Aeol— I mean, the First Hunter told me, my lady," she replied.

The queen pushed back Latera's hair and ran a slender finger across her ear. "You're not fae," she stated.

"I'm not, my lady. I'm human."

Asherah studied Latera's features for a moment. "You look elfin to me. Are there elves in your family?"

"I don't think there are any elves in Gannera." When Asherah's brows peaked, Latera added, "That's where I'm from, Gannera. It's in the mortal realm."

"Fascinating," Asherah murmured.

"I want Latera trained as a hunter," Aeolmar said. "She has good instincts, and can already wield a sword better than most. Latera will be an asset to your court."

Asherah's gaze slid between Aeolmar and Latera. "You've never been wrong about hunters in the past, Aeolmar, I will admit that. Your judgment has always been sound." Asherah turned to Latera and asked, "What do you think of Aeolmar's request? Do you wish to devote your life to killing vermin and keeping Parthalan's borders safe?"

"I...I think I would like being a hunter," Latera responded. "Aeolmar assures me I will do well."

"You will," Aeolmar said, so emphatically Asherah raised an eyebrow.

"Then I've decided," Asherah said. "Latera may enter the *sola*, but first I want to hear how you came to be in my land, so very far from your home."

Asherah indicated they should follow her from the hall to her private sitting room. "No, Aeolmar," Asherah said, when they reached the door, "this time is for Latera and me, alone. I'll send for you when we're through."

Aeolmar scowled and stalked off, and the queen and her newest *nuvi* settled before the hearth. After Asherah sent her *saffira-nell* to fetch refreshments, Latera told her everything, from how she'd been taken from her home, to her time alone in the woods, to her six winters as a stable hand. Lastly, she told the queen about her astonishment over the immense weight of Aeolmar's sword, and how she used it to kill two demons. Asherah listened to every word, never interrupting.

"You weren't scared of the demons?" Asherah asked when Latera had finished her tales.

"I wasn't. My only thought was to keep them from the horses. And Aeolmar," she added.

"Are you scared of me?" Asherah asked.

Latera frowned. "No, my lady, I'm not."

The queen studied Latera's face as she continued. "I get the impression that very little frightens you."

"That's true," she responded. "The first time I remember being frightened was when I thought my sisters would be harmed, on the day I was taken."

"Was the last time when Mersgoth fell dead upon you?" Asherah asked.

Latera shivered. "I wish I hadn't forgotten about him. It was a mistake I won't repeat." The queen regarded Latera for a time, and divined what Latera was trying not to ask.

"You want to know what they are," Asherah said.

"I cannot believe demons really exist," Latera said. "We used to hear stories when we were children, but we never thought they were real." Latera turned her wide eyes to Asherah's dark, glittering pools, and the queen was struck by how young the girl next to her really was. "What are they? Where do demons come from? Why do they hate us so?"

"They are the descendants of banished gods trying to influence the daylight realm."

"Banished gods? How did that happen?"

"Long ago," the queen began, "Olluhm cast the old gods from the sky. He cursed their followers, and demons are what they've become."

"They seemed partly human," Latera said.

"They probably were. Dark magic cannot create life, only remove it. Therefore, demons have to take a female to procreate. They will use a female of any kind, whether it is a horse, or a faerie, or a human." Asherah's dark eyes clouded over. "The overlord of the demons, the *mordeth-gall,* Asgeloth, is said to have fae blood."

"I have never, ever imagined that something so vile could exist," Latera said. "You have my word, I won't let these foul creatures harm any that I can defend."

"Latera, you remind me of myself when I was younger," Asherah said. "I do not believe Aeolmar is wrong about you."

Latera and the queen sat together for a time, sharing tales both big and small. Asherah spoke of her youth, of the first demon she killed, and how factions of *mordeths* had enslaved the fae at the old king's behest. She spoke of Torim, how they first met Harek, and of her mate, the elf king Lormac.

"You loved him?" Latera asked.

"I did," Asherah replied. "I love him still."

Latera sighed, her face wistful. "I wish someone loved me that much. It must be grand, being the center of another's world."

Asherah smiled. "I'm sure you'll know. Let's summon Aeolmar. We've let him stew long enough."

"Stew?"

"Like as not he's been waiting right outside the door."

"Surely he has better things to do," Latera said, but the queen pressed a finger to her lips and walked toward the door. She flung it open, revealing Aeolmar leaning against the far wall.

"I trust you're done distracting my *nuvi*?" he demanded.

"I am," Asherah said. "I'd say we've become fast friends."

"May all the living gods help us," Aeolmar muttered. To Latera, he said, "Now, I will bring you to the *sola*."

The queen and Latera said farewell, and Aeolmar walked Latera to the *sola*, where she finally met the other *nuvi*. There were twenty *nuvi*, including Latera, but the only other female was Alia. She had green eyes and long straight hair the color of hay at the end of summer. She swept Latera away from the First Hunter and showed her around. There was a large central room with many cots against the wall, which was where they slept. Adjacent to that room was a bathhouse on the left, and to the right a large eating area. A long corridor led from the eating area to the arena. Latera mentioned that the arena seemed smaller from the inside. Alia was surprised to learn that Aeolmar had personally escorted her around the palace grounds.

"I asked him to," Latera said. "Doesn't he show all the *nuvi* around?"

"No," Alia replied, "he hardly speaks to anyone. Some wonder if he has a tongue at all."

"I find that hard to believe," Latera said. "We spoke of a great many things on the journey here."

"Maybe your fiery hair brings out the conversationalist in him," Alia said with a knowing glance. Latera frowned, but then she saw a familiar face and smiled.

"Adhaire," Latera called, her smile widening when he joined them. "I thought you were already a hunter. Why are you in the *sola*?"

"My final Trial was in Brennus," he replied. "Thanks to the ambush I couldn't prove myself, so Aeolmar told me I couldn't be named a hunter." He looked around the *sola* as if he'd been confined to a dungeon.

"Oh, then you probably just need to complete your Trial," Latera said.

"It's not fair," Adhaire cried. "These tests are only held once a year. I've completed the other Trials; I should be named! Aeolmar is too greedy with his titles."

"How long have you trained?" Latera asked.

"Ten winters." He glanced around before he continued. "You know, Aeolmar didn't even train. He was given his rank by the queen herself." Alia nodded, murmuring that it was true.

"She just made him First Hunter?" Latera asked.

"No, she named him a hunter. He became First some winters later," Adhaire replied, sounding deflated.

Latera thought for a moment. "Will I have to train for ten winters?"

"Probably not." He draped an arm around her shoulders. "You've already killed two. I didn't even see a demon until my fourth winter here. Everyone's calling you Demon-killer," he added with a wink.

"Who's calling me that?" Latera demanded.

"The other hunters and *nuvi*."

"Aren't the other hunters demon-killers as well?"

"Yes, but they're *hunters* killing demons, whereas you're a girl killing demons with the First Hunter's sword." Adhaire looked around, then asked, "So, are you still under his protection?"

"Whose protection?" Latera shot back.

"While we were in Brennus, Aeolmar made it clear that he was standing between you and the rest of us," Adhaire explained.

Latera smiled. "Did he?"

"Adhaire, leave her be," Alia said, pulling Latera away from him. "She's just the latest to fall under his spell, for all the good it will do her. Follow me; I'll get you set up with a cot."

Latera followed Alia into the dormitory, and wondered what else the coming days would bring.

Chapter Four

After leaving Latera in the care of the *sola*, Aeolmar strode into Asherah's chamber without knocking, and found the queen seated at her map table. He sat opposite her and tossed a small knife onto the table between them.

"Bringing me gifts?" Asherah asked.

"That's how I killed him," Aeolmar muttered. "After all this time, and all those missed chances, I killed Mersgoth with the knife I keep in my boot."

Asherah picked it up. "Perhaps it's what we should have tried all along." She glided a fingertip across the flat of the blade. "You're certain he's dead?"

"I burned him myself," Aeolmar replied. "Best thing I've ever done."

Asherah slid her hand across the table and grasped his forearm. She was one of the few who understood Aeolmar's obsession with Mersgoth: the *mordeth* had murdered Aeolmar's entire family. "Is there anything you need from me?"

"What? No. I'm fine. No, I'm not, but..." He blew out a breath and scrubbed his face with his hands. "And would you like to know the worst of it?"

"Worst?"

"I should be elated. I should be dancing on his grave, getting drunk and taking women to my bed."

"Celebration is certainly your right," Asherah said.

"Instead, I can't stop worrying," Aeolmar finished.

"I thought you said you burned him yourself?" Asherah asked. "Yet you worry he lives?"

"He's dead. Of that, I'm certain." Aeolmar raised his head and fixed Asherah in his gaze. "It's Latera."

"Ah." Asherah shuffled a few of her maps. "Does she know what killing Mersgoth means for you?"

"No," he replied. "I tried to tell her, but the words wouldn't come."

"Aeolmar, the great communicator."

Ignoring the gibe, Aeolmar leaned back in his chair and stared at the ceiling. "Gods, Asherah, why did I bring her here?"

Instead of answering him, the queen rose and retrieved a flagon of brandy and two cups.

"I hate brandy," Aeolmar said when she set them on the table.

"Which is why you've consumed every drop I've ever poured for you," Asherah said. "You do realize she's not human?"

"She believes she is," Aeolmar replied. "What I'd like to know is who lied to her."

"She has the reddest hair I've ever seen," Asherah said. "You know what race has red hair? Thurndian elves."

"Sibeal's hair is paler than yours," Aeolmar countered.

"She takes after her father," Asherah said. "The prior Lady of Thurnda, Elvasla, had hair as red as the moon."

"Still," Aeolmar said, "I highly doubt Latera is in truth an elf from the north."

They sat for a time, sipping brandy. "Why did you bring her here?" Asherah asked at length.

"You should have seen her kill those demons," Aeolmar said. "She'd never even touched a sword before, but she wielded mine as if she'd been born with it in her hand. It was beautiful...she was beautiful." Aeolmar frowned at his empty cup. "Asherah, you've gotten me drunk."

"You drank it yourself," she retorted. "And you've a stronger constitution than that," she added, refilling his cup.

Aeolmar drank, then glowered at the queen. "When she's named, I won't have her going to one of the borders. She'll stay here."

Asherah raised a brow. "Is she skilled enough for the palace contingent?"

"She is," Aeolmar insisted. "You'll see. She is."

"I will, because I will oversee her training myself," Asherah declared. When Aeolmar complained, she continued, "Aeolmar, if Latera is to forgo her border assignment she must have a certain level of competency. I'm willing to grant your request, but I must be certain."

Aeolmar frowned. "I...understand." He glanced up. "Thank you for indulging me."

Asherah smiled. "Of course."

Chapter Five

Asherah speaks

After Aeolmar finished his third cup of brandy he stalked off to do whatever surly drunk men do. Perhaps he went to the arena to sweat out some of the brandy, or inform the instructors yet again that they were teaching the nuvi *incorrectly. He wasn't normally a mean drunk, but he was adamant that I'd tricked him into telling me his feelings about Latera. Apparently he'd forgotten that he was the one who brought her to Teg'urnan in the first place.*

Perhaps Aeolmar had gone to seek out his nuvi, *this girl who'd made such an impression on his stony façade. There had been no talk of Aeolmar being with a single person in the years since he'd handed me over to Finlay, and I wondered if his solitude was over. Whether it was or wasn't, it had certainly gone on long enough. If that man didn't find release soon, he would give himself a seizure.*

Leaving aside thoughts of my First Hunter, I stepped onto the balcony. I liked watching the bustle of the palace square, the merchants and hawkers going about their days. Sometimes, I became so engrossed in the daily minutia of the palace I forgot that my life had ever been anything but that of a queen's.

Movement near the castle gates caught my eye. A cart was laden with some sort of goods, and my Second Hunter was speaking with the gatekeeper and merchant. The latter two were not happy with one another, and each pleaded their case to Finlay. Eventually, Finlay turned the merchant away, much to the gatekeeper's satisfaction and the merchant's obvious displeasure. Having concluded whatever business that was, Finlay strode across the square toward the palace. When he was almost underneath my balcony he glanced upward. I didn't meet his gaze, but I did place my hands, palms up, on the stone railing. It was one of our signals, and it meant that I was alone in my chambers.

I remained on the balcony, enjoying the fresh air and waving at those below, until I heard my private entrance open and shut. My body humming with anticipation, I withdrew and met my mate in our bedchamber.

"Beloved?" I called.

"Have you any idea how much I've missed you?" Finlay demanded, taking me in his arms. He wasted no time lifting me against him, and I wrapped my legs around his hips as he carried me to bed.

I opened my mouth, intending to say how much I'd missed him as well, when Finlay closed his lips over mine. We landed on the soft cushions, and he proved with every stroke and caress how he loved me. Gods, how had I survived all those winters without a mate?

Our coupling was hard and brief, but that was all right. I knew he'd love me again later, once the palace was asleep. Even though we both had tasks to attend, we lolled about in bed for a time.

"Tell me about the Trial?" I asked.

"We were attacked," Finlay said. "Mersgoth nearly killed Aeolmar, then Aeolmar's stable girl saved him." Finlay drew a length of my hair between his fingers. "Didn't Aeolmar already report to you?"

"He did, but I wanted to hear it from you." I rolled until I was above Finlay, and held his face in my hands. "Were you hurt? Do you need anything from me?"

"No, and a few things," he replied, pulling me in for another kiss. When we parted, he asked, "Aeolmar bring her by?"

"Yes, he did. I rather like Latera."

"We all do. She's smart, quick of mind and foot."

"Aeolmar asked for her to be a nuvi. *He went so far as to tell me that when—not if, but when—Latera is named as a hunter, she'll stay here. The thought of sending her to the border terrifies him."*

Finlay chuckled. "You should have seen her ordering him around on the journey back here. He didn't argue once, just did whatever she asked." A shadow passed across Finlay's face. "Did you see me with the merchant at the gate?"

"I did. Why was he turned away?"

Finlay frowned and dropped my hair. "He was hauling a certain type of powder," he replied. "A single spark could set one canister ablaze like a volcano."

"What?" I demanded, sitting up. "I've never heard of such a thing."

"I have. It's common across the sea in Ysr." Finlay's summer blue eyes met mine. "Harek sent it here."

"Did he?" I said. "I received a message from him not two days ago, telling me he'd uncovered some sort of new threat to Parthalan. It mentioned nothing of a powder that burns."

Finlay snorted. "A new threat? Hopefully this one is actually threatening."

I swatted his arm. "Need I remind you that he helped me lead Parthalan through eight centuries of peace?"

In one deft move, Finlay had me underneath him. "Need I remind you that I've heard those tales all my life?" He bent to kiss my neck, and added, "No more talk of that fool."

"Agreed. When must you leave?"

"I shouldn't be here now. You know how Aeolmar gets when things aren't done in a timely manner."

My heart fell; it pained me to keep my mate a secret, but I needed Finlay safe. After the fates that had befallen my last lovers, there was no way I would risk his life. Finlay had almost died once, and while I didn't know if he'd been targeted because of me, I wasn't taking any chances with my man from the desert. "Maybe the queen can intercede on your behalf."

Finlay smiled, warming me to the tips of my toes. "As I've said many times, Parthalan has a gracious and beautiful queen."

Chapter Six

Latera spent the rest of autumn and the entire winter in the *sola*, where she trained with the other *nuvi*. While she was there she learned how to fight with swords, spears, and her bare hands. Latera demonstrated adequate skill with a broadsword, but she soon learned that two short swords better fit her frame and speed. She wore them strapped across her back, and before long she perfected drawing them in an instant.

Every few days, Aeolmar visited the *sola* and observed the *nuvi* train. He watched them from the gallery, scowling down into the arena as they went through the motions of swordplay. On occasion, Latera caught him watching her. Once, he almost laughed as Latera knocked Adhaire onto his backside in the dust.

The winter proved mild, and soon enough spring burst forth across Parthalan. With the season's change the Prelate, Harek, returned to Teg'urnan from his winter abode in the south. The *nuvi* watched from the palace gates as he marched inside the palace, along with the *con'dehr*.

"Are Harek's soldiers hunters, too?" Latera asked Adhaire.

"Anyone can be a soldier," he replied. "If you prove yourself good with a sword and can follow orders, they'll welcome you into their ranks. You need to be selected in order to join the *sola*."

"Then we outrank the soldiers?"

"We do. We're trained to engage demons, whereas soldiers are only trained in standard combat. They cannot make fire, and they aren't trackers like we are. But Harek outranks Aeolmar, and he doesn't let the First Hunter forget it."

"I didn't think anyone outranked Aeolmar," Latera said.

"Only Harek and the queen do," Adhaire continued. "Harek was with Asherah when she took the throne, and has been loyal to her ever since."

The day after his return Harek inspected the *nuvi*. They lined up according to rank inside the arena, with Latera in the last position since she was the newest. He walked past the first nineteen individuals, stopping at every third or fourth *nuvi* to speak with Asherah, as Aeolmar followed them.

"I still don't understand the ultimate purpose of that powder," Asherah was saying. "And would it really be safe to store it here in Teg'urnan?"

"It's a well-known weapon in the southern lands," Harek replied. "And safe enough when handled properly." He stopped before Latera, and she got her first good look at the Prelate. He was a short, stocky man with a chest like a barrel, small club-like hands, and coarse brown hair. He stood at least a head shorter than the queen and First Hunter, his rough face a sharp contrast to their delicate features, and Latera wondered if some troll blood coursed in his veins. As Latera contemplated Harek's heritage, Aeolmar spoke.

"This is Latera," Aeolmar said. "She's our newest *nuvi*."

"Where do you hail from?" Harek barked.

"Brennus, my lord," Latera replied; normally she would have replied Gannera, but she'd learned to not draw attention to her race.

The Prelate's face hardened. "This is the one you told me of? She's too small to hunt. Any demon could rip her in two."

"No," replied Aeolmar, "one could not. I'm standing here today because she defended me against three demons. *Mersgoth* is dead because of Latera."

Harek scrutinized Latera. She smiled. The Prelate scowled. "We shall see," he grumbled, and then he, the queen, and Aeolmar continued on their way.

***

Five days after the Prelate's return, the Trial by Combat was held. As the *nuvi* readied themselves, and wagered on who would win this round, Adhaire bragged about winning the last Trial by Combat.

"I expect I'll win this bout as well," he said, as he strapped on his gauntlets.

"What will that change?" Alia asked. "You've won the last three, yet you're still a *nuvi*." The other *nuvi* laughed as Adhaire scowled, but Alia waved him off. "Be calm, Adhaire. You know we all want you to win again."

"If for no other reason than to get him out of here," Latera muttered.

It was well after midday when the *nuvi* entered the hot, dusty arena. Every last seat was filled with Parthalan's citizens, eager for both the spectacle and the celebration that would be held afterward. Latera saw the queen seated on the gallery with Harek and Aeolmar flanking her, an outpost of calm amidst the excited crowd.

The *nuvi* formed a circle around the edge of the perimeter, and waited. Latera flexed her hands as she concentrated on her breathing, as her gaze darted among her opponents.

Earlier today, we were friends.

A gong sounded, and the Trial by Combat began.

Three *nuvi* rushed Latera at once, and she evaded two as she disarmed the third. She tripped over a fourth, but rolled away from another attacker. Latera crouched with her back against the arena's wall as she watched the battle. Dust churned across the arena, obscuring the *nuvi's* faces. Latera grit her teeth, and plunged back into the fray.

Out of the corner of her eye Latera saw another enter the arena: the unknown warrior. He slowly made his way across the playing field, waiting for his opponent. He was clad in gray leather, with a matching helm that covered most of his face. Taking his helm was key to winning the Trial by Combat, and Latera meant to win.

Latera had barely glimpsed the unknown before she spun to face her next opponent: Alia. Latera struck, and Alia couldn't parry in time. As Alia fell into the dust, Latera turned to the next opponent and learned that only she and the unknown remained.

They circled one another. The unknown drew his sword with a flourish. Latera remained still. When the unknown rushed at Latera, she parried and stepped aside.

The unknown rushed her again. She evaded him, but the tip of his sword caught the end of her braid.

"That all you've got?" Latera taunted. "Did you come here to cut hair, or to fight?"

Unaffected by her goading, the unknown advanced toward Latera with a great arching blow. Latera lowered her stance and crossed her swords, blocking him mid-strike. As they struggled, Latera glanced toward the gallery—but only Asherah and Harek were there. In a burst of recognition, she twisted out from under the unknown's sword and snatched his helm. As Aeolmar's chestnut hair fell around his shoulders he pulled Latera's back against his chest, his sword at her throat.

"You did very well," Aeolmar breathed into Latera's ear. She twisted free of his arms and faced him.

"That is not your sword," Latera snapped.

"Of course not. You would have recognized mine."

Latera glared at the First Hunter, her face hot. Before she could properly accuse Aeolmar of trickery, the hunters and *nuvi* crowded around them, congratulating Latera as the victor. Then they parted for the queen. Asherah took the unknown's helm from Latera's hands, and proclaimed her the winner.

"I don't feel like I won," Latera protested. "Aeolmar had his sword at my neck."

"You outlasted the rest of the *nuvi*," Asherah stated. "And you took the unknown's helm. That is a great accomplishment, especially when the unknown is the First Hunter."

The *nuvi* lined up against the side of the arena, and cheered as Asherah tied a red sash around Latera's waist. *Saffira* led them to the great hall, where the victory celebration was already underway. Latera caught up with Adhaire, who was nursing his wounded pride.

"A toast to the victor," he said, as he handed Latera a cup of wine.

"I wish I'd been able to disarm Aeolmar," Latera grumbled.

"No one bests him. He excels at everything," Adhaire said bitterly.

"You don't love our leader?"

"What's to love? He gives us impossible tasks he knows we can't accomplish. He sets us up for failure to reinforce his own ego. It's not fair." Adhaire clenched his fists.

"Maybe he only wants the best," Latera said.

Adhaire put his arm around Latera's shoulders and led her to a bench. They sat, Adhaire straddling the bench as he faced Latera. "You'll see," he said. "You're still new, but you'll see how he treats us."

Latera frowned, so Adhaire told her funny stories until she laughed so hard tears rolled down her cheeks. At some point, Adhaire took her hand. Suddenly Adhaire fell silent, and Latera realized that the First Hunter was standing over them.

"May I speak with my lady?" Aeolmar asked.

"Your lady," Adhaire muttered.

Latera stood. "Of course."

"Follow me," Aeolmar said. Adhaire held onto Latera's hand until she was out of his reach. Aeolmar noticed but said nothing. Latera followed Aeolmar out of the hall and across the courtyard, until he stopped at the far end. She watched his features outlined in the torchlight, emotions warring on his face.

"Is something wrong?" Latera asked.

He shook his head, but his expression didn't change. "I wanted to commend you. You fought well today."

Why couldn't he have told me that inside? "I only wish I'd disarmed you as well. Next time, I'll expect you."

"There won't be a next time for you."

Latera's heart sank. "Have I done something to displease you?"

"What? No, no," he said quickly, "you've exceeded all of my expectations. Your teachers tell me that you're the best student they have ever had...and you're the best *nuvi* I've yet encountered."

"Thank you," Latera replied, bowing her head, "But if that's so..."

Aeolmar turned away from the torchlight. "I've spoken with the queen," he said. "In two seasons, the next hunter will be named. That hunter will be you."

"Is that fair?" Latera asked. "Others have trained for far longer than me."

"You are the one who deserves it," Aeolmar replied. "There is no set amount of time one needs to spend in the *sola*. Some hunters didn't enter the *sola* at all. Finlay was never a *nuvi*, and you're a better fighter than he. I wasn't a *nuvi*, either. The honor is given to the one who deserves it the most, not the one who has spent the most time in training."

"But I haven't completed the next Trials. What if I fail?"

"I know you can call fire," he answered, "and I'm sure that poor horse remembers as well." Latera looked at her feet, hiding her continued shame over burning Petal. "Asherah has decided to continue your training herself over the next two seasons. She will oversee your Trial by Stealth."

"I thought you would train me," Latera said, with unexpected disappointment. "Surely the queen has more important matters to deal with than me."

"You forget, the queen is a huntress. You couldn't find a better teacher in all Parthalan," Aeolmar said. "She has decreed you will be her burden. Not that training an excellent student is ever a burden," he added.

"I appreciate it, but it does concern me that I'll be named before the others."

The troubled look returned to Aeolmar's face. "Are you afraid it will cause a rift between you and Adhaire?"

"I'm afraid it will cause a rift between me and all of the *nuvi*, not just him."

"I saw him holding your hand. I thought there was something between you," Aeolmar said carefully.

"There's nothing between us but friendship." Latera sat on the edge of the fountain. "Do you always enter the Trial?"

"No. Usually the unknown is played by one of the other hunters, or one of Harek's *con'dehr*; someone the *nuvi* are unfamiliar with."

"Then why did you enter today?"

Aeolmar gave her a wry grin, and Latera realized that she'd rarely seen him smile since they left Brennus. She liked his smile. "I wondered if you could best me."

Latera rose and beckoned Aeolmar to follow her away from the courtyard ad back to the playing field. It was a ghost of the earlier spectacle, now deserted and lit only by the ruddy moonlight.

"Show me how to best you," Latera said, then she drew her swords. Aeolmar moved toward the stack of wooden practice swords, but she blocked him. "No, with your own sword that inspires such fear in the *sola*."

"I could kill you with this sword."

"Then show me how to stay alive."

Aeolmar drew his sword and advanced toward her with another arching blow. Latera blocked him as she had before, and asked, "What did I do wrong earlier?"

"Act as if you'll take my helm, slowly." As Latera reached toward his head he shifted his weight and she fell toward him. Once again, he pulled her around so her back was against his chest. "Your error was your curiosity," he said, and Latera shivered at his breath on her neck. "When you looked toward the gallery, you moved your focus away from your opponent. I did not, and used your distraction to my advantage."

"I had to know if it was you," Latera said.

"Why?" Aeolmar asked. Latera slid out of his arms and faced him.

"I couldn't embarrass the First Hunter in front of the queen, and all the hunters and *nuvi*. It was my duty to let you win." Latera circled him, waving her sword under his nose.

"Is that a challenge, beautiful girl?"

Latera halted. "Why did you call me that?"

Aeolmar grinned. "Where's your focus now?"

Latera rushed him, but he blocked her. He shouted directions, and Latera altered her attack accordingly. Every time Aeolmar called out suggestions, Latera followed them to the letter. While she couldn't break through his defenses, neither did he break through hers.

They fought on until Latera wondered if Aeolmar had any vulnerabilities or if he was the God of Swordplay himself, when he stumbled and fell to his knees in the dust.

"You win," Aeolmar cried as Latera dropped beside him, both panting.

"You let me win," Latera said when she caught her breath.

"I've never let anyone win. Before tonight, the only other who had the honor of disarming me was the queen. None of the other *nuvi* could have fought with me for this long, nor could most of the hunters. When I say you deserve to be chosen, I mean it." He rose and extended a hand. As he pulled Latera to her feet, the cord that restrained her hair fell away.

"You shouldn't bind your hair," Aeolmar said. "It's a shame to keep something so lovely wound up in knots."

Latera's cheeks warmed, and she turned toward the lightening sky. "It's almost first dawn," she said. "Do your lessons often last all night?"

"No one has ever asked me to teach them before," Aeolmar replied, gracing her with a smile.

"I wish you weren't so sullen all the time," Latera said.

"If only I had more things to be cheerful about." With that they turned to greet the elder sun; while they recited the prayer, Latera realized he hadn't released her hand. When the prayer was complete, Aeolmar turned to Latera and said, "Now I must leave you, my lady." Aeolmar kissed her hand, and added, "If you'd like another lesson, you have but to ask."

When Latera returned to the *sola*, the rest of the *nuvi* were beginning to wake. She drew several interested looks, and Alia caught up with her as she headed to the bathhouse.

"Where have you been all night?" she asked, looking over Latera's dusty attire.

"Aeolmar was teaching me swordplay," Latera answered.

Alia grabbed her shoulders. "Aeolmar?" she asked. "*The* First Hunter? You spent the *entire night* with him?"

"He was showing me how to best him," Latera said.

Alia rolled her eyes. "I bet he was," she said. Latera's icy glare made Alia change her tone, but not the subject matter "Nobles from all across Parthalan struggle to catch his eye. It's rumored that he's turned down every woman in Teg'urnan, even Innetha herself." Latera stared at Alia, shocked. Innetha was regarded as the most beautiful woman in Parthalan, save for Asherah.

"Why does he turn everyone down?" Latera wondered.

"Forget them. What will poor Adhaire say?" Alia mused.

"Why does everyone ask me about Adhaire?" Latera countered.

"Who else has been asking you about him?" Alia demanded. Latera bit her lip, and Alia continued, "No matter who. Adhaire has decided that you should be his. When he learns how the First Hunter favors you, it won't go well."

"I'll hear no more of this nonsense," Latera said. She entered the baths and slammed the door, shutting out the rest of the *nuvi* along with Alia's foolish notions, but part of her wondered if Alia was right.

Chapter Seven

Asherah Speaks

Three mornings after the Trial by Combat I slipped into the sola before first dawn, intent on waking Latera. Since I'd decided to oversee her training, I wanted to get on with it. After moons of hearing Aeolmar wax on about Latera's immense skill, I needed to witness it myself, especially if he thought I'd let her have a place in the palace contingent. It wasn't that I didn't trust Aeolmar's judgement, because I did. However, I couldn't make an exception and risk Latera not being ready for an assignment at Teg'urnan, especially not when Harek had already questioned her ability.

Soon enough, I found Latera's cot. I touched her cheek, and her eyes fluttered open. "Would you like to begin your training today?" I asked.

She sat up and replied, "I would."

"Dress quickly, and meet me outside."

In a short time, Latera exited the sola, and we made our way to the stables. By the time the elder sun rose we had left the palace grounds and were atop the Hill of Torim. I reined in my horse, and Latera did the same.

"Aeolmar tells me you're doing well," I said, after we'd dismounted and sat near the crest of the hill. "Have you enjoyed your training thus far?"

"Yes, my lady."

"You seem to have taken to it well," I said, and she agreed that the sola suited her. "Do you miss your life in Brennus?"

"I miss the people that took me in, but I don't miss being a stable hand." Latera laughed shortly. "I was a stable girl in every meaning of the word. If the inn was full, Ingvarr reclaimed my room and sent me to sleep with the horses. I often wondered how many travelers thought I was addled, and the innkeepers were caring for me out of charity."

I wondered if the innkeepers themselves were addled. Anyone with a measure of sense would have attempted locating Latera's family, if for no other reason than to claim a reward. She was a princess, after all. "Do you know whom this hill is named for?" I asked.

"Your companion, Torim," Latera replied. "She died here, didn't she?"

"She did." I stared at the gnarled oak tree that Caol'nir had planted in her honor, all those years ago. "I love Parthalan," I said. "I would give my life for it, just as Torim gave hers for me. I must know if you feel the same."

Latera looked from me to the palace, then to the tree. "Parthalan has become my home. I won't allow it to be overrun by evil."

"What of Gannera?" I pressed. "You don't feel honor-bound to return to your birthplace?"

"It's been seven winters since I was taken." She pulled up handfuls of grass as she spoke. "They...never came for me."

My heart went out to the girl. I knew all too well how it felt to be alone in the world, abandoned by those who'd once claimed to love you. Before I could say as much, Latera looked up and speared me with her gaze. "Have you ever known another like me? A human who came to Parthalan, whose ears and eyes changed like mine?"

"I've known quite a few humans," I replied, "but never one whose appearance changed from that of a mortal to fae, or elfin," I added; despite Aeolmar's protestations I still thought Latera had a bit of elf blood. "I once knew a human who had been here much longer than you, well over a century, and he only ever looked like a human."

"Over a century," Latera murmured. "How is that possible?"

With a pang I remembered that humans were one of the truly mortal races. How would Aeolmar react if his fiery nuvi left him after a scant few decades? "That's something else I can't answer. Why this realm will choose to alter the appearance of one and not another is a question for a sorcerer, or perhaps a scholar, but not a simple queen like me. But I will say that, for you to look like one of us, you must have had a bit of nonhuman blood to begin with."

Latera frowned, and tore at the ground with renewed vigor.

"Would you like me to speak to my sorcerers? Perhaps they can return you to the mortal realm."

She didn't hesitate in her reply. "I may have been born in Gannera, but I've become a Parthian. I will remain in your service as long as you command it."

I smiled, relieved and a bit surprised at my relief. "Latera, you've made me very happy. It pleases me to no end that you consider Parthalan your home."

We grinned at each other, and I realized that I liked the girl, and... I didn't know how I felt about that. I'd already decided that Aeolmar was only infatuated with her, but she was as sharp-witted as he claimed, and her fighting skills had been plain during the Trial by Combat. And if the rumors were true, Latera had not only defeated Aeolmar during the Trial, but again later that night during a private training session. That made her only the second person to disarm Aeolmar since he became First Hunter.

I'd been the first.

"Has Aeolmar told you that he wants you to be named in the fall?" I asked. When she nodded, I continued. "There is much to teach you in so short a time. I've been told that you're adept at calling fire, but I do need to learn what sort of tracker you are."

"All right. What shall I track?"

"For now, nothing." I retrieved a few maps from my saddlebags, and unrolled one between us. "I want you to be familiar with Parthalan's landscape. Are you adept at reading maps?" As it turned out, Latera was skilled with maps (not that I was surprised), and we spent the day discussing political boundaries, different types of terrain, and other topics that would have bored anyone but her and me.

Latera and I continued to meet every few days, and she continued to impress me. I showed her battle sites, and explained what had gone well or poorly at each of them. We visited locations where demons had infiltrated in the past, saw where they were likely to hide, and divined the best ways to flush them out. I taught her everything that couldn't be learned in the sola, and Latera soaked it all up like a sponge.

Near midsummer we rode north, and camped at the edge of a wide river. As we set up our camp, Latera noticed a furrow in the ground. It was a small depression, hardly as deep as the width of my finger, but it was there nonetheless... and more depressions led away from the river and into the trees. Latera motioned for me to follow, and she tracked the depressions through the forest, and we discovered a demon camp.

A demon camp, well within Parthalan's borders. The area was enormous, the size alone telling us that it must have been established some time ago. I clenched my fists, furious that Harek and his band of fools were always going south, when the threats to our home clearly were not there.

"No one knew this was here," I whispered. "I've not seen them so bold in over a century."

"How many are there?" Latera asked.

"I see four wooden domes, some tents, and at least twelve of them milling about," I replied. "The twelve alone are too many for us, and we don't know how many are inside the domes."

Latera nodded, her gaze never leaving the camp. "Forgive me for asking, but can you call fire?"

"Yes, of course."

"Why don't we burn them out?"

I couldn't help it, I grinned. "Yes, that is what we will do."

Under cover of night Latera and I returned to the demon camp. We said the words to call fire, and watched flames lick the wooden domes. The demons screamed in terror, as Latera and I watched from the safety of the trees.

"Their numbers are more to my liking now," I said, after the domes had burnt to the ground. "Let's make sure those that survived the fire never return."

We ran into the camp and dispatched anything bearing claws or teeth or a smelly, filthy pelt. Soon enough, all of the demons had fled or perished.

"Are you hurt?" I asked Latera.

She shook her head. "I understand why they call you Asherah the Ruthless."

I leaned on my sword, panting. Aeolmar would have scowled for a week if he'd seen how I let the tip of the blade rest in the dirt, but he wasn't there to reprimand me. "Do they still call me that? I've been called many things in my time, and I daresay that's a compliment."

After a short rest, we disposed of the remaining bodies and extinguished the flames, then returned to our camp and the tent we never did erect. Latera moved toward the heap of canvas, but I stayed her.

"Latera, you have completed your Trial by Stealth," I declared.

Her pale eyes went wide. "But the Trial is something that needs to be set up, planned. This was just something we happened upon."

"You found the tracks and followed them to their camp. You found a veritable city of demons, and now it is no more." I smiled at she who would be my newest huntress. "The Trial is passed, my friend."

"There is one thing I would ask of you, my lady," Latera said.

"Anything, you have but to name it."

"We've only been training for a short time, but I feel that I have so much more to learn," she said. "Must it end now?"

"I will never understand how Aeolmar found one so suited to this life in a stable," I murmured. "I've enjoyed our time together as well. Yes, we will continue to train together until you are named in autumn."

And so we traversed the countryside for the rest of the season. I kept my peace about Latera having already completed the Trial by Stealth, although everyone rightly assumed she would be the next named. On the last day of summer, we again rode to the burnt-out demon camp and surveyed our handiwork.

"You may leave the sola tomorrow," I said as we picked our way among the charred debris. "I've chosen rooms for you that are near my own."

"I'm to have a room in the palace?"

"Yes, all of the hunters have rooms in the southern tower, even those not assigned elsewhere. Did you think you were to remain in the sola?"

"I hadn't really thought about it," Latera said. "Won't the room be wasted if I'm assigned to the border?"

I gazed out over the burnt remains of the demon village as I responded. "Latera, it's very lonely to be queen. I can speak to you as an equal, and while you've shown me respect, you've also shown me friendship. You aren't afraid to question me, and you always answer me as truthfully as your heart allows, not like others who only tell me what they think I'd like to hear. Therefore, I've decided that you'll stay in Teg'urnan. It's a selfish decision on my part, but as queen I am allowed to indulge myself occasionally."

Latera bowed her head. "I'm glad that you've enjoyed my company, as well." She paused, then asked, "The palace contingent is led by Aeolmar, is it not?"

"Yes, it is. He also requested that you remain in Teg'urnan."

"Did he say why?"

"I didn't question his intentions," I replied, which wasn't really a lie. I knew exactly why Aeolmar wanted her to remain, even though he hadn't said as much aloud. "Would you like me to?"

"No, no," Latera said, shaking her head. "I'll ask him myself."

I felt a smile touch my lips; Aeolmar finally had someone who would question his every move. I couldn't wait to see how that played out.

Chapter Eight

The next day a *saffira* showed Latera to her new rooms. Alia accompanied her, and they both gasped when they entered Latera's spacious new chamber.

"My father's home is large, but it has no rooms like this," Alia said.

"I'm a king's daughter, yet I don't believe I've ever seen a room so fine," Latera said.

The room was a large, open space with three arched doorways on the left that opened to a balcony. To the right was a large sleeping platform, which was several steps above the main level and piled high with cushions and furs. The walls were covered with dark blue and gold mosaic tiles that extended up to the vaulted ceiling, and many ornate metal lanterns hung from sturdy chains. In the rear of the room was a sunken bath. The *saffira* opened the tap, and steaming water flowed into a basin large enough to swim in.

"Is everything to your liking?" the *saffira* asked Latera.

"Yes," Latera replied, "more than yes."

The *saffira* bowed her head and departed, leaving Alia and Latera to wander about the chamber.

"Do all the hunters get rooms this wonderful?" Latera asked.

"I certainly hope so," Alia replied. "When may I partake of your bath? I suddenly find bathing in the *sola* beneath me." She leaned down and splashed Latera with the warm water.

"Never, if this is the way you'll behave," Latera replied, darting out of the spray. Alia looked over Latera's shoulder, and gave her a knowing glance.

"I think I'll leave you now," she said through her smirk. Latera followed her gaze to find Aeolmar standing in the doorway. Alia gave him a respectful nod as she passed, and shut the door behind her.

"What do you think?" Latera asked, spreading her arms wide. "Isn't this room grand? I can't believe I'm going to live here!"

"It's quite a change from the *sola*," Aeolmar agreed. "Asherah certainly favors you."

"I suppose she does," Latera said. "She's very kind to me."

"You'll be named tomorrow, at second dawn. Are you prepared?"

"I've been trained well. I'm as prepared as I could be."

Aeolmar favored her with one of his rare smiles. "Good. You've proven that my faith in you was sound."

"Thank you," Latera said as she ducked her head. Aeolmar was the first person to ever have any sort of hopes for Latera. In Gannera she was merely expected to be pretty and docile, and Ingvarr and Elma had never pushed her to do anything more than care for the horses; they probably wouldn't have minded if she'd reduced herself to peeling vegetables. But Aeolmar had shown Latera that she could be more than a vapid princess or a grubby stable hand, and she appreciated that beyond measure.

Aeolmar held her gaze for a moment, his blue eyes searching for something but he didn't say what, before he walked out to the balcony. Latera followed, and they watched the courtyard below.

"The queen said that I'll be assigned to the palace contingent," Latera ventured.

"Yes, that's correct."

"Why aren't I being sent to the border? Aren't all new hunters sent there?"

Aeolmar's gaze remained on the courtyard. "Would you prefer the border? It's a rare privilege to guard the queen."

"What of Adhaire?"

"What of him?" Aeolmar snapped, facing her at last.

"It's not his fault he didn't complete the Trial in Brennus," Latera replied. "He feels slighted by fate."

"Adhaire feels slighted by many things. You worry too much for him."

"I implore you, my lord, he deserves to be named," Latera continued.

"Do you ask this to keep him near you? So you two may patrol the border together?" Aeolmar demanded.

"Why do you always ask if I want him near me? He's my friend, my fellow *nuvi*. I want for him the same things I would want for Alia," Latera replied, irritation creeping into her tone.

Aeolmar ground out, "You don't ask me to name Alia, only Adhaire."

"What business is it of yours if I do want him near me? You're just as infuriating as he is!" Aeolmar's eyes widened, and Latera worried she'd gone too far.

"I'm sorry," she said. "I spoke out of turn. Forgive me if I've said something to offend you." Latera turned away and stared straight ahead at nothing in particular, wishing he would just leave. Her knuckles were white from gripping the stone wall, and she considered leaving Aeolmar alone on the balcony with his ridiculous notions.

After Latera had fumed for a time, Aeolmar touched her hand. Latera didn't react, determined to ignore him for as long as possible.

"Latera, please. Look at me." She did, and saw that the anger was gone from his face. "I'll speak to the queen about Adhaire, but I make no promises. It's Asherah that names the hunters, not me."

"Thank you, for hearing my request," Latera said.

"I fear I can deny you nothing," Aeolmar sighed.

Latera smiled. "Then I'll be sure to make my requests important."

They remained on the balcony together, watching the activity below. "My lord," Latera began, but Aeolmar held up his hand.

"I've asked you not to call me that, especially when we're alone."

"Very well, Aeolmar." He smiled when Latera said his name. "I don't want to make you angry, but please tell me why you questioned me about Adhaire."

The troubled look returned to his face. "I know what he's like, and you deserve better."

"I can take care of myself in these matters."

"That doesn't mean I can't offer you advice." Latera thought that he wasn't offering advice so much as telling her with whom to associate. Rather than say this directly, she tried a softer approach.

"You will assign him to the border if he is named?" Latera asked.

"Yes," Aeolmar replied. When Latera looked at him expectantly he added, "With you added to Teg'urnan's contingent, there are ten. There is no room for him here."

"Is that the only reason?"

"Would you like it to be the only reason?" They had barely resumed their contest of wills when Aeolmar threw up his hands. "I don't want to argue with you," he said. "Please, I'll fight with you again tomorrow, but no more today."

Latera smiled. "As you wish, Aeolmar," she said, and they remained on the balcony together until the elder sun set, and didn't speak of Adhaire or contingents again.

Chapter Nine

The next morning, Asherah stood atop Teg'urnan's central steps above the palace square, clad in the armor that marked her as the she-wolf of Parthalan. The First Hunter stood to her right, and behind him hunters were assembled by rank while the *nuvi* were lined up on the queen's left. The palace square was as crowded as Latera had ever seen it, with onlookers having shoved themselves into any available space; some were sitting atop the hawker's carts, and others shoved themselves onto balconies and window ledges. Latera wondered if all of Parthalan had turned out for the naming ceremony, and the feast that would follow.

As the elder sun rose Asherah looked toward the square, her silver armor shining. Her gauntlets were set with blue stones that flashed as she gestured, and the helm was shaped like a wolf's head. Asherah led her Parthians in the prayer to the elder sun, and once the child sun began his ascent she removed the helm and addressed the *nuvi*.

"As the child sun follows his father across the sky, so the *nuvi* follow the hunters. Today, the best of you is named." Asherah turned to Aeolmar, and asked, "First Hunter, who shall be named?"

"Latera," he replied, his voice booming across the square.

Ignoring the butterflies in her stomach, Latera approached the queen and knelt before her. Asherah placed her metal-gloved hand on Latera's head and proclaimed, "Latera, you are hereby my huntress.

Rise and join your brothers and sisters, for you are honored among them."

Latera stood and took the place of the newly named at the First Hunter's right. Aeolmar beamed at her, and she couldn't help but return his smile. When Latera was in position Aeolmar looked forward, and called, "My queen, there is another. Adhaire!"

Adhaire's eyes widened, then he too approached the queen.

"Surprised?" Asherah asked.

"A little, my lady," Adhaire admitted, as he knelt.

"Don't be. You deserve the honor." Asherah placed her hand on Adhaire's head, and said, "Adhaire, you are hereby my hunter. Rise and join your brothers and sisters, for you are honored among them."

The assembled people cheered, breaking the solemn atmosphere of the naming. Adhaire took his place beside Latera, as the onlookers cheered. As Latera gazed across the square packed full of happy Parthians, she wondered if she'd ever felt so content.

Following the naming there was a celebration in the great hall, and everyone from the square packed themselves inside. Latera arrived long after the festivities had begun; sick of wearing her riding leathers day in and day out, she'd changed into a purple silk gown. The fitted bodice and sleeves were edged in silver embroidery, and the full skirt trailed behind her. Latera's freshly washed curls bounced across her shoulders and almost to her waist, restrained only by a simple clasp.

Latera stood at the entrance to the hall, excited and overwhelmed by the gathering. She'd regularly attended state functions in Gannera, since ad the king's heir her presence was all but required. With a pang, she realized her sister Jannei was now heir by default. She shoved those memories away; remembering her sisters made her heart ache, and today wasn't a day for sadness.

A hand shot out of the crowd, and Adhaire grabbed Latera's wrist. "We've both had such good fortune," he said. "This is a sign from the gods."

"Is it?" Latera asked. "A sign of what, exactly?"

"That we should stay together."

"I fear we won't be together for long," Latera said, freeing herself from his grasp. "I'm staying in Teg'urnan, while you're to go on to the border."

Adhaire's brow furrowed. "All new hunters are sent to the borders. It's been that way for many winters."

"The queen has decreed otherwise." Latera remembered Aeolmar insistence that there wasn't room for Adhaire in Teg'urnan, but didn't mention it.

"Then we'll make the most of our time together," Adhaire declared. Something across the room caught Adhaire's eye. He made his apologies to Latera, and rushed off. Latera made her way through the crowd, and found Alia.

"I don't think I've ever seen so many people," Latera said as they sat. "I didn't think there were this many people."

"They're excited,'" Alia said. "Two hunters haven't been named at once in over one hundred winters, not since before the last great battle was fought here."

"Great battle?" Latera repeated. "You mean the Battle of Esguth?"

"That's the one. However," she continued with a sly smile, "the people aren't only discussing the many strong warriors in our midst. Everyone saw how Aeolmar smiled at you."

"He was pleased that I did well," Latera said. "That's all."

"He looked like he was besotted with you," Alia said. Latera glared, but Alia was undeterred. "And when Adhaire was named our First Hunter didn't even hazard a glance in his direction."

"Are you expecting me to defend Aeolmar's facial expressions?" Latera turned away from her gossip-hungry friend, only to have her gaze land upon Aeolmar. He was standing near the center of the hall, deep in conversation with Finlay. Instead of his usual battle gear he wore a fine blue tunic that made his dark blue eyes shine, and black trousers tucked into boots. His chestnut hair was loose, and fell in a shining wave well past his shoulders. Ever the warrior, his sword hung at his side.

Alia followed Latera's gaze, and rolled her eyes. "Oh, not you too."

"Not me what?" Latera demanded.

Alia pointed at Aeolmar, but Latera grabbed her hand and held it down. "You see?" Alia asked. "If he isn't gazing upon you, you stare after him, and neither of you will admit it. If one of you doesn't say something soon you'll spend eternity staring at each other. Just talk to him."

Latera glanced at Aeolmar, and for all her bravery she couldn't move. "What could I possible say to interest him?"

Alia replied, "It doesn't matter what you say. If you speak, he will listen."

With that, Alia smiled sweetly and shoved Latera off the bench. As Latera made her way through the crowd Finlay walked away from Aeolmar, and she hesitated. She was prepared to engage him in conversation with another present, but confronting him on his own was an altogether different matter. If Alia hadn't been watching her like a hawk Latera would have fled the hall. Then Aeolmar saw Latera, thus ending her planned retreat. For long moments they watched each other, then he took the last steps toward her.

"I've never seen you in anything like this," Aeolmar said, indicating her purple gown. "You look wonderful."

"I could say the same of you," Latera said. She caught herself staring into his eyes and looked away. Her gaze traveled to his hands; he was holding an object wrapped in black silk. Before she could ask what it was, Adhaire erupted from the throng and grabbed her elbow.

"Dance with me," Adhaire said as Latera yanked her arm away from him. Undeterred, he grabbed her waist.

"Not now, Adhaire," Latera snapped.

Adhaire looked from Latera to the First Hunter, and dropped his hands. "Very well, you've made your choice." With that, he turned around and shoved his way through the crowd.

"I think he's had too much wine," Latera said.

"It's given him the courage to approach the most beautiful one here," Aeolmar said.

Latera's cheeks heated and she looked down; she couldn't even concentrate on Aeolmar's feet so she focused on the floor. "I wanted to thank you. Not for...that," she clarified, her face going even hotter, "but for your faith in me. You were right, I'm much happier here than I ever could have been in a stable." Latera glanced up, and Aeolmar's warm smile eased her.

"You are very welcome, my lady," he said. He fingered the silk-wrapped object as he beckoned Latera to follow him, and they left the bustle of the hall for the deserted courtyard. Latera closed her eyes and stretched her arms toward the suns.

"On a beautiful day like today, they cram themselves inside," Latera said. She spun around, letting her skirts twirl about her ankles. When she opened her eyes, Aeolmar was standing before her. He placed the silk-wrapped object in her hands.

"This is for you," he said. When Latera just looked at the lump of silk, Aeolmar frowned and unfolded the cloth, revealing a gold cuff set with a red stone. Underneath the stone was Asherah's royal mark, the she-wolf.

"It's called a hunter's gauntlet," Aeolmar explained. "It's only given to the best of the hunters. Surya was the last to earn one, and Finlay before her."

"Does Adhaire get one as well?"

"Adhaire did not earn one. By me giving it to you privately we can spare his pride."

Latera smiled. "You are very kind, First Hunter."

He returned her smile with a smirk of his own. "Don't let that get around." He placed the cuff on Latera's left wrist; he held her hand after it was in place, tracing the outline of the stone. "This is a bloodstone, to remind us of those who have fallen before us."

"Like those you lost, when you were made First Hunter?" Latera asked.

Aeolmar released her hand. "Even though it's called a gauntlet I'm afraid it will offer you little protection in battle. Those of us who have them hardly ever wear them."

"I don't think I'll ever remove it." She traced the stone as he had.

"You'll feel differently after a demon claws at your wrist, trying to take it from you." Aeolmar glanced toward the hall; they could plainly hear the revelers within. "And now, I'll take my leave of you."

"You're not staying?"

"I'm not one for crowds and gatherings. I've offered to patrol, so the rest may enjoy themselves." He turned away, pausing when Latera touched his arm.

"May I accompany you?" Latera asked. "I'm not fond of crowds, either."

"This celebration is for you," he protested. "You've earned this."

"I'm sure Adhaire can create enough merriment for both of us," Latera replied. "I don't think I'll be missed, and I too prefer to have the sun on my face and the wind at my back than to sit in a stuffy hall."

"I'm only patrolling the perimeter," he said.

"As I'm now a huntress assigned to Teg'urnan, I beg you to show me my duties."

He nodded, and without another word they went to the stables, their finery earning them a few curious glances from the grooms. Soon enough, they were off.

***

They left the palace complex, their horses galloping as if chased, and crossed the plain below the Hill of Rahlle. Aeolmar led them to a rocky outcrop, where they stopped to rest. They sat in the tall grass against the rocks, and Aeolmar told Latera about the Battle of Esguth; much of it had taken place where they were sitting. He described being separated from the others and fighting his way back to his commander, only to find him dead at Esguth's feet. What's more, Esguth had killed all the hunters, along with the *nuvi* who'd been pressed to fight that day. As Aeolmar approached the demon it snapped the neck of a *nuvi* named Mena.

"I was too late, even for her," he said. "She was so young, far too young to be in such a battle, and she never stood a chance against anything like Esguth. But Mena had the heart of a warrior, and when the alarm was raised she picked up her sword and went out to fight. He waited to break her neck until I was close enough to hear it. I've never felt so helpless."

"Is that how you felt when you saw me with Mersgoth?" Latera asked.

Aeolmar squeezed her hand. She hadn't realized he'd taken it. "I did, but you proved me wrong. Esguth was maybe half as despicable as

Mersgoth, yet you survived. When you're told that you've earned your place as a huntress, neither I nor the queen say such things lightly."

Latera smiled tightly. "What became of Esguth?"

"I killed him. Then, being that the rest were dead and she had no other options, Asherah named me First Hunter." Aeolmar grazed his thumb across Latera's knuckles. "Mersgoth also attacked that day, but he escaped. When I saw him grab you…" He shook his head, and began again. "I was terrified that yet another would perish, all because I'd never had the strength to kill him. Latera, if you only—"

"Stop."

Aeolmar looked up. "Stop what?"

"Making yourself suffer." Latera withdrew her hand from his, and folded both in her lap. "The *mordeths* are evil. Demons are evil. It's not your duty to destroy them all, First Hunter or no. It's not your fault they did terrible things."

Aeolmar's eyes narrowed. "What do you know of their deeds?" he demanded. "I tell you one story, and you're an expert?"

"I don't need to know anything more about them. I need you to stop hurting yourself." When Aeolmar frowned, she continued, "Aeolmar, you're a good man, a kind man. You deserve to be treated better than you're treating yourself."

"If only I had—"

"If only nothing," Latera said. "Haven't you ever spoken of these events before? Told anyone how these deaths made you feel?" She moved closer and asked, "Why do you let these burdens rest solely on your shoulders?"

Aeolmar's shoulders slumped, his hair falling across his face. "I'm not like you," he said. "I don't have anyone like Alia to confide in."

Latera tucked his hair behind his ear, the softness of it surprising her. She ran her fingers through the long strands, straightening them against his shoulder. "You're wrong again. You have me."

"So you want me to tell you everything that weighs upon my soul? So you can share my burden, as it were?" he asked.

"If you need to, you can," she replied as she dropped her hands. "Or I can just sit here with you, and you'll know that you're not alone."

Aeolmar brushed her cheek with his fingertips. "My lady, I'm awed by your compassion."

"Thank you, my—" Latera frowned. "Why is it that you correct me when I call you 'my lord', yet you refer to me as your lady? It's hardly fair."

"The title doesn't suit me. I'm a farmer's son, and have never been any sort of lord. You, on the other hand, are mine," he replied.

"I don't think anyone can call me theirs," Latera pointed out.

"That's where you're wrong," he said. "You were named today. That makes you my huntress, my lady, my Latera."

"Are we all yours? All of the hunters?"

"Of course."

"So you're *our* First Hunter? If anyone asked Bron, he could claim you as his Aeolmar?"

Aeolmar laughed. "I don't think Bron would want to designate me as his. Or any of the rest, for that matter."

"Then you can be my First Hunter, mine alone," Latera declared. He reclaimed her hand, and kissed her fingertips.

"I suppose that's only fair, my Latera," Aeolmar said. She dropped her gaze as her cheeks reddened. Worried that he'd made her uncomfortable, Aeolmar changed the subject. "Have I told you how much I like your dress?" Latera smiled and straightened her skirt, smoothing the purple silk over the grass. Satisfied with her efforts she leaned back on her hands, and Aeolmar saw her shiver.

"Are you cold?" Aeolmar drew her close and wrapped his arm around her shoulders. Latera held herself still for a moment, then she relaxed against him. She leaned her head on his shoulder and fingered the edge of her sleeve.

"You're so different outside the palace," she said. "Today, you're like you were in Brennus." She looked up at him. "I'd like to make a request of my First Hunter."

"Anything," he said, and he meant it. He would have drawn down the moon if she'd asked him to.

"I understand if you feel the need to act somber and gruff around the others, but with me I want you to be this Aeolmar, the one with no walls built up around him, the one that laughs...my Aeolmar."

"I can try," he said softly. Latera smiled at her victory; when he returned her smile, she blushed and dropped her gaze. Aeolmar chuckled and looked at the sky, and saw that the elder sun was dipping toward the horizon.

"We should return before nightfall," Aeolmar said as he stood, pulling Latera to her feet. "Arknen and Luth are likely already patrolling." When they reached the horses, Latera faced him with her hands on her hips.

"I need you to look away while I mount up."

"Afraid I'll peek up your skirts?"

"No! My shoes are very soft, and I almost slipped out of the stirrup earlier." She raised the hem of her dress and revealed her delicate footwear.

"You think I wouldn't catch you?"

"I think you'd laugh, which is what I'm trying to avoid."

Latera made a valiant effort at a stern face, but Aeolmar strode toward her, grabbed her waist and lifted her onto her saddle. The movement was so quick she was still stunned as Aeolmar mounted his own horse.

"So you wouldn't slip," he explained. "I'll even help you get down."

When they returned to the stable, the lack of grooms told them that the naming feast went on without them. They put up the horses themselves, and Latera proceeded to tell Aeolmar that he did everything the wrong way. Aeolmar responded that since he has been brushing horses longer than she had been alive, maybe she should listen to his advice?

Once the horses were in their stalls, they took the long way back to the palace. The sounds of revelry filtered toward them, and Latera was certain she could hear Adhaire begging girls to dance with him. When they reached Latera's door she bade Aeolmar a good night, but he caught her hand.

"I need you to know something," Aeolmar said, drawing her against him. "What you asked of me at Esguth's Rock. You see the man I used to be. I don't know if I can be him again."

"You're already that man. I see him now." She placed her palms on his chest and gazed up at him.

Aeolmar traced Latera's cheek with his fingertips. "I haven't been that man in a very long time, but I'll try to be him, for you." She smiled, and leaned her forehead against his chest. He wrapped an arm around her shoulders as his other hand stroked her hair.

"I only hope I'll be worthy of your faith in me," Latera said against his chest. "I imagine I'm the first stable girl to become a huntress for the queen. I hope I'll make you proud of me."

"Every time I look at you, I'm proud. You've exceeded every expectation of your instructors, and the queen...and of me. You'll be a fine huntress, never doubt that for a moment." He kissed her hair, and heard her breath catch in her throat. "Don't worry so. You're perfect as you are."

He drew back but held on to her hands; he wanted to see her inside her chambers, but he didn't want to overstep. Aeolmar pressed his lips to Latera's fingers as he bowed low, enjoying how she giggled at his overly formal gesture.

"Until morning, beautiful girl."

"Will my First Hunter have an assignment for me?"

"Yes, my Latera, I will."

Chapter Ten

Soon after she was named, Latera learned that while guarding the queen was a rare privilege, it was also rather boring. Finlay told her that no demon had approached the palace in over fifty winters, and he would know since he was the one who killed it. Since her duties consisted solely of patrolling every other day, Latera took to training in the afternoons. One blazing hot day near midsummer found her in the arena, sparring with Alia while Luth and Innetha looked on from their seats in the shade.

Surya entered the arena, and sat beside Innetha. "Who's winning?"

"Latera, though Alia's too stubborn to give up," Innetha replied.

Surya stood, and grabbed one of the wooden practice swords. "Perhaps I'll help out."

"Help which?" Luth asked, but Surya didn't answer as she approached the pair. Latera immediately struck at Surya, pitting herself against both huntresses.

"'Neth," Luth murmured against Innetha's hair. "Go show the girls how it's done."

"You think I can best the Demon-killer?" Innetha countered.

"'Course you can. You have help."

Innetha sighed at the almost-compliment, then rose and grabbed a practice sword of her own. Latera went on the offensive against Innetha as well, then Surya caught Latera's left sword on her hilt, bearing down on the smaller woman until Latera went to her knees.

Innetha knocked away Latera's right sword, as Alia came up behind her.

"Enough," Aeolmar shouted. He strode up to the four, glaring at the panting huntresses. He stopped before Latera, who was still kneeling in the dust.

"When my father taught me swordplay, if I did something foolish he slapped me with the flat of his sword," Aeolmar said, extending his hand to help her up. "Why would he have slapped you today?"

Latera ignored his hand and got to her feet under her own power. "He'd slap me for practicing?"

Aeolmar's frown deepened. "You were overmatched. If these hadn't been practice weapons you'd be in the healers' ward."

"Shouldn't I be overmatched when I'm practicing?" she countered. "How am I supposed to improve if I don't push myself?"

"It's one thing to push yourself, another to invite injury," Aeolmar said. "From now on, spar with only one opponent at a time."

"No."

"Excuse me?"

"You heard me. No."

Aeolmar moved closer to Latera, so close she had to tilt back her head to meet his eyes. "You dare defy me?"

"Defy you? You've hardly given me any orders," Latera shot back. "All I do is lounge around this palace, and ride around it every day or so." Latera realized she was yelling, and didn't care. "And now, instead of allowing me the opportunity to better myself, you tell me to stop. So yes, I am defying you. I will keep pushing myself, harder every day, until I'm as good a hunter as you."

Latera threw her practice swords aside and stalked toward the baths. After a moment, the other hunters followed.

"Coming?" Innetha called over her shoulder. It wasn't an unusual question; like the *nuvi*, the hunters often relaxed in the common baths together. Aeolmar had never bathed with Latera present, originally because he worried he'd make her uncomfortable. Now he worried he'd made her hate him.

***

Latera flung her gear against the wall of the bath house, spouting curses that would have made even Bron blush. She was still cursing when she sank into the steaming tub.

"Infuriating man," she muttered. Latera leaned her head back against the tiled edge, letting the hot water unwind the knots in her shoulders. It did nothing for the knots in her gut.

"It's my fault," Surya said, settling on the bench beside Latera. "I shouldn't have interfered with you and Alia."

"Shouldn't have mattered," Luth said. "We've trained as such before. Once the entire contingent went against Aeolmar. He defeated us without even breaking a sweat."

"Aeolmar abides by his own rules," Innetha said, sliding between Luth and Surya. "Some days he's calm, and other's a lunatic. We've all grown accustomed to him."

Latera closed her eyes, and replayed Aeolmar stalking toward her. She'd never seen him so furious, his dark blue eyes blazing, and all over a training session. "If he thinks I'll abide by his stupid rules, he's a fool."

"Aeolmar's many things," Innetha said, "but a fool isn't one of them."

***

When Latera exited the baths, she found Aeolmar waiting for her beside the door. "I don't suppose I could just walk by you?" she asked.

"If you do, I'll follow."

"Fine. Follow."

They walked for a time before Aeolmar spoke. "You're not happy here."

"I never said that."

"Didn't you?"

Latera halted, and faced him. "I like being a hunter. Truly, I do. It's just..." Latera pursed her lips and turned away. They were at the entrance to the marketplace, and Latera watched the patrons milling about.

"Just what?" Aeolmar prompted. When she didn't answer Aeolmar placed his hand on her shoulder, and moved so he was in front of her. "Latera, if you don't tell me what's wrong, I can't help."

She glanced at his face. "I just get so bored."

"Bored?" Aeolmar repeated. "I brought you from a stable in the woods to the heart of Parthalan, and you're bored?"

"Yes," she replied. "When I was in Brennus, there was always something to do, be it repairing tack or a stable wall or even helping Elma around the inn. Now that I'm a hunter, I patrol, and wait for a demon to attack." She looked up at him, eyes narrowed. "When *was* the last time a demon attacked?"

Aeolmar didn't answer that. "So you thought training was the best way to fill the time. An excellent plan, but having everyone attack you at once would like as not end up with you injured, and laid up in the healers ward. How boring would that be?"

"They were wooden swords," Latera grumbled.

Aeolmar touched her upper arm, and the bruise that was beginning to swell. "I saw Surya strike you. Didn't you agree on a safe word?"

"We did," she replied. "How am I supposed to learn if I don't push myself?"

Aeolmar watched her for a moment, stroking his thumb along her arm. "Is that what you truly want? To learn?"

"Yes," she replied. "You forget, I still know very little of Parthalan."

He had forgotten, being that his huntress looked as fae as the rest of them. "Come with me," he said, and he led Latera inside the palace.

"Where are we going?" she asked.

"Where all your questions can be answered."

They followed the corridors to the northern tower, and to a tall oak door. They entered the dark, quiet chamber, and Latera was confronted by rows and rows of shelves that stretched from floor to ceiling.

"This is the royal archive," Aeolmar explained. "Here, you can learn about most anything you'd like to know."

Latera walked to the center of the chamber and turned in a slow circle, drinking in the sight. She'd often spent time in the archive at Gannera castle, though that room wasn't nearly as grand as this one. Latera noticed a few smaller corridors radiating from the center of the room, which she imagined led to even more books.

"How will I ever find anything?" she asked.

Aeolmar led her to the far wall. A set of parchments hung there. "Here's a map," he explained, and indicated the symbol key. "Books on Parthian history are here, Tingu here, and so forth."

"What are these books?" Latera asked, indicating an unfamiliar symbol.

"Sorcery."

Latera shuddered. "I think I'll avoid that section." She scrutinized the hanging and asked, "What should I start with? What does my First Hunter suggest?"

"History, perhaps?" He noted the location of the history tomes on the scroll, then led Latera to the proper area. Latera followed, and looked up at the tall shelves.

"I'll never reach the top books," she said.

"I'll get them for you," he said. "Latera, I want you to be happy here. I'll do anything you need done."

Latera smiled. "And you'll ensure my happiness by retrieving books?"

"If you need me to, yes." Aeolmar selected a volume from the top shelf, and read the title. It told of when Parthalan had gone to war against the island nation of Ysr. "Did you know that Parthalan once had a navy?"

"A navy?" Latera repeated, her eyes brightening. "Tell me more." And so the First Hunter and his huntress spent the afternoon reading each other stories of past battles. By the time they left the archive, Latera was confident she'd never be bored again.

Chapter Eleven

Aeolmar speaks

"*A*ny idea what this is about?" I asked Finlay.

"None at all," he replied. We'd been summoned to Asherah's receiving chamber by Harek for a meeting of the utmost importance. However, his message neglected to include what the subject of said meeting was to be. The Prelate did enjoy his dramatics.

"Asherah didn't give you a hint?" I pressed. I resented that Harek had commandeered my morning, not that I'd had anything planned. Actually, that was the point; I had an entire half day to myself, and that arse had ruined it.

"Sher said—" Finlay caught my interested gaze and began again. "Asherah said she didn't know, either."

"Sher?" I repeated. "Is that what you call her when you're alone?"

"Wouldn't you like to know."

"Yes, absolutely."

"You'd only torment her with it."

"Of course. Why else would I want to know?"

We entered the queen's receiving chamber, and saw Harek standing before the garden doors with his con'dehr fanned out about him. Asherah and Innetha were seated across the room, their heads close in conversation. I wondered if Asherah had summoned Innetha as some sort of armor against the Prelate. While no one had ever claimed to like Harek, since Innetha's mate, the con'dehr Olwynn, had died while under Harek's command, she barely concealed her hatred of him. It was one of the few things I liked about her.

Finlay and I took up positions flanking Asherah and Innetha, and the four of us looked as one toward Harek. It was as if we were opposing forces about to do battle. Asherah gestured for me to speak.

"We're here," I said. "What's this all about?"

"What this is about is keeping Parthalan intact," Harek replied. "My con'dehr and I have uncovered Asgeloth's latest scheme."

"Oh?" Asherah asked, arching her brow. "And how did you manage that?"

"I sent spies into his nest."

Asherah rose to her feet. "Spies? Did I not expressly forbid you to send spies to the underworld?"

"It had to be done," Harek insisted. "And now, as a result of their courage we have invaluable information to hold back the mordeth-gall!"

"The new mordeth-gall has shown no sign of attacking," I said. "Since he came to power he's only harried the outer lands."

"Building strength," Harek said. "Garnering support. Asgeloth means to strike Parthalan once, and win."

I frowned, and glanced at Asherah. I didn't approve of Harek's actions any more than she did, but if he had uncovered information we might as well hear it. After a moment, Asherah nodded.

"We have learned of an ancient champion," Harek began, "one called a deva'shi. In times past it was an old, feared warrior. Asgeloth means to raise the power of the deva'shi and create a new champion, one that will decimate Teg'urnan."

"Decimate how?" Asherah asked. "I doubt one lone warrior could do much against the might of my hunters."

Harek scowled at the mention of the queen's hunters, but continued, "He will do much with a demon army at his back."

It was Asherah's turn to frown. "You really believe this threat?"

"I do, with all my heart."

"Very well. How do we stop it?"

"That, I don't yet know," Harek admitted. "I will need the aid of the sorcerers to learn how."

Asherah blew out a breath, and looked to her scribe. "Prepare a writ for the sorcerers," she ordered, "and one for the archive. I want every scroll and tablet scoured for any mention of this deva'shi."

"What language is that?" I asked.

Harek blinked. "What language is what?"

"Deva'shi. What language?"

"A form of ahm'ri, I assume."

"It's not," I said. "I speak ahm'ri as well as the gods, yet I've never heard that word." I looked toward Asherah. "By your leave, a linguist should assist in the archive. If we determine what language that word is from, perhaps we can learn where this supposed champion hails from."

Asherah nodded. "As you say."

Harek frowned, but held his tongue. After all, what could he really complain about? We were taking him, and this possible threat, seriously. I'd hate to laugh in Harek's face today, and have this deva'shi come calling tomorrow.

"Very well," Asherah said. "We will turn our resources toward this threat, and learn how to combat it. Thank you, Harek, for bringing it to my attention."

Harek nodded, then he gathered his con'dehr and departed. Once the door was shut behind him, we let our true opinions show.

"Idiot," Finlay muttered.

"Blowhard," I concurred.

Asherah looked from her mate to me. "Agreed. But if we don't at least look into it, we could be setting ourselves up for attack. I'd rather caution than bravado."

"There's more to this," Innetha said. "He's lying about something."

"How do you know?" Asherah asked.

"I don't know how I know," she admitted. "I just do."

Asherah looked at the scribe. "Leave us," she ordered, and he gathered his things and scuttled from the room. When he was gone she continued, "I will find out when Harek's people are in the archive. When they are not, I want you to conduct your own research. Report only to me."

Innetha nodded. "I'll start now, before they arrive. If I don't find anything in the archive, I'll petition Atreynha to enter the vaults." With that she left, the three of us staring after her.

"I thought you had to be pure to enter the vaults," Finlay said.

"Pure of heart and deed," Asherah said. "Innetha believes that Harek led Olwynn to his death. If there's the slightest chance she can avenge her mate, she'll take it."

"She's held on to that after all this time," Finlay mused.

Asherah fixed him in her gaze. "If I thought Harek had harmed my mate, I'd do nothing less."

They stared at each other, and I sensed something happening between them. I also knew that there were many hours yet left to the morning, and I didn't want to waste my rare free time in the queen's chambers.

"If there's nothing more you need of me, I'll go as well," I said. When Asherah only nodded, I added, "Don't be too hard on him, Sher."

Asherah's head snapped from Finlay to me, then back to Finlay. As I closed the door I saw Finlay back up a step.

***

I wandered through the palace, wondering what I should do with myself. In the past, whenever I'd been given the gift of time I got Myrnnhe saddled, and we rode away from Teg'urnan as far and fast as we could.

Since I only had a free morning I couldn't go too far, but I could still put some distance behind me.

I descended the palace steps and saw a crimson braid on the far side of the square; Latera, heading toward the stable. Being that I couldn't think of anyone else I'd rather spend my time with, I followed.

"Latera," I called. She halted, and waited for me to catch up. "Are you patrolling?"

"No, not for a few days yet," she replied. "Why? If you need me to I can."

"No, it's not that." I rubbed the back of my neck. "I seem to have found myself with a free morning."

"Have you," she said with a smile. "Let me guess, my First Hunter is bored."

"A bit."

Her smile widened. "If you like you can ride with me. I'll warn you, it won't be an exciting adventure like you're used to."

If she only knew that this conversation was the most excitement I'd had in years. "I'd love to. Where are you taking me?"

"Berry picking."

***

She was serious.

Latera Demon-killer, the slip of a girl that had killed two, nearly three demons with my sword, was taking me berry picking. The patch in question wasn't far from Teg'urnan, and soon enough we were dismounting.

"Have the cooks decided to apprentice you?" I teased. "Last I checked, they made all sorts of tarts and pies with berries."

"Stop," Latera admonished. "A tart just isn't the same as eating a berry freshly picked. And," she added, her sky-colored eyes glinting, "this is the best brambleberry patch in all of Parthalan."

"The best?" I asked dubiously.

"Yes!" Latera grasped my hand, and walked backward up the hillside with me in tow as she went on about the succulent berries. All I knew was that she was lovely in the morning sun, and I wished she was mine.

It had been nearly a full turn of the seasons since Latera had been named a huntress, and I'd resolved to win her heart. It wasn't going well, since I, slayer of mordeths *and defender of the queen, lacked the courage to tell one woman how I felt. I had managed to spend time with her; indeed, the few bits of idleness I possessed had been occupied with Latera, but those small slices of time were few and far between.*

As I watched her bouncing step, heard her laughter, I knew that today was the day. It was the perfect opportunity; we were alone on a sunny morning, far from Teg'urnan's prying eyes and ears. After we picked berries for a time I'd ask her to sit beside me, then I'd lean close...

"Stop!"

Latera halted immediately, never questioning my order. She was a well-trained huntress, which was something I took immeasurable pride in. "Demon?"

"No." I reached down and withdrew the knife I kept in my boot. The knife I'd used to kill Mersgoth. "Slowly, reach toward me."

I tossed the knife in my hand, catching it near the tip of the blade. Latera realized I was aiming for a point above her shoulder, turned slightly and saw the tree snake bearing down on her. Green scales glittered on a body the width of my thigh, and yellowed fangs protruded from its maw as it reared back to strike.

"Oh," Latera cried as the snake lunged at her. I threw the knife as I snatched Latera into my arms, swinging her about so my body was

between her and the snake. She trembled against me, and rightly so. The venom caused one's limbs to blacken and die, and there was no antidote.

"You're all right," I murmured against her hair, as much for my own benefit as Latera's. I rubbed her arms and back; when that had no effect on her trembling, I tucked her face against my neck. "It's dead."

"Thank you," she whispered, her breath ragged. She glanced at the snake, and saw my knife in its skull. "It would have bitten me."

"You think I'd let a snake bite my beautiful girl?" I asked, and she laughed. She shifted in my arms, but I wasn't done holding her. I pressed my face against her hair; she smelled sweet, like sun-warmed honey. "You're always safe with me."

"I know." She rubbed her cheek against my throat. "I never feel safer than when I'm with you."

If she'd said those words any other day, I would have dragged her to the ground and spilled my heart. That day, I merely kissed her hair before I released her. "We should go." I retrieved my knife and wiped it on the grass. "I've no desire to meet this snake's family."

She nodded, and we returned to Teg'urnan. After we'd returned the horses, we again crossed the great square.

"I wish we'd gotten some berries," Latera grumbled.

"You'd risk getting bitten for a few berries?"

"The season is very short," she explained. "Soon enough they'll all be bound up in pies."

"Mm." I looked toward the suns; it was almost noon, which meant that my time with Latera was over. "The Trial by Combat is tomorrow," I said. "Perhaps you'll be able to console yourself with a pie or two at the feast."

"Perhaps."

I left Latera before the royal archives, and made my way to the sola. *Despite what I'd said, there was no way I'd let Latera go berryless.*

Chapter Twelve

Latera leapt out of her bath, barely pausing to dry herself before she dressed. The Trial by Combat would begin soon, and she didn't want to enter the arena late. If she did, not only would she not be able to sit with her fellow hunters, she might be stuck sitting near the *con'dehr*. No one wanted to sit near the *con'dehr*.

She'd just found her boots when there was a knock at her door. "Yes," she said as she flung the door wide. The First Hunter was standing there, holding a cloth sack. "Aeolmar, what brings you here?"

Aeolmar's gaze traveled from her wet hair to her bare feet. "I assumed you'd be late, and came to hurry you along," he replied as he stepped inside. "I brought you something." He held open the sack, and Latera grinned when she saw the contents.

"My First Hunter risked a snake attack to pick some brambleberries?" she inquired with a coy glance.

The corner of his mouth curled up. "I only take such risks for you."

"Sit with me?" Not waiting for his response, she took the sack, and her boots, out to the balcony. When they reached the balcony Latera settled herself on the bench, where she had left her comb and gauntlets. Aeolmar sat behind her and straddled the bench.

"Eat your berries," he said, then he began combing out her hair. Latera hesitated for a moment, and then swung her leg over the bench to mirror Aeolmar's posture and set the berries in front of her. She selected a plump berry and held it over her shoulder.

"What are you doing?" Aeolmar asked.

"Since you picked them, you deserve the first," she replied. "You did brave the mad snakes."

Aeolmar ate the berry, and admitted, "Maybe you're right about that being the best brambleberry patch near Teg'urnan."

"Told you."

Latera dug out more berries, and Aeolmar teased, "Don't get purple fingers."

"Hush, mean man."

Aeolmar finished combing her hair and began braiding it, and Latera resumed feeding him berries over her shoulder. He ate the first, and the second, but caught her wrist when she offered the third.

"Why are you feeding me berries?"

"Because I want you to eat them." She twisted around to look at him. "Don't you want any more?"

"Mates feed each other," he said softly. "Sharing your mate's food is one of the oldest traditions in Parthalan. It honors how Olluhm fed honey to Cydia while she was with child."

"Oh," she said. "I didn't know that."

"I know you didn't."

"Should I stop?"

Aeolmar frowned, then he leaned forward and selected a berry, his gaze not leaving hers as he brought it to her lips. Latera glanced at the offering, and gently took the berry with her teeth. Aeolmar similarly took the berry Latera offered him, then he finished braiding her hair.

"Am I your mate now?" Latera asked.

"Most definitely." Aeolmar tied off the braid and moved closer to her, his thighs bracketing her hips. "I'll have my things moved to your chamber immediately."

"Will they call me First Huntress?" Latera leaned back against Aeolmar's chest. He slid his arms around her waist, his cheek against her temple.

"If you'd like."

"It's certainly better than Demon-killer." She thought for a moment, and said, "Maybe we should start calling you Snake-killer."

"What?"

"The demon and snake killing mates," Latera declared as she giggled.

"We're going to be late," Aeolmar said against her skin, then he kissed her temple. Latera closed her eyes and sighed, and wondered if being late to the Trial was such a bad thing.

Aeolmar was up and moving a moment later. Latera gathered the berries and her gauntlets, and set the sack on the ledge above her hearth.

"Give me a moment." Latera slipped a gauntlet over her arm, then took one of the laces in her teeth. Aeolmar strode up to her and took the laces, finishing one and then the other. The task complete, he dropped her hand and left the room, Latera following close behind.

Once they were in the crowded corridor Aeolmar placed his hand at the small of Latera's back as they moved through the throng, and they made their way to the arena. When they reached the stairway to the gallery, where Aeolmar would stand beside the queen while she watched the Trial, Latera said that she would find a seat in the arena.

"Wait." Aeolmar caught her elbow and drew her toward the base of the stairs, away from the crowd. "I must ask you something."

"Is something wrong?" Latera asked, squaring her shoulders.

"No, nothing," he replied. "Will you go riding with me tomorrow?"

"Will we be patrolling?"

"No." He cupped her face with his hands, and continued, "I'm not ordering you as your commander. I'm asking you, as a man. Will you go riding with me?"

Latera recalled his arms about her waist, the way he'd kissed her temple. "I will very much enjoy riding with Aeolmar, the man."

"You will?"

"I will."

"Then I'll come for you at second dawn." He swept his thumbs across her cheekbones, and kissed her forehead before he released her.

"There you go again," she said as she turned away. "Kissing the top of my head, like I'm your favorite pet." Aeolmar grabbed Latera's shoulders and pulled her back against his chest.

"I kiss the top of your head because you're so tiny, it's all I can reach," he said.

"You could have said something," she continued. "I would have found a rock, or a tree stump—"

Aeolmar lifted Latera and set her on the second stair, and their height disparity was gone. "You would have found a rock or stump to do what, exactly?"

Latera licked her lips, her face hot all the way to her neck, but she held his gaze. "To be the same height as you."

"Would you?" Aeolmar murmured, lacing his fingers with hers. Latera nodded and squeezed his hand, her heart pounding against her ribs.

"Aeolmar."

The First Hunter cursed softly, then looked over his shoulder at Asherah. "My queen," he greeted.

Asherah looked at the two, and smiled. "Latera, would you like to join us on the gallery?"

"No. I-I—" Latera began, her face hot for a new reason. Aeolmar turned his back on the queen and led Latera to the arena's entryway.

"I'll come for you tomorrow," he said, and then he kissed her hand. "I'll be on the lookout for stumps and boulders," he warned. Latera smiled, then she nodded a farewell to the queen and fled around the corner. She leaned against the wall, pausing to catch her breath, and overheard the conversation between Aeolmar and the queen.

"Have you finally spoken to her?" Asherah asked.

"No." He was silent for a moment, then continued, "I picked her some berries."

"Berries?" Asherah asked.

"Brambleberries," Aeolmar clarified.

"Those are her favorite," Asherah said.

The gong sounded, and Latera made her way to the arena. She wondered what that was all about, what Aeolmar was waiting to tell her. Her fingers grazed the spot where Aeolmar had kissed her temple, and then the braid he'd worked while she ate the berries he'd picked for especially for her.

Mates feed each other, he'd said before he'd offered her the berry.

Gods, what in the nine realms does he want to talk about?

Chapter Thirteen

Latera entered the arena, determined to enjoy the Trial and not dwell on whatever Aeolmar and the queen had been talking about. For all she knew, Aeolmar wanted to ask her something about his horse.

She scanned the seats, and saw the hunters clustered together in the higher benches. Latera moved toward them, then she noticed Innetha sitting alone.

"Mind if I sit with you?" Latera asked. Innetha nodded, and Latera sat beside her.

"You're wondering why I'm not with the others."

"A bit."

Innetha remained silent, and Latera turned her attention to the field. The *nuvi* were entering, and taking up their positions around the edge of the arena.

"I can't be near Luth right now."

Latera turned back to the huntress. "Did he upset you?"

"No, he's been wonderful. He's always wonderful." Innetha looked at her lap, her hands folding and unfolding. "Did I ever tell you about my first mate?"

"You had a mate before Luth?"

Innetha snorted. "Luth is not my mate."

"But, don't you sleep with him?"

Innetha snorted again; Latera didn't know if she should be irritated or embarrassed. "I've slept with many people. The act alone doesn't make someone a mate." Innetha leaned close and whispered, "One of my former partners is on the gallery right now."

Latera looked at the gallery, occupied solely by the queen and First Hunter. "Aeolmar?"

"No, Asherah."

Latera exhaled a great breath as her shoulders slumped. Innetha asked, "Why is that such a relief to you?"

"It's not," Latera replied. "It's just…"

The gong sounded again, and the Trial began. "You were saying you had a mate," Latera prompted.

"Yes. His name was Olwynn. He was a *con'dehr*, and as magnificent a warrior as there ever was."

"A *con'dehr*?" Latera glanced toward Harek's men.

"He was nothing like those fools," Innetha snapped. "He was kind, and loyal, and I loved him as I never thought I could love another. Would you like to know the last thing he ever said to me?"

"Tell me."

"We were dressing for battle, and he pulled me to him and ordered me not to die because he'd hate to go to sleep without loving me." Latera's eyes widened, and Innetha laughed. "You practically ignore that I've bedded royalty, yet you're shocked that I made love to my mate?"

"I didn't ignore what you said about Asherah," Latera replied, "and I'm really not accustomed to such frank talk." Latera glanced around, noting that all the spectators seemed to be focused on the Trial. "Well? What was it like?"

"With Olwynn?"

"No. Asherah."

Innetha's smile widened. "She's very playful, and very attentive."

"Do you still...go there?"

Innetha laughed. "How are you so ignorant?"

"I am not." Latera pouted. "I remember the *sola*, the goings-on there."

"The *sola* has more than goings-on, and we both know that." They laughed together. "I'm sure Surya would give you a bit of instruction, if you're curious."

"Not you?" Latera fluttered her eyelashes.

"Careful," Innetha said, nodding toward the gallery. "The First Hunter seems quite interested in our conversation."

Latera turned toward the gallery and yes, Aeolmar's gaze was fixed on them. "If he frowns any harder he'll crack a tooth," Latera said.

"I wonder what's gotten him so worked up," Innetha said.

Latera turned so Aeolmar couldn't see her face, and said. "Aeolmar kissed me."

Innetha arched a graceful brow. "When was this?"

"It all started yesterday," she replied. "We went to pick berries but we were attacked by a tree snake. Aeolmar killed it, then he stood there holding me and kissing the top of my head."

"He was holding you? You weren't holding him, as well?"

"I was," Latera replied. "It was...nice? No, nice is not the right word." Latera thought for a moment, then continued, "Anyway, he went back and got the berries, and gave them to me this morning. Then he braided my hair and we fed each other berries and he kissed me here." Latera pointed at her temple. "Then he asked me to go riding, and he kissed my forehead, and I said he was treating me like his pet, then Asherah caught us and asked Aeolmar if he finally spoke to me. He speaks to me all the time! What could they have been talking about?"

"I was wondering how with all this kissing, he keeps missing your mouth," Innetha said.

Latera looked at her hands. "I was wondering that, too."

The spectators began shouting, and Latera looked toward the playing field. All the *nuvi* were down, and the unknown warrior was removing his helm.

"Padashen," Innetha muttered when the unknown revealed his identity. "That explains why no one won."

Latera nodded. "He's too competitive for his own good."

"Think you'd have beaten him?" Innetha asked.

"No idea," Latera replied. "I hope I never find out."

The huntresses followed the throng and they left the arena for the main hall. The atmosphere was jovial even though no one had beaten the unknown, with the *nuvi* consoling each other over cups of wine and speculating as to next year's victors. Latera found herself near the smaller hearth when Innetha and Alia both rose to refill their wine. A moment later, Aeolmar sat on the bench across from her.

"Wine?" Aeolmar asked as he handed her a cup.

"Thank you." Latera accepted the cup, and noted it was golden wine rather than the usual red. "Do you prefer the gold wine?"

"It reminds me of home. I saw you talking with Innetha earlier. Is everything all right?"

"Oh, yes," she said quickly, having no intention of telling Aeolmar what their conversation was really about. "She misses her mate, one from some time ago."

"Olwynn?"

"You knew him?"

"I did. He was one of the best men I've ever met."

Latera put down her cup. "I don't know why anyone bothers with mates."

"Why do you say that?" Aeolmar asked.

"If something happens to one, then the other is just set drifting, bereft." She glanced at Aeolmar, then at Asherah on her dais. "It's not just Innetha. Look at Asherah. Everyone knows she lost her mate long ago. And there she sits, alone."

"Asherah moved on," Aeolmar said, "as did Innetha. Their mates wouldn't have wanted them to dwell on their losses. Their mates wanted them to be happy."

"That's just it," Latera said. "I don't know if I could go on. I mean, I think being mated is wonderful, but to be the one left behind…"

Aeolmar squeezed her knee. "Does that mean you'll make sure you'll die first?" he asked, and Latera swatted his hand. "I thought we were mates, after earlier. Do you think I could go on without you?"

Latera snorted. "If we're mates then I'll definitely end up miserable. No one is more likely than you to go off and get yourself killed."

Aeolmar took her hand, kissed her fingertips. "So you'll miss me."

"Perhaps."

Innetha and a wine jug-bearing Alia returned. While Alia refilled everyone's cups, Innetha said, "The First Hunter needs to work on his aim."

"It's better than yours," Aeolmar said.

"Not this time."

"What is wrong with you?" Aeolmar demanded. "If you have something to say, say it."

"I believe I did."

"Stop," Latera said, rising to her feet. "Both of you, stop."

They both stared at Latera, so she turned and left the hall. When she was in the corridor, Aeolmar caught her elbow. "I'm sorry," he said. "We learned some unsettling news yesterday, and it's put us all on edge. I suspect it's why Innetha's missing Olwynn, too."

"Unsettling?" Latera said. When he nodded, she placed her hand on his arm. "If you need to talk, I'm here."

He scrubbed his face with his hands, then he pushed back his hair. "Not here." Aeolmar took her hand, and led her to her chambers.

They encountered a *saffira* along the way, and liberated a wine jug from his cart. Once inside her chambers Latera poured the wine, and they sat before the hearth.

"Harek called us—by us I mean myself, the queen, Innetha, and Finlay—to a meeting yesterday," Aeolmar began, and he told her everything that had transpired in the queen's chambers. By the time he was done recounting the events they were sitting on the floor, and had the sack of berries between them.

"Do you think this threat has merit?" Latera asked as she fed Aeolmar a berry.

He swallowed, and replied, "Truthfully? I've no idea. However, we should at least look into it. I'd hate to endure Harek's gloating if he was right and we all ignored him."

"Good point. And none of you have ever heard of a *deva'shi* before?"

"Not a one, not even Asherah or Atreynha." Aeolmar fed Latera a berry. "What do you think?"

"If this legendary warrior hasn't been around for centuries, and no one has ever heard these stories save for a few obscure bards, then he's not all that legendary, is he? Like as not Harek heard some campfire tale and took it too seriously."

Aeolmar chuckled. "Exactly what I thought." He refilled their cups, and asked, "What if the threat is serious?"

Latera shrugged. "Then we will fight."

Aeolmar cupped her face with his hand, stroking his thumb over her cheekbone. "My mate is wise." Latera's cheeks warmed and she ducked her head. "You see how mates comfort one another? Still think they're not worth the bother?"

"Maybe a small bother." Latera glanced at his other hand, and said, "Get your purple fingers out of my hair."

Aeolmar smiled as he withdrew his hand. "The berries were your idea."

"Not this morning."

"Two out of three, then." Aeolmar leaned against a chair leg and sipped his wine. "Have you ever had a mate?"

"Me? You're joking." She eyed him over the rim of her cup. "And you, First Hunter?"

"Never," he admitted. "Who would put up with me?"

"I've no idea," she said. "Not even a lovemate?"

"Long ago, yes," he replied. "But I never felt as I should with a mate."

"Like Luth and Innetha, then," Latera murmured.

"Yes, like them."

"Gods, that must be worse than being mated. Being with one who will never love you..." Latera drank more wine. "It's terrible."

Aeolmar took her hand. "You think you wouldn't be loved?"

"I think it would break my heart if I wasn't." She rubbed her thumb across his palm. "Why are you always kissing me?"

Aeolmar pressed her knuckles to his mouth. "I like kissing you. Do you want me to stop?"

"I just wish your aim was better."

Aeolmar examined her hand in his. "I was wondering why you never kiss me back."

Latera blinked. "I never thought to."

Aeolmar blew out a breath and released her hand. Latera bit her lip, then she set down her cup and knelt before him. Slowly, she took his hand and brought it to her mouth.

"You usually kiss me here," she said, pressing her lips to his knuckles. She released his hand, and kissed his forehead. "And here." She moved on to his temple, and said, "I liked it when you kissed me here."

"Did you?" he asked.

"I did." Latera stroked his cheek, the shadow of his beard rough against her fingertips. "Have you ever kissed my cheek?"

"No. Never once."

She leaned forward and pecked his cheek, then she sat back on her heels. "There, then that one's from me."

Aeolmar took her hands, then he saw her empty wine cup. He stood and pulled Latera into his arms.

"What are you doing?" she asked when he lifted her.

"You're drunk, and I'm putting you to bed," he replied. "It's what mates do for one another."

Latera wound her arms around his neck. "I could never do this for you. You're so big I could never lift you."

"All the better for me to protect you."

Aeolmar laid Latera on her bed, frowned, and set about removing her boots and gauntlets. Once that was done, he pulled one of the furs across her body and tucked it under her chin. "Rest well. We're still riding tomorrow."

Aeolmar bent down and kissed her cheek; by the time he straightened, Latera was asleep. "Sleep well, *nalla*."

Chapter Fourteen

Latera Speaks

I woke achy and cramped and not at all comfortable, mainly because I'd slept in my clothes. What had possessed me to do such a thing? My gaze traveled around my chamber to the sack of mostly-eaten berries, my empty wine cup ... two empty wine cups.

"Gods," I muttered, remembering my ramblings about mates and kissing. With any luck Aeolmar had had more wine than I, and had no memory of last night. Then I remembered how he'd carried me to bed and kissed my cheek. And called me nalla. *What in the nine realms could that mean? Something good, I hoped.*

Maybe he could remember a little bit, just not everything.

Much like the day prior, I'd just gotten myself bathed and dressed when Aeolmar himself was pounding at my door. "Wet hair again?" he asked when I opened the door.

"Perhaps if you ever bathed your hair would be wet too," I snapped. Embarrassed by my outburst, I turned my back and busied myself with my gauntlets. A moment later, I felt a series of gentle tugs as Aeolmar began braiding my hair.

"How much do you remember of last night?"

I debated my answers; everything, or nothing? "Enough. You?"

"Everything."

I shuddered, rather obviously since he settled his hands on my shoulders. "Latera, I would never—"

"Never what?" I asked, turning around. "Yell at me? Punish me? You've done both."

To my surprise, he smiled. "Fair enough. Shall we eat before we ride?"

"Please."

We went to the hall, and after a simple meal, and many bowls of tea for me, we got our horses and were off. After a time we found ourselves atop the Hill of Torim. We set the horses loose to graze, then we sat under the old oak and surveyed the plain below.

"The Trial by Combat was disappointing," I said. "Will you be the unknown in the next Trial?"

"That honor will belong to another," he said with that smile I only saw outside the palace walls.

"I wish I could compete again, and best you in front of everyone."

"You wouldn't. That one time was luck."

"Oh, I could, and I will. Spar with me now."

Aeolmar rose as I drew my swords, but instead of reaching for his own he grabbed the spear he kept behind his saddle. Before I could adjust for the unexpected weapon he knocked the sword from my left hand.

"Not a good beginning," he said.

"I only need one sword to defeat you," I retorted.

We circled each other for a time. I easily evaded the spear by blocking his strikes against my upper body, and jumping over the blows aimed toward my legs. Aeolmar lunged at me, and I tossed my sword to my left hand and caught the shaft of the spear with my right, plunging it into the ground at my feet. I poked the tip of my sword under his chin and smiled.

"My lord," I purred.

He responded by kicking my feet out from under me. I fell and Aeolmar caught me, pulling me against his chest. "My lady," he said, his eyes glinting.

"Not fair. You have a longer reach."

"*Battles aren't fair.*"

"*Aeolmar, let me go. People will talk if we're seen like this.*" *Despite my words, I put my arms around his waist.*

"*Let them.*" *He stroked my cheek.* "*Beautiful girl, do you know what you mean to me?*" *he asked. Before I could respond, he saw something behind me.* "*Hells,*" *he cursed. I twisted around and saw Brynne's contingent, returning early from the Eastern Border. They were dragging a litter behind them. They had lost one.*

I freed myself, but Aeolmar's hand moved from my cheek to the back of my neck, drawing my face close to his. "*We're not finished here,*" *he said. I nodded, then we mounted and galloped toward the returning hunters.*

I checked all the faces in the contingent, but one wasn't there. While Aeolmar spoke with Brynne I left my horse and approached the litter, and drew back the covering.

It was Adhaire.

I screamed, backing away from his body and stumbling into Aeolmar. He tried to turning me away but I couldn't stop staring at Adhaire's face. His right cheek was burnt, and there were long gashes across his neck. His eyes remained open, frozen in fright. I couldn't imagine what horrors he'd seen.

"*Let them continue on to Teg'urnan,*" *Aeolmar said.* "*Let them bring him home.*"

I nodded, and Aeolmar signaled to Brynne. We stood by the side of the road and watched them until they disappeared behind the palace walls.

"*What happened?*" *I croaked.*

"*Brynne said he was on watch, and he saw a pack of four in the distance. Rather than wait for the others he went after them himself.*"

"*That sounds like Adhaire, always wanting to be the hero.*" *Aeolmar put his hands on my shoulders and I leaned my forehead against his chest.*

"He'll be remembered as a hero. Latera, I know he was your friend. I wish I could have kept you from seeing him like that. When Brynne told me who it was I wanted to stop you, but you already knew." I must have lost my balance, since Aeolmar's arms wound around my waist and held me to him, his lips so close I felt his breath. My mind was blank, and I let the numbness wash over me and soak its way into my soul. It didn't help.

At length I asked, "Do you need to speak with the queen?"

"Yes, but that can wait," he replied. "Brynne will speak with her first." I pulled away and looked for my horse, who was nowhere to be found. Understanding my confusion, Aeolmar told me that he had asked Brynne's hunters to bring our horses to the stables. I nodded, not trusting my voice. We started down the road to the palace, but when we were close to the gates I halted. They were already constructing Adhaire's pyre in the square.

"I need to be alone," I said as I turned away. Aeolmar tried catching my hand but I evaded him. "I know you only want to help, and I appreciate it. Go, speak to Asherah. I know you have obligations." He reached for me again, and I didn't move away.

"My obligations can wait." With his thumb Aeolmar tilted my face up to his, forcing me to meet his eyes. "Mates comfort one another, remember?" He wasn't looking at me with sadness, or pity; it was empathy, something I didn't deserve.

I couldn't look at him and walk away, so I looked at the pyre. "I'm not your mate," I said as I pulled myself free.

He grabbed my shoulder. "Latera, I didn't mean anything by that."

"I know. Go to the queen," I said as I walked away. He didn't reach for me again, and I didn't turn back. I walked like one possessed through the busy streets of Teg'urnan, and almost without knowing where I was headed my feet brought me to the sola. I found Alia inside, curled up

on the cot Adhaire used to call home. I sank down next to her, and we mourned our fallen friend together.

***

Adhaire's body laid atop the pyre for the rest of the day, wrapped in white fabric that did a poor job of hiding his wounds. When the child sun was going to rest, Asherah took her place at the head of the pyre. She spoke of Adhaire's life, and declared that stories of his bravery would be told for many winters. The queen then lit his pyre, and the hunters formed a ring around the flames, guarding Adhaire's ascent to the next world.

I couldn't bring myself to approach the blaze, so I watched from the gatehouse. As he always did, Aeolmar found me. I should have asked why he wasn't at the pyre, for as First Hunter shouldn't he be making a speech or something? But I was too exhausted to care, and we watched the flames together.

"It's my fault," I said.

"It is not," Aeolmar said. "Did you send demons to ambush Brynne and her people? Did you strike the blow that killed him?"

"I may as well have. You knew he wasn't ready, but like a fool I begged you to name him. It should be me upon the pyre."

"Would that make you happy? Death?" he demanded. "Do not make yourself suffer for his death the way I made myself suffer for Mena and the others. You told me that was wrong. Prove to me you meant it."

I turned my back; my death wouldn't make things right, but I knew what would. "Assign me to the Eastern Border."

"No!" Aeolmar grabbed my shoulders and turned me around. "You will stay where the queen has assigned you."

"You mean where you assigned me!" I wanted to beat his chest with my fists, rail at him that he shouldn't have listened to me. Didn't Aeolmar know not to place such importance on the requests of an insipid girl? That he should have reprimanded me for daring to ask such things of him? I was so angry with him—with myself!—I could hardly see, or even speak. So I cried.

I covered my face with my hands and turned my back, but Aeolmar drew me to him and cradled my head against his shoulder. He whispered that everything would be all right, soothing me, gentling me. We ended up sitting on the stone floor, his back against the wall and his knees drawn up. I pressed my cheek against his chest, listening to his heart. It was strong and steady, just like the man that held me.

When I thought my voice wouldn't fail, I said, "Please, send me to the border to replace him. Let me finish his assignment."

"It won't bring your friend back," he said, brushing tear-soaked hair from my cheeks.

"I know." I looked up at him. "You know it's true, I should have gone to the border. I'm only in Teg'urnan because you wanted me here." He frowned, but let me continue. "You say you can deny me nothing. Let me make this right." I held his gaze and waited for him to argue with me. Instead, he closed his eyes and rubbed his temples.

"Must you leave me?"

"I must fulfill my duty." My head ached, and I laid it on Aeolmar's shoulder. I loved the feel of him against me, as if I was absorbing his strength to replace my own. I would have sat on the floor of the watchtower in his arms forever, if only I could.

"You made this bearable for me. I don't want to think of how hard it will be to watch you leave."

"So you'll miss me."

Aeolmar lowered his hand, and I was taken aback by how striking he was in the firelight. I wanted to retract my words and tell him I would stay, but I couldn't. I had to right this wrong. He nestled me closer, and kissed my forehead.

"I'll miss you," he said, his lips against my skin.

"I...I'm sorry."

"I know."

We sat together until Adhaire's pyre burned out. The combination of the night air and stone floor made us stiff and awkward, and we bumped against each other as we rose. The great square was deserted, the only sound our footfalls echoing on the stone steps. When we reached my door he pulled me into his arms.

"I'd beg you to stay, or forbid you from going, if I thought it would do any good," he said against my hair. "If you need anything while you're there, send word and it's yours. If you wish to return, let me know and I'll retrieve you myself. And please, my beautiful girl, return to me."

I placed my hands on his shoulders and stood on my toes, making myself as tall as possible. "I will. All of it. I promise."

If he had asked me to stay at that moment I would have agreed, but he didn't. Aeolmar pressed his lips to my forehead once more, and then he was gone.

***

The next morning my stomach was so knotted I could hardly greet the elder sun, all because I had to tell Asherah that I was going to the border. Gods, leaving her was almost as bad as leaving Aeolmar. I found her alone in her chambers seated at her table, sorting through heaps of maps and scrolls.

"So, you've decided to become one of Brynne's?" she asked without looking up. Before I could ask how she knew, she continued. "Aeolmar

came here after he left you at your door. I don't think he approves of your decision."

I sat across from her. "Do you approve, my lady? Am I a fool to want to take Adhaire's place?"

Asherah grasped my hand. "Whether or not you and I are fools is a question scholars will debate long after our demise. Do I think you need to do this? No, I don't. But I do know something of duty and obligation, and I understand why you want to do this." She gave my hand a gentle squeeze.

"I'm sorry," I said softly. "It isn't that I want to leave, but I shouldn't have been here at all. If I hadn't asked Aeolmar to speak to you about Adhaire I would have been sent to the border, and Adhaire would be alive in the sola."

"Aeolmar wouldn't have sent you to the border for any reason." I raised an eyebrow at that. Asherah explained, "He insisted that you stay here. For all his confidence in you, he feared for what would happen to you out there."

"I didn't know that." Aeolmar had never mentioned any concerns he had for me, either at the border or elsewhere. I couldn't imagine what would happen there that he would shield me from, yet have no qualms over sending others to that same fate.

The queen offered a gentle smile. "There is much you don't know about him, enigma that he is." She pushed a map across the table. "Here, I've made notations for you."

"You aren't angry with me?"

"Not at all. You feel a wrong has been done, and you wish to right it. I would feel the same, were our roles reversed. I cannot be anything but proud of you."

"Thank you," I said, tears rolling down my cheeks. Asherah stepped around the table and embraced me, stroking my hair.

"Now, none of that. Two winters will pass in the blink of an eye, and we'll all be here when you return. There will always be a place for you in Teg'urnan as long as I am queen."

I remained with Asherah until the child sun rose. We shared our morning meal while she shared advice about the Eastern Contingent. Before I departed from the queen she handed me the map she'd marked up, a gift to help me over the next winters.

It wasn't so easy convincing Alia that I was doing the right thing. To her what had happened to Adhaire was fate, controlled by no one save the gods. I told her that I'd asked Aeolmar to consider Adhaire's naming, but even that didn't sway her.

"You think you're responsible simply because you made a request, and Aeolmar honored it?" she asked. "Aeolmar did so because he loves you, don't you see that?"

That shocked me into silence. Aeolmar had never behaved as if he had any sort of feelings for me; well, maybe that wasn't true. There were the berries, the kissing, the pretend mates... Gods, I was an idiot. When I shared these instances with Alia, she agreed.

"For someone who is touted as the bravest and most intelligent among us, your skull is incredibly thick," she said. "If he were any more in love with you it would be written on his head."

I clasped and unclasped my hands. "Have you ever heard the word nalla?"

"It means beloved. It's what mates call each other."

"Oh."

Alia's brows lowered. "Has someone called you that?"

"Yes. Someone has."

I left Alia and searched the palace for Aeolmar, but he was nowhere to be found. I did, however, find his second.

"Finlay," I called, as I ran to his side. "Have you seen Aeolmar?"

"He took his horse and left," Finlay replied. "That was just after first dawn."

"Where did he go? Did he say when he would return?"

Finlay shrugged. "I don't know where he went."

Gods, he was gone. Just when I was beginning to understand what I felt for Aeolmar, he was gone. "Thank you, Finlay." I turned to leave, but Finlay touched my arm.

"He'll return soon," Finlay said. "Trust me, Aeolmar won't let you leave without saying goodbye."

"I fear he already has."

"Sweetheart, he'll be here. I'm sure of it."

I nodded, and went on my way. Despite Finlay's insistence, I was certain that Aeolmar didn't want to see me. I'd missed my opportunity with him, if one had ever existed to begin with.

The next day my new contingent assembled to leave, and the entire palace came to see us off. Asherah gave a short speech of how we were going off on a noble quest to defend Parthalan, but I hardly heard it. Aeolmar still hadn't returned, and his absence was breaking my heart. He had always watched the contingents depart, and now he was avoiding Teg'urnan because of me and my foolishness. I hoped that once the palace was out of sight I could turn my thoughts to other matters, and forget about him.

I turned to mount my horse, but Bron captured me in one of his great bear hugs.

"Can't get away from us that easily, little one," he rumbled. He set me on my feet and the hunters of Teg'urnan clustered around me, giving me advice, such as which taverns had the best (and worst) ale, where the best blacksmith was located, and the cheapest suppliers.

"Remember, Brynne's all talk," Finlay whispered. "You'll do well."

"Yes, you will," Innetha said as she smoothed my hair. "Send word if you need us."

"I will."

Lastly, I embraced Asherah, and then Alia, and then I mounted up and followed my new commander down the royal road and away from Teg'urnan.

As we passed under the stag and doe, my head hanging low as I studied my horse's ears, Brynne called for us to halt. I twisted around in my saddle, and saw Aeolmar riding toward us at a furious pace. He stopped before Brynne and gave her a quick instruction, and the hunters continued onward as he motioned for me to remain.

"I told Brynne you'd catch up," he said when he reached me. "I'm sorry I'm late; I meant to return long before you set out." He dismounted, so I did the same.

"You're exhausted," I said. "Where have you been?" His eyes were rimmed in red and he looked as if he hadn't slept in days. He held out a bundle, urging me to take it.

"I went north, to get this for you." I let the bundle unfold, and discovered it was a cloak made from fine gray wool. It had long sleeves and a hood, and the whole of it was lined in dark brown fur. I rubbed the fur on my neck, stunned that Aeolmar would journey for two solid days just to bring me a gift.

"Why are you giving me this?"

"It gets very cold at the border, and I won't be there to look out for you."

I started say that I could look out for myself, but it wasn't the time to be stubborn. "Thank you, Aeolmar. I'll miss you."

"Not nearly as much as I'll miss you." He placed the cloak around my shoulders, and then wrapped his arms around me. I flattened my hands on his chest, the lump in my throat keeping me from speaking. "Remember, we're not finished here."

We stood like that for a moment, and before I could talk myself out of it I stood on my toes and kissed him. I'll never know what gave me the boldness to do so. I meant to quickly touch my lips to his but he held on to me, and for once there were no games, no half-spoken declarations. There was just he and I. My blood ran hot as his lips were on mine, and he grasped me harder, pulling me against him. I clung to him as if I was drowning and he was my only hope of breath, and took all he could spare.

Once we parted Aeolmar pressed his forehead to mine, and I fell into the endless blue of his eyes. "Why haven't you ever done that before?"

"I never thought you'd let me," Aeolmar replied, stroking my cheek with his thumb. "Please don't cry, I can't bear your tears." I smiled but another fell unbidden; as he kissed it away I heard my horse fidgeting. Out of habit I looked at her and saw that my new contingent was beyond the crest of the roadway, almost out of sight.

I hid my face against his chest. "I have to go."

Aeolmar tightened his hold on me. "The only reason I'm letting you go is because you believe you're doing the right thing."

"Thank you, for believing in me."

"Always." Aeolmar shifted so he was holding my shoulders. "Two winters, no more. When you return, I'll be waiting for you right here."

"Asherah said that time would pass in the blink of an eye."

He smiled that half smile, the one that had made me love him so long ago. "May Cydia make it so."

Aeolmar walked me to my horse and watched me mount up. "Don't forget me."

"Never."

I flicked the reins and followed the others. Two winters. For Aeolmar, I could definitely wait two winters.

Chapter Fifteen

If there was one thing Latera was certain of, it was that she hated the Eastern Border.

Her hatred of it began the day she arrived. It wasn't that the outpost was in a remote location, with the hunters' home, a wooden structure called the Long House, perched near the edge of a cliff. It wasn't the bitterly cold wind, or that there was nothing but sharp rocks and dirt as far as the eye could see. It was because the first thing Brynne's second, a man called Kemen, had asked upon meeting her was if she was Adhaire's girl.

"He was my friend," Latera replied, clenching her fist in an effort to control her temper. "We spent time in the sola together. I don't know what you mean by 'his girl'."

Kemen handed Latera a mug of ale. "Adhaire talked about his Latera every day, saying he couldn't wait to return to the palace and claim you."

Latera lifted her chin. "That's a lie."

The hunters erupted in laughter. "Of course it's a lie," Kemen said. "What sort of woman would wait around for the likes of him?"

"Don't you care that he's dead?" Latera demanded. The laughter ceased.

"Everybody dies," Kemen said, "and out here, people die faster than normal. You either make peace with it, or you end up dead with them."

Latera finished the ale, then she left the Long House. While she hadn't expected to immediately befriend this lot like she had the palace hunters, nor had she expected this crude bunch who laughed rather than mourned Adhaire's death.

Maybe this is where the awful people are sent, to keep them away from Teg'urnan. Maybe this was why Aeolmar didn't want me to come here.

But, she was at the border, and she was honor bound to complete Adhaire's assignment. Latera cast one last glance toward the Long House, then she erected the tent she'd traveled with next to the stable. That night she slept alone, wrapped in the cloak Aeolmar had given her, wondering if she'd made a huge mistake.

Two winters. After two winters, I can go home.

The first demon she killed at the border was almost an afterthought. Latera had finished her watch and was heading back to her tent, when it leapt out at her from the shadows. She dispatched it with one clean stroke. As she stood over the corpse, her first thought was that she needed to report the kill to the First Hunter, but that was a leftover of palace life. Brynne was uninterested in kill reports; she assumed that if the hunter was alive and the demon dead things must have gone well, and left it at that. Latera knelt and ripped an eyetooth from the beast, and burnt the body. Afterward, she entered her tent and plunked the tooth into a clay bowl, a tangible reminder to make her report to Aeolmar.

Latera volunteered for the third watch, mostly so she could spend every night alone. Her days were spent either sleeping in her tent or caring for the horses, only interacting with the others when necessary. One night when the wind was frigid and howling, Brynne visited her.

"How long are you going to keep this up?" she asked.

"Keep what up?" Latera countered.

"This," Brynne replied, spreading her hands. "You'll freeze to death if you remain up here every night, and alone in your tent all day."

Latera sighed. Her tent wasn't built for the east's frigid winds, and she'd woken up with blue fingers more than once. "You're probably right. I'll move my bedroll to the Long House tonight, after my watch is over."

Brynne smiled. "You'll come to enjoy it there. Even though you didn't start off well with Kemen, I'm sure he'll welcome you to his bed."

"I would never sleep near him, let alone with him," Latera said, disgusted.

"Then it's true about you and Aeolmar." Latera held her tongue, but Brynne continued, "Of course it is, you're perfect for each other."

Intrigued, Latera asked, "How's that?"

"You both enjoy making yourselves miserable. Tell me, does he still lug around that gigantic sword just to make himself suffer?"

"How could his weapon make him suffer?"

"He took it from a demon called Esguth. Maybe you've heard the story."

Latera remembered the day they'd sat at Esguth's Rock, and how Aeolmar had recounted the horrors from that battle. "I have."

"Aeolmar declared that he'd carry the sword in memory of all that had fallen that day, or some nonsense."

"His sword is quite heavy. The first time I held it, I almost dropped it."

"You've touched the First Hunter's sword?" Brynne sneered. Latera, feeling foolish for being the butt of Brynne's lewd humor, looked away. They stood together for a time before Brynne spoke again.

"Regardless of how you feel about him, he's not here. If he was, he wouldn't shiver alone when he could find warmth with another."

"Aeolmar would not. He's far too noble."

"Is that so?" Brynne asked. "I've known Aeolmar much longer than you have. I knew him when he was first named, and when he served at this very border. And," she leaned closer to Latera, "it's well known that Innetha and Asherah both call him to their beds. Do you think he's alone, even now?"

Latera bit the inside of her cheek, and swallowed hard. "How would you know that?"

"Everyone knows," Brynne replied. "It's been going on for many, many winters."

Latera squeezed her eyes shut, tears freezing on her lashes. She felt like a fool, freezing cold and pining away for someone who probably didn't even remember her name.

"I know it seems like I'm being cruel, but I only want you to know the truth. It will ease your time with us." Brynne took Latera's elbow and led her into the Long House, where the other hunters slept in twos and threes before the hearth. She watched as Brynne joined the two closest to the fire, then Latera retreated to the farthest corner. The next night she moved her bedroll to the stable and slept with the horses, much as she'd done in Brennus.

***

A sennight later, a clutch of demons invaded the stable. Out of thirty horses, only six survived. If Latera hadn't been sleeping in the last stall, they would have lost all of them.

The next morning, Brynne departed for to Teg'urnan to request replacement horses from the queen. While she was gone Kemen was in charge, enjoying and abusing his position. The rest of the hunters also enjoyed it when Brynne was away, since they lounged about the Long House emptying cask after cask of ale. Latera alone kept to her patrols, and once Kemen and his usual companion, Lura, decided that she wouldn't tell Brynne about their questionable behavior, they left her alone.

A moon passed, then Brynne returned with fifteen horses. Leading the way was a fine golden mare, who was easily the most beautiful horse Latera had ever seen.

"She's for you," Brynne told Latera, as they settled the horses into the rebuilt stable.

Latera thought she'd misheard her commander. Not only did all hunters share the horses, this mare was fine enough for Asherah, not a simple huntress like Latera. "Why do I get my own horse, when others do not?" she asked.

"Your First Hunter selected her for you. When I told him how you preferred to sleep in the stable instead of the Long House, he must have thought you were terribly lonely." Brynne watched as Latera combed her fingers through the mare's thick mane. "He's named her Enna."

"Why did he decide on Enna?" Latera wondered.

"If you don't know who Enna is to him, you obviously don't know him as well as you think," Brynne snapped. Latera ignored Brynne; she was so overjoyed with the Enna before her she had no interest in her horse's namesake. Well, almost none.

The days stretched on, and Brynne went to Teg'urnan in the autumn as she did every year. As soon as she was out of sight Kemen began pursuing Latera more relentlessly than he'd ever pursued any foe, demonic or otherwise. On the third day these annoyances he crept up behind her in the stable, while she was brushing Enna. Latera spun around and shoved him face first into the wall.

"Did Aeolmar teach you how to do that?" Kemen asked, his voice muffled by the wood.

"He taught me many ways of dispatching vermin." Latera released him, and stood with her arms crossed over her chest while he straightened himself. Kemen was an attractive man, nearly as tall as Aeolmar with black hair and striking green eyes, but Latera felt nothing for him, save contempt.

"What is wrong with you?" she demanded. "You know I have no interest in you. And won't Lura be offended if you run around chasing others?"

"Lura's tired of me for now," he said, rubbing his wrist.

"I can't imagine why." Latera turned back to her horse.

"She's just like everything else out here, hard and cold," Kemen continued. "You know how long I've been here? Fifty-four winters! What I wouldn't give for a season in Teg'urnan's warmth."

"Why have you been out here for so long?"

"My father's long shadow. He's a priest of the old gods, and Asherah believes he wants to have her dethroned."

"Is Asherah right?"

Kemen shrugged. "I've no idea. I haven't spoken to my father in decades, and I've never once spoken to him about the queen." Kemen watched Latera for a moment; once she looked up, he said, "However, if a huntress who had the queen's ear took a liking to me, and brought me to the palace with her..."

Latera glared at Kemen. "And who would this huntress be? Surely you don't mean me. I can't wait for the day when I leave this wretched place, and you, behind."

He leaned close and whispered, "You can only remain alone for so long out here."

"I'd rather freeze to death than accept anything you have to offer."

As he left the stable, he called over his shoulder, "If that happens, I'll enjoy warming your corpse."

Latera flung the brush into the hay. *If Kemen dies first, I'll push his corpse off the cliff and leave it to rot at the bottom.*

Soon enough, winter began its frigid reign. The cold weather didn't dampen Kemen's pursuit of Latera, so she kept sleeping in the stable. Fortunately, her sleeping arrangement was what kept the newly replaced horses alive. Latera heard some scratching, and caught three demons trying to break down the walls. Latera called fire to run them off, and accidentally burnt down half the stable in the process. The commotion roused the others, and as they spilled forth from the Long House more demons poured up and over the cliff.

Fighting alongside the demons, the hunters saw something foreign to even the most seasoned among them: a monstrous beast, larger than the horses or any animal Latera had ever seen. It had two curved horns jutting from the sides of its head, a maw packed with sharp teeth, and massive cloven hooves. It rampaged through the battle, and didn't seem to care if wounded a hunter or one if its demon handlers.

The battle wore on, and the beast trapped Kemen against a boulder, its head thrashing wildly about. Latera ran towards them, and watched in horror as the beast gored Kemen. Latera killed the beast and retrieved Kemen, though Brynne doubted he'd survive the night. He managed to pulle through, though he was confined to the Long House thereafter.

After that day, the attacks came in earnest. While the wind howled as strong as ever, Latera never felt the cold as the sweat of battle ran down her face. If she hadn't already earned the name Demon-killer she would have that winter, and she soon needed a larger jar for her grisly trophies.

Gods, I cannot wait to go home.

Chapter Sixteen

Aeolmar Speaks

I followed the two senior sola *instructors, Jase and Ren, as we made our routine inspection of the arena; the Trial by Combat was being held in two days' time, and this inspection, while not mandatory, was as much of a tradition as the Trial itself. What's more, the impending Trial meant that Latera had been gone for almost one full turn of the seasons.*

It also meant that in just one more turn of the year, she would return to me.

A wise man would concentrate on the second fact. A rational man would throw himself into his work, and ignore the passage of time as the date of her return moved ever closer. I have never been wise nor rational about Latera.

I missed her so much my heart ached, my head pounded, and my skin burned with the need to touch her. To hold her again. We'd become so close in the days before she left, and part of me wondered if we'd be able to pick up where we'd left off, or if we were over before we'd ever properly begun.

No. I would not allow us to be over. Not without a fight.

"My lord? Is something wrong?"

Ren's question roused me. I followed his gaze and realized I was scowling at the wall, my fists clenched as if I was going to start pummeling the stones. "Boredom, nothing more," I replied, flexing my fingers. "We should be done soon, yes?"

"There is the tunnel that passes under the seats, and that should be the end of it."

The instructor indicated the tunnel's entrance. I grabbed a torch and ignited it with a word, enjoying how the other two flinched. I was glad they wouldn't have my back in a hunt, but it did make me wonder why we let this spineless lot teach the nuvi.

With me at the lead, we entered the tunnel. It went on, as tunnels do, and my companions made note of any cracks in the walls, and where the ceiling needed shoring up. I continued around the curve that mirrored the layout of the seats above, and found a wooden barrel set in the center of the path.

"That wasn't here before," I said, to no one in particular. I approached, and saw the Prelate's mark, a golden sun, painted on the barrel's lid, and snorted.

Times past, when Parthalan was new, the first Prelate to the crown was Solon, Olluhm and Cydia's firstborn son. In time Solon became the child sun and passed the mantle of Prelate on to his firstborn, as did the next, and so it was until Asherah took the throne. Officially, the old king's Prelate had died during the Battle for Teg'urnan and left no issue, but some stories claimed Asherah pardoned him, and he left the palace and took his family far to the west. No matter which version of the story was true—and I was certainly not going to ask Asherah to relive those days just to settle a bit of gossip—it meant that Harek, while Prelate in title, was not descended from Solon.

Had anyone ever called him a fraud? To my knowledge, not within his hearing. But there were those who said Asherah needed a true Prelate. I thought Asherah ruled the land just fine on her own, but Harek's ego was as fragile as the thinnest eggshell, and he created his Prelate's mark to compensate for his lack of interesting heritage; he had a ring forged, too, just in case we forgot his title while speaking to him face to face. There were rumors about what else he was compensating for, but I ignored those. The less I knew about Harek, the happier I was.

But as for this mysterious wooden barrel, I was intrigued. "Is this supposed to be here?" I called out.

The instructors hurried to my side, and gaped at the barrel as I had. "Is it ale?" asked Jase.

It did resemble a keg. "Only one way to find out."

I grabbed the knife from my boot and pried off the lid. Instead of golden ale, the barrel was filled with black sand.

Why is there a barrel of sand underneath the arena? I moved to touch it, but Ren grabbed my forearm. "That's not sand, my lord," he said. "Keep your torch clear of it."

I moved it away. "Why?"

"One spark, and that powder will explode."

"Ren, scout for more barrels," I ordered, and he was gone a moment later. "Jase, I need the log books. I want to know every person who entered the sola and arena, starting the day after the last Trial."

Jase nodded, and went to retrieve the log books. I stared at the black powder, wondering how—and why—Harek had done this.

***

After we'd finished our sweep of the sola and the arena, Jas, Ren, and I enlisted the nuvi *to search the whole of Teg'urnan. In the end we turned up two hundred and fifty-four barrels of powder, all of them marked with Harek's seal. Two hundred and fifty-three of them had been hauled into the center of the arena while we decided what to do with them. One sat in the middle of Asherah's receiving chamber as the queen paced around it.*

"Why did he do this?" Asherah asked for easily the hundredth time. "Of all things, why this?"

"I don't know," I said. "But we will find out."

In addition to the queen and me, the full palace contingent was present as well as Asherah's saffira-nell, *Attia. The latter had provided the most useful insight on the black powder.*

"Where I'm from, this powder is quite common," she said. "It isn't only used as a weapon. If you mix it with other powders and set it up properly, it will fly skyward and create a shower of colored sparks."

"Sparks," I repeated. "Which lead to fire."

"Harmless sparks," Attia clarified. "Relatively so. They're common during celebrations."

"Perhaps Harek meant to celebrate the Trial by Combat," Asherah murmured. She glanced at her hunters, and frowned. What she saw on our faces told her otherwise.

"He tried bringing in this powder here before," Finlay said. "Remember the day we returned from Brennus, when I stopped the shipment at the gate?"

"I do," Asherah said. "Which means he smuggled it in."

"My queen," I began. "What do you want to do?"

Asherah glanced at the suns; Harek had already been summoned to her chamber, and would arrive soon. "I don't know," she said. "We should at least hear him out."

"I agree," I said. "But, then what?"

"I suppose that depends on what he says," Asherah replied.

Innetha, Luth, and Surya stood, the three of them holding hands. "We've spoken among ourselves," Innetha said, using her free hand to gesture toward the other hunters. "Whatever you choose, we stand beside you."

Asherah let out a sigh of relief, and guilt stabbed me in the gut. Had she really thought otherwise? We were Asherah's hunters, beholden to her alone. I made a mental note to discuss this with Finlay, after Harek had been dealt with. I would not have the queen feeling isolated among us.

"You do realize that this will pit us against Harek and the con'dehr?" Asherah's gaze moved around the room, meeting all of us in turn. "I understand that neither Harek nor his soldiers are favored by anyone in this room. If we stand up to him today, if we tell him to remove this powder from Teg'urnan once and for all, it may cause a rift that will never heal."

"I'll dig that rift myself," I said. "I stand with you, Asherah."

Finlay took her hand. "I stand with you, always."

Attia grabbed her other hand. "As do I, my queen."

"As do I," said Innetha, the rest of the hunters repeating the declaration. Asherah's eyes shone as she gripped Finlay and Attia's hands.

"Thank you, all of you," she said.

"Hunters belong to the queen," Finlay said. Attia grunted, so he added, "As does only the best saffira-nell."

Attia preened at his comment. As for Asherah, the queen beamed at us. It was one of the rare moments when I felt being First Hunter was my calling, rather than something I'd stumbled into like a drunk bumbling through an alleyway. For once in my life, I was proud of myself.

Harek flung open the chamber door, scowling when he saw the queen's hands entwined with Finlay and Attia's; as Second Hunter and saffira-nell, he thought both were beneath her. In truth, Harek was so far beneath them he was practically entombed.

"My queen," Harek said, inclining his head toward Asherah. I noticed ten con'dehr waiting in the outer chamber. Quite a lot of protection for a simple conversation. "Why am I summoned?"

Asherah looked to me. I stepped aside, and Harek's gaze fell on the barrel. "I found something of yours beneath the arena," I said. "Then I found over two hundred more barrels. Planning something, Harek?"

"I don't answer to you," he said.

"Then answer to me," Asherah said. "Why is this powder here? Why, after Finlay specifically rejected it more than three winters past, is there enough of this substance in and around the palace to destroy it?"

Harek glanced behind him. I strode past him and shut the door, separating him from his con'dehr. *"Was that necessary?" Harek asked.*

Leaning on the door, I shrugged. "You tell me."

Harek scowled at me, then he turned to the queen. "If what I've learned is true and the mordeth-gall *does attack, we may need to take extreme measures to defeat him."*

"Destroying our home is not an extreme measure," Asherah said. "It's suicide." She paused, worrying her lower lip. "Why did you do this without my knowledge, or consent? Anyone else would be cited for treason and thrown into the dungeon. Why shouldn't I do that now?"

"Deliverer, I—"

"Do not call me that." Asherah stepped closer to Harek, her black eyes blazing. "You have lost the right to address me as anything other than queen. See to it that every grain of this... this fire sand is removed from Teg'urnan by sun rest today, or you will be spending time in a cell."

Harek's brows lowered. "When the mordeth-gall *comes, you will run to me for help."*

Asherah took the last step toward him, meeting his gaze with a scowl of her own. "If the mordeth-gall *comes, I will cut off his head myself and throw it from the ramparts."*

Harek's nostrils flared, then he stalked toward the door. I stepped aside—though I would have welcomed any attempts to move me—and the noble Prelate threw it open and stomped out of the room in a huff.

"Seems he left his dignity elsewhere this morning," Attia said.

"Agreed," Asherah said, then she bent her head toward Finlay. "Can you speak to the gatekeepers, try to determine if we've found all of the barrels? I don't..." She cleared her throat. "I don't trust Harek to remove them all."

Finlay took her hands, then pressed his forehead against hers. "I will." They separated, and he scanned the hunters. "Bron, Luth, with me. The rest of you, keep your eyes open. If you see the Prelate or his followers do anything out of the ordinary, report to me."

Finlay left the room. The rest of the hunters did as well, each murmuring words of encouragement to Asherah as they passed. When it was only the queen, Attia, and I left in the room, Asherah sat heavily and cradled her head in her hands.

"What is happening?" she asked. Attia sat beside the queen and put her arm around her shoulders. I should have offered her comfort as well, but my mind wouldn't stop replaying Harek's words. I put my hand on the barrel of black powder, and realized what had stood out.

"He said when the mordeth-gall *comes, not if. When." I spun around and faced Asherah. "How would he know when the* mordeth-gall *is coming?"*

Asherah covered her mouth with her hand. "Blessed Cydia. Do you think he's acting as Sahlgren did?"

I hadn't heard the old king's name spoken out loud in so long, it took me a moment to realize what she was asking. Sahlgren had formed an alliance with the previous mordeth-gall, *Ehkron. If she thought Harek was doing the same...*

"How can we know if he is?" I asked. "What did Sahlgren do, in the beginning?"

"All I know is hearsay," Asherah replied. "He closed all the temples and brought the priestesses here, then he selected a group of soldiers to work with the demons. They emptied villages, and set up the slave camps."

I remembered that Asherah had been enslaved as a part of Sahlgren's plans. "Then the con'dehr *may be the key," I said. "I will watch them, see what I can learn. Hopefully, there is nothing to learn."*

"Be careful," Asherah said. "If Harek suspects you, he will stop at nothing to make your life miserable."

I grunted, and turned toward the window. I would not let Harek put our home in jeopardy, regardless if he thought he was doing the right thing. As I tracked the child sun across the sky, I considered how far I would go to stop him.

The answer was easy. As far as it takes.

Chapter Seventeen

As spring turned into summer the demon attacks increased at the Eastern Border. Latera became Brynne's second while Kemen continued to recover from the beast's goring, and her ferocity against the enemy earned her enough respect to sleep in the Long House in peace. The whole of the contingent soon followed Latera's ways, and no longer neglected their duties. Talk around the hearth changed from the bawdy tales Kemen was fond of telling, to stories of past victories. Brynne herself recounted the Battle of Esguth, and everyone sat in silent awe as she described how Aeolmar slew the *mordeth,* and then claimed the fallen demon's weapon as his own.

When Brynne made her next trip to Teg'urnan, her intent was to return with the newly named hunter. Latera was overjoyed when the new hunter arrived, and saw it was her dear friend Alia.

"Tell me everything that's happened these past winters," Latera said, after they'd greeted each other.

"We need to speak of things at the palace," Alia said, "alone."

The two entered the stable, and Alia relayed how the barrels of black powder that were found underneath the arena, and how the Prelate was ultimately responsible for placing them there. Alia was very clear in that all of this had been done behind the queen's back.

"I've heard storied about this powder," Alia concluded. "If they're to be believed, that amount of powder could have destroyed Teg'urnan."

"There's a similar power in Gannera," Latera said. "They pack it into dry gourds and fling it toward the enemy. When it explodes, it injures many at once."

Alia shuddered. "That's awful."

"It is." Latera chewed her lip. "But the powder was dealt with, yes?"

"There's more," Alia said. "Aeolmar has not done well without you. He's miserable, much worse than he was before you came to the palace. Everyone avoids him, and he lashes out at those few foolish enough to approach him."

"How is Aeolmar's mood more important that Harek trying to blow up the palace?" Latera demanded.

"It's not," Alia said, "not to Parthalan at large. But isn't it important to you?"

"I don't know why he's so lonely, when he has Asherah and Innetha to amuse him," Latera said, then she told Brynne's tales to Alia.

"You believe that nonsense?" Alia demanded. "Do you think if he were bedding random women in Teg'urnan he would behave this way? Of course he wouldn't. He misses you, and you miss him." Latera was quiet, raking her fingers through Enna's mane. "She is a fine horse," Alia admitted.

"Aeolmar sent her for me," Latera said. "I'm the only one here with my own horse."

"When will your time be up?"

"Next spring."

"Soon, then," Alia said. "Soon, you can return to him."

Latera's finger's stiffened in Enna's mane. After all she'd learned, she didn't know if she ever wanted to see Teg'urnan, or Aeolmar, again. The stories had hurt her so much, and if they turned out to be true...

"It would be easier to let him go," Latera said.

"Easier, yes, but would it be better?" Alia took her friend's hands. "If you do that, you'll never know what might have been."

***

During Latera's final winter at the border, the weather was their true foe. The wind sought out cracks and crevices as it invaded buildings and clothes alike, and the hunters moved the horses into the Long House to share their warmth. Latera still slept in the far corner, but Alia now joined her to help stave off the cold.

Toward the end of winter the wind abated, and the demons returned in earnest. The demons climbed up the side of the cliff, clawing and scratching and tearing their way through the hunters' ranks. Their caustic blood froze as soon as it hit the ground, and the hunters skidded across frosty red rivers.

Soon enough the ground thawed along with all that spilled blood, and the camp became a muddy, gory swamp. The hunters set small fires to burn off the blood, which created billows of black smoke and only worsened the stench. Then out of the smoke clouds demons poured up and over the cliff as three beasts thundered toward the Long House.

Latera killed two of the beasts, turning the battle in the hunters' favor. Alia and Latera made their stand by the cliff when a demon snaked over the rocky ledge and grabbed Alia by the ankle. Alia yelped, and Latera turned in time to see her dragged over the edge. Latera screamed, certain her friend had perished, and was taken over by a blind fury worthy of Aeolmar. Moments later she surveyed the bodies, and heard a scraping against the cliff. Latera spun around, certain it was another demon, but it was Alia, her hair caked with so much blood it was as red as the moon.

"Are there any more?" Alia asked.

"How did you climb back up?" Latera asked. "How did you not die from the fall?"

"I landed on a beast instead of the rocks, and I climbed many trees in my youth; climbing up rocks is much the same. Don't worry, the beast is dead."

Latera grabbed Alia's hand and gave her a wicked grin. "We have work to do," she said, and they ran back into the fray.

By autumn there was a lull in the siege, and Brynne was confident that she could make her scheduled journey to Teg'urnan, both to return Latera to the palace contingent and bring back the newly named. Latera went to Brynne the morning of her departure, and asked to remain.

"But you've completed Adhaire's time, as was agreed," Brynne said. "You don't like it here. Why do you want to stay?"

"There are too many demons," Latera replied. "I'll remain here, where I'm needed, until the threat has lessened."

Brynne snorted, and again drew comparisons between Latera's love of misery and Aeolmar's own self-flagellation, but agreed that the onslaught was the worst she had seen in years. As Latera watched Brynne ride to Teg'urnan without her, she buried her emotions in the farthest corner of her heart. She would see the demon threat lessened. It was her duty.

She hoped Aeolmar would see it that way, too.

Chapter Eighteen

Asherah Speaks

It was a beautiful spring day, and I was standing at the apex of Teg'urnan's steps waiting to greet Brynne and her hunters upon their return from the Eastern Border, as I always did. Flanking me were my First and Second Hunters, though one was a great deal more anxious than the other.

"Aren't you supposed to meet Latera out on the road?" I teased Aeolmar. "Wasn't that part of your grand promise to her?"

"It was," Aeolmar replied, suppressing a smile. "I'll wait until I can see them before I go down, so I'm not standing there like a fool for half the day."

"No, he's never done anything foolish before," Finlay muttered. Aeolmar must have been in an extraordinarily good mood, since he ignored both Finlay's gibe and my laughter.

"Ah," Aeolmar said, having spotted the hunters in the distance. "They approach."

Aeolmar was off without another word, descending the steps and crossing the palace square so he could finally reunite with Latera, which left Finlay and I alone together. While it wasn't unusual for him and me to be seen in public, I did try to avoid it. Even after all this time I was afraid a careless glance or caress would reveal my heart, and thus endanger Finlay. He, however, held no such qualms.

"How long will you be with Brynne?" Finlay asked.

"Not long. Why?"

"Just wondering when I can have you all to myself."

I glanced at him over my shoulder. "My, you're bold today. I remember when you blushed at the sight of my ankle."

"You do have lovely ankles."

I laughed, then I composed myself and stared straight ahead. The hunters had nearly reached Aeolmar. While I leaned this way and that, straining for a glimpse of Latera's bright hair, Finlay stepped closer and touched my hand. I didn't hesitate before lacing my fingers with his.

"Careful," I said. "One of the saffira saw you leaving my bedchamber. Attia said she's been spreading rumors that you're my latest lover."

Finlay snorted. "Better that, than the rumors about Aeolmar."

I squeezed his fingers. "No one knows more than you how untrue that it."

He squeezed back. "I am in a position to know the goings on in the queen's bed."

I began to speak, then stopped. Where would all of this banter lead us? Only to more rumors that we'd have to quell, when in fact they were all true. I told myself, loudly and often, that keeping my and Finlay's binding secret was for the best. At times like this, when I all I wanted was to throw my arms around his neck and laugh, I wondered if I was afraid of something else.

"Why do you go along with my whims?"

"Which whims are we discussing now?"

"This." I tugged his hand. "Us. Why did you agree to hide us?"

"Because it's what you wanted." Finlay stepped in front of me, and tilted my chin up. "Sher, I'm not hiding that I love you. Everyone in Teg'urnan—hells, everyone in Parthalan—knows that I love you. Most just assume you can do better than a merchant from the south."

I smiled, tears pricking my eyes. He was so sweet, so perfect, and my greatest pain—very well, one of my great pains—was keeping him at a distance, when I only wanted to rest in his arms. I touched his cheek, a *moment away from declaring our ruse ended, when a commotion in the square drew our attention.*

"What's happening?" I asked.

Finlay turned around, and assessed the situation. "Aeolmar's yelling at Brynne."

"That's certainly not unusual." I followed Finlay's gaze; yes, Aeolmar was yelling a bit louder than usual, but screaming matches between he and Brynne were common enough. Wondering what had gotten him so worked up I looked around the square at the returning hunters, gasping when I realized who wasn't there.

"Blessed Cydia. Where's Latera?"

***

My initial thought was that Latera had been hurt, but evidently she had remained at the border of her own free will. What was worse—in my opinion, not Aeolmar's—was that Brynne's second, Kemen, had sustained a grievous wound and was currently in the healer's ward.

"How long will he remain here?" I asked Brynne. I didn't want Kemen in Teg'urnan a moment longer than necessary. In fact, had I known who his father was all those winters ago when he entered the sola I never would have named him a hunter in the first place. "Will he depart with you?"

"I've no idea," Brynne replied. She and I, along with Finlay, Aeolmar, and Innetha were in my receiving chamber. I'd summoned Harek as well, but per usual my Prelate ignored me. We didn't miss him.

"His injuries are terrible," Brynne continued. "He was gored by the beast's horns, and lost much flesh along with the shattered ribs. If Latera hadn't—"

"If Latera hadn't what?" Aeolmar demanded.

"If Latera hadn't killed the beast, I doubt he'd have survived," Brynne replied. "She and Alia are the only hunters who have killed any of those beasts."

"Explain these monster's again," I said.

"They're larger than a mordeth," Brynn said. "They walk on all fours. All have thick hides, and sharp horns."

"This past winter is the first time you've seen them?" Finlay asked.

"Yes," Brynne replied. "Every attack brings a few beasts. The only good thing is that they're dumb as posts. I've seen them eat lessers when the demons get in their way."

"And you left Latera there," Aeolmar said.

"The rest of my hunters are there, too," Brynne snapped. "And I did not leave her. She stayed of her own accord."

Brynne and Aeolmar stared at each other, until he shoved back from the table so fast his chair toppled over, and he stalked toward the hearth. Brynne settled back in her chair, with her arms crossed over her chest and a smirk on her face. Latera not being here was hurting Aeolmar, and Brynne was enjoying his pain a bit too much.

"Brynne," I began, "go to the Prelate, and tell him everything you know about these beasts. I'll have him send a company of soldiers with you when you return."

"As you say," Brynne said, bowing her head. "Would you like to hear the rest of my report?"

"No."

Brynne's face went white, then red as she looked from Aeolmar to me. "As you say," she muttered as she stood and left the chamber.

"Gods, what a shrew," Innetha said. "You'd think she'd be over Aeolmar's rejection by now."

"Apparently it's all that's keeping her warm," I said. "About these monsters appearing alongside the demons; Aeolmar, do you think they could be orcs?" Silence. "Aeolmar? Aeolmar!"

"What?" he roared, spinning around to face us. Behind him the flames in the hearth roared as well. Gods, was he so upset he'd influenced the fire?

"First of all, calm yourself before you burn down the palace," I said. He looked at the hearth, and the fire died in an instant. "Second, I sent Brynne away because she was glorifying in your pain. However, if what she said is true, and Latera stayed behind to hold the border, then she truly is the huntress you hoped she'd be."

Aeolmar sat in Brynne's empty chair, his hair falling in front of his face. "If that's why she stayed."

"Why don't you just ask her?" Innetha suggested.

Aeolmar snorted. "She isn't here to ask."

"Then go get her."

Aeolmar looked up. "She's at the border, six days east!"

Innetha glanced at the window. "You still have some daylight. Leave now."

"I can't just leave," he said. "I have obligations, and—"

"Truth be told, I'm surprised it's taken you this long to go get her," Finlay said. "We had wagers on how long you'd last."

Aeolmar's brows lowered. "Who had wagers?"

"Everyone," I replied. "If you leave today, I believe Attia's the winner."

Aeolmar stood and glowered rather impressively, even for him. "And what was your guess, Sher?"

I'm going to kill Finlay for telling Aeolmar that pet name. Just as well few know of our binding. "I said you were so stubborn you'd go to your grave before you retrieved her."

"I gave you a moon," Finlay said.

"I said a sennight," Innetha said.

"*Interesting, that the queen's* saffira-nell *is the wisest person in Teg'ur-nan,*" *Aeolmar growled, then he stalked out the door. Innetha, Finlay, and I sat staring at the door for a moment, all of us wearing shocked expressions.*

"Is he really going to her?" Finlay wondered.

"Gods, I hope so," I said.

Chapter Nineteen

F ive and a half days after he stalked out of the queen's chambers, Aeolmar arrived at the Eastern Contingent. Hunters and *saffira* alike stopped what they were doing and gawked at him, since none of them could remember the last time the First Hunter set foot at the Eastern Border. Aeolmar scanned the faces, and urged his horse forward when he found Alia.

"Where is she?" he asked.

"The lookout point," Alia replied. Aeolmar nodded, and Alia took Myrnnhe's reins. "Go. I'll see to your horse."

Aeolmar dismounted and headed toward the point, ascending the rock-cut steps as he had so many winters ago; since he and Brynne regularly butted heads, he'd often been assigned the post. He wondered if Latera found Brynne as difficult as he did, and if he and his huntress were more alike than he'd ever realized. As he climbed the hill, hope sparked in his breast.

He reached the cliff, then his breath caught in his throat when saw her for the first time in two winters. Latera was standing at the very edge of the cliff, her shoulders hunched and her cloak wrapped tight around her, fiery braid blowing in the wind. Aeolmar watched her for a moment, his heart thundering against his ribs.

"You look like you're going to jump," he called. "Please don't."

Latera straightened, and cocked her head toward his voice. She looked over her shoulder, and broke into a run when she saw him.

"You're here," she said, throwing herself into his arms. "You're really here."

Aeolmar wrapped his arms around her and pressed his face against her hair; it felt just as soft, smelled just as sweet as he remembered. "You missed me?"

"You have no idea. I hate this wretched place."

"Then why are you still here?" When she didn't reply, he added, "I was waiting for you, on the road."

Latera looked up at him. Her lips were chapped and cracked from the cold, there were dark smudges under her eyes, and her cheekbones were sharper than before. She was still the most beautiful woman he'd ever seen. "You were?"

"I'd never break my word to you." A single tear fell from her lashes, and he wiped it away. "Don't cry, love, you know I can't bear it."

Latera smiled, then she nestled herself against his chest. "What made you come all the way out here?"

"I'm here to bring you home."

"I can't leave," she said. "What with so many wounded, if I go—"

"You're leaving," he declared. "They will fight on without you."

"I can't do that," she insisted, pulling away from him. "I have a debt to honor."

"A debt that isn't yours," Aeolmar said. "Your intent was to finish out Adhaire's time, which you have." His eyes narrowed. "Unless your reasons for being here have changed."

"What other reason would I have?" she demanded. "How dare you come here after all this time and act as if you know what it's been like? Have you been running over rocks and getting burnt and trying not to die? No, you haven't!"

"You forget, huntress, I was here for ten winters," Aeolmar growled. "I know exactly what it's like, better than you ever will."

"You don't know what it's like now," Latera said. "Arrogant man, who do you think you are?"

"I'm First Hunter, and you will obey me!"

"I'll jump off that cliff before I obey you!"

"Go ahead. Jump."

Latera backed toward the edge, Aeolmar assuming it was all a bluff. An instant later she was gone, and Aeolmar rushed to the edge. He found a rope wound around a boulder, and remembered the cave situated just below the rocky overhang. As he gripped the rope, Latera severed it.

***

By the time Aeolmar had climbed down from the cliff, then climbed up to the cave, he had sweated and bled out most of his anger. When he stepped into the cave he found Latera huddled inside, staring into a small fire.

He sat next to her, and they were silent for a time. "Is that the cloak I gave you?"

"A fool man assumed I didn't have enough sense to keep myself warm," she replied. "So yes, it's the one you gave me."

"I gave it to you because I wanted to keep you warm myself, but couldn't," Aeolmar said. "Why are you so angry with me?"

"I'm not," she said. "I didn't mean to disobey you, but I couldn't leave, not with all the attacks…"

Aeolmar reached for her, and she let him gather her against his chest. "You don't have to defend all of Parthalan alone. Brynne told us about the increased attacks, and the beasts. Asherah's sending a company of soldiers here to help."

"She is?" Latera looked up, her brow pinched. "You didn't tell me that."

"You were busy jumping off a cliff." Latera frowned and ducked her head. "Why didn't anyone send word? I would have sent help moons ago."

"I don't know. It never occurred to me to ask for help. I just wanted you to be proud of me."

"I was already proud." He tugged her braid until she raised her head. "Brynne said you're a scourge among the demons, your swords moving so fast you can hardly see them."

Latera smirked. "And you told me not to train so much."

"I was wrong. And I was wrong to let you go." Aeolmar stroked her cheek before he kissed her. "Come home with me. Please."

Latera laid her head on his shoulder. "Will we be like we were before? Dancing around each other and arguing at every turn?"

Aeolmar laughed to himself; the Latera of two winters ago never would have asked such a direct question. "We'd argue less if you listened to me more."

"We'd also argue less if you spent more time listening to my reasons rather than just assuming your way is the only way," she countered.

"Maybe you have a point." Aeolmar pressed his lips to her temple, and asked, "Find any rocks or tree stumps to stand on?"

Latera grinned. "A few."

Chapter Twenty

Latera Speaks

*A*eolmar and I sat together for a while longer, enjoying the fire and each other's company. I'd spent so long convincing myself that my feelings for him were false, but now I understood that those thoughts were merely armor used to keep my heart intact. The moment I turned and saw him—no, the moment I heard his voice behind me—all of that armor was rendered to so much dust.

Gods. He'd come for me.

After the meager firewood had burned itself out we climbed down from the cave, and went to the Long House. The evening meal had just been served, and Lura was poised to tap the ale. All movement ceased when the First Hunter stepped into the room. Aeolmar glanced at me, and I shrugged.

"I've no idea what's gotten into them," I said.

Alia stepped forward, and explained, "They're wondering if Brynne's remaining at the palace, and if you'll be sending a replacement."

"Replace Brynne?" he scoffed. "I don't want the likes of her in Teg'ur-nan." A murmur coursed around the Long House.

"Say something," I insisted. "They deserve to hear from you." Aeolmar frowned, then he cleared his throat and addressed the hunters.

"For those of you who don't know me, I'm Aeolmar. I'm the First Hunter," he began; there was the sound of a plate crashing near the back of the room. "Brynne has informed us in Teg'urnan about the conditions here, and we are sending reinforcements. You've all done very well, and the queen and I thank you."

I touched my fingertips to his palm. "Very good," I whispered.

"Who will the reinforcements be?" someone asked. "More hunters?"

"A company of soldiers." Aeolmar's reply was met with groans across the room.

"Soldiers?"

"Not con'dehr, I hope."

"Is Harek coming too?"

"No Harek, and no con'dehr," Aeolmar assured them, then he moved toward the serving tables. He indicated a cask, and asked, "Is that ale from the tavern in Dreen?"

"It is," Lura replied, then she filled a mug and handed it to him; her sour face when he didn't give her a second glance more than made up for the nights she and whoever she was with had kept me awake. After Alia and I had full mugs as well, we sat at one of the tables.

Aeolmar looked around the great room, his gaze settling on the bedrolls at the far end. "Which is yours?"

"After the delegation left, Alia and I took Kemen's room," I said, nodding toward the door. "It's quieter."

"Kemen's? Isn't Brynne's room larger?" Aeolmar asked.

"Kemen's was cleaner," Alia replied.

"Gods," Aeolmar grumbled, "some things never change."

Platters of food were passed to us, and after I filled my plate I slipped off my cloak; it was my prized possession, and I wasn't about to have it marked by food stains. I'd no sooner draped it across the bench beside me than Aeolmar's hand shot across the table.

"When did this happen?" he demanded. He'd grabbed my hand and was turning my arm this way and that, examining my blood burns. They did look rather terrible.

"Which ones?" I yanked my hand from his and tore into my bread. "We ran out of the burn salve a sennight ago. We've all got burns atop burns."

Aeolmar's mouth was a thin, white line. "Have you more?"

"Yes."

"After we eat, you'll show me the rest."

"What a brilliant way to get me out of my clothes."

"Olluhm's Balls, just go to our room and get it over with," Alia said, rolling her eyes. "I'm trying to eat."

"Alia," I hissed.

"What? He's obviously here to claim you."

Before I could respond, the gong sounded. "Up," I shouted. "All of you, to weapons."

"Attack?" Aeolmar asked.

"Yes," I replied. "Good thing the First Hunter's here. We'll need you."

I shouted orders, and we took up positions along the edge of the cliff face. I ran to the promontory, Aeolmar at my side.

"You're taking point?" he asked.

"Always do." I stood with my hands loose at my sides, waiting for the enemy to show itself. Then Aeolmar grabbed my shoulders and kissed me.

"You're amazing, Demon-killer," he said against my lips. "Be my mate."

Did he mean that? "Ask me again if we live."

He smiled, then he kissed me again. "I can do that."

"Swords out," Alia called. "Time enough for love later."

We parted and I drew one of my swords. Gods, these demons were taking their time. "Want to know what I thought when you kissed me in the cave?"

"Tell me," Aeolmar said.

"That you're worth waiting for."

Aeolmar grabbed my hand. "Stay alive, and I'll show you what else you've been missing out on."

Then the demons came, up and over the cliff like a sickening wave. Aeolmar grinned, and pulled me into the battle.

***

I suppose the battle went well.

No hunters died, lots of demons did, and the only wounds we sustained were a few burns and scrapes. All in all, it was a good day.

Once it was over, Aeolmar barked a few orders that sent the rest scurrying, doing things like burning bodies and checking weaponry. While the rest of the contingent was otherwise occupied, he took my hand and drew me inside the Long House's kitchen area.

"Leave us," he said, and the saffira *disappeared. When they were gone Aeolmar began raiding the larder.*

"What are you doing?" I asked.

"I'm going to treat your burns," he replied. "The tea I sent last Winter's Eve, is there any left?"

I will never forget when the messenger arrived, bearing a tin of fragrant tea from my First Hunter. "Yes, in my chamber."

"Not the good tea," he clarified, "the chaff I sent for the rest."

"Oh. Yes, it's over here."

"Can you brew up a cauldron full?"

"All right." I found a pot and filled it at the well, then I set it on the stand to boil. "Why am I making a lake's worth of terrible tea, when the best tea I've ever had is two rooms away?"

He glanced over his shoulder. "You liked it?"

"I loved it."

"Good." He turned back to the shelves and resumed his search. "You're going to bathe in it."

"I—what?"

Aeolmar set a few things on the work table; a pot of honey, a pail of goat milk, a sack of grain, and lastly a length of cheesecloth. "Your arms are so raw and red you could be a mordeth. Not surprising if you always take point," he added.

"I look nothing like a mordeth," I grouched. "We're just out of the salve. I'll heal well enough, it will just take a bit longer."

"You will heal, because I'll help you." He gestured to the cauldron. "First you'll bathe in the tea, which will take the sting away. After your bath, I'll make you a poultice of oats, honey, and milk that will draw out the burn."

I stared from the ingredients to him. "What of the others with burns?"

"I'll make enough for them, too."

"Where did you learn how to do this?"

"I wasn't always First Hunter," he replied. "When we burnt ourselves as children, this is how my mother treated us."

"You had blood burns as a child?"

"From the oven, mostly." He nodded toward the cauldron. "Make the tea strong. I'm going to have a tub put in your room, and locate a mortar and pestle."

He left the kitchens, leaving me dumbfounded. Gods, was I going to have to bathe in front of Aeolmar?

***

A tub was brought to my chamber, the tea was brewed, and then Aeolmar hauled the cauldron off the stand over the kitchen fire, and dumped it *into the tub with the rest of the water, all without burning himself or spilling a drop. It was rather impressive.*

"While you soak, I'll make the poultice," Aeolmar announced, then he left me alone with a tub full of tea. With a sigh I removed my gear, then I slid into the blissfully warm water. It was relaxing, and my burns did feel much improved. But, he never told me how long I should remain in the bath. By the time Aeolmar returned the water had long since cooled, and I was shivering like a fool.

"Why are you still in there?" he asked, grabbing a length of toweling. "You must be freezing."

"I-I d-didn't know how l-long I should s-stay in," I chattered. I stared up at him, my knees drawn up to my chest. After a moment he bowed his head. Figuring that was the only concession he'd make for modesty, I stood and wrapped the toweling around me so fast I splashed him.

"You'll bathe in front of all the hunters and nuvi, *but not me?" he teased.*

"I never cared if the others saw me naked," I grumbled. I sat on the edge of the platform that served as my bed and asked, "Well? Where's this magic potion of yours?"

Aeolmar stood before me with his arms crossed over his chest, frowning. "Where are you burnt?"

I extended my arms; one had a just small burn near my wrist, but the other was burnt up to my shoulder. After Aeolmar inspected both of them, he asked, "Where else?"

"My leg." I drew the linen higher. The area above my knee was red as the moon, and looked scorched in places.

"Gods, Latera," he said as he knelt before me, "how did this happen?"

"I killed a larger one. I thought it was a mordeth *but Brynne claims it wasn't," I replied. "I shoved my sword straight up into its throat, and the beast's blood poured out like a waterfall. It ate right through my leathers."*

Aeolmar touched a tender spot on my knee and I sucked in my breath, then he looked up at me with the most furrowed brow I'd ever seen. "To leave this bad of a burn it probably was a mordeth. *Blessed Cydia, you're the smallest woman I've ever seen wield a sword, yet you're out here killing beasts and* mordeths."

"Lessers, too." I knotted the linen above my breasts, then I stood and retrieved my clay pot. When I returned to the bed I handed it to Aeolmar.

"What's this?" he asked.

"There's a tooth from every kill I've made, from those that had teeth," I said. "I took them so I'd remember to report each one to you."

He pried off the lid, eyes widening when he saw how many teeth were in the jar. "It will take you two, maybe three winters to report on all of these."

I shrugged. "I didn't take any earlier. I figured that since you're here, you know as much as I."

Aeolmar set the jar aside, then he grabbed a bowl of what I assumed was the poultice. "We'll do the leg first."

Wonderful. I raised the linen as high as I dared, then Aeolmar scowled and pushed it up higher. He spread the thick, sweet smelling gunk across the burn, giving me almost immediate relief. When he was done he wiped his hands, then set about winding bandages around my leg.

"It feels better already," I marveled.

"Didn't you trust me?"

"Obviously. I let you steep me in tea, and now you're spreading some kind of sweet cake batter across me. This is either trust or stupidity."

He gave me a look that made me shiver in places I did not know could shiver. "Careful, or I'll take a bite out of you. Arm."

I held out the arm that was worse off, and he got to work battering me and wrapping me up. After that, the burn on my wrist was done in the blink of an eye.

"Can I cover the bandages?" I asked, though I didn't see how. My bandaged arm was easily twice its normal size, and I could hardly bend my elbow. "Not that my shirt will fit over this."

"Don't you have a night dress?"

"If I'd gone about this place in a night dress there's no way I'd still be—"

And, I shut my mouth. Aeolmar was learning far too many details about me. However, he inferred a different meaning.

"Are they that bad?" When I remained silent he sat beside me and slid his hand along the back of my neck. "Did anyone try anything with you?"

"Everyone tries with everyone here. It's a game, to them." I met his gaze. "I don't think it's a game. Once I made that clear, they left me alone."

Aeolmar drew me close and kissed my forehead. "I don't think it's a game, either. I want you to know that."

I nodded. "I still need something to wear."

Aeolmar grinned, then he stood. "You can wear one of my shirts, if you'd like."

"All right," I said, since his shirts were so much bigger than mine it would be like wearing a tent. He started to pull his over his head, but I held up a hand. "Don't you have a spare?"

"I do."

"Then give me the spare. I don't want the smelly one you've been riding and killing demons in."

After another look that made me shiver, Aeolmar retrieved his spare shirt and held it before me. "Will this do?"

"It's perfect. Give it here." He tossed it to me before turning his back, and a moment later I was clothed. "Not bad," I said, since it fit better than I'd hoped. It also fell to my knees, which was convenient.

"You'd be beautiful in anything." He kissed my knuckles, and said, "I'll see you in the morning, love."

"Where are you going?"

"To tend the rest with burns."

"I'll help," I said, but Aeolmar stayed me.

"Latera, you've done more than enough." He scooped me under my legs and laid me on the bed, then he pulled a fur over me. "Rest, love. You've earned it."

"Why do you keep calling me that?" I asked. "I thought I was beautiful girl."

"You can't be my beautiful girl and my love?"

I gripped his hand, so grateful that he'd come for me. "I can do that."

***

I woke some time later, and heard someone moving about the room. Assuming it was Alia, I tried sitting up, and swore when my bandaged arms and leg made that difficult.

"Latera?" Aeolmar came to my bedside; evidently he'd been the one making all the noise. He'd also stripped off his shirt, and when I looked past him I saw a basin in front of the hearth. He'd been washing up. "Are you all right?"

"I'm fine," I said. "It's just hard to move with these bandages. Are the others well?"

"They are." He helped me to my feet, and said, "The poultice has likely done all the good it can. Let's get it washed off you."

I followed Aeolmar to the hearth, and sat on a blanket he'd already spread out. I stretched out my bandaged leg, but Aeolmar began with my wrist. Once he'd unwound the bandage he soaked a rag in the basin, and rinsed away the dried poultice.

"It feels like I was never burnt," I said as I flexed my wrist. The raised welts remained, but they were utterly painless. "Perhaps you should put up your sword and open an apothecary."

"Perhaps."

Aeolmar went to work on my other arm, and I watched the firelight play off his hair. He was a beautiful man, and I'd missed him so much over the past two winters that at times my heart ached. Then he'd asked me to be his mate, and part of me—a large part—wanted to say yes. The rest of me wondered if Aeolmar and I finally being together was too good to be true.

"Aeolmar," I began. "We should talk."

"We should." He wadded up the bandage and tossed it into the fire. "Do you remember Mersgoth?"

Reliving past battles was not what I'd had in mind. "Of course I do."

Aeolmar didn't look up from washing my arm. "Mersgoth killed my family."

It took a moment for his words to sink in, then I felt gutted. "All of them?"

"Yes." He moved on to my leg, and I winced when he unwound the bandage. "Maybe we should leave this on a bit longer."

"No, it's fine," I said, and he resumed cleaning off the poultice. When he was finished, I asked, "When did that happen?"

"A long time ago," he replied. "I was hardly more than a boy. I'd spent the morning swimming, and when I returned home..." He cleared his throat. "Only my mother still lived. It was she that told me Mersgoth was responsible...and then she died."

"Gods, Aeolmar." I crawled toward him and into his arms, and wrapped myself around him. "I'm so sorry."

We stayed like that for a time, silent save for the crackling fire. Eventually I coughed, and Aeolmar unwound himself from me and retrieved a pitcher and two cups. He filled one of the cups and offered it to me.

"Thank you," I said after I'd sipped it. "I didn't know there was any wine to be had."

"I brought it. I tried to get you some berries, but they're hard to come by this late in the season."

I smiled, remembering the sack of berried he'd once given me. "What made you tell me about your family?"

"I tried to tell you about them, many times. I wanted to tell you before I asked you to be with me, but it didn't happen that way."

"With you." I stared into my cup. "Aeolmar, about that."

"I don't just want to be with you. I want to be bound to you." My head snapped up, my mouth slack but with no words. He took my hand, and asked, "Do you know what it is to be bound?"

"Not really," I replied. "I know that the bond is strong, and it can only be held by two immortals. I don't understand how it works, or how the bond is created. But since I'm mortal, I don't need to know. I'll never be bound."

"Are you so certain you're mortal?" he asked. "If you were, magic wouldn't respond so readily to you. For a mortal to learn the workings of magic takes many, many decades of study, yet you mastered calling fire in less than a day. I can see magic on you, flowing over you like sunlight."

"I'm human," I protested, but Aeolmar pulled me closer, his forehead against mine.

"Not entirely," he insisted.

"How can you be so certain?"

"I'll find out how we can know," Aeolmar promised. "If I'm wrong and you're human, I'll share my immortality with you."

"You would do that?" I asked, shocked.

"Latera, I would do anything for you."

My head spun, my thoughts racing with the implications of what he'd said. If Aeolmar shared his immortality with me, that meant that if my life ended his would as well. Granted, either one of us could be felled by any number of reasons; for all I knew we wouldn't survive the next demon attack. But, that wasn't what Aeolmar was saying. By offering to share his immortality with me, he was saying that he wouldn't want to go on without me.

At least, that's what I hoped he meant. "Aeolmar, we've been apart for two winters."

He took my other hand. "I thought of you every day."

"I thought of you, too." I watched my hands in his for a moment. "I'm a different person now. How do you even know if you'll like her?"

"How different can you be? You're still my Latera."

I shook my head. "Don't you realize how long two winters is for me? I remember Asherah saying that the time would pass in the blink of an eye. For you, and she, I'm sure it did, but two winters is one tenth of the time I've been alive." I swallowed hard. "No matter how badly you want me to be your fae huntress, I'm still a human girl."

Aeolmar dropped my hands and held my face. "You're my huntress, fae or no. Do you really think your race, or your age, matters to me?"

"It matters to me." I touched his cheek, ran my fingertip along his jaw. "I think, before we have any more talk of mates and bindings, we should get to know one another again."

Aeolmar stared into the fire. "Is your answer no, then?"

"My answer is that I want to choose you so badly I can taste it, but I must do it for the right reasons."

For a moment, I worried that I'd made him furious... Then he smiled. Gods, how I loved his smile.

"You're not angry?"

"Not at all." Aeolmar repositioned us so we were facing the fire, with me leaning against his chest. "I have a proposition for you."

I glanced up, noted his mischievous grin. "What kind of proposition?"

"I've already asked you to be my mate, and I have no intention to recant," he replied. "Choose me when you're ready. I'll wait until then."

"You will?"

"I will." Aeolmar kissed my hair. "And, you were wrong."

"Wrong about what?"

"Our time apart did not pass in an instant for me. I lived through endless lonely days, wishing I could see you, talk to you... Wishing I could hold you again."

I nestled myself against him, and traced a scar that meandered across his ribs. "Were you wearing a shirt while you pined away for me?"

Aeolmar tilted up my chin and kissed me. "Imagine it however you'd like."

"Well, then."

Chapter Twenty-One

It took Aeolmar and Latera eight days to return to Teg'urnan instead of the usual six, and Aeolmar accepted the full blame for their slow progress. He found that he just couldn't rise at first dawn as long as Latera was asleep beside him, and she never rose before the child sun. So he let her sleep, and after second dawn Aeolmar became serious about waking Latera, and experimented with kissing her hands, neck, and face, to determine which method was fastest.

Of course, that was all he kissed. Being that they were traveling they slept in their clothes, and Aeolmar was careful with her. He had no intention of claiming her amid the roadside dust, or anyplace else until Latera expressly said that she wanted to be claimed. She hadn't even agreed to be his mate yet, something Aeolmar attributed to her youth. Aeolmar hoped her reluctance didn't signify anything more.

Around noon on the eighth day they crested the eastern foothills and saw Teg'urnan rising in the distance. Aeolmar had always seen the palace as a prison, but now that he was bringing Latera home with him, there was no place he'd rather be.

Once they had entered the palace complex and the horses were seen to, Aeolmar and Latera met with the queen. Even the Prelate's insistence that he should join them couldn't dampen Aeolmar's mood.

After greetings had been exchanged, Latera reported on her time at the border. Harek became positively bored with all the talk of blood burns and chilling winds, and ignored most of Latera's report. He only showed interest when Latera began describing the strange and terrible beasts.

"You say they're horned?" Harek asked.

"Not all of them," Latera answered. "Many had horns, or tusks, and I recall one with a barbed tail. The one that gored Kemen had horns."

Asherah and Aeolmar looked to each other, both of them with pursed lips and pinched brows. "How many of these creatures did you encounter?" the queen asked.

"Beginning last winter, we saw them almost every day," Latera replied. "Every attack had at least one of them; they would just set it towards us and we would run out of the way. The demons themselves grew in number after this, and almost all of our time was spent defending ourselves."

Asherah turned to Harek, and asked, "Do you think these beasts are a sign of the *deva'shi*?"

He replied, "I don't know, but I suspect it has something to do with it. I will investigate further."

Aeolmar produced Latera's trophy jar from the folds of his cloak. He pried off the lid and poured the contents onto the smooth tabletop, covering the polished wood with rotting teeth.

"What is this supposed to be?" Asherah demanded.

"Each tooth represents one of Latera's kills," he replied, "only one."

The queen sat back in her chair, letting this news of the Eastern Border settle in her mind. "Brynne did not suggest that things were this bad," she murmured. "And these beasts..."

"Brynne is proud," Aeolmar reminded her. "Perhaps too proud."

Asherah turned to Harek. "I want those soldiers to leave for the border today," she said. He frowned, but agreed. Asherah grasped Latera's hands across the table, careful to avoid the heap of demonic teeth.

"You look as if you've been at war these past winters," she said, "and from what you've said you may as well have been. I had no idea things were as dire as this, but fear not. We will hold our borders."

"I have no doubt," Latera said.

Asherah glanced between Aeolmar and Latera, and said, "Go, both of you. We'll deal with these demons and beasts on the morrow."

Aeolmar bowed his head, then he and Latera left the queen's receiving chamber.

"Are you happy you're back in the palace?" he asked, once they reached Latera's chamber door.

"I hated the border. I'm very, very happy to be home," Latera replied.

"Home is here, then?" Aeolmar asked. "Not Brennus, not Gannera? You've spent more time at both places than you have here."

Latera smiled. "Home is here."

"You do realize I'm never letting you leave again." He'd meant to sound stern, but his smile made it difficult. "I hereby permanently assign you to the palace contingent."

"Good." She bit her lower lip. "I'd like to rest before I see the rest of the hunters."

"Of course. You'll be in the hall this evening?"

"I will."

Aeolmar kissed her goodbye, and watched Latera enter her chamber alone. As he walked through the wide corridors he remembered the blood burns on Latera's arms and leg, and turned toward the healers' ward. Despite his homemade burn poultice, a small patch on Latera's arm remained red and angry, and while she claimed it didn't hurt, he wanted to put a stronger ointment on it.

He also knew that Brynne's second, Kemen, was in the healers' ward. Aeolmar wanted to speak with him, to assess his progress but mostly to hear yet another tale about his excellent huntress. Aeolmar found Kemen in the ward's solarium, tossing dice with Finlay.

"My lord," Kemen said, inclining his head toward Aeolmar. Kemen had been at the Eastern Border longer than anyone, save Brynne, and Aeolmar could hardly remember the last time he saw him. He hadn't even seen Kemen upon his return a few sennights past, on account of Aeolmar's rush to retrieve Latera.

"You look much improved," Aeolmar said. "Have you spoken with Mallia?"

"I have," Kemen replied. "She assures me that she can loosen these infernal scars. Worry not, First Hunter, more vermin will fall before me," he added with a grin.

Aeolmar nodded, then he asked Kemen about the beast that had dealt him the injury. Kemen described the creature in great detail, then his eyes glazed over with an emotion Aeolmar didn't care for when he spoke of how Latera had rescued him.

"Watching her fight is a feast for the senses," Kemen said. "Such grace, such beauty... It's what first brought my attention to her."

"Your attention?" Aeolmar asked.

"It gets very cold out there," Kemen replied. "I couldn't let the poor girl freeze."

"And how long did she have your...*attention*?" Aeolmar asked.

"Not long," Kemen replied. "But don't worry, she was never cold."

"What do you mean, never cold?" Aeolmar demanded.

"One of her beauty is never alone for long," Kemen said. "That red-headed huntress broke many hearts at the border, mine included."

Anger tinged with pain welled up inside Aeolmar. He finally understood why Latera hadn't returned with Brynne; she'd had a companion at the border. He closed his eyes and made a fist, then he was vaguely aware of his second dragging him from the healer's ward.

"What are you doing?" Aeolmar growled.

"I don't want you to kill Kemen over a few words," Finlay hissed. Aeolmar leaned against the wall and rubbed his eyes. "You don't actually believe him, do you?"

"She didn't come back once her time was over."

"She's here now."

"Because I dragged her here."

"When has Latera ever done as ordered?" Finlay asked, and Aeolmar admitted that Finlay was correct; Latera, king's daughter that she was, cared little for orders regardless of who issued them.

"You know she cares for you," Finlay continued, "and you care more for her than I thought you were capable of. Personally, I would forget what Kemen said. But I know you won't, so just talk to her."

Aeolmar nodded and left without another word. He climbed the stairs to his rooms in the southern tower, bypassing his bedchamber and heading directly to the balcony and its lone chair. So many nights he'd spent sitting there staring eastward, hoping beyond hope that he would see Latera on the road, returning to Teg'urnan long before she was due. In his fantasy, he rode out to meet her and she tumbled into his arms, claiming that she couldn't bear to spend another night away from him.

While Latera hadn't returned to him in the dark of night, she had run into his arms at the border, and had slept beside him every night since. She'd also refused to become his mate... yet. She'd refused to become his mate, yet.

Aeolmar decided that Finlay was correct. He needed to speak with Latera, and ask her, once and for all, what she felt for him. If her answer was nothing, well...

It can't be nothing. Please, Cydia, don't let it be nothing.

Aeolmar entered the hall shortly after the elder sun set, and found Luth spinning Latera about in his arms.

"Our little one has finally returned," Luth bellowed while Latera beat his shoulder and demanded to be put down. Aeolmar tapped Luth's shoulder, and the hunter released his indignant captive. Out of the corner of his eye, Aeolmar saw Kemen enter the hall.

"Yes, she certainly has," Aeolmar said. Latera had barely escaped Luth when his brother swept her into a bear hug.

"Little Demon-killer," Bron rumbled. "Have you left any for the rest of us?"

"There are one or two left for you," Latera said, squeezing him with all her might. Bron set Latera down as the rest crowded around her.

"You haven't gotten any taller," Arknen said, ruffling her hair.

"You haven't gotten any better looking," Latera retorted.

"That I haven't," Arknen agreed.

As the night wore on the hunters drifted away until Aeolmar, Innetha and Latera were all that remained before the hearth. Aeolmar hoped Innetha would leave as well, but she sat there prattling on about something Luth had done. Latera eyed Innetha as if she were a viper, then leapt to her feet and left the hall. Aeolmar followed, and caught up with Latera in the corridor.

"What's the matter?" he asked.

"I could ask the same of you," Latera countered. "You've been frowning all night." He pursed his lips, but when it was plain that Latera was waiting for him to speak, he continued.

"I spoke with Kemen earlier," he said. "He told me...many things."

"What could he have possibly said to upset you?" Latera asked. Aeolmar remained silent, but his face answered for him. "And you believe him."

"I don't want to, which is why I'm talking to you now. You act as if you know what he's told me."

"I can imagine," she muttered. Latera stopped walking and glared at Aeolmar. "Why do I have to defend myself to you?"

"What?"

"You've known me four winters, and you yourself admit you hardly know Kemen. Why do his words have more weight than mine?"

"Should his words have weight?"

"No," Latera replied. Aeolmar wanted her to explain what she had been doing—and with whom—for the two winters she'd been away, but he knew that would only end with a shouting match. Before him stood the most stubborn hunter ever to grace Teg'urnan, far more stubborn than he ever was.

"Latera, I don't want to fight with you," Aeolmar said.

"Then don't."

Unable—unwilling—to let her walk away from him, Aeolmar pulled Latera into his arms. He worried she would push him away, but she wrapped her arms about his waist and laid her cheek against his chest.

"I'm sorry," he said. "I don't know why I let him upset me. I believe you, always you."

"Thank you," she said. "I'll always believe you, too."

"When I imagined the night you returned to Teg'urnan, it wasn't like this," Aeolmar said, his forehead pressed against her hair.

"What was it like?"

Two *saffira* clamored into the corridor, startling Latera into pulling away from him. After the *saffira* had gone, Latera continued to her chambers. Aeolmar followed, but when he touched her wrist she flinched away. He had been so distracted by Kemen's tales, he'd forgotten about the burn salve.

"Tell me what Kemen said," she implored.

"It doesn't matter."

"Do you trust me?"

"With my life," he replied. They reached Latera's door, and Aeolmar placed his hand on her shoulder. "May I—"

"I'm really so very tired," Latera interrupted. "We traveled for eight days, and arguing with you makes me wearier still." She dropped her gaze and stared at her hands, and Aeolmar realized that just because she'd slept beside him as they traveled didn't mean she was comfortable with him in her bed, and his accusations had made it worse. He needed to rebuild her trust in him, one step at a time.

"You're sending me to bed alone?" he asked. "I don't know if I can sleep without you."

"I'm sure you'll manage."

"Then sleep well, love." Aeolmar embraced her, and silently berated himself for almost ruining Latera's first night back at Teg'urnan. As he buried his face in her silky red curls he decided that he didn't care what had happened at the border, not as long as she remained with him.

"I'm so glad you're home," he murmured.

"I never thought you'd miss me so," Latera said, smiling. Aeolmar traced her cheek with his thumb.

"I felt your absence every day," he said. He stepped back, and once he released her he kissed her hands. "Will I see you in the morning, beautiful girl?"

"I hope so," she replied. Aeolmar squeezed her fingers, and smiled as she entered her chamber, his grin not leaving his face as he traversed the empty corridors. The night had not worked out as he'd expected, but Latera was home. Maybe tomorrow, she would choose him.

Chapter Twenty-Two

Latera speaks

*D*espite my weariness the night before, I woke before first dawn as wide-eyed as ever. I'd had a hard time sleeping without Aeolmar beside me, not that I'd ever tell him that. I also wasn't telling him that I'd woken before him every day of our journey home, but I'd been so warm and content in our shared bedroll that instead of rising, I remained in his arms. That bit of deception led to eight wonderful mornings, and I didn't feel a bit of guilt.

Waking up alone hadn't been nearly as fun, but at least I'd slept in a bed instead of on the ground. Searching for something to do with myself, I rummaged through my still-packed belongings and found one of Enna's nicer brushes. After I dressed I made my way to the stable to visit my golden friend.

"Do you like your new home?" I asked, petting her neck. Even though Enna had been thoroughly cared for the day before, I checked her over for sore spots, and made sure her hooves were in good condition. I brushed her mane even though there wasn't a single tangle on her, since Enna loved being fussed over. I'd moved on to her tail when I heard boots crunching the hay behind me. I spun around, dagger in hand, and almost stabbed Kemen.

"Gods, Kemen," I said, lowering my dagger. "What are you doing, sneaking around like that? And should you really be walking?" I asked, nodding at his cane.

"I figured you'd be here," he replied, ignoring my second question. "You and your horses."

"Me and my horses." I went on brushing Enna, Kemen standing sentinel. I glanced up at him, and he dropped his gaze.

"I don't mean to bother you," Kemen said, "It's just that I have no one to talk to here."

"You did a wonderful job with Aeolmar yesterday," I said. "What in the nine realms did you say to him?"

"Nothing too bad," he replied. "I get so few chances for fun, and watching him turn all shades of red was the most amusement I've had in moons."

"Careful, or all that red will be your blood after he beats it out of you."

"All right, I'll stay out of his way. But only until I can run again."

Kemen kept me company until Enna was thoroughly brushed and combed. After I kissed Enna's nose and promised to return with a treat, Kemen and I walked out in time to greet the child sun. As we crossed the palace square, we also crossed the First Hunter's path.

"My lord," Kemen said as he bowed his head, a gesture I was also supposed to perform but never did. Aeolmar himself did something he had never done in front of another: he greeted me by kissing my hand.

"Where are you coming from?" Aeolmar asked me, not Kemen, while he retained my hand.

"The stable," I said.

"Where are you off to?" he continued, still ignoring Kemen.

"To join you, of course," I replied, as Aeolmar's grip tightened. Kemen sensed he was not wanted, not that Aeolmar's intent was difficult to determine. He muttered an apology and limped away from us.

"You were with him, just now, in the stable?" Aeolmar asked.

"Yes. He doesn't know many here, and wanted someone to talk to."

"So you obliged him"

I snatched my hand away and hissed, "What is the matter with you?" His brows peaked, so I went on, "You're acting like I'm your property."

He rubbed his eyes. "Forgive me. When I saw you with him it aroused my protective instincts."

I'd been back less than a day and twice Aeolmar had found cause to mistrust me. "I appreciate that you want to protect me, but I can take care of myself. You don't need to chase people from me." I noticed we were the object of several interested glances. Aeolmar noticed as well, and led me inside the palace and to a small alcove.

"Again, I ask your forgiveness." He set his hands on my shoulders. "I know you're quite capable. Am I wrong to want to care for you?" I wanted to stay angry, but his pleading eyes and soft voice won me over.

"I suppose not," I said, falling into his arms. I rested against him for a moment, and asked, "Why were you looking for me?"

"You're mine. Do I need a reason?"

I pushed him away. "I am not!" He grabbed my shoulders, halting me.

"You're my huntress," he said, "You know that well."

I had to concede his point. I was his, to order as he wished, and he could only be overruled by the queen. However, I questioned what he meant by "his". I kept on glaring until he threw up his hands.

"I won't argue with you," Aeolmar growled. "You know I don't pretend to own you. I sought you this morning to ask how you slept, if you were well, if you needed anything. Say the words, and I won't seek you again."

I flinched, but he was right; I'd overreacted. I swallowed my pride and said, "Now I must ask you to forgive me. I've been away too long, and become unaccustomed to life within the palace. Will you help me adjust?" I placed my hands on his chest, looked up through my lashes and smiled.

The anger bled from Aeolmar's face, and the corner of his mouth curled up. "If you keep looking at me with those eyes, I might make you mine right here."

My face went hot, and I ducked my head. It was one thing for Aeolmar to kiss me awake while we were traveling, but now that we'd returned all this talk of claiming made me nervous.

"Love." Aeolmar tilted my chin up. "I'm only teasing you."

I let out a breath I hadn't realized I was holding. "I know. And," I added, standing on my toes to kiss his chin, "maybe I'll make you mine."

"Does that mean you've chosen me?"

"Maybe."

Our moment was interrupted by Ren, one of the instructors from the sola, *who respectfully informed the First Hunter of each and every* nuvi's *progress. Aeolmar listened to the reports and sent Ren off with a few words of advice, assuring him that he'd follow in a moment. Once he was gone Aeolmar pulled me down the corridor in the opposite direction of the* sola. *I pressed my hand over my mouth, laughing as Aeolmar held a finger to his lips.*

"Hush," he said. "They find me wherever I go, and your lovely laugh will alert them all the sooner."

"Are you avoiding your duties?" I asked in mock outrage. "For shame, First Hunter, for shame."

"I plan on avoiding them for the rest of the morning, or for as long you will keep me company."

We went to the palace square and wandered amongst the shops and tradesmen, until our path brought us to an apothecary. Aeolmar exchanged a few coins for a tiny pot of ointment meant to relive blood burns, I assumed for the sola *but he murmured it was for me alone. He gently massaged the ointment into my hands, carefully following the raised welts around my wrists, and I didn't know if the warmth that spread through my body was the result of the salve or his touch. I had* no idea how to react to his ministrations, not knowing what to say or do other than wish I hadn't worn long sleeves so he could continue up my arms.

"Thank you," I said, though the words did not come close to expressing what was on my mind.

"You're very welcome, my beautiful girl."

Chapter Twenty-Three

Latera was smiling when she woke the next day, though she couldn't remember her dreams. After she kicked her way free of the bedclothes she went to her balcony, and saw nearly every resident of the palace running about the courtyard. After her winters at the border, Latera had forgotten how the warm air incited such a flurry of activity around Teg'urnan.

Since Latera didn't want to take part in the flurry—at least, not yet—she made her way to the north watchtower. She climbed to the uppermost ledge and sat on the railing, grateful for a few moments of solitude.

"I hope you won't jump."

"Why does everyone think I'm going to jump?" Latera muttered. She looked around and saw Kemen, of all people, on the landing.

"I thought this was the one place no one would find me," he said as he sat beside Latera.

"Teg'urnan has a few lonely spots," she said. "Do the crowds unnerve you too?"

"Oh, yes," he replied. "I was at the border for so long I'd forgotten what Teg'urnan looks like. Never thought I'd say this, but I miss the border's emptiness."

"I know," Latera agreed. "When I first got to the border I only thought of coming home." She leaned her elbows on her knees. "All I really wanted was to be warm again."

Kemen snorted. "You don't know what cold is. I remember one winter—long before you arrived—when it snowed. At first I thought it was beautiful, but after a few days I hated it with every fiber of my being. It fell in never-ending drifts, and it piled up higher than our heads. Higher than our roof by winter's end."

"I wish there'd been snow while I was there," Latera said. "Instead, I got ground crusted with ice, and freezing fogs. It's a wonder we all didn't freeze to death."

Latera and Kemen spent the rest of the morning at the watchtower reminiscing about their time at the border. It was the first time Kemen had spoken to her as an equal, and Latera enjoyed the camaraderie. Close to midday they went their separate ways.

Days passed, and Latera continued spending her mornings at the watchtower with Kemen. They talked about many things, such as the protocol and procedures associated with palace living, and other freedoms they missed from the border. One morning, Kemen tried to kiss Latera.

"No," Latera said, shoving him away. He had the decency to look a bit sheepish.

"I wasn't going to bite you," Kemen said. "Where I'm from, girls like to be kissed."

"I'm sorry," she said, "I didn't mean to react that way." The offense in his eyes became a question, so she explained, "I've only ever kissed one man, and I'm not looking to add to my numbers."

"Who is the lucky one?" he asked.

"Aeolmar," Latera sighed.

Kemen snorted. "Of course it is. I certainly cannot compete with the First Hunter. How long have you two been mates?"

"We're not mates," Latera admitted. "Not yet." Latera held her head in her hands. "You could say he and I are complicated."

"What's so complicated?" Kemen asked. "If he kisses you and you kiss him back, it's quite straightforward."

"We were just becoming close, and then I went to the border." Latera laughed through her nose. "Two winters later, Aeolmar went to the border to bring me home."

"He must love you like Olluhm loved Cydia if he went out there for you," Kemen said.

"I have no idea if he loves me."

Kemen put his hand on her knee. "If he doesn't, I know of a man who will care for you."

"Oh. Thank you." Latera stood, and said, "I'm due in the stables."

Kemen watched her leave, then he smiled. If Aeolmar couldn't manage to claim her, he would.

Chapter Twenty-Four

Latera speaks

I climbed down from the watchtower and headed toward the stables; I wasn't due there for any sort of reason, but it was the first excuse I'd thought of. When I saw Aeolmar walking toward the sola, I altered my path.

"Where is my beautiful girl off to?" he asked, folding me into his arms.

"Nowhere, really," I replied. "Do you have a moment?"

"For you, always."

We moved to the side of the sola's entrance, and all I did was stare at him. My mind was swirling with thoughts, yet no words would come out of my mouth. Aeolmar cupped my chin in his hand, his brow pinched.

"Latera, what's wrong?" Aeolmar asked. "You can tell me anything. I'll help you with anything."

"Do you love me?"

Aeolmar blinked. "Of course I do. I've loved you for a long, long time."

"Why haven't you ever told me before?" I pressed. "And how long is a long time?"

"Since Brennus," he said. "I thought I had told you. Forgive me."

"Brennus?" I repeated. "Gods, man, you're as silent as a corpse."

Aeolmar smiled and drew me closer. "I keep my secrets, and the ones I love, close," he said. "What brought this on?"

I took a deep breath; he wasn't going to like this. "Earlier, Kemen tried to kiss me."

"What?" Aeolmar demanded, holding me at arm's length. "Are you all right? Did he hurt you?"

"I'm fine," I replied. "We were sitting at the watchtower, and he...tried."

"Gods, Latera, I wish you wouldn't sit there with him," he muttered. When I looked at him quizzically, he added, "I do know of the many hours you and he sit together, staring at the horizon."

"We only sit there, talking," I said. "I can talk to whomever I wish."

Aeolmar frowned, which explained how he felt about me talking to other men. "What were you talking about this morning?"

"I don't even remember. Then he tried to kiss me and I told him about you, and he asked me how long we've been mates," I said in a rush. "And I said we're not mates, because we aren't." Aeolmar's frown deepened, and I continued, "Then I realized that I don't even know if you love me."

"Is that why you haven't chosen me?"

I opened my mouth to protest, but nothing came out. "I don't know."

Aeolmar's deep blue eyes bored into me, then he gathered me against his chest. "Forgive me, love," he said against my hair. "You mean more to me than I could ever put into words. Perhaps if I'd been more forthcoming we would have been mated these last two winters and not on opposite ends of Parthalan."

"Too bad we weren't mated when we fed each other berries."

He laughed, a low rumble deep in his chest. "Do you know how hard it was for me to leave your chamber and go to the Trial? I wanted to claim you right there."

I shivered. "You probably would have terrified me. That was before you'd properly kissed me."

"Good thing we got that out of the way," he said. "About Kemen."

I looked up at him. "You're not going to kill him, are you?"

"No, but only because I've got better things to do." He smoothed my hair back. "Stay away from him, at least for now. I don't want him anywhere near you, not until his attraction to you has ended. If he tries approaching you, I want you to find me immediately."

"I will," I promised. "I won't go back to the watchtower, either. At least, not alone."

"Good. I just want you to be careful." Aeolmar kissed me, then he asked, "You're patrolling later?"

"Yes, with Finlay."

"I'll find you afterward, and spend the night telling you how much I love you." He looked toward the suns and frowned. "I'm expected in the sola, or I'd do that now."

"I know you're busy," I said. "I'll miss you."

"And I, you."

As I walked toward the stables, Aeolmar called out, "I love you, beautiful girl."

I looked over my shoulder. "I love you, too."

Chapter Twenty-Five

Finlay ended up trading shifts with Arknen that night, and Latera rode with him for the second watch. The wind was calm and the sky cloudless, and the ruddy moonlight illuminated the plain below the palace almost as thoroughly as the suns. They took advantage of the pleasant night and rode farther afield than usual, enjoying the crisp air, and were well out of sight of the palace when Latera motioned for Arknen to halt.

"Listen," she whispered. Arknen cocked his head, and nodded. They could hear the distinctive sound of demon claws scratching up the trees.

"There, in the oak grove," he said, pointing with his sword.

They approached the grove, and found six demons hiding in the treetops, and a beast on the ground. Latera whispered that the beast was similar in size to the one that had gored Kemen, though it had tusks instead of horns.

"Olluhm's Balls," Arknen whispered, nodding toward the beast, "look at that monster. We should return to the palace, get the others."

Latera shrugged. "I've killed bigger. We can handle this one. Let's send back the horses."

Once the horses had galloped away, the hunters approached the grove. Arknen silently dispatched the two demons standing watch. Another wandered into the night, presumably to look for the other two, and Latera slit its throat, the only sound the demon's blood flowing onto the dirt.

Now that half of the demons had been dealt with, Latera didn't need the element of surprise. She climbed a tree above the beast, and dropped onto its back. It bucked and shook itself, trying to throw her, but Latera plunged her sword into the back of its neck and held on. The beast roared as she jabbed it over and over, repeatedly burying her sword where she was certain its spine should be. Her sword cracked at the hilt, its bones proving too strong for the blade.

Latera cast the ruined metal aside and crawled forward on its head, grabbing on to the beast's coarse, slimy bits of hair to steady herself until she was alongside its eye. She plunged her dagger into the cloudy orb, digging her fingers into its skin as the head thrashed about.

"Latera," Arknen screamed, throwing himself onto the beast's back.

"Stay clear of the teeth," Latera shrieked, dragging herself further up its skull, forcing her arm further inside its head until she was in past her elbow. Again it roared but she pushed harder, now in it to her shoulder, and twisted her dagger in its brain. Finally, it let out a bellow and collapsed in its death throes.

Arknen grabbed Latera's free arm and pulled her away from the beast's corpse. "I can't believe you killed it," he panted. "Or that you've killed others like this."

"Their blood isn't caustic like demons," she said with a nod toward his red legs, "believe me when I say that you should always opt for the beast."

"If the gods smile upon me I'll never encounter one again," Arknen said as he stood. He and Latera dragged the demon bodies around the beast and burnt them, but not before Latera broke off one of the beast's tusks. When Arknen raised an eyebrow, Latera shrugged.

"Trophy," she said. "Old habit."

Once the bodies had been reduced to ash, they walked back to Teg'urnan. Aeolmar met them outside the gates, astride Myrnnhe and scowling like a thundercloud.

"What happened?" he demanded. "Your horses returned riderless shortly after you set out! We've been searching the area for you!"

"We came upon six demons and one of their beasts" Arknen said.

Aeolmar dismounted. "Tell me everything."

Latera produced the tusk and the remains of her sword as evidence, and Arknen gave a full report to Aeolmar while they walked back to the gates. Aeolmar ordered the gatekeeper to send out a scout, and a report to the queen's chamber. Once they were inside the palace complex Arknen offered to take Myrnnhe to the stable, and Aeolmar and Latera continued on alone. He was silent as he walked Latera to her rooms, but once they were inside the chamber he pulled her into his arms.

"I'm covered in gore," she protested. "Let me at least wash the beast from me."

"I don't care what you're covered in," Aeolmar said. "I just want you safe."

"I am safe." When he didn't release her, she added, "You're not going to let me wash, are you?"

"Are you hurt?" he asked. "The truth."

"I'm fine," she replied. "I'm not cut, and the blood only got my back."

"The things that went through my mind," he said. "Fear when your horse returned without you, then when I saw you laughing with Arknen..."

Latera pushed him away. "You thought what?" she demanded. When he remained silent, she went on, "Do you think I'm some kind of wanton? That I run off into the night with whoever's available?"

"You know what you mean to me," Aeolmar shouted.

"Do I?" she shouted back. "You distrust me when I've given you no reason to! You believe everyone else over me!"

"Latera, I—" he began.

"Kemen tells you a pack of lies, and you believe him," Latera continued. "You see me laughing with Arknen, so obviously we were doing something. Didn't you notice the blood, the beast's tusk?"

"Of course I—"

"When are you going to believe me?"

"Latera, I always believe you!"

"It doesn't feel that way." Latera crossed her arms and turned away. "I'd like you to go."

"Latera, no." Aeolmar moved to grab her shoulders, but she evaded him.

"I said go."

Aeolmar recoiled as if she'd burnt him, then he spun on his heel and left. The door slammed shut behind him.

Chapter Twenty-Six

Latera Speaks

I leaned against the door, my body shaking. I had thrown the First Hunter out of my rooms. Me, one with no authority to speak of, a girl half or maybe a third of Aeolmar's size, had ordered him away. More, he had gone.

I didn't like that he was gone. I liked less that he trusted me about as far as he could throw me. No, Aeolmar could probably lob me quite far. He trusted me as far as I could throw him.

If he can't trust me, I can't love him.

I covered my face with my hands. Gods, I don't know how not to love him.

I peeled off my gear and finally washed away what was left of the beast. It went quickly, since most of the gore had been on my clothing. I'd just pulled a shift over my head when a knock sounded at my door, and my fury returned full force. How dare he return so soon after I'd thrown him out? I flung open the door, but it wasn't Aeolmar standing there.

"Finlay," I greeted.

"I hope I'm not, ah..." Finlay looked away. I glanced downward and saw that my wet hair had soaked the front of my shift, making it nearly transparent. Wonderful.

"A moment," I said as I stepped back and grabbed a shawl. "I thought you were Aeolmar. He—"

"I know," he said. "Half the palace heard you screaming at him."

"Did you hear about the demons?" I asked. "And the beast?"

"Yes, I read the message he sent to the queen." Finlay stepped inside and shut the door. "Would you like to talk about it?"

"The demons, the beast, or Aeolmar?"

"Any of the three, though I believe you handled the first two quite well."

"No. Yes." I stared at my hands, and continued, "I don't know what's wrong with Aeolmar. He believes gossip and rumors; I tell him the truth and he still thinks the worst of me. Rather than ask me what's in my head, or my heart, he just avoids me, or leaps to conclusions." I laughed, or maybe it was more of a sob.

"First, he thought I had something with Kemen; no, first he thought I had something with Adhaire. Then there was Kemen, and now Arknen. I haven't so much as laid a finger on any of them, nor they on me. I tell him this, but he doesn't believe me. I don't know what he wants from me." My head drooped even further, and I came to the inevitable conclusion: whatever I'd had with Aeolmar was over, and it had hardly begun.

"What he wants," began Finlay, "is for you to be his, and his alone."

"He did ask me to be his mate, but even that's...stalled."

"Asking you was part of his plan."

"How do you know?"

"He spoke of you and nothing else for days, moons even, after we met you in Brennus. We'd be riding together and he would see something that reminded him of you, like a flower the color of your eyes, and he would go on and on about you."

"He did?"

Finlay nodded. "After you two had your moment the day you left for the border he was the happiest I've seen him. He started planning for your return right away, plotting out the good life he would give you."

"Has he ever told you of these plans?" While most of me hoped that Aeolmar had told Finlay everything, that flame of anger ignited again.

Fat lot of good it had done Aeolmar to tell his second how he felt while leaving me in the dark.

"Many times he said he would meet you on the road, take you away somewhere peaceful, and love you until you were his."

I blushed and turned away, remembering how Aeolmar asked me to spend the night with him. "Is that all he wants me for?"

"No, sweetheart, no," Finlay said, taking my hands. "I'm sorry. I shouldn't have said it that way."

"Tell me more," I implored. "But leave out anything that will make me blush!"

He smiled and continued, "Aeolmar feels very strongly for you, and he has felt this way since the moment he set eyes on you. For some time now he has seen you as his mate, and he thought you would feel the same. He hoped you'd bind yourself to him."

I leaned back in my chair, considering Finlay's words. Aeolmar hadn't brought up bindings again since that night at the border, and I assumed he'd forgotten about it. But for Finlay to know as well, along with Aeolmar's other plans for us...

"Why doesn't he say these things to me?" I asked.

"I don't think he knows how. For all his great skill and experience, very little of it has to do with love," Finlay replied.

"Stubborn man," I muttered. "We could have learned of love together."

Finlay snorted. "Sweetheart, I understand more than anyone how stubborn Aeolmar is. May I ask, have you ever told him how you feel?"

"I thought I had," I murmured, unsure if I was being fully honest. When he ordered me away from Kemen, was he trying to protect me? And tonight, was he worried about me, and had I overreacted? I remembered the look on his face as he approached Arknen and me; it was of concern, not jealousy. My heart sank; I had finally, irrevocably ruined things between us.

No. We are not ruined. I will fix this.

"Will he ever forgive me?" I asked.

"He will," Finlay replied. "I'm certain of it."

"Will you help me find Aeolmar? I want to speak with him tonight."

***

I walked to the arena, which was where Finlay had last seen the First Hunter. I stepped onto the sandy field and found Aeolmar sitting in the shadows. He didn't bother raising his head or otherwise acknowledging me when I sat beside him.

"I've been told that your plan upon my return to Teg'urnan was to take me somewhere and have your way with me," I began.

"Finlay," he muttered.

"Don't be angry with him," I warned, "he only answered what I asked. Why haven't you ever told me these things?"

Aeolmar looked up, his blue eyes gleaming in the moonlight. "I thought I'd been quite clear."

I leapt to my feet, pacing in the moonlight. "Then why the secrets? Why the jealousy? You bare your heart to Finlay, but leave me in the dark!"

Aeolmar remained seated, clenching his fists. "I wanted to tell you everything that day on the Hill of Torim, but you left me anyway, all for another man."

"Do not speak ill of the dead," I railed. "You told me nothing that day! You didn't even say anything when I kissed you goodbye! You only want me now because you worry others may beat you to me!"

"Are you looking to add me to the list, along with the others?" he demanded.

"What others?" I demanded. "Gods, Aeolmar, there are no others!"

"Then why won't you choose me?"

"Maybe because of your arrangements!"

"What arrangements?"

"With the many women who share your bed!"

"Just so you're aware," he growled, "no one has seen my bed in a very, very long time."

"What, you think all the men bed down with me?" I wailed. "If you need it said plain, fine. I want you, Aeolmar. Only you."

"Do you mean that?" he asked.

"Yes," I replied, "gods, yes. Why are you so quick to assume I want another?"

"You could have anyone, why would you want me." I looked at him in the moonlight, his tall form and handsome face with those eyes you could so easily lose yourself in, and beneath all of that was his generous, loving heart. I wondered how anyone could not want him.

"Tell me what Kemen said to you," I implored.

"That you and he had something while you were at the border," he replied, "and you left him after a time, and moved on to others." I was shocked, hardly able to breathe at the thought of forsaking Aeolmar for Kemen.

"That's a lie," I hissed. "He chased me relentlessly, so much so I slept with the horses, until he was wounded and bedridden. Still, he tried to get me to join him. I imagine he's bitter over being rejected time and again."

"Did he hurt you?" Aeolmar demanded. "If he's done anything to you I'll kill him."

"No, Aeolmar. He never touched me." Aeolmar let out a great breath and pulled me into his arms.

"I'm sorry," he said with such sadness my anger bled away. "I'm so, so sorry. Ever since we've met I've tried to do right by you, but I can't even manage that."

"You can, and you do," I said. "And, I'm not innocent here. I'm sorry, too."

"Can you ever forgive me?" he asked, pressing his forehead to mine. "You deserve so much more than I can give you. I belong alone with my misery."

"Please don't be alone," I said. "If you're alone I won't be with you, and I so want to be with you." He bowed his head, burying his face in my hair. While his fears had been calmed, I still needed to allay suspicions of my own.

"I need to ask you something," I began. "I've heard that Innetha takes you to her bed."

He held me at arm's length and turned my chin up, his brows lowered. "Who told you this?"

"Brynne." Gods, please let it not be true.

"It seems Brynne is also bitter over a past rejection." He stroked my cheek, and his eyes warmed as he continued. "I wouldn't lie with Innetha if she was the last woman in Parthalan, nor have I in the past." Relief washed over me, and I asked my second, less-awful question.

"And what of Asherah?"

"The queen? Please understand, if she made such a request not only would it be a great honor, but I would be bound to comply." I stiffened, but he smiled. "But, if Asherah had made such a request in the last five or so winters—which she hasn't—I would have declined and suffered the consequences." Relief cascaded over me, and I let go of my last shreds of doubt. "Has this truly been bothering you?"

"A bit," I replied, and realized that I understood exactly how Aeolmar had felt when he heard rumors about Adhaire and the others. "I think I could have made peace with you and the queen, but not Innetha."

"I'd castrate myself before I'd lie with Innetha," he grumbled. "For too many years she and I were the only hunters in Teg'urnan. Asherah was afraid she would find Innetha dead with my hands around her throat. Moreover, Innetha already has an arrangement, if you want to call it that, with Luth. You knew that."

"I did," I said. "I'm just amazed that such arrangements exist."

"They're more common that you realize," he said, his eyes glinting. "The queen herself has one, with Finlay."

"The queen and Finlay? Actually, that explains quite a bit," I said. "I wonder if that's why he switched with Arknen tonight, so he could be with Asherah."

"Finlay traded his shift, and his replacement encountered demons?" Aeolmar said. "Gods, my second is a fool."

"Perhaps he's just in love," I said.

"Perhaps." Aeolmar's teasing voice trailed off, and his manner became serious. "You haven't said if you'll forgive me. I would understand if you refused, for I am undeserving of your affection." I moved my arms from his waist to his neck, standing on my toes.

"I will, with two conditions."

"Name them, name anything."

"Don't castrate yourself, not for Innetha or anyone."

"Done." He kissed me, beginning at the hollow of my throat and slowly traveling up my neck, the combination of his warm lips and soft breath driving me mad.

"And the second condition?" he asked.

"All the things you wanted to tell me, but never did," I began. "That day on the Hill, and all the other days. Tell me now."

"All of it?"

"All of it."

He drew back, his gaze meeting mine. "It comes down to this; I've been trying to tell you I'm in love with you since the day we met," Aeolmar said. "I couldn't tell you while you were in the *sola*; others would have thought that you were named so quickly because I favored you. As it was, whenever I went to observe the nuvi others would say that I was only there to admire you. I suppose that much is true."

"You admired me?" I fluttered my lashes in that way I knew he liked. "Had I known I would have worn nicer leathers."

"My beautiful girl," he said. "Still, I had to wait... You were so young, and I had power over you. I never wanted you to feel like you were forced to be with me."

"I never did," I replied. "Even when you were affectionate with me, I felt you holding back."

"I tried to be careful with you. Then you were named, and I tried to tell how I felt you whenever we were alone, but my courage failed me again and again. It failed me so many times... Then the day came when you left for the border, and the day came when you did not return to me, and I thought it was too late for us."

"When I stayed at the border, I thought I was needed. I thought Brynne needed me. There were so many demons, and they just kept coming and coming...they were endlessly coming... And I wanted you to be proud of me... I'm so sorry I didn't come back sooner. I never meant to hurt you." Tears rolled down my cheeks. "When I was standing on that cliff and heard your voice behind me, I hoped for the first time that you loved me like I love you." Aeolmar stroked my cheek with his thumb, wiping away my tears.

"I've always been proud of you," he said. "Brynne told me that you remained because the attacks were unending, and it made me want you to return to Teg'urnan all the more. Every time Brynne came to the palace I only asked about you, until she demanded to know if I had any interest in the other hunters."

"She never told me," I said.

He uttered a small laugh. "Typical of Brynne. I gave her direct orders to give you messages, and she refused." I stepped back and wiped my face with my shawl. The quick tug pulled it off my shoulders, and I stood before him in the thinnest gown I possessed. Aeolmar placed his hand on the nape of my neck, and drew me into his arms.

"My beauty," he said as he kissed me. I wound my arms around his neck, then he lifted me against him. His hands gripped my thighs as I wrapped my legs around his .

"Am I too heavy?" I asked.

"Never," he replied, then he dropped to his knees, keeping me in his arms. Aeolmar's hand found its way under my dress, then he shifted his weight and I was on my back. The sand scraped the bare skin of my arms and back, but then Aeolmar was kissing me and all I could think of was him.

My hands slipped under Aeolmar's tunic, the muscles of his back rock hard with the strain of holding me. I felt his cock straining against his clothes, pressing against my leg as his mouth caressed my breasts. I heard my dress tear and remembered where we were, and what we were about to do.

"Aeolmar," I cried, catching his head between my hands. "Not like this."

Aeolmar opened his eyes, and saw me crumpled beneath him. "Gods, what was I thinking?" He withdrew his hands and helped me sit up. After I shook the sand from my hair, he said without meeting my eyes, "Gods, Latera. You deserve much better than me."

"What I deserve is another question, but I only want you. Surely your great plan didn't involve making love in the dirt?"

"I may have considered it," he said, and we laughed. Aeolmar pulled me to my feet and I flinched, so he turned me around and touched my back. My skin was damp, and sand was sticking to my gown. "Your burn is weeping," he said. "How much demon blood got on you?"

"A small amount, I think," I replied. "It may have pooled inside my vest."

Aeolmar wrapped my shawl around my shoulders and led me inside the sola's infirmary, where he retrieved a few ointments and some bandages. Once he had what he wanted, I turned to leave but he stopped me. "You cannot walk back in this state," he said, then he saw my feet. "You're not even wearing shoes."

"Oh, I forgot about shoes. I rushed out of my chambers, my only thought to find you." He put the ointments and such into a satchel, slung it over his shoulder and scooped me into his arms. "I'd really rather walk."

"Not this time," he said. "Not only are you hurt, you're barefoot." I sighed, and laid my head against his shoulder as he carried me through the darkness. He didn't set me down until we were inside my rooms, then he launched into an explanation of the various creams he had brought with him.

"I think I need another bath," I said.

"Then bathe," Aeolmar said. He dragged a chair around and started mixing his creams and oils together, his back to my bath. Since he obviously had no intention of giving me any real privacy, I set about peeling away my ruined shift. I bit my lip as I pulled it free, knowing that if I made the slightest noise Aeolmar would be at my side in an instant. Clothing dealt with, I washed quickly. When I stepped out of the bath I wrapped a length of linen around me and sat on the low bench alongside the basin.

"All right," I called. I heard the chair move on the stone floor, then felt Aeolmar's hands as he moved my wet hair over my shoulder.

"Lower this," he said, tugging at the linen. "Is this like the last time you wouldn't let me see your back?"

"That was different," I said, relaxing my grip. I remembered well how I'd ended up half-dressed the day we'd met, and was still mortified.

He pulled the linen from my back and touched the welt. I hissed out a breath and flinched. "This may be the worst blood burn I've ever seen, far worse than your leg was at the border."

"Will it heal?" I asked, peeking over my shoulder.

"Of course it will," he reassured, as he spread ointment across my back, "but I will bring a healer to look at it."

"I've never needed a healer for a simple burn in the past," I scoffed. "At the border we enjoyed the warmth."

Aeolmar rose and took my hand. "You're no longer surrounded by Brynne's lawless ones," he said. "I'll order you to a healer, if I have to." He led me to bed and told me to lie on my belly. He pulled a blanket up to my waist, explaining that the ointment needed to dry before it could be covered, and pulled away the damp linen. I crossed my arms under my chin, laughing to myself.

"What's so funny?" Aeolmar asked.

"Some hunters are in such awe of you they won't speak your name aloud," I replied. "What would they say now, if they saw you acting as my nursemaid?"

"If they saw me now I'd chase them from the room, to keep them suitably afraid of me." He sat on the floor in front of me, and I touched his hair.

"I'd fall in love with you now, if I wasn't already in love with you," I said, then he turned his head and kissed my palm.

Aeolmar leaned forward and touched the burn, kissing my shoulder on the way. "The salve has dried," he said as he brought the blanket up to cover the burn.

"Will you get me something to sleep in?" I asked.

"If you insist." Aeolmar smiled; apparently he liked that I was naked. "Your clothes are here?" he asked, indicating a trunk.

"They are."

Aeolmar opened the trunk, and selected a pale green gown. "I like this one," he said.

"Around," I said, making a twirling motion with my hand. Aeolmar turned his back, smiling the entire time.

"All right, I'm decent."

Aeolmar turned around, and found me clothed and lying on my belly. "I'll let you rest now," he said. "Sleep well, love."

"No. Stay here, with me," I said, my heart in my throat.

Aeolmar crouched before me, so close our noses almost touched. "Are you sure you want me to stay, after earlier?"

"I'm not trying to taunt you." I closed my eyes, since I didn't think I could bear it if he declined. "Would it be wrong for you to stay?"

He placed his hands on my shoulders, and kissed my forehead. "I don't think it's wrong," he said, his lips warm against my skin. "Cydia save me, I hope it's not wrong for me to want to stay with you."

I heard the rustle of clothing, and felt him move onto the bed. I grabbed my favorite fur coverlet and pulled it between us before I opened my eyes. When I did, I saw a shirtless Aeolmar leaning on his elbow and waggling his eyebrows. I laughed, burying my face in the fur.

"When my saffira comes in the morning, I don't know how I'll explain all of this. She'll never believe we were only sleeping."

"I charmed the door. Now, it will only open for you and me." I'd forgotten how adept Aeolmar was with magic. After Finlay had taught me to call fire, I hadn't learned a single other spell, and I liked it that way.

"I'm sorry, about earlier," I said, looking at him through the silky strands of fur.

"Sorry for what?" he asked, pushing back my curls. "For making me admit I was a fool? I'll never doubt you again, love."

"I'm not sorry for that. If I'd known I only needed to yell at you in the middle of the arena to get you to talk to me, believe me I would have."

He smiled, and I told him the true reason for my apology. "I mean...for afterward. For making you stop like that. That's what I'm sorry about."

"I'm the one who should apologize," he said. "I shouldn't have let things get to that point. You were right; of the many nights I dreamt of making love to you, it was never in the dirt like an animal. You're far too dear to me for that." I nestled closer to him, and Aeolmar draped an arm around my shoulders.

"These dreams...what are they like?" I asked, grazing his smoothly muscled chest with my fingertips. He brought my hand to his lips and kissed it, then placed my palm over his heart.

"I'd rather show you than tell you," he said with that grin of his, "but not tonight. My love, you're safe with me."

"Aeolmar..."

"What, love?"

"Do you still want me to be a nalla?"

Aeolmar chuckled. "Yes, more than anything."

I stroked the skin over his heart. "Will you be my nalla too?"

"The man is called nall," he began, then he understood what I really meant. "Latera, what are you saying?"

I raised my gaze to his. "Aeolmar, beloved, I choose you."

Aeolmar crushed me against him. "Beloved, you've made me so happy," he said. "Once the burn has healed, I'll make you mine."

"Promise?"

"Promise, beloved."

"Call me your beloved again," I said, resting my head on his chest.

"My beloved, my heart, my soul," he said, "You're all of these things to me, and more." My eyes were heavy, and I yawned.

"Rest now," he whispered, "I'll be here when you wake up."

Chapter Twenty-Seven

Aeolmar Speaks

I lay in bed, eyes closed yet wide awake, happier than I'd ever been. Latera loved me, she was here in bed with me, and once she was healed from this blood burn I'd make her mine. I'd almost accomplished that earlier in the arena, but Latera had stopped me, rightly so. It would have been wrong to claim her in such a way. Latera deserved more than that. Let's face it, Latera deserved more than me, but I was who she wanted.

Latera wanted me. No fact in all the nine realms was more important to me than that.

Now I was in her bed, with her warm body curled against me; I suppose it didn't matter that I hadn't loved her yet, being that we'd ended up in the same place. I kissed her forehead, noting her damp skin. I guessed that was due to the blood burn, then I realized her hair was still wet. I stroked her neck, and learned that it wasn't still wet, it was wet again. Latera was sweating as if she was in the middle of the High Desert.

"Latera?" I whispered, rolling her onto her back. The fire had burned low, but there was enough light for me to see her flushed cheeks, and the sweat pooling in the hollow of her throat. Panic squeezed my heart, and I shook her. "Love, wake up."

Her eyes fluttered open, and she coughed. "Water," she rasped. "Please, water."

I jumped out of bed, casting my gaze about her rooms as I searched for a pitcher, a mug, anything. Then I heard the bedclothes rustle, and turned to find Latera sitting up and tearing at her dress.

"Latera, wait." I ran to her and grasped her hands. "Let me help you."

"I need water," she said, then she slumped against me. I stared down at the woman I loved, unconscious and soaked in sweat, and did the first thing that came to mind. I went to Innetha for help.

Chapter Twenty-Eight

Latera opened her eyes, squinting at the bright light. She wasn't in her room, since her bed wasn't this bring or this lumpy. Wherever she was, she was too warm, too uncomfortable, and the white curtains that surrounded her on three sides weren't very reassuring. The smooth gray stone of the one bare wall told her she remained in Teg'urnan, but that was all it told her.

Remembering the blood burn, she felt her back and discovered thick layers of bandages, and that she was wearing an unfamiliar garment to match her unfamiliar surroundings. Blankets and shawls were heaped upon her, and she was terribly thirsty.

Hoping she remained among friends, Latera called out for water. A curtain drew back from the cot and Aeolmar appeared. He sat beside her, and held a bowl of something warm to her lips.

"It tastes awful, but you need to drink this," he said. Aeolmar held the back of Latera's head with one hand and tipped the bowl with the other, and something akin to swamp mixed with fire flowed into her mouth. She tried pulling away but his grip was firm, and he held her until she finished every drop. Once Latera had drained the bowl Aeolmar put it aside, then he wrapped his arms around her.

"Gods," she said, wiping her mouth with the back of her hand. "I would have preferred water."

Aeolmar kissed her hair. "I know, but water won't heal you."

"And that potion will?" she rasped. "Where am I?"

"The healers' ward. After you fell asleep you were taken by fever dreams."

"Who put this awful tunic on me?"

"Innetha. Your own dress was torn, and I couldn't bring you here like that." Latera wrinkled her brow, and Aeolmar explained, "Her rooms are next to yours."

"What happened?" she asked. "Am I sick?"

'The matriarch says the demons were poisoned, and they passed it to you by way of the blood burn. We've been waiting for your fever to break since yesterday," he replied. She took in his bedraggled appearance; he was wearing what she'd last seen him in, and looked as if he hadn't slept in days.

"Arknen," Latera said. "Was he poisoned as well?"

Aeolmar indicated a second curtained area across the room. "We're still waiting for him to wake. His burns are much more severe than yours. If you hadn't asked me to stay with you, you might have died before morning," he said softly. "After we brought you here Innetha went to check on him, and she was almost too late." He drew her against his chest, and she nestled into his arms.

"The demons were a trap, then," Latera concluded. "They poisoned their own to poison us." She gazed up at her First Hunter, pale eyes shining. "Thank you, for keeping me safe."

"I'll keep you safe forever, beloved," he said, smoothing her hair as he stifled a yawn.

"You must be so tired," Latera said, then she made room for him on the cot. "Rest here with me."

"I have a chair."

"And you'll be more comfortable here."

Aeolmar blew out a breath. "Only for a moment," he said, but in a short time he was asleep with his head in Latera's lap. She ran her fingers through his long hair, watching over him as he'd done for her.

Latera watched the as the healers came and went, their arms laden with their foul-smelling decoctions and bundles of herbs. Eventually, one stopped by Latera's cot with a mug of cool, clean water. After Latera had drained the mug, and asked for another, she asked after Arknen.

"He still sleeps, but is responding to care," the healer replied. She scurried off after that, and Latera sighed, bored with lying about on a cot. She's even lost interest in Aeolmar's hair.

After a time, Finlay and Innetha appeared at her bedside. Latera moved to wake Aeolmar but Finlay shook his head, then made his way toward Arknen. Innetha sat in the bedside chair and asked how Latera felt.

"As if I've been packed full of desert sand," Latera said, "I've drunk two mugs of water yet my throat's still dry."

"You were on fire when I came to you," Innetha said, "and so slick with sweat I could hardly lift you."

"Aeolmar said how you helped me. Thank you."

"We hunters look out for each other, little one," Innetha said, patting Latera's arm. "I believe I helped your First Hunter more than you. He was in quite a state, raving of how he couldn't wake you. It would have been faster if he'd just brought you here himself."

"True," Latera said. "It's not like I would have cared who dressed me." Latera turned her attention back to her sleeping charge. Aeolmar was so tall and broad he barely fit on the cot, and if he had lain flat on his back his feet would have dangled off the edge. As it was his body was curled around Latera's, with his arms encircling her waist. Latera smiled down at him, stroking his hair.

Innetha said, "You two make quite the pair."

"Yes, we do," Latera replied.

"Despite his many faults, he'll be good to you."

"Faults?"

"Impatience, jealousy, the way he flies into a rage over the slightest offense," Innetha said with a wave of her hand. "I'm sure you've seen all of that, and more." Latera dropped her gaze, unwilling to agree with her.

"When he acts this way, it's only because he knows of no other way to be," Innetha continued. "He's very protective of those he cares about. Hells, he's protective of me, and we've been at each other's throats since the day we met." Latera looked up, and saw sincerity in Innetha's doe-like eyes. "He's lost almost everything and everyone he cares for, and he will fiercely hold on to whatever is left. Remember, little one, he only behaves like a madman for those he loves."

Latera stared at Innetha, confounded by her efforts to make Latera see Aeolmar as a good man. Wasn't it obvious that she already knew? Finlay returned, explaining that the healers had chased him away so Arknen could rest.

"I fear I don't have the presence of Aeolmar," Finlay said.

"What does that mean?" Latera asked.

"The healers have been trying to get him to leave right along, but he flat out refused," Finlay replied, "He's hardly let them touch you, and only he has given you the healing drinks."

"I have him to thank for this horrible taste in my mouth?" Latera asked with a wry grin.

"Yes, him alone," Finlay replied with a smile of his own. "Come along, Innetha. Let's go before he knows we were watching him sleep."

Innetha stood and said over her shoulder, "Latera, please let me know if you're ever in need of my services. I did so enjoy our time together."

Finlay raised an eyebrow. "Services?"

"Wardrobe services," Innetha purred.

"Away, both of you," Latera said. When they were gone a healer asked if Aeolmar could be moved to his own cot, but Latera refused.

The healer insisted, and Latera explained that she and Aeolmar were not to be separated, not for any reason save a demon army at the gate. The healer shook her head as she left, muttering about unruly hunters.

Once the healer was gone Latera slid down the cot until she and Aeolmar were face to face. She stroked her fingertips along his stubbled jaw, caressing him until he woke. Aeolmar's eyes blinked open, and she greeted him with a smile.

"You are wonderful," she said, "the kindest, most wonderful man that has ever lived, and I love you with all my heart."

"I love you, too," he said. "What have I done to deserve all of that?"

"Finlay and Innetha were here. They told me how you've been caring for me."

"They saw me sleeping on your cot?" He rubbed his eyes. "I'll never hear the end of this."

"It's worse," she whispered, grinning, "Innetha told Finlay that she needed to dress me. In the future, I give you leave to dress me yourself."

"I can do that," Aeolmar answered, pressing her fingers to his lips. Latera sat up as a healer rushed over, and told Aeolmar that Arknen was awake. Latera moved to rise, but Aeolmar halted her.

"You need to rest," he said. Latera frowned but stayed put. The healer tucked the many blankets around Latera, prattling on how about how she needed to stay warm. Latera hardly noticed the woman as she watched Aeolmar crouch next to Arknen, and quietly spoke to his hunter. Aeolmar called for water, and once Arknen had slaked his thirst Aeolmar told him to rest and build his strength. Aeolmar exchanged a few words with the healers, and then returned to Latera's side.

"His burns are much worse than yours," Aeolmar shared. "His arms and neck are covered, as well as one of his legs. You were fortunate to dispatch the beast."

"I don't feel fortunate," she said, and he squeezed her hand. "When may I leave, and return to my rooms?"

"When you are well."

"When will you leave?"

"When you are well," he repeated, "and not a moment sooner, to the matriarch's great displeasure."

They sat together for a time, each dozing off in turn, until Latera insisted she'd go mad if she spent another moment on that cot. She begged Aeolmar to tell the healers' matriarch, Mallia, that she was as well as she was going to get in that ward, and after much cajoling he did. Mallia examined Latera herself, tutting and clucking as she felt various points on her neck and arms. In the end she agreed that Latera could depart the ward, provided that she continued resting and kept herself as warm as possible. Aeolmar was sent to fetch Latera some fresh clothing. While he was gone Mallia rewrapped Latera's bandages herself.

When Aeolmar arrived with the clothes, Mallia drew the curtain to help Latera dress.

"I can manage," Latera said, then her knees give way when she stood. Mallia caught her, and settled her on the edge of the cot.

"You haven't used your legs in days," she admonished, "give them a moment to remember what they're for."

Once Latera was dressed Mallia brought her to where Aeolmar impatiently waited. "Listen well, hunter," Mallia began. "You must support Latera when she walks, but don't let her walk too long or far. You must keep her warm and well covered, and she's not to be left alone for at least three days. I'll know if you don't abide by these rules, and if so I'll have Latera returned here in an instant. Do you understand?"

"I do," Aeolmar said, slipping his arm around Latera's waist, "and I will do as instructed."

Mallia sniffed. "See that you do."

With that, Aeolmar and Latera left the ward. When they reached her chamber door it opened of its own volition, startling Latera. "An effect of the charm," Aeolmar explained.

"Magic," Latera muttered. She looked around her chambers, feeling as if she'd been gone for much longer than two days. Latera walked toward the balcony, declining Aeolmar's assistance. It proved to be more of an exertion than she expected, and when she didn't protest as he slipped his arms around her waist.

"You should rest," he said.

"I've slept for days. My eyes refuse to close," she said, leaning against him. "How long can you remain with me, away from all a First Hunter does?"

"You heard Mallia; you cannot be left alone for some time yet. You're now my charge." Ignoring her protests, Aeolmar brought her to bed. Despite her talk of being rested, Latera was soon asleep.

CHAPTER TWENTY-NINE

Aeolmar was true to his word, and never left Latera's side during her recovery. He also kept his word to Mallia, and continued pouring those foul, swampy teas down Latera's throat. Latera drank them without protest, but secretly swore to give Aeolmar the same teas if he ever showed the slightest hint of sickness.

The third morning after Latera left the healer's ward, Innetha visited them with news that the queen wished to see Aeolmar. Latera promised that she would be fine on her own, and with a kiss on her forehead and the assurance that he would return as soon as possible, Aeolmar left her alone for the first time in days. What did she do with her newfound freedom? Naturally, she bathed.

After her bath, Latera pulled on a clean tunic and leggings. Re-bandaging her back turned out to be more difficult that she'd anticipated, and eventually she just left it alone. When Aeolmar returned he found her sitting on the edge of her bed, struggling to pull on her boots. He laughed at her plight. She scowled and he laughed harder, then he knelt in front of her and took her boots in hand.

"You know I'll help you," he said, easing the boots onto her feet. "Why didn't you just wait for me?"

"You don't need to do everything for me. I'm not an invalid."

"I understand, but you can't be exerting yourself right now."

"I'm not exerting myself. I just can't bend far enough to reach my feet."

"How is the burn?" Before Latera could protest Aeolmar sat beside her and lifted the back of her tunic, and found the wound bare.

"I'll assume you wanted me to do this for you." Aeolmar salved the burn and covered it with fresh linen.

"You're good at this," she said. "Where did you learn such excellent wound care?"

"It's the result of tending many injuries, both on myself and others." He finished bandaging her and tucked the loose ends under. "Is that better, love?"

"Yes," she replied, leaning against him. She felt so small next to Aeolmar, like a pebble resting against a mountain.

"You're such a big man," she said, comparing the size of their hands. "I never realized how big you are until you were in bed with me." Aeolmar stifled a laugh. When Latera met his amused gaze, she flushed and looked away.

"I understand your meaning," Aeolmar said, lips against her forehead, "and I appreciate the compliment." They laughed, and he continued, "Asherah wants to speak with the hunters. We're to meet in her chambers."

Latera got to her feet and offered Aeolmar her arm. She liked being silly with him, mostly because she loved his smile. "Well, then, let's be off."

Aeolmar and Latera were the last to arrive at the queen's receiving chamber. The Prelate sat at the queen's left, with two of the *con'dehr* standing behind him. Latera sat next to Finlay, and she noticed that her latest trophy—the beast's tusk—was in the center of the table. Once Aeolmar took his seat at Asherah's right, the queen began speaking.

Asherah recounted to the group of how Arknen and Latera were poisoned by demons' blood, and advised that her scholars were researching the origins of the poison; no one knew if the poison was a sort of hex, or something as mundane as the demons poisoning themselves earlier that day. When asked, neither Arknen nor Latera recalled the demons consuming anything that could have been poisonous as they hacked them to bits, and they hadn't detected any spellcraft, not that they were looking for such things.

"And, there is the matter of these beasts," Asherah said. "They appear to be unique creatures, and not any known variation of troll or orc. I cannot help but wonder what their presence truly means."

"Until we do know," Harek continued, "no hunter is to engage any demons traveling with beasts. They are dangerous and likely cannot be killed. Best leave the beasts for the soldiers."

"Perhaps we should douse them in black powder and set them alight," Innetha suggested.

Harek's eyes flamed as he opened his mouth, but the queen gave both the Prelate and her huntress a quelling look. "Are there any serious suggestions?"

"I doubt they're unkillable, since Latera took care of this one," Padashen said, pointing at the tusk. "That means we can kill them, too."

"You should have seen her, she was amazing," Arknen added, flashing Latera a grin.

"Latera has killed other beasts, too," added Kemen. "She killed the one that gored me, and two others at the border."

"That was a matter of luck," said Harek, "not skill."

"My lord Harek, I beg your pardon," Latera interjected, "do I look lucky?"

"Yes," Harek growled, "you look lucky to be alive."

"I disagree," she said. "I'd say I look like a well-trained huntress, and one who has had much success against this new foe."

"You haven't been trained to combat these creatures," he said. "We don't know what they are, or where they come from, yet you claim you're skilled enough to defend us against them?"

"You've doubted my ability from the instant you set eyes on me," Latera said, remembering the day they met in the *sola*. "Even now, after I've been a huntress for three winters and the evidence of my victory is plain before you, you still find cause to doubt me. I'd like to know what I've done that prejudiced you against me." Harek opened his mouth, then he glanced around the table and saw every hunter staring at him.

"By all means then, go after any beast you'd like," he hissed. Latera kept her gaze on Harek until he looked away.

"The new protocol," Asherah said, her gaze darting between Aeolmar and Harek, "is that if any of you encounter a demon, with or without a beast, afterward you are to report to the healers immediately. Whatever they're using to poison us works quickly and the recovery is not pleasant, as Latera and Arknen will attest."

As soon as the words were spoken Harek rose and stalked out of the room, his *con'dehr* rushing to keep up with him. The hunters left slowly, first paying their respects to the queen, and then reassuring Arknen and Latera that they were looking much better. Kemen also approached Latera, but Aeolmar's glare chased him away. In a short time only Finlay, Innetha, Arknen, Aeolmar and Latera remained with the queen.

"Forgive me, for speaking to Harek that way," Latera said to the queen.

"You were correct in challenging him," she replied. "You and Arknen both displayed great skill, and if not for you two who knows what the demons would have done." Asherah smiled indulgently. "I'd forgotten that you're a king's daughter, and you acted as such."

"Harek needed to be challenged," grumbled Finlay. "He's been treating hunters as lower beings for too long, and his soldiers follow his example."

"I'll speak to him," Asherah said. "His arrogance is a problem. Still, I shudder to think of what would become of Parthalan without him"

Latera placed her hand on Aeolmar's arm. "I must return Latera to her chamber," he declared. "Innetha, see to Arknen."

"I can manage on my own," Arknen said, with a glance toward Innetha that said he'd long since tired of her attention. Asherah nodded her approval, and he departed.

Latera and Aeolmar stood to leave, only to have Innetha block their way. "Princess Latera," she purred. "Please, accept me as your loyal servant."

"Oh. Um. Thank you." Latera looked up at Aeolmar. "I think I'd like to rest now."

After glaring at Innetha, Aeolmar walked Latera to her chambers. After the door shut behind them, Aeolmar said, "Please don't pick fights with one of the two people I can't order away from you."

Latera fell into his arms, more exhausted than she was willing to admit. "He's just so hateful."

"I know." He tucked her head underneath his chin. "He thinks of us as little more than barbarians."

"I'd like to see his reaction to a great tusked beast," Latera mumbled. Aeolmar called for fire in the hearth, then he swung Latera into his arms as if she was weightless. He sat on the floor before the crackling blaze, with her nestled against him.

"Stop pretending you're strong," he said. "I know you wanted to seem well in front of the others, but you don't need to pretend with me." She nodded, stretching her feet toward the fire as she drifted off to sleep.

When Latera's eyes next opened she was in bed, shivering in spite of the many furs wrapped around her. She heard voices across the room, and strained to hear what they were saying.

"Harek angered her, and she used all of her strength in challenging him," Aeolmar said. "She fell asleep soon afterward, and went cold as death."

"The same has happened to Arknen," said a female voice; the queen, perhaps? "Mallia assures me that this coldness is part of the recovery, and we must keep them as warm as possible."

"Why don't we just dump Arknen in bed with the princess? Seems like a quick solution." Latera fought her way to the top of the bed-clothes and saw Aeolmar scowling at Innetha, and the queen seated before the hearth.

"Oh Innetha, you know I'd rather share your bed," Latera quipped, to which Innetha raised an inviting brow. Asherah approached Latera's bedside, and touched her forehead.

"You're absolutely frigid," she said. "How do you feel?"

"As if I've been packed in ice," Latera replied. "I preferred being hot." Innetha brought over a bowl of tea, not the disgusting teas from the healers but real tea, and Latera gladly accepted it. "How is Arknen?" she asked, the warm bowl thawing her fingers.

"He has been returned to the healers ward," Asherah replied, "and I was about to order Aeolmar to return you, as well. He seems to think that you'll fare better here."

"Please don't make me go back there," Latera implored. "That place is all smelly herbs and lumpy cots. I'll heal faster here."

Asherah looked at Latera, her brows pinched and her lips pursed as she felt the huntress's cold cheeks, and even colder fingers. "I won't lose you, or Arknen, to this illness. You may remain here tonight, but if you're not improved by morning I'll carry you to the healers on my back, if I have to."

Latera nodded. "As you say, my queen."

"I will be here by second dawn to learn of your progress," Asherah warned, then she and Innetha went toward the door. Latera saw the queen whisper a few words in Aeolmar's ear, then he returned to the bed. Before her eyes he pulled off his boots, and then his shirt.

"What are you doing?" she asked.

"The queen ordered me to keep you warm," he replied, climbing into bed, "and I intend to follow her to the letter." He wrapped his arms around Latera, and said, "Rest, love. I'm here."

"Promise me you won't send me to the ward."

"Latera—"

"Promise!"

"All right. I promise."

Latera smiled, then she kissed Aeolmar's throat. "Thank you," she murmured, drifting off to sleep.

Chapter Thirty

Aeolmar speaks

*A*t first we did rest, and Latera was warm and content in my arms. I was rather warm and content myself, being that we'd slept together every night since Latera's release from the healers ward. Of course, we'd only been sleeping, but that was to be expected. Latera was still healing, and even I wasn't bastard enough to claim a wounded girl.

It was past midnight when Latera began shivering, her shoulders shaking hard enough to wake me.

"Am I not enough to warm you?" I asked. She didn't answer, asleep as she was, so I rose and shut the balcony doors. When I returned to the bed Latera's skin was like ice. I knelt over her, chafing her arms.

"How are you so cold?" I wondered aloud. "I'll make you some tea."

Her eyes rolled back into her head as she trembled; no, she shook, an icy seizure that terrified me as demons never had. I scooped Latera up, bedclothes and all, and laid her before the hearth. When her shaking didn't slow, I ripped off my clothes, and then hers, pressing my warm body against her cold one. I called for the fire to increase in both size and heat, and put her as close to the flames as I dared. Sparks leapt out and caught on the fur blankets, making it smoke and crackle. I stamped them out with my hand and turned Latera's back to the fire, holding her face against my chest as I shouted for it to burn hotter.

Eventually Latera's skin went from frozen to merely cold, and when she was warmer than a corpse I let myself breathe again. She ended up with her face pressed against my throat and her legs drawn up against my chest, my arms wrapped around her. When she woke she coughed, her hair having fallen across her mouth.

"Are you warm?" I asked, brushing the hair from her face.

"I am," she replied, "as much as I can remember what warmth is." She tried stretching, but I kept her body against mine.

"No," I said. "Is isn't yet first dawn. You cannot rise until the suns have risen. It will be too cold otherwise." Latera's brows peaked, then she looked over my shoulder at her closed balcony doors. "When I got up to shut them, you started shivering," I said, following her gaze, "and it was all I could do to warm you afterwards. That's why we're here, so you could be closer to the fire. I thought I'd have to put you in the fire, but then you stopped shaking and curled up like a sleeping kitten." She smiled, tracing my cheekbone with her fingertips.

"It seems that I owe you my life, once again."

I took her hand and moved it to the wound on my leg she'd tended in the woods outside Brennus. It seemed like it had happened a lifetime ago. "I've owed you mine for some time."

Her hand clasped my leg, her thumb tracing the scar's path. "Does it still hurt?"

"No. I had a girl with me, the loveliest girl I've ever seen, and she looked after me. But then she tried to feed me the worst food I've ever tasted, and I wondered if she was a spy sent to poison us all." We laughed, remembering the stew she'd made for dinner. To this day, Luth tells the story of Latera's Dirt Soup. I kept her hand over the scar, enjoying how she stroked my leg. Then her eyes widened, and she understood what I'd done.

"Forgive me," I said, "but the best way to share warmth is skin to skin." I thought Latera would be angry, or at least embarrassed at the both of us lying naked on the floor. Instead, she dragged her hand up my side, seeking each and every scar I bore. When her fingers rested on one of the marks that scored my ribs, she paused.

"I remember seeing this on you, before. Is it from a battle?" she asked, stroking her fingertips across my skin. Gods. "A demon's claw, perhaps?"

I laughed. "It was nothing like that. I stumbled, and landed on a dead branch. It wouldn't have healed so badly if I hadn't taken care of it myself."

"So proud, First Hunter." Latera rubbed the scar with her palm. Then she drew the blanket aside and kissed it, and I almost lost the few shreds control that remained. I closed my eyes, allowing myself to enjoy the moment, before dragging her away from my multitude of old wounds and covering her up.

"You're not to move," I said, tucking the fur around her chin, "and not to remove any of these coverings, not until I'm certain you won't be chilled again." She gave me a look, but didn't protest.

"How can you remain here with me for all this time?" Latera asked. "Who is looking after the other hunters?"

"They're grown. They can look after themselves."

"What I mean is how can the First Hunter remain here for five days, neglecting all of his duties, for one sick girl?"

"We've all stopped what we're doing, holding our breath while you and Arknen recover," I said, taking her hand beneath the blankets. "I don't think you realize how serious this is. In Asherah's long reign, a hunter has never been poisoned by a demon, and her scholars can't find any reference to demons ever having used poisons. This, coupled with the appearance of the beasts, may signify a new foe, one worse than any demon. As for why I remain to care for you, Innetha and Surya have been assigned to watch over Arknen. I assumed he would prefer them over me," I added.

"Then Finlay must be overseeing your obligations," she said.

"Finlay is seeing to the queen, with the added benefit of annoying Harek with his presence." I placed my hand on her neck, drawing her closer. "None of us are doing anything, except trying to find out who or *what has done this."* Latera slipped an arm around my neck, then she glanced over her shoulder.

"I believe the burn's healed," Latera said.

"Has it?" I sat up and said, "Let me see." Latera rolled onto her belly, and I tugged the fur down to her waist. I grazed my fingers across her smooth skin, and saw her shiver. I snatched her back into my arms, wrapping myself and the fur around her.

"I'm fine," she said. "You don't need to bundle me like this."

"I saw you shivering."

"No, Aeolmar," Latera said, "I...um... It wasn't the cold."

"Wasn't it?" I asked, nuzzling her neck.

"You've ruined me," Latera said, stretching her neck for more kisses. I obliged. "Every night I fall asleep in your arms, and when I open my eyes, I see you smiling at me. I don't want to be well if it means giving this up."

"You could never be ruined," I said. "I'm not leaving you as long as there's the slightest chance you remain ill. And once you're well, I'll stay for as long as you'll have me." As she laid her head on my shoulder, we saw light around the balcony doors.

"It's after first dawn," she said. "The queen will be here soon."

I turned my back as Latera rose; after last night I thought it was rather needless, but I wanted her to be comfortable. After she dressed, she returned wearing a dress that fastened behind her neck and left her shoulders and upper back bare. The rational part of my mind understood that the skin where she'd been burnt would be unusually sensitive for a few days, and leaving it bare was more comfortable. The rest of me wanted to explore every bit of exposed skin.

"I would like to request," she began, dropping my clothes in a heap before me, "that you stop shredding my wardrobe to bits."

"I had to tear them," I said, pulling my shirt on. "You were freezing to death, and I didn't have time to fumble with buttons and fastenings."

"I noticed that none of your clothes were torn."

"Of course not. I know how to take my own clothes off." I stood to pull up my pants, and Latera turned toward the fire. Once I was clothed I stood behind her, caressing her arms. "You should be more covered than you are. I don't want you to be cold."

"So warm me." She leaned back and kissed my chin. In another moment she was in my arms, and I pulled us onto the chair next to the fire. With Latera on my lap, I did indeed start exploring her neck, and then her shoulders. After an all too short time, we were interrupted by a knock at the door.

"Can we ignore it?" Latera asked.

"It's probably Asherah."

I stood, keeping Latera in my arms, then sat her in the chair and placed the fur across her lap. I tossed a shawl over her shoulders for good measure, and went to admit Asherah. Two saffira followed the queen inside the room, one of them bearing a pot of something hot, while the other carried a platter of bread and fruit. The platter was set on the low table alongside the hearth, while the pot was placed on a stand next to the fire. Once the girls departed, Asherah took a seat next to Latera.

"Latera, you look better than I expected," Asherah began. "How do you feel?"

"I'm warm, and that's something," Latera said. "How is Arknen?"

"He hasn't fared as well as you," Asherah replied. "He's still cold to the touch, but no longer shaking. Innetha and Surya set braziers on either side of his bed to warm him." She looked at the tangled knot of blankets on the floor. "I see you employed a similar tactic."

"Yes," I said, sitting across from the queen, "the fire was a great solace to her." Asherah's gaze travelled between myself and Latera, then she indicated the platter set before her.

"Eat," Asherah said. "I'm sure you must be starved." I offered some fruit to Latera, but the queen held up her hand. "This is for you alone,

Aeolmar. Mallia has given me strict orders that Latera is only to have the contents of this pot, whatever they may be. As you know, not even I dare to defy her," she concluded, her black eyes twinkling.

Latera moved toward the pot, but I blocked her. "I will get it."

"As you wish, my lord," Latera said as she sat. My eyes narrowed, but I refused to get into a teasing match in front of Asherah. That would only lead to her—and Finlay, and probably Innetha—teasing me as well.

I ladled the hot liquid into a bowl, frowning at the acrid smell. "This might be worse than the teas," I muttered, and handed it to Latera. Her nose wrinkled, but she drained the bowl in one draught. Latera watched me tear off a piece of bread, and I resolved to feed her real food once Asherah was gone.

"What does it taste like?" Asherah asked.

"Dirt and death," Latera replied. "I'd rather lick Enna's hoof."

Yes, I would definitely feed her real food, as soon as Asherah was gone so she wouldn't tell Mallia. "Tell me what's been happening," I said.

"We still require an unknown for the Trial by Combat," Asherah began. "Both Luth and Surya have volunteered."

"It's already time for the Trial?" Latera asked. "Gods, how long have I been ill?"

Asherah patted Latera's knee. "Not long, and you will be well soon," she said. "Who would you prefer as the unknown?"

"Not one of the con'dehr,*" Latera said.*

"Agreed," Asherah said.

"Kemen would be a good choice," I said, surprising both of the women before me. "He's quite skilled, and mature enough to realize he will be facing a neophyte, not a seasoned warrior, and will adjust his attack as such. If we sent Surya I don't know if she would show the same restraint."

"And Luth would probably let them win," Latera added.

I sighed; Luth's big heart would someday be the death of him. "I'm sure he would."

"Then it is decided," Asherah said. "I will have Finlay inform Kemen, as I assume you wish to remain with your charge." The queen smiled at Latera, and continued, "If only Arknen was faring as well as you. Perhaps I shall have him relocated here, so he may also receive Aeolmar's attentions. You have quite the healthy glow."

Latera blushed and looked at her hands. "That is probably from the soup Mallia sent."

"Enough," I barked, grabbing Asherah's elbow. "No one teases Latera but me." Latera gasped and Asherah laughed, but I ignored them both as I directed the queen toward the door.

"Really, Aeolmar, I mean no harm," Asherah said.

"I know," I admitted. "But she was so ill, and I don't want to tax her, and—"

"And you're finally with her, as you've always wished," Asherah finished. "Worry not, my friend. Latera will be well before you know it, and the two of you will have your life together."

"May Cydia make it so," I muttered.

Asherah squeezed my arm. "I will send Innetha with instructions from Mallia by midday. Until then, enjoy your time with your nalla."

Asherah departed, and I returned to Latera. "Did she give you any orders about me?" she asked. I set her empty bowl on the table, and put her back on my lap.

"No, but I have some of my own," I said. "I will not let you out of my sight or arm's reach, for if anything happened to you, when I have just now been able to be with you, I fear I'd never recover." I smoothed back Latera's curls, hoping she would agree. Latera was easily as strong-willed as I, and had never taken orders well. She chewed her lip for a moment, then she repositioned herself so she was straddling my waist and looked me in the eye.

"Then you have to stay in my sight, as well," she said. "I won't allow anything to happen to you, either."

Gods, just when I thought I couldn't love her more. "Agreed, beloved."

Latera watched me, her crystal blue eyes searching my face while her fingers traced the edge of my collar. "I've chosen you."

"By doing so, you've made me the happiest man in Parthalan."

"I want you to claim me. Now."

Chapter Thirty-One

Latera Speaks

*A*eolmar stared at me as if I'd asked him to stick a frog in his ear. "Now?"

"Yes, now." I tugged at his collar. "I don't want to wait any longer. I'm sick of waiting."

"You were hurt," he said. "First the burns, then the poison."

"The poison's gone." I tugged off the shawl and placed his hand on my back. "The burns are healed." Aeolmar's fingers traced little circles on my skin, but otherwise he was as still as a statue. "I want to be yours."

"Once you do this, you can never go back," he said. "I don't want you to give me anything you're not ready to."

"I want to go forward." Despite his words, I felt him harden against me. "What's the saying about Cydia's gift?"

"Cydia gave Olluhm a gift that only she could give," Aeolmar replied. "A part of herself that he carried in his heart for all time."

I rocked my hips against him. "I have a gift for you." I leaned forward and pressed my lips to his. "Give me something of you that I can carry in my heart, as well."

"What...what would you like?"

"You, Aeolmar. I want you."

He stared at me, and I was torn between screaming in his face and getting off his lap and burying myself in a hole. I had the grand misfortune of loving the most honorable man in Parthalan, one who would rather I went to my grave a virgin than risk taking advantage of me.

And gods, if he didn't claim me now I didn't know if I'd ever get up the nerve to try this again.

I unfastened the button behind my neck and let my dress fall to my waist. "Don't you want me?"

Aeolmar's gaze dipped lower, then he kissed me hard. "I want you more than anything," he said, his lips traveling to my throat. "Let me take you to bed."

"No," I insisted, rocking my hips again. "Here."

He pulled back. "In the chair?"

"If we get up you'll just think of another excuse. No more excuses!"

His mouth curled up in his lazy, half smile. "I don't think up excuses." Then he moved and laid me on the floor, right on top of the blankets we'd slept beneath. "I just don't think the chair is the ideal location."

"Oh," I said, then I lost my breath as his mouth traveled across my jaw and down my neck. He slid his hands up my sides, then he kissed the hollow of my throat.

"You're sure?" he asked, his kisses traveling lower.

"Gods, Aeolmar, if you don't get on with it I'm never speaking to you again!"

He laughed, and I balled my fist. Then he kissed my breasts, taking one in his mouth as his hand kneaded the other. A moment later his other hand moved to my thigh.

"You're so beautiful," he said. "Perfect, in every way."

I arched my back and a moan escaped me; I enjoyed his hands and his words. I looked at my fully clothed almost-mate. "I want to see you."

Aeolmar kissed me between my breasts, then he sat back on his heels and pulled his shirt over his head. His deep blue eyes never left mine, which was horrible because I wanted to rake my gaze over him. Then he distracted me by unfastening his belt, and standing to remove his boots.

"Why did you put your boots on?" I wondered, drunk on the sight of him.

"So Asherah wouldn't ask why I was barefoot."

Naked, he knelt between my knees. Aeolmar had said I was beautiful, and by that comparison he was godlike. His smooth, firm muscles were wrapped in soft golden skin, the rich hue scored by many pale scars. His cock, wide and tall and more than a bit intimidating, blushed red at the tip. I was so entranced I forgot to blush.

Aeolmar touched the rumpled mess of my dress. "Off."

I nodded and pushed the dress lower, then Aeolmar's hands were on my hips, lifting my bottom and divesting me of my only garment. He spread my thighs apart and knelt between them, his gaze so heavy it was like a caress. Then he leaned forward and kissed me.

Gods, I'd never felt anything like that...never knew I could feel anything like that. I was inexperienced, yes, but I wasn't ignorant, and in both the sola and the Long House I'd seen others in the act of love. In the past, I thought the screams and moans were just them showing off; now I realized that with pleasure this intense they couldn't contain themselves.

My hips bucked upward and Aeolmar pushed me down, his strong hands holding me against the floor. He kissed me, licked me, drove me insane... Then my world shattered, my body shaking and stars exploding behind my eyes. Aeolmar kissed his way up my body as I fell back to earth; when I opened my eyes he was smiling above me.

"How do you feel?" he asked.

"Like I was flying," I replied, and his smile stretched into a grin. I grasped his cock, and asked, "Is it your turn?"

"That's not what I want." He unwound my fingers, and positioned himself where his mouth had just been. When he nudged me I gasped.

"Have you ever done this before?" he asked. When I shook my head he drew back and regarded me. "Love, are you certain? You're certain you're certain?"

I reached up and caressed Aeolmar's neck. "I'm certain. Let me show you how much I love you."

Aeolmar kissed me hard, and while I was distracted he pushed forward. I yelped, the sound muffled by his mouth, but he didn't stop. After the initial shock passed, I didn't want him to stop either

Finally, we were one.

"You're my mate," he said afterward, affection shining from his deep blue eyes. Aeolmar propped himself up on an elbow beside me, his fingers tracing a line from my neck to my navel. "Now and forever, bound or not. You're mine."

"You're mine, too." I moved onto my side, my hands under my head as I looked up at him. His hand stroked my belly and then my leg, and followed the contour of my hip before coming to rest on my waist.

"I'll never understand why you chose me," he said. Gods, was he joking?

"Aeolmar, you're the most desired man in Parthalan. Every woman in the palace tries to catch your eye, but you don't even look at them. Some assumed you were a monk," I added.

"They never wanted me," he said, rolling onto his back to glare at the ceiling. "They wanted to be the First Hunter's woman. I was an aid to their ambition." He met my eyes. "I'd been alone for a long time when I met you. Before tonight I hadn't been with anyone since... Gods, longer than I can remember."

"So your loneliness drove you to look for shy girls behind stables."

"Beautiful girls behind stables." Aeolmar kissed my forehead. "I wish I'd done things differently. Perhaps we'd have been long since mated, and you never would have gone to the border. While you were gone all I could imagine was you finding love with someone else, someone who could tell you what you needed to hear... Someone who wasn't like me."

"I promised I'd come back to you," I said, hating the pain in his eyes, hating myself for causing it. "I shouldn't have gone. I was wrong to leave you." Aeolmar kissed my wrist, then he draped my arm across his chest.

"I was wrong not to have faith in you," he said. "By giving yourself to me you've honored me. I never thought I'd be so blessed as to have someone like you love me."

I held his hand over my heart. "You asked why I chose you, and the answer is so simple I can't believe you've never seen it. You made this choice for me all those winters ago, when you held me and told me I was safe with you. For me there was no choice, save you or nothing."

Aeolmar smiled. "Have you really loved me that long?"

I kissed his throat. "I've loved you that long."

There was that grin, the devious one I loved so. "I've loved you longer. Let me prove it?"

I let him.

Afterward, Aeolmar held me close and pressed my fingers to his lips. "You make me so happy, beautiful girl," he said.

We stayed together for the rest of the day, sharing stories and endearments. As the day wore on it got cooler, and Aeolmar lit a new fire. After the suns set we watched the night sky through the balcony doors, and Aeolmar told me the name of every constellation within our view, and did not become cross with me when I promptly forgot them all, and he had to start again from the beginning.

CHAPTER THIRTY-TWO

Two uneventful days passed at Teg'urnan, then the *nuvi* were due to compete in the annual Trial by Combat. After Latera's many conversations with Aeolmar and the queen, and their many conversations with Mallia on her behalf, she was allowed to attend the event; after all, she was a huntress and witnessing the Trial was her right. At least, that was Latera's argument.

Arknen was also allowed to attend, though he was still accompanied wherever he went by Innetha and Surya, whom he now referred to as his girls. Latera suspected he liked the arrangement a bit more than he let on.

Latera entered the arena alone, and found a seat in the stands directly across from the queen's gallery. When she looked up, she saw Aeolmar watching her from his place at the queen' right. Latera nodded toward a certain portion of the playing field, where not so long ago they'd been locked in each other's arms. He responded with that half smile of his, the one she adored that appeared only for her. While Latera ruminated on their time in the arena, Finlay and Bron claimed the places on either side of her.

"Did you make your wager?" Bron asked.

"I bet on the *nuvi*, of course," Latera replied; it was tradition for all hunters to wager on the *nuvi*, and whatever funds were collected were put toward a celebration in the *sola*. "Though I don't know if any of them will be able to best Kemen."

The announcer entered the field, and the audience cheered. A moment later the unknown entered and jogged about the perimeter, and the cheering increased twofold. The unknown disappeared as quickly as he appeared, and the announcer began listing the rules of combat.

"I have to tell you, sweetheart," Finlay said, once the stands had quieted down, "we've all been trying to keep Kemen away from Aeolmar."

"Whyever are you doing that?"

"It seems he was drinking with this lout," Finlay indicated Bron, who looked positively pleased by that description, "and went on about how he's a better mate for you than Aeolmar could ever be. What's more, he said that if given half a chance he'll steal you away, and perform a certain duty that he claims Aeolmar is not."

Latera, who'd always had a glass face, purpled at Finlay's words. "Why—he—no," she squeaked.

Finlay took her hand. "I'm not trying to embarrass you, but he was very loud, and as you know the walls have ears." Latera looked from Finlay to Bron, who nodded.

"I tried to quiet the boy down, but he would have none of my sage advice," Bron said.

"Were there many others present?" she asked.

"No," Bron answered, "but it only takes one."

Latera looked at her hands. "Does Aeolmar know?"

"He hasn't beaten Kemen senseless, so I'm guessing no," Finlay replied, "which is why keeping them out of each other's sight is for the best right now."

"Why are you protecting me?" Latera asked. "Is it because of Aeolmar, or would you also do this for Innetha, or Surya?" Bron patted Latera's head.

"We take care of our own, little one," Bron said, "and by doing this we are keeping you and Aeolmar out of harm's way." He leaned in close and whispered, "As for Kemen, now that is something else altogether. The fool needs to learn that he cannot sway a heart that has already found a home elsewhere." Latera beamed at him until red dusted his cheeks. "Stop that," he grunted. "I've a reputation to maintain."

The first gong sounded, and the hunters turned toward the playing field. The *nuvi* entered the arena and circled the perimeter.

"Bad form," Bron muttered. "Lining up to be picked off."

Latera nodded. "Have either of you ever played the unknown?"

"Not I," Bron declared. "My shape is rather distinctive," he added, resting his hands on his ample belly.

"Oh, Bron, you're my favorite lunk," Latera said. "And you, Finlay?"

"Many times," Finlay replied, "but the only *nuvi* who ever beat me was Kemen."

"Kemen," Latera repeated, wondering if that previous victory was why Aeolmar had suggested him as the unknown for today's match. "How many times has Aeolmar been the unknown?"

"Only once," Finlay replied with a grin. "When you took his helm and he whispered in your ear I thought he'd kiss you, right there on the field."

"I was furious," Latera said. "If he'd done that I would have struck him." They laughed at the idea of Latera attacking the First Hunter in the middle of the arena, while all of Teg'urnan watched.

"We all knew you'd win over the other *nuvi*, but besting the First Hunter as you did is unheard of. However, Aeolmar was worried you wouldn't defeat him, and he didn't want to be the reason for extending your stay in the *sola*. He was in quite a state," Finlay said.

"If he was so concerned then why didn't he have someone else face me?" Latera wondered.

"Because," Finlay replied, "he didn't trust anyone else."

"He didn't sleep at all the night before," Bron said. "I kept telling him to relax but he paced the hall for hours, muttering away to himself." Bron leaned closer, and said, "You see, he wanted to be closer to you, but he also wanted to wait until you were a full hunter. If you lost, he'd have to wait another year."

"He told you all of this?" she asked.

"What was there to know? From when he first saw you, you've made him happy, and little else has ever made him happy."

The second gong sounded, signifying the start of combat. All turned to the playing field, except Latera. She watched Aeolmar until she caught his attention. He looked up and smiled, and the world fell away around her. With her attention focused on her mate, she didn't notice a single swing or blow or anything else happening in the arena.

At length, the crowd cheered. Aeolmar nodded to the field, and Latera saw that the *nuvi* had prevailed and the unknown's sword was in the dirt. Kemen removed his helm and slowly turned in a circle, his gaze searching the stands. Once Kemen found Latera, he held his helm aloft and gave her a great, glittering smile that tied her gut in knots.

"You see, little one?" asked Bron. "All can see Aeolmar's devotion to you, save he who chooses not to."

Latera nodded, then she followed Bron and Finlay as they made their way to the playing field to congratulate the victor. Bron went first, his great girth clearing a path through the crowd. Finlay guided Latera with a hand on her shoulder.

"I do know the way," Latera said.

"I've strict orders to not let you out of my sight until Aeolmar joins you," Finlay replied. He had no sooner said the words when Latera felt hands on her waist, and Aeolmar pulled her into his arms.

"We've been apart too long," he said. "I was jealous of Bron and Finlay, for being closer to you than I was."

"They were telling me stories of how dearly you wanted me to win my own Trial," she said, sliding her arms around his neck.

"All true." He tucked a curl behind her ear. They stood together, and island of calm amidst the chaos, until the throng moved past them and toward the feasting hall. "Now, while no one is watching," he said, pulling Latera toward the exit.

"But the feast," Latera protested.

"I told Asherah you need to rest, but we're not going to your rooms. I'm getting you out of Teg'urnan before these walls drive you mad." Aeolmar led Latera to the stables, where Myrnnhe and Enna were already saddled and waiting for them. They rode west, and stopped at Esguth's Rock.

"Why are we here?" Latera asked, once they set the horses loose to graze. "I thought you hated this place."

"Not any longer." Aeolmar took her hands and held them over his heart. "Not after being here with you. When you were named, and we left that loud, crowded feast and came here... The way you listened to me, not because it was your obligation, but because you cared about me... When I told you that you made life bearable for me, that was how. I was so much happier after that day, knowing I had the chance to win your heart."

"You won my heart long before that day," Latera said.

"I have so much time to make up with you."

She reached up, stroked his cheek. "Let's start today."

Aeolmar led her to the same spot they'd occupied three winters past, setting his back against the sun-warmed rock. He pulled Latera into his arms and, out of habit, she moved onto his lap.

"You're like a kitten," he said, nuzzling her ear, "crawling onto my lap whenever you have the chance."

Latera scowled. "If you insist on calling me a baby cat, I'll have to act like one," she said, then she licked his neck.

"You enjoy testing the limits of my restraint."

"What are your limits, First Hunter?" She tested her teeth against his skin.

Aeolmar pushed Latera onto her back, and tickled her until tears rolled down her face. Eventually he released her from her torment, and wiped her cheeks with his thumbs.

"No tears, not for any reason," he said, kissing away the last of them. He rolled onto his back and they lay in the tall grass, enjoying the warm sunlight and watching the clouds scurry across the sky.

"When do we need to return?" Latera asked.

"Not until nightfall. The feast will keep them occupied until then."

"Won't they wonder where we've gone?"

"Finlay and Innetha are available, and if I'm needed Innetha can track me."

Latera remembered what he'd said in the arena. "You lied to the queen! She thinks we're in the palace."

"I did not lie," he said, "I told her we'd go to your rooms, and we will. She didn't ask when."

The mates returned to Teg'urnan as the elder sun set, the guards' foul moods telling them that the feast continued on without them. Aeolmar took Enna's reins from Latera, bidding her to go on to her chamber while he returned the horses. Latera did, and found Kemen waiting in front of her door.

"Kemen," she said. "What are you doing here?"

"I was going to wait for you inside, but your door's locked," he said.

"It's charmed. Only Aeolmar or I may open it."

"Charmed?" Kemen repeated. "How does the charm work?"

Latera shrugged. "Aeolmar's the magician here, not me."

"I didn't see you after the Trial," Kemen continued, "I hope you're well."

"I'm fine," Latera replied with a smile. "I just don't care for crowds. I hardly attended my own celebration when I was named."

"Did you see me compete?" he asked. Before she could reply, Aeolmar strode up beside her. He placed his hand on Latera's shoulder, and she covered it with her own.

"We did," the First Hunter said, "you fought very well." Kemen bowed his head; a compliment of that magnitude from Aeolmar was a rare occurrence.

"Will you join us at the feast?" Kemen asked.

"We cannot," Aeolmar replied. "Now, we will take our leave of you."

As they left Kemen standing alone in front of Latera's charmed door, she asked, "Where are you taking me?"

"Have you ever been to the peak of the southern tower?"

"I have not."

"Then I'm honored to be the first to bring you there."

Aeolmar led her up the tower's stairs, an elegant spiral that eventually brought them to a plain wooden door. Beyond the door was a small living area, the far corner piled high with dusty wooden boxes. The center of the room was dominated by a copper tub, and beyond that were stone steps that led to a sleeping area, nestled high in the corner like a bird's nest.

"Whose rooms are these?" Latera asked.

"Mine," he replied.

Latera blinked, then looked around the room again. "You bathe here?"

"You bathe in your chamber."

"How do you get the water up all those steps?"

"Magic," he replied with a wink. "Follow me, I want to show you something."

Aeolmar opened a small door on the far side of the room, and they climbed up yet another staircase. This one brought them to a balcony that overlooked the palace gates, and the village below.

"Beautiful," Latera murmured. "Do you have these rooms to keep watch?"

He laughed softly. "They used to belong to one of the cooks. I requested them after you left for the border, and Asherah gave me quite a struggle in obtaining them. She said they weren't suitable for me."

"She's right," Latera said. "You deserve more than those tiny, lightless rooms. What made you want them in the first place?"

Aeolmar lit a candle, illuminating a solitary chair pointed toward the east. Aeolmar sat in the chair and pulled Latera down beside him, and pointed toward the eastern horizon.

"I sat here every night, looking east. I had this misguided hope that you would ride back to me in the middle of the night, and I'd rush out to meet you."

"You weren't misguided," Latera said, and then she told him about all the nights she stood watch at the border staring west, and how the rest of the contingent thought she had no sense of direction because the demons would be coming from the opposite way.

"You see, love," Aeolmar said, "we were always meant to be together."

Chapter Thirty-Three

Latera speaks

I woke in the half-light before first dawn, wondering why my bed was so close to the ceiling. As my senses returned I remembered sitting with Aeolmar on his balcony, the two of us exchanging stories of our imagined midnight meetings while I was at the border and he remained here in Teg'urnan. That we shared the same fantasy made it seem like we'd always been destined to love one another.

That's why the ceiling is so close, this is his bed. *I shifted and saw Aeolmar sleeping next to me, his arm curled around my waist. I rolled over and my stiff muscles protested, since Aeolmar had brought me to bed fully dressed. Gods above, when would he accept that I liked it when he undressed me?*

I tried sitting up so I could get out of my clothes, but Aeolmar tightened his hold on me. I lay still for long moments, ensuring that he was still asleep, before I moved again. He retaliated by burying his face in my hair. Realizing that resistance was futile, I snuggled against his bare chest and amused myself by tracing his scars.

Asherah once told me that Aeolmar was deeply scarred, but that he bore his marks on his soul. I considered where I was, lying in his bed. Aeolmar had never brought me to his rooms before; in fact, before last night I'd had no idea of where he slept when he wasn't with me. Aeolmar had spoken very little about his past, but what he had shared told me he was deeply hurt. The heap of boxes shoved against the far wall told me he couldn't, or wouldn't, let go of whomever or whatever had hurt him.

Yet here I was in his rooms, the foolish human who'd caught his eye. The fact that he'd brought me here, to his most secret place, meant more to me than any spoken declaration. Anyone can say a few endearments, but by inviting me into his private world Aeolmar had proven how much he loved me.

If I loved him any more my heart might burst.

I looked up at Aeolmar, once again struck by his handsome features. I remembered the despair in his eyes when he asked why I wanted him, and I'd give anything to keep him from feeling such sadness ever again. I felt an overwhelming need to protect him—which was ludicrous; if anyone did not need protection, it was Aeolmar—and silently proclaimed myself the defender of his body, and his heart. I refused to let whatever had hurt him in his past ever harm him again.

I moved closer to him, brushing my lips against his cheeks, his lips, until Aeolmar responded and his mouth found mine. He pulled me underneath him and I put up no defenses, enjoying that he was a bit less gentle than he usually was with me. We remained in this blissful embrace, until his fingers brushed my belly and I giggled. Roused by my laughter, his eyes snapped open as he moved to the side.

"Forgive me," he said, "I thought I was dreaming."

"You were, at first," I said, "I kissed you until you woke up." I touched his chest, tracing small circles with my fingertips. "Are these dreams frequent?"

"Yes," he replied. "Promise me something."

"Anything."

"Wake me that way every morning."

"Gladly."

Chapter Thirty-Four

Shortly after second dawn, Aeolmar and Latera returned to her chamber so she could get ready for the day. After doing so, they took a moment's rest in front of the hearth.

"When can I patrol again?" she asked.

"Do you feel well enough?" he asked, and she nodded vigorously. "When Finlay is available, you can patrol with him."

"Why can't I patrol with you?" she asked, looking at him through her lashes.

"Did you learn how to do that with your eyes to bend me to your will?" he countered, pulling her into his arms. "If you went with me I wouldn't be looking for danger, but a spot to rip your clothes off."

"You rip my clothes off all the time, right here in this room. Why would you need to take me somewhere?" Latera asked.

Aeolmar sighed. "I must meet with the queen at midday, but we can go riding together until then." Latera kissed him, but not for long. She didn't want him to change his mind about their outing.

They rode north from the palace. Aeolmar chose that route because the area had been quiet of late. Aeolmar was ahead of Latera when she noticed leaves fluttering on the trees, and felt the ground roll. Latera sidled up next to Aeolmar, and asked, "What are these tremors?"

Before he could respond they noticed an odor emanating from a nearby ravine: the telltale stench of demons. They left the horses a safe distance from the edge, and climbed down the rough path, cruelly carved from the living rock by the stream at its base, and crept along the water until they reached a bend in the terrain. Aeolmar looked downstream, then he turned around and shoved Latera against the ravine wall.

"What is it?" she asked. Aeolmar covered her mouth with his, pinning her against the rocks.

"Stay still," Aeolmar breathed into her mouth. He crept toward the streambed, and Latera saw a line of demons marching down the waterway. Then the source of the tremors, one of their huge, lumbering beasts, came into view. It was as big as four horses and had thick, scaly skin the color of dried blood. Three curved horns protruded from its head, and it was led by chains attached to a metal collar around its neck. As it passed, pebbles and other debris shook loose and rained down upon them.

More demons, and two more beasts, each larger than the last, passed by Latera and Aeolmar. None of the monsters so much as glanced toward the hunters.

Why don't they notice us? Latera tore her gaze from the nightmare procession to Aeolmar, and saw beads of sweat on his brow. *He's hiding us.* She felt his magic washing over her, so powerful it lifted her off the ground. Aeolmar was pressed against her as his spell wrapped around them, silent save for his heart thundering against hers.

When the last of the demons had passed, Latera tapped Aeolmar's shoulder, signaling that it was safe. Aeolmar ended the spell and they fell to the ground in a tangle of limbs, gasping for air.

"Did you count how many?" he panted.

"Fifty four and three beasts."

"Olluhm's Balls, you've killed those monsters?"

"I'd rather take on a beast than a demon. How did you hide us?"

"With a glamour. I'm sorry for not warning you, but I needed to maintain skin to skin contact in order to hide you as well."

Latera raised an eyebrow. "And all you could think to do was kiss me?"

"I also needed you to stay quiet."

"Next time, cover my mouth with your hand."

"Next time, I'll use you as a distraction while I evade them." Latera propped herself up on her elbows and looked down at Aeolmar, and brushed the hair from his brow.

"You're always taking care of me," she murmured.

"Always, love," Aeolmar said, then he rolled and trapped her beneath him.

"You do love getting me on my back in the dirt," she teased, sliding her arms around his neck.

"You have no idea."

"I think I do." She moved her hips against him. Aeolmar shifted so she was immobile, and kissed her breathless.

"Always testing my limits." He got to his feet and pulled Latera along with him. "We must go to the queen. There haven't been that many demons so close to Teg'urnan since Esguth's time."

"Explain that glamour to me," Latera said as they walked toward the horses.

"It's a simple spell," he said. "It lets me blend with my surroundings, like casting a fog over me. It's good that we were near the ravine's wall. The glamour doesn't work if I'm standing out in the open."

"What if we'd been lying on the ground?" she asked.

"Then one of the beasts might have stepped on us."

Latera shuddered. "When we started seeing those beasts at the border, we thought they were walking nightmares." Latera turned to mount Enna, but Aeolmar grabbed her wrist.

"You're walking dream for me," he said. "I hope I can make you happy."

"You already have," she said. "I can only promise to love you in return."

He kissed her wrist. "I'll hold you to that."

Chapter Thirty-Five

Latera speaks

I patrolled with Finlay that night, both of us relieved we didn't encounter any demons or beasts or whatever new monster was lurking in the dark. Our shift was almost over before I worked up the courage to ask him about Aeolmar.

"Has he said anything?" I asked, as we approached the palace gates.

"Has who said anything?" Finlay countered. When I frowned, he continued, "Yes, Aeolmar has been in a better mood of late, and much easier to deal with. Keep him happy, please, for all our sakes."

We passed under the gates and dismounted. "Give me your reins," I offered. "Go, get some rest. Or visit the queen. Although, if you go to her then neither of you will be resting."

Finlay's ears went pink. "I...how..."

"You're not the only one Aeolmar confides in." When he looked panicked, I added, "Do you really think I'd tell anyone about your arrangement?"

"Thank you," Finlay said, relief washing over his features. "I'm sure the queen will thank you, too."

As I led the horses to the stable, I hoped Finlay would visit Asherah. I liked the idea of them together. After I left the stable, Kemen crossed my path.

"I'm leaving at the next full moon," he announced.

"I thought you were staying in Teg'urnan."

"So did I. Aeolmar's sending me to the Western Contingent."

"I wonder why," I mused.

"Why do you think?" Kemen snapped, as he stalked away.

I shook my head, and continued on to my chambers, where I found Aeolmar asleep in my bed. I changed into a nightdress, but my thoughts raced too quickly for sleep. Since the night was warm, I went to the balcony and combed out my hair. Aeolmar joined me a short time later.

"May I?" he asked.

"This task isn't beneath the First Hunter?" I teased. He admonished me with a glance as he took the comb, and gently untangled my hair.

"Would you like me to braid it for you?"

"I thought you didn't care for it braided."

"I don't. If it were up to me you'd never bind it, and leave it loose every day."

"That wouldn't be practical."

Without another word, he grabbed handfuls of my hair and twisted until it hung down my back in a fiery rope. While he tied off the end, I told him about my encounter with Kemen.

"He's not just being sent to the Western Contingent, he'll lead it," Aeolmar clarified.

"I thought you were sending him away because of what he said to Bron." As soon as the words were out of my mouth, I realized I shouldn't have spoken. Aeolmar dropped my braid and placed his hands on my shoulders.

"I wasn't aware of anything he said to Bron." When I remained silent he moved in front of me, leaning against the short stone railing. "Are you going to tell me, or should I send for him?"

I debated running, but his gaze held me fast to my seat. "Kemen was drinking with Bron, and said that he wanted to take me from you, and perform a, um, certain duty. I thought you already knew, or I would have told you sooner," I added.

Aeolmar knelt before me, and said, "It's not your responsibility to report every drunken word said in the hall. Bron, however, should have told me."

"He and Finlay didn't tell you because they thought it would make you angry."

"Finlay?" he asked, raising his brows. "My second keeps things from me as well?"

I pressed my lips to his, part distraction and part apology. "Promise me you won't be mad at Bron and Finlay. They were only trying to protect you, and me, and they mentioned you may beat Kemen senseless, so they just wanted to protect him, as well."

"What if I promise not to be angry with Bron and Finlay, remain angry with Kemen for speaking of you in such a manner, and discuss with you this certain duty?" Aeolmar countered as he pulled me off the bench. My legs curled around his waist as his mouth went to my neck.

"What if instead of discussing these duties, you demonstrate them," I said. "I can name a willing participant."

"Are you sure?" he asked. "You know I'd never demand it of you."

"What if I demand it of you?" I asked. "I do enjoy showing you how much I love you."

"You show me every time I look at you," he said, "every time your eyes find mine, and you smile, I know." He kissed me with such passion if I wasn't already sitting I would have fallen. "You don't need to do anything for me."

"That's too bad," I said, threading my fingers into his hair, "I like playing with you."

Aeolmar kissed me as he stood, my legs wrapped around his waist and his hands under my thighs. He didn't break our kiss as he crossed the room and climbed the stairs to bed.

"Go ahead. Play," he said as we fell onto the soft cushions. Aeolmar moaned as I touched him, a low, throaty noise that aroused me in ways I

never thought a sound could. His hands moved under my dress, caressing my hips as I moved closer to him. His mouth traveled to my breasts, then a shaft of daylight found us, and he swore.

"Hells," he hissed as he moved to the side of me.

"What in the nine realms is wrong?" I demanded.

"Nothing with you," he replied. "Don't think that for a moment. I must meet with Asherah at second dawn, about Muirin."

"What is a Muirin?"

"Not a what, who. She's nuvi *who won the Trial by Combat."*

"I didn't notice the winner," I said, stroking his chest. "My attention was captured by another. How long will this meeting be?"

"Afterward, I need to speak with Harek about the demons we saw yesterday." Aeolmar rubbed his eyes, then he rolled onto his back and blew out a breath. Like so many of Aeolmar's days, this one had been scheduled from second dawn to dusk. It was a wonder he ever slept.

"We have now," I said. Aeolmar propped himself up on his elbows, his hair falling around me like a shining chestnut curtain.

"Are you propositioning me?"

"Perhaps."

"Only if you'll come to this blasted meeting with me."

"I'll go to Asherah's, but not Harek's."

Aeolmar dipped his head and kissed my throat. "If those are your terms you'd best love me exceptionally well."

"I accept that challenge."

CHAPTER THIRTY-SIX

When they reached the queen's chambers later that morning, Latera was shocked when Aeolmar simply pushed open the door. "You enter her rooms without even a knock?" she asked.

"Only I and one other may do so," he replied, and as the door opened they saw Finlay pacing inside. When the Second Hunter saw them, he halted.

"You really won't say anything?" he asked Latera.

"Of course she won't," Asherah said, as she brushed past Finlay. She took Latera's hands and let her toward a table heaped with food.

"Forgive him," Asherah implored, casting a glance over her shoulder at Finlay. "I fear it's in a man's nature to be suspicious."

"Agreed," Latera said. "Do you eat this much every morning?"

"I don't, but Finlay has an amazing appetite," she replied. "I sometimes wonder if his mother ever fed him."

"Not as well as you do, Sher," Finlay said, kissing her cheek.

Latera raised an eyebrow. "Sher?"

Aeolmar opened his mouth, but Asherah silenced him with a glare. "Don't, not if you know what's good for you. Come, let's eat while the food is hot."

The four of them gathered around the table, and Asherah personally served her guests. After they'd eaten—and Finlay had seconds—and discussed the upcoming Trial by Stealth, Asherah brought up a new topic.

"I don't know how much Aeolmar has told you already," Asherah began, with a nod toward Latera, "but we've decided to send our First Hunter northward."

Latera turned toward Aeolmar. "North?"

"It's the best course of action, for now at least," he replied. "The demons and beasts we intercepted yesterday were coming from that direction, and Harek claims there have been other reports of activity in that region. Not that he informed me of these reports," he added. "Harek seems to think that someone or something is aiding a *mordeth* in the area, and possibly aiding Asgeloth himself. I'll visit each of the five elfin lands. Hopefully, the local lords will have noticed something out of the ordinary."

"You're leaving?" Latera asked, her tone betraying her irritation over being the last to know.

"Yes, and you're coming with me," Aeolmar said.

She blinked. "I am?"

"I can't stand being away from you for half a day. You think I could go an entire season without you?" He wrapped an arm around Latera's shoulders and pulled her close. "Will you accompany me on this mission?"

"You know I will," she replied.

"Well, that's settled," Asherah said. "Shall we plan this little adventure?"

Asherah hauled over her maps and the four of them discussed the pending journey. Throughout it all Latera marveled at Asherah's easy manner with Finlay. When they'd first arrived the two had remained formal with each other, but as the day wore on their deep affection was plain to see. Asherah's gaze softened as she looked at Finlay, and if Latera didn't know better she'd have said that the queen was in love with the Second Hunter. As for Finlay, he found many ways to subtly touch the queen, be it a graze of his hand across hers or a caress to her shoulder. Latera thought they were the sweetest couple she'd ever known, save for her and Aeolmar.

As the morning wore on Aeolmar relaxed as well. After his third glass of wine he laughed out loud, something the queen did not let go unnoticed.

"Why Aeolmar," she said, "I haven't heard you laugh like that in at least ten winters."

"Twenty," Finlay chimed in.

"Your fiery huntress may yet break down your defenses," Asherah teased. Latera blushed, but Aeolmar put his arm around her and kissed her temple.

"She already has."

Aeolmar and Latera remained with them until midday, and when they left the door swung open of its own accord. "Have you charmed that one as well?" Latera asked once they were in the corridor.

"Yes," he replied, "It only opens for me, Finlay, and the queen, but she has asked me to alter the spell so it will open for you, as well."

"I believe she has more than an arrangement with Finlay," Latera said. Aeolmar frowned, then he led Latera into a little-used hall. They sat in an alcove, and Aeolmar took her hands.

"Asherah and Finlay are bound," he said. "Very few are aware of this."

Latera cocked her head to the side. "Does that mean Finlay's the king?"

"Don't give him any ideas," Aeolmar warned.

"Why would they keep something so wonderful a secret?"

"The queen believes that if their binding was common knowledge it would make Finlay a target," he replied, "thus endangering his life. That's why we don't quell the rumors about Asherah and I, as a bound woman would never seek another's bed."

"Perhaps these rumors are fueled by the First Hunter wandering in and out of the queen's chambers without knocking."

Aeolmar grinned. "Perhaps."

"Who else knows?"

"Aside from Finlay and Asherah, only me, Innetha, the High Priestess, and now you. Most suspect there is something between them, but no one knows of the binding."

"Not even the Prelate knows?"

"Harek is loyal to Parthalan, but he's a terrible person," he replied. "If he knew he'd deride Asherah as weak for wanting another's company." Latera was about to voice her treasonous thoughts about Harek, when Aeolmar placed a finger on her lips. "I don't want to talk about any of them right now. I want to talk about you and me."

"What about us?"

"Have you thought more on binding yourself to me?"

"Does it matter? I'm still human."

"You're not," Aeolmar insisted, "not wholly. I'll find someone—a sorcerer, maybe—who can determine your exact heritage."

Latera frowned, wondering why her bloodline had suddenly become so important. No one, not even the queen, had ever shown an interest in Latera's race. As she watched the emotions play across Aeolmar's face—uncertainty, hope, concern—she realized how much he wanted to be bound to her. Latera also realized that she wanted a binding, too.

"You want to be bound to me so badly?" she asked. He caressed her cheek with his knuckles, his other hand playing with the end of her braid.

"Latera, I love you, more than I ever thought I could love another. I've already wasted so much time with you, and I don't want to lose another moment." He let his hair fell across his face, and Latera waited for him to continue. "If you do me the honor of binding yourself to me, I'll love you and protect you for all eternity."

"And you chose to ask me something of such importance in a dark, dusty hall?"

"It's not the location that matters, only the answer."

Latera looked at him, memorizing his striking face, how his blue eyes gleamed in the dim light. She wanted to tell him yes, but she knew that bindings were broken by nothing, not even death. She refused to let Aeolmar suffer, alone forever, if she died as a mortal... And she didn't want him to share his immortality with her. She couldn't do that, since it meant his life would end when hers did.

"If you can find a way to determine my heritage," Latera began, "and it tells me—without any doubt—that I'm not wholly mortal, then yes." Aeolmar's eyes went wide as his jaw dropped. Latera tucked his hair behind his ear, and smiled. "Don't look so surprised. Surely you knew I'd say yes. I love you, Aeolmar. Never doubt that I do."

Aeolmar's face was taken over by the widest grin Latera had ever seen, then he pulled her against him. "I'll spend my life making you happy."

"I'm already happy. I have you."

Aeolmar rained kisses onto her face and neck, holding her so tightly she lost her breath.

"Gently, or I'll tell anyone who asks how you tricked me into a binding in the servant's passage."

"I'll tell them of the day we met, and how you threw a saddle at me."

"I did nothing of the sort. What were you doing, standing in my way like that? I thought you were quite rude," she added.

"I had to see where you went," Aeolmar said, stroking her cheek with his thumb. "I caught the briefest glimpse of you as you went behind the stable, and I had no choice but to follow. I've been smitten by my beautiful girl ever since." When Latera laughed, he asked, "And what is so funny?"

"Finlay told me a version of that tale the night I followed you to the arena."

"Finlay," Aeolmar grumbled, "He tells you everything I say."

"If he hadn't, I wouldn't have gone after you that night," Latera said. "And if you are to be my bound mate you need to say such things to me, not him."

"I suppose you have a point," Aeolmar conceded, then he pulled her upright. "Come, love, let's return to your chamber."

"Why, First Hunter, whatever for?"

"If you must ask, I'll need to spend the rest of the day showing you what I mean."

"What of your meeting with Harek?"

"He can wait. My mate needs me."

Latera looped her arm with his. "I do."

Chapter Thirty-Seven

Latera had always counted herself lucky to avoid the Prelate in most matters, and she soon learned just how fortunate she'd been. Harek had deemed it necessary to review every detail of her and Aeolmar's journey north, and state his opinion on all matters. Seven days after messengers had been sent to inform the elf lords of their plans Aeolmar burst into Latera's chamber, his irritation filling the room like a gust of cold air.

"What did he do now?" she asked. Aeolmar sat and rubbed his eyes. Latera stood behind him, massaging his neck.

"Dealing with Harek was more frustrating than usual," he said. "He made me plot out every step we'll take, what order we'll visit the regions, even how long we plan to remain in each"

"That doesn't seem unreasonable."

"Harek has never cared where I was before. Why he cares now is beyond me. I've been gone from Teg'urnan for entire seasons without informing him."

"Perhaps Asherah is worried."

"Perhaps." Aeolmar hauled Latera onto his lap and nuzzled her neck. "I've done something that will make you happy."

"Oh?" She stretched her neck for more kisses. "And what was this great deed?"

"Guess."

"You've learned how to turn demons into toads?"

"That would be handy, but no."

"Make yourself invisible around Harek?"

"Another useful spell, but no."

She thought for a moment. "Toads into demons?"

He nipped her neck. "You're not even trying."

"Why bother? You'll tell me eventually."

He nipped her again. "I've sent for Alia to return to Teg'urnan."

"You have?" Latera drew back, her pale eyes shining. "For me?"

"For you," he replied.

"But why now?" Latera asked.

"The queen and I believe we are coming into dark times. More protection is always better than less."

"Alia is the only one I know of who's killed a beast, other than me. One dragged her right off the cliff, and she fought her way back up."

"That drop is deadly. From what Kemen said, you two were a deadly combination."

"You have conversations with Kemen now?" Latera asked, raising an eyebrow. "Careful, First Hunter, or others will realize you're not nearly as awful as you pretend to be."

Aeolmar grabbed Latera's braid and tugged. "Hush. That's our secret."

Latera freed her braid and swatted his shoulder with the tufted end. "Must you meet with Harek again today?"

"Thankfully, no. Asherah has invited us to join her midday meal," he said. "She wants to offer us some advice about the elves. And," he added, his eyes twinkling, "Harek will not be attending." Latera giggled, feeling like his conspirator.

When they arrived at Asherah's door, Aeolmar bade Latera to approach first. She had forgotten that he reworked the door's charm and jumped back when it opened for her.

"Doors don't bite," Aeolmar said, as he caught her waist.

"You just wanted to get your hands on me," she accused. "Mean man, scaring me on purpose."

"Correct on two counts," Aeolmar said, and they entered the queen's receiving chamber.

"Aeolmar, Latera," Asherah said as she rose from her map table. "Thank you for joining me."

"Thank you for the honor," Latera said, nodding toward the door.

"It won't seem like an honor when I summon you at odd hours of the night, as I do with Aeolmar," Asherah said with a smile. "Follow me, the others are already here."

They followed Asherah into her sitting room, and saw Finlay and Innetha seated at a table heaped with nearly every map in Teg'urnan. Attia moved around the edge of the room, depositing little plates of food and steaming bowls of tea in the few uncovered spots on the table. While they ate and drank Innetha shared her knowledge about the northern region, and Latera learned that Innetha and Aeolmar once made those northern treks together.

"And you no longer travel together?" Latera asked.

"We stopped for the good of Parthalan," Innetha said.

"Indeed," Aeolmar agreed. "It didn't reflect well on Asherah to have us bickering across the countryside."

"No, it certainly did not," Asherah murmured.

Once the plates had been cleared away, and Attia replaced the bowls of tea with ale or wine, Asherah unrolled several maps. Innetha outlined the best routes through the elflands, as well alternatives in the event of heavy snow.

"Snow?" Latera repeated. "I haven't seen snow since I was in Gannera."

"You'll see so much of it in the north you'll come to hate it," Innetha said. "Even in summer the mountains stay white, and once you reach Thurnda it will likely be knee deep."

While Aeolmar and Innetha bent low over the maps, the queen showed Latera the careful notes she'd made for them. Asherah listed the specific gifts she'd chosen for each region, and gave instructions as to how to present them. Apparently, one of the lords, Micon of Rael, had a habit of deliberately misinterpreting messages. Innetha rolled her eyes when she heard Micon's name, as Aeolmar and Finlay laughed.

"We're laughing, because?" Latera asked.

"Micon is enamored with our Innetha," Finlay explained. "Aeolmar and Innetha went to Rael—how long ago was it? Almost a hundred winters past, I believe, back when Micon was first made the local lord—and he's been captivated by her ever since."

"Micon wouldn't leave her alone," Aeolmar added. "He followed her everywhere she went, begging her to stay in Rael and become his lady." Innetha shoved Aeolmar so hard he almost fell, but he caught himself on the table's edge. "He even asked me to speak to Innetha about him."

"And did you?" Latera asked.

"No," Aeolmar replied, shielding himself from another blow. "I was afraid she'd stab me if I mentioned Micon."

"A wise decision, for once," Innetha grumbled. She asked the queen to excuse her, and Asherah graciously let her go. After Innetha departed Finlay related how Micon had sent her gifts for many winters, each more extravagant than the last. When she ignored the gifts Micon came to Teg'urnan, to see her for himself. Innetha retaliated by going to the Northern Contingent, and staying there until she was certain he'd gone.

"Aeolmar, you should be leaving as well," Asherah said with a glance toward the suns. "Aren't you due to meet with Harek shortly?"

Aeolmar scowled. "Unfortunately, yes." He rose and took Latera's elbow. "I'll walk you to your rooms."

As Aeolmar and Latera left the queen's room, she stole a backward glance. She saw Finlay take the queen's hand and lead her to her sleeping chamber, where they would clearly not be sleeping. Latera's cheeks flushed, which amused Aeolmar.

"It's no different that you and I," he said with a wry grin, "I'm leading you to your chamber."

"I just didn't expect them to be so intimate," Latera said. Aeolmar said nothing further, but once they were within her chamber he pulled her to him, kissing her in that way of his that turned her knees to jelly. He led her to the balcony and they sat on the stone bench.

"I can hardly think when you kiss me like that," Latera said.

"Good," he said. "I'll be with Harek for a long, long time today. I'm sorry I can't spend the afternoon with you."

"I understand. I know you have many obligations."

"I mean, I'm sorry I can't spend it with you the way Asherah and Finlay are spending theirs." Latera's cheeks went scarlet, but she held his gaze.

"And now you test my limits, First Hunter," she said. Aeolmar cursed softly and stood; Latera looked across the courtyard and saw Harek standing on the opposite balcony. He stared at them while he barked orders over his shoulder. Aeolmar and Latera retreated inside her chamber and sat on the rug before the hearth.

"I'll enjoy being away from him for a time," he said a length.

"Do you think he was looking for you?" Latera asked.

"I don't know," he replied, rubbing his eyes, "and I'm beginning to not care." He opened his eyes and regarded Latera with his warm gaze. "While I'm with him, I'll only think of you waiting here for me."

"If I'm to wait here until he's out of breath I'll starve."

They laughed, and Aeolmar said, "What if I promise to bring you supper?"

Latera rested her head on his shoulder. "That will do."

Chapter Thirty-Eight

Two more sennights came and went before Alia returned from the Eastern Border. Latera and Aeolmar waited for the hunters on his balcony, since it offered the farthest view. Or rather, Aeolmar waited, while Latera paced across the small space.

"The contingent rarely arrives before midday," Aeolmar reminded her, "and once you catch sight of them you'll still have plenty of time to go down to the square and meet her." Latera leaned over the balcony's railing and frowned at the road.

"Beloved, sit with me," Aeolmar said. Being that the road remained infuriatingly vacant, Latera sat beside him.

"You should have demanded that they arrive by first dawn," she said.

"Now you know what it was like when I waited for you," Aeolmar said, as he kissed the top of her head. "The queen's messenger is due to return from the north today. We'll be departing soon."

"I can't wait," Latera said. "We should travel as slowly as possible, and whenever we find a lovely inn we can remain there for days at a time, never leaving our room."

"We must travel quickly to our destinations," he said, "but we can take our time on the journey back."

The suns climbed higher and Latera admitted that Aeolmar was correct, Alia wouldn't arrive for some time yet. They retreated to his rooms to escape the heat, his stone chamber much cooler than the unshaded balcony. As Latera stretched the weariness from her limbs

Aeolmar embraced her from behind, and suggested a way to pass the time.

"You're insatiable," Latera said.

"And you never say no," Aeolmar countered as he pulled her to bed.

Afterward they lay entwined despite the heat, enjoying their stolen moments. "I've spoken with then queen," Aeolmar said.

"Have you?" Latera asked, her cheek against his chest. "About what?"

"She believes we can determine exactly what sort of blood flows in your lovely veins," he replied, brushing his lips against her wrist.

"Did you tell her why you want to know?"

"No, but she probably assumes the reason."

"Will our binding be secret, like hers?" Latera pressed. "Has a First Hunter ever taken a mate before?"

"I don't know. Does that make a difference to you?"

"No," she replied. "I don't care who knows, or doesn't know. I'll love you either way." Aeolmar pressed her fingers to his lips.

"You make me happy to no end, beautiful girl."

Latera untangled herself from his arms. "We're supposed to be watching for the hunters."

"How could I forget?" Aeolmar returned to the balcony, then reappeared a moment later, and said, "I can just make them out on the road." Latera leapt to her feet and grabbed her clothes, but Aeolmar caught her, and kissed her until she was breathless.

"What was that for?" she asked.

"Do I need a reason?" he countered, caressing her cheek with his thumb. "I think you'll be with Alia long into the night, and I need to kiss you now while I can." Latera held him for a moment, then they dressed and left to meet their friends.

The returning contingent was still a fair distance down the road, so Aeolmar and Latera waited in the watchtower. They were joined by Finlay and Surya, and then Bron and Luth. To pass the time Bron told bawdy stories that would have made the whole of the Eastern Contingent proud. Latera laughed so hard she forgot what she was waiting for, until Aeolmar whispered that Alia was staring at her.

Latera ran down the steps of the tower, and almost knocked Alia over as she dismounted. "I'm so glad you're home," Latera cried, throwing her arms around her.

"Me too," Alia said. "I saw you with the First Hunter. I take it things are going well?"

"They are," Latera replied. "Perhaps better than well."

Aeolmar approached them, and said, "Welcome home, Alia."

"Thank you," Alia said, bowing her head. Aeolmar squeezed Latera's elbow, then he moved on to speak with Brynne.

"You'll tell me everything, and soon," Alia said.

Latera smiled. "I will."

Brynne and Aeolmar left the square for their meeting with Asherah, with Latera and Alia in tow. During the short walk to the queen's receiving chamber, Latera noted Alia's appearance. When Latera returned from the border she'd been covered in blood burns and bruises, but Alia didn't have a single mark on her. In fact, Alia seemed as well and hale as she'd ever been, and Latera couldn't understand why.

Once greetings had been exchanged and all had settled around Asherah's map table, the queen asked Brynne, "Were the soldiers helpful?"

"I'm sure they would be, but we're hardly attacked of late," Brynne replied. "We see one, perhaps two demons every ten days."

"It doesn't sound like the same border," Latera said, remembering all the teeth she'd collected.

"It's quite unusual," Brynne continued. "I first thought they were lulling us into complacency, but they seem to have abandoned their prior plan of attack."

Alia nodded. "Despite the lessened activity, we kept to our patrols. No one wanted to be caught unawares."

"And what of the beasts?" asked Aeolmar.

"We haven't seen one since Alia dispatched the behemoth at the cliff," Brynne replied. "I don't like this calm. Makes me think they're plotting."

"Could it be the *deva'shi*?" Latera asked

"What in the nine realms is that?" Brynne demanded.

"The *deva'shi* is a sort of demon champion," Aeolmar said. "Harek uncovered the information a few winters ago."

"Why wasn't I told about this champion? Why am I out at that border defending it, if I don't know what to defend it from?" Brynne demanded.

"I didn't wish to concern you over something we couldn't prove true," he replied. "I don't need you spreading more lies among your people."

"Are you questioning if I'm a fit leader?" she seethed. "I dare you to find another like me."

"I agree, there's no one like you." Aeolmar said.

"Enough," Asherah said, silencing them both. "Brynne, go."

Brynne stood and stalked out of the room, nearly knocking Finlay over as he entered. Once she was gone Aeolmar turned to the queen.

"She needs more discipline," he said, "She's been at the border too long."

"And who would replace her?" Asherah asked. "It's an assignment no one wants, and everyone but her see it as punishment. What's really bothering you? Is she really spreading lies?"

"Brynne speaks whatever lies work for her at the time," Alia said, when Aeolmar remained silent. "Her aim is to make one think that the border is the one place they will be happy, far from the rules that govern life elsewhere. I know of the lies the First Hunter speaks of, and they were enough to convince Latera to remain with her instead of returning to Teg'urnan."

"Is this true?" Asherah demanded, and Latera nodded.

Asherah sighed. "She will be dealt with, but not until after your journey" Asherah said. "This news that the onslaught to the east has lessened, in addition to the increase of demons near the palace, makes me eager to know if someone in the north really is assisting Asgeloth. I will have my scholars research this *deva'shi* further." With that, the queen dismissed all but Finlay, and the three hunters made their way to the great hall.

"Her lies made you stay," Aeolmar said. "I thought you were fighting demons."

"That is why I stayed," Latera insisted. "The attacks were as horrible as you've been told."

"Brynne is a bitter, spiteful woman," Alia said, "with a heart as cold as the winter wind." She darted in front of them, and said, "Forgive me, my lord, but you should have told the queen."

"I'll not speak of such trivial matters before the queen," Aeolmar declared.

Undaunted, Alia continued, "Is it trivial that Brynne so undermined Latera's faith in you?"

Aeolmar's gaze moved from Alia to Latera. "Was there more?"

Latera looked at the floor. "Yes."

Alia said, "Brynne furthers her own agenda, not the queen's."

"Alia, go on without us," Aeolmar ordered. After she walked away Aeolmar grazed his thumb along Latera's jaw, tilting her chin up.

"A lie against the queen is treason," he said. "Tell me what Brynne said."

"She didn't lie about Asherah," Latera said. "She said that Teg'urnan is restrictive, and unfair to hunters. She told me things of your past, of women you'd been with, but I don't care about anyone you were with before you met me." She placed her hands on Aeolmar's chest and looked up at him.

"Please don't look at me like that," he said, "I'm not angry with you. But a lie spoken against me is also treason." He wrapped his arms around her and kissed her hair.

"What will you do about Brynne?" she asked.

"Asherah said it will be decided when we return, I'll leave it until then."

"I think I'm becoming a bad influence on you, First Hunter," Latera teased. "A few seasons ago you would have taken Brynne to task. Now, you're almost docile." Aeolmar glared at her in mock anger.

"You should be punished for that insolent tone," he said. "Give me a moment to come up with the proper torture."

"May I offer suggestions?" she teased. Aeolmar pushed Latera against the wall and kissed her, far more passionately than normal for the palace corridors; when a *saffira* walked by them, she gasped and ran off. They laughed, then Aeolmar draped his arm around Latera's shoulders and they continued on.

***

That evening, Alia and Latera retired to the latter's chamber. Latera wanted to hear about the state of the border, but Alia was only interested in the details of Latera's relationship with Aeolmar. Latera told her nearly everything, from their shouting match in the arena to the way he'd cared for her during her illness.

"Such tenderness," Alia said. "I never knew he had it in him."

"He's much gentler than he lets on."

"Apparently so. Now, tell me everything that has since transpired with you and your Aeolmar," Alia said. They sat on the steps before Latera's bed, Alia clutching a cushion to her breast.

"Things have been well, between us," Not caring for the vague reply, Alia swatted her with the cushion. "Perhaps better than well," Latera added with a grin. "Soon, we'll journey north."

"Just the two of you?"

"Well, us and our horses. Probably a pack animal, maybe two."

"All that time alone," Alia murmured. "At this rate, you'll have a babe before winter." Before either could continue, Aeolmar strode into her chamber.

"You let him saunter in whenever he wants?" Alia asked. "My, how things have changed." Aeolmar ignored Alia and sat beside Latera, his eyes dark as thunderclouds.

"What happened?" Latera asked.

"Brynne and Harek have been screaming at each other for the better part of the day," he replied. "He wants his soldiers returned. She thinks they should remain at the border and is outright refusing."

"Brynne doesn't even like the soldiers," Alia grumbled, "She just wants to make trouble."

Aeolmar's head drooped forward and he rubbed his eyes. "I cannot wait until we're gone from this place," he said, and Latera took his hand. He dropped his other hand from his eyes and stroked Latera's cheek, drawing her toward him.

"Remember me?" Alia asked.

"Apologies," Aeolmar said, "I'm not used to anyone being with us."

"We'll speak again tomorrow," Alia said as she rose. After Alia departed, Aeolmar laid his head in Latera's lap and closed his eyes. Aeolmar was frequently irritated after dealing with his many obligations, but she'd never seen him sad. Worse, if his dealings with Harek were the cause of his depression, she didn't know if she could help him.

"Tell me what's wrong." She raked her fingers through his long, soft hair, and waited for him to speak.

"I don't know how this became my life," he began. "My days consist of hearing mindless disputes where others speak before they think. I don't care where Harek's soldiers are stationed, yet I'm forced to listen to him complain. I don't care about the nonsense that courses through Brynne's head, yet I must hear her out. I wasn't made to administer matters of state; that's a job for Finlay I'm First Hunter, yet I hardly ever hunt."

"Tell me of a time you were happy," Latera said.

"When I was young, and still with my family. We were poor, having little more than a home and the clothes on our backs, but we were happy.

"My sisters and I would watch our mother bake bread," he continued. "Hers was the finest in our village. Sometimes she'd let us help and we'd make a mess of her kitchen, getting more flour on each other than in the dough." Aeolmar laughed quietly. "When I was older, I helped my father in the fields. My brothers, who were much older than me, worked in the mill. Our life was hard, but good."

"You hardly ever speak of your family. It seems like such a happy time."

"It was." Aeolmar moved onto his back. Latera pushed his hair back from his face, enjoying how the strands slipped between her fingers. "Do you miss your family?"

"Yes. I'd give anything to see my sisters again. My mother is harsh, but fair. Innetha reminds me of her, with her sour demeanor and great heart."

Aeolmar snorted. "I doubt Innetha has a heart. What of your father?"

"My father is a wonderful, kind man," I replied. "He's patient, and wise, and always puts his people first. All of Gannera love him, or at least that's what I was told. I don't know if I ever told you, but I was only ten when I was taken."

Aeolmar ran his thumb along her jaw. "Ten?" he repeated. "No, you never told me the details of how you came here. Tell me now." Latera recounted the events as best she could remember, from the swirling water in the pond, to the cottage filled with shadowy men, and to her eventually stumbling into Brennus.

This hovel of sorcerers was in the west?" he asked, once she'd finished.

"I believe so," Latera replied. "I walked through the woods for at least six days before I reached Brennus. Well, I can only remember six of the days, maybe there were more."

"I know of no sorcerers that congregate so, but there is evil hidden in the western hills." He then had Latera describe every detail of the cottage and its occupants, pressing her for every clue. When she couldn't remember any more, his gaze softened.

"To think of what you endured at such a young age," he said. "I'm awed by your courage." Aeolmar sat up and wrapped his arms around her. "You never looked for a way home?"

"At first, I didn't think I could," Latera replied. "There weren't any magic handlers in Brennus, and once Ingvarr and Elma took me in I just assumed that would be my life. Asherah once offered to look into it, but I said no. It's not like my family ever looked for me."

"How do you know?"

Latera dipped her head. "If they did, wouldn't they have found me?"

"Beloved, do you want me to find you a way home?"

"My home is with you," she answered. "You wouldn't like Gannera anyway; I'm first born, heir to the kingdom."

"That explains your arrogance," he teased. "If you'll be happier in your homeland I'll find a way to get you there. And, beloved, don't be so quick to assume your family hasn't looked for you. Magic is difficult to work with, and they may be searching for you even now."

Latera's mind spun; having long since given up hope, it hadn't occurred to her that her family might still be looking for her. But, there were other reasons she couldn't leave Parthalan.

"I've sworn fealty to Asherah; I cannot return to Gannera." She stroked his jaw, and smiled. "But I'd love to bring you there. It's beautiful, with high mountains in the north, and thick forests throughout."

"Is it as beautiful as you?"

"I like to think I'm better looking than a tree."

Aeolmar laughed, then he rose and led Latera to the balcony. They sat on the stone bench, and he coaxed her gaze skyward.

"Tell me about the stars from your home." Aeolmar loved the stars like Latera loved horses, and she frequently found him staring upward, looking for patterns among the blackness.

"I wasn't taught about the stars," she said. "My parents didn't think it was appropriate for princesses to learn about astronomy."

"You mean you never had stories about the night sky?" he asked, eyes glinting. Latera sighed and told him the only story she could remember, of a sea serpent that created the world from her body. He listened in rapt attention, and when the tale was complete Aeolmar looked toward the sky.

"Do you see her stars here?" he asked.

"No," Latera wailed. She hadn't meant to wail. "The sky here is different from Gannera. We only have one sun, the moon is white, and the stars are in different places."

"One sun?" Aeolmar repeated, and she nodded. "How is that possible?" Latera could see the memories of his youth flitting across his mind.

"When you're ready, will you tell me more about your family?" she asked, and Aeolmar nodded. Latera kissed his hand and tucked herself against his chest. "What kind of life do you want to have?"

"What do you mean?"

"If you're not happy with this life here in the palace, tell me what will make you happy."

"If I could, I'd take you far from here," Aeolmar began, his mouth against her ear, "far away from any demons and beasts. We would go to the west, or maybe the south, near the sea."

"I used to love the sea," Latera said.

"I'd build you a house, a simple home with as many rooms as you wanted. I know I couldn't expect you to be a baker, since your food is terrible." He smiled at her offended face. "After all, we'll want the other villagers to like us."

"What would we do with all those rooms?"

"We'd fill them with children," he said. "I'm from a large family, as you are. Wouldn't you like a home with many small feet running about?"

"I never thought I'd be so blessed." As she sat with Aeolmar in the moonlight Latera realized that all she wanted was a cottage near the sea, with nothing more in it than him and their children. Her cheeks were wet, and she hid her face against his chest

"What's wrong, beloved?" Aeolmar asked, kissing away her tears.

"Nothing," she replied. "I never realized how perfect you are for me." She wiped her face, and looked into his bottomless blue eyes. "You truly are my beloved. I couldn't find a more ideal mate if I had eternity to search." She rose, and led him to bed.

"I need to feel you," she said, unlacing his shirt. "Sometimes, I feel as if you are all that is real to me. The six winters I was in Brennus flew by like a dream. My winters at the border are a blur. But when I'm with you, my Aeolmar, my beloved, I'm aware of every moment, of every twist and turn my life takes." She pushed his shirt off his shoulders and they tumbled onto the cushions.

"Beloved," Aeolmar began, "I'll find a way to give you what you need. What we both need. We'll find out what Asgeloth is planning, and we'll stop him. If the threat is over Asherah will release us, and we can make a life for ourselves."

"You would walk away from all you have, for me?"

"All I have is nothing compared to you, beautiful girl."

Chapter Thirty-Nine

Three more days passed, and the messengers Asherah sent to the north still hadn't returned. Latera wondered if she and Aeolmar would leave the palace before autumn. Since Aeolmar had already delegated away his duties, and reassigned Latera's patrols, they spent their mornings exploring the parts of the palace they were normally too busy to visit. On this rainy morning they were in the archive, searching for information about the northern regions. As usual, Latera had trouble reaching things.

"Mar," she called. "Can you get this for me?"

Aeolmar cocked his head to the side. "Why did you call me that?" he asked, as he retrieved the book she'd indicated.

"I don't know, it suits you. Do you not like it?"

A smile ghosted across his face. "My youngest sister called me Mar."

"Oh, I'm sorry—" she began, but he touched his fingers to her lips.

"It's good to hear it again."

Latera set the book on the table, the surface hardly visible under the heap of maps and books. "My youngest sister called me Tera," she said. "She had a terrible time learning my name."

"What was her name?"

"Sasha," Latera replied, remembering her sister's bubbling laugh. "She looked nothing like me, all golden curls and rosy cheeks."

His smile widened. "I'm sure she's beautiful, just like her sister."

"What was your sister called?"

"Enna."

Latera laughed aloud as Aeolmar cringed. "I suppose you think I'm a bit foolish for naming your horse Enna," he said.

"I think it's a beautiful name, for a beautiful creature." Latera tapped her fingers on the closed book. "Where did you get your sword?"

"It's a troll sword. I've had it for many years. Why?"

"Brynne told me it's Esguth's sword. She said that you took from him in battle, and it's so heavy because it was the *mordeth's*."

He exhaled heavily. "She's partly right. I did take Esguth's sword, but I broke it in battle not long afterward. Grelk, the troll king, crafted the sword I carry now. His dens are near the elflands. If you'd like I can take you to his forge."

"Your sword was made by the troll king himself?" Latera asked, raising her brows.

"He owed me," Aeolmar replied. "What else did Brynne tell you?"

"Nothing that matters." Latera looked toward the windows; the downpour continued. "Is it punishment enough that she needs to ride back in the rain?"

Aeolmar shook his head. "Not nearly."

The queen's *saffira-nell* entered the archive, and advised them that the messengers had finally returned from the north. Aeolmar and Latera went to Asherah's receiving chamber, and saw the emissaries standing before the queen and the Prelate, soaked to the bone. Quickly—probably because they were freezing—they relayed the elfin lords' responses. All five of the regions were willing to accommodate them; however, Tingu had been difficult. Asherah's head drooped, and Harek only waited for the messengers to leave the room before complaining.

"Leran," Harek spat. "He continues to be a thorn in our side."

"Do *not* speak ill of him," the queen hissed. "Leran is a good man, easily as good a man as his father. Give me a moment." Asherah stood and went to her private chamber. Harek opened his mouth, but Aeolmar shook his head.

"If you say anything about Leran, we will tell the queen," Aeolmar said.

"That elf is a menace," Harek growled.

"Perhaps, but he's my menace," Asherah said as she reentered the room carrying a small wooden box.

"When you arrive in Tingu present this to Leran. Tell him it contains a gift from me," Asherah said, handing the box to Aeolmar.

"It will be done," Aeolmar said. "Shall Latera and I depart the day after next?"

Asherah nodded. "That is as good a day as any."

***

Six days after Aeolmar and Latera departed from Teg'urnan they arrived in Rael, the smallest of the elfin lands, and the closest to Teg'urnan. The capitol of Rael was a walled city dominated by a turreted castle.

"That castle," Latera said as they approached. "It reminds me of Gannera."

Aeolmar squeezed her hand. "You know I'll find you a way back to your family."

Latera squeezed back. "I've never doubted you."

Micon, Rael's administrator, proved to be an excellent host. He said time and again that he was honored to have the First Hunter and his mate in his home, lest Aeolmar didn't hear him and forget to tell the queen. Micon regaled them with stories about Asherah's bravery and kindness, and how he appreciated her continued good favor. He also asked Aeolmar for the latest news concerning the lovely Innetha, which Aeolmar managed to relate with a straight face. Latera, on the other hand, couldn't stop laughing, and excused herself.

That night, Micon held a feast in Aeolmar and Latera's honor. She wore the purple gown from her naming day, which brought back many pleasant memories for Aeolmar.

"You wore that when you were named," Aeolmar said.

"I'm surprised you remember."

"I'll never forget how you looked that day. If I had any sense, I'd avoid this feast entirely and keep you in our room."

Latera's cheeks went hot, and she swatted his shoulder. "Wonderful. Now I must appear in Micon's court blushing like a maiden."

Aeolmar laughed. "One dress, and the Demon-killer becomes a demure princess."

Latera swatted him again. "My swords are sharp as ever, terrible man."

Aeolmar grabbed her hand and kissed her knuckles. "I've no doubt."

The festivities stretched into the small hours of the night. Tray after tray of food passed before Aeolmar and Latera, some bearing exotic dishes they couldn't hope to identify. Aeolmar watched as Micon heaped local delicacies on his plate, which he neither wanted nor appreciated. Latera surprised herself at how much she enjoyed the fare, and the revelry; she felt more at home with the elves than she ever had in Parthalan.

Once the meal ended the musicians stepped up the beat and all in attendance began dancing, from the lord of the land to the scullion girls. Micon insisted Latera join him, and he pulled her into the mass.

Latera spun and twirled until her feet couldn't take any more abuse, and begged a moment to catch her breath.

Latera returned to her table, but Aeolmar was gone. She gazed about the hall, wondering where he could be, when she spied him in the corridor.

"Hiding so you won't have to dance?" she asked.

"I was waiting for you," he replied, as they walked to their rooms. "After your naming, I dreamt of getting you out of that dress for weeks."

"Oh?" Latera paused, her hand on the door. "And how did these dreams play out?"

"I'll show you," Aeolmar replied, and made good on his words. The next morning, Latera blushed fiercely as she brought her ruined gown to the palace seamstress, with the bodice ripped in two.

During their time in Rael, Aeolmar and Latera made formal inspections of his guards, with Micon agreeing to every recommendation Aeolmar made. Fed up with Micon's sycophantic manner, Aeolmar suggested that the training field be filled with snow, especially during the summer moons. Of course, Micon agreed, until the First Hunter said he was joking. Micon clapped him on the back, laughing as he praised Aeolmar's robust sense of humor.

While their days involved time with elfin warriors, their nights were spent with Aeolmar speaking with Rael's commanders about any local demon activity, while Latera was relegated to socializing with the women. Elfin women were not warriors, and Latera found those nights more boring than waiting around for a demon to attack Teg'urnan. She imagined Aeolmar trading war stories with the men, while she watched the women practice their embroidery.

After a few boring nights, they determined that if anyone in the north was assisting Asgeloth, they were not in Rael. On the fourth morning they left, and Micon gifted them trinkets for both the queen and Innetha, and made Aeolmar promise he wouldn't wait a century before he returned.

"I lied to Micon," Aeolmar said as they rode away from Rael. "I never want to see him again."

Latera laughed. "With any luck he'll forget he knows us."

"That would be some luck, indeed."

"What are the rest of the elflands like?" Latera asked. "Are they all as welcoming as Rael?"

"We'll next visit Tingu," Aeolmar replied, "and you'll meet the menace himself, Leran."

"If Harek dislikes him, I'm sure we'll be great friends."

Aeolmar snorted. "We'll see about that."

Chapter Forty

Latera speaks

*F*our days after we left Rael, Aeolmar and I reached the southern edge of Tingu. It was a vast and remote land, and Tingu's lord was once the king of all elfdom. The legends tell how Asherah, after escaping a life of slavery, begged the elf king, Lormac, for aid, and that he'd been so entranced by her strength and beauty he made her his queen. Lormac had died during the Battle for Teg'urnan, but Asherah remained Lady of Tingu to this day. I wondered how Finlay felt about that.

We arrived at Tingu's southern keep as the child sun went to rest; when I asked why we weren't meeting Leran, the current Lord of Tingu, at The Seat, the ancestral home of the elves, Aeolmar replied that it was an additional ten days travel over land so rough it made the Eastern Border seem like a rolling meadow. Still, I'd expected a bit more from Tingu than a single stone tower surrounded by a few wooden structures.

We were greeted by Leran himself, who stood before the keep with what looked like his entire guard fanned out around him.

"Welcome," Leran called. "Why does the queen see fit to send the First Hunter all the way to Tingu?"

"Greetings, Leran," Aeolmar said. And, they stared at each other.

"Well?" Leran asked at length. "What is so important for you to journey so far?"

Aeolmar bristled; it was a breach of hospitality to demand the nature of a guest's visit before inviting them inside. "Would you prefer to speak inside?" he asked.

"Here is as good a place as any."

"Demons have been seen coming from the north," Aeolmar said. I was amazed, both that Aeolmar's tone remained respectful, and that he hadn't called out Leran's bad behavior. Yet. "The queen desires to know if you require assistance."

"We haven't seen a demon here in hundreds of years, and if we did we'd take care of it ourselves," Leran stated. "Elves take care of elves, as faeries should."

"I would ask that you consider your words carefully, Leran," Aeolmar said, "for an insult to the queen is a grave matter."

"We did not request your presence here," Leran said, "nor do we welcome the intrusion. Tingu does not exist merely to furnish the queen with warriors whenever she sends out the call." Leran's men became restless. His words were dangerously close to treason.

"Asherah is Queen of Parthalan and Lady of Tingu, which makes you her subject twice over," Aeolmar retorted.

"But not her concern."

A dead silence settled over the crowd. I had no idea of how we could turn this mess around; while Aeolmar was in the right, the elves severely outnumbered us. Aeolmar held his composure, and asked Leran the one question for which the wrong answer would result in the elf's head on a pike.

"Are you denying me entry, Leran?" Aeolmar demanded.

"Would it matter?" Leran countered.

Aeolmar's eyes flashed, and the crowd murmured. Aeolmar was known for his rage as much as his bravery, even as far away as Tingu, and Leran was perilously close to learning the truth behind those tales. Leran ignored Aeolmar's fury, and whispered a few words to the man beside him. After the man retreated inside the keep, Leran faced us.

"Our evening meal is now ready. Please, join us. I'll have my men speak with you, and share any information that could help in your quest for demons," Leran said, then he turned on his heel and entered the keep.

"Well, that was simple," I muttered.

"Dealing with Leran never is," Aeolmar replied.

As we followed him inside the keep, I realized that Leran had been so busy provoking Aeolmar he hadn't once looked at me or asked who I was. I wondered if he had some kind of vendetta against the First Hunter, or maybe a death wish. When we were seated, a much more mundane reason became apparent; all the women in Leran's keep were either saffira, or relegated to the smaller hearth at the back of the hall. I ignored the obvious inequity and sat next to Aeolmar, but Leran's men complained about a woman at their table. I moved to rise, but Aeolmar caught my wrist.

"Is there a problem with my huntress sitting beside me?" Aeolmar demanded. "She can best any one of you in a fight, fair or otherwise."

Leran shrugged. "I care not where she sits."

I stayed where I was, and the muttering ceased. The meal turned out to be quite fine, with Leran offering us the best of his larders. The food was plain but hearty, and I enjoyed it a great deal more than Micon's fancy dishes. Once the food was laid out Leran relaxed somewhat, and he and Aeolmar spoke of casual matters. By the time the food was gone, and the platters were replaced with casks of ale, Tingu's guards approached us, at first only to verify that I could use the swords on my back. As the ale flowed Leran and his men opened up further, and spoke of their exploits. In the elves' minds no faerie could hope to match the bravery of an elf, and they meant to prove it.

After we'd all talked for a while, Aeolmar presented Leran with the wooden box that contained Asherah's gift. "What's this?" Leran asked.

"The queen requested I give it to you," Aeolmar replied. "I've no idea what's inside."

At first, Leran merely traced the carvings on the box's lid. After staring at the box for some time he opened it, only to set it down and leave the hall. I leaned forward, and saw that the box contained a silver armband set with five stones. Four were green like polished malachite, and one was as red as blood.

"What does that armband mean to him," I muttered.

"I'll go after him," Aeolmar began, but I stayed him.

"Stay with his men," I said. "I'm better at talking, remember?"

Aeolmar frowned, but didn't protest. "Be careful, beloved."

"Always."

I grabbed the box and went after Leran. I found him at the top of the keep standing before the battlements.

"Did the First Hunter send you to follow me?" he asked. "Are you worried I plot against the queen?"

"No one thinks that," I replied. "I wanted to make sure you hadn't misinterpreted the gift. Asherah meant no offense." He glanced at me, then turned back to the night.

"That armband was my father's," he said at length. "He gave it to Asherah when he pledged his loyalty to her."

"The Sala," I whispered, now staring at the box in my hands. It all fell into place: Leran's animosity toward all things faerie, and Asherah's willingness to overlook Leran's insubordination. How had I not realized this sooner?

"Your father was Lormac," I stated.

"You know of him?"

"Everyone knows about Lormac," I replied, for it was true. Even in Brennus tales were still told of the elf king who gave his heart, and his life, to the faerie queen. "I'm sorry, Leran. To live with such pain must be terrible."

"What do you know of my pain?" he demanded. "You've been here less than a day. Hells, you didn't even know who my father was until a moment ago."

"You wear your sorrow as if it were a noose around your neck," I replied. "It's strangling you, and makes you hate us for being what we are."

"I don't hate you," he said. "We did not belong in your fight."

"Lormac must have felt differently."

"He was wrong!" Leran clenched his fists, his arms shaking. I touched his elbow, and he stilled himself.

"Your father must have been a good man, and a wise man, for you to still grieve him so. He must have been a strong leader as well, or Parthalan and Tingu alike wouldn't still mourn him, and tell stories about his greatness." Leran snatched his arm away, then he stared out into the darkness for what seemed like half the night.

"What do you know of loss?" he asked.

"I was kidnapped when I was small, and I haven't seen my family since. I feel their loss every day like a knife in my breast." I placed the Sala on the edge of the battlement. "I believe Asherah offers this to you as an apology. She knows it cannot return your father to you, but hopes it will bring you some comfort."

Leran ran his finger along the edge of the Sala. I left him to his thoughts, and found Aeolmar waiting for me at the edge of the shadows.

"How long have you been there?" I asked.

"Long enough," he replied. "Your compassion humbles me."

I glanced back at Leran. "I only hope I helped him understand."

When we got to our room we found that no fire had been lit, and we could see our breath in little white puffs. We thought nothing of it until we entered the inner chamber and saw the incredibly small, elf-sized bed we'd been provided with. Elfin beds consisted of a wooden frame surrounding a mattress, similar to a human bed, in contrast to the faerie custom of large flat cushion placed directly on the floor. Aeolmar disliked the elfin beds, a fact he'd made me well aware of while we were in Rael.

"Leran is not the most considerate host," Aeolmar said.

"I don't think half of you will fit on that," I said.

I started a fire, and while Aeolmar dragged the blankets off the bed and laid them before the hearth I went to our packs and retrieved a comb. I returned and saw that he'd assembled a cozy nest from all the cushions in the room. I raised an eyebrow, and Aeolmar shrugged.

"What? I just want you to be comfortable. You put up with me always wanting to sleep outside..."

I placed my fingers on his lips. "And I loved every moment." With that, we undressed and tried out Aeolmar's bed. It was rather nice.

I woke in the twilight before first dawn, lying atop Aeolmar's chest. I tried moving but he tightened his arms around me.

"Stay," he whispered, "just a little longer." I laid my cheek against his chest, and listened to his heart.

"How did you know what to say to Leran?" he asked.

"I understood that it was the memory of his father that pained him. I knew what he needed to hear."

We remained in our blissful cocoon for a short while longer, and as the elder sun rose we decided to depart. While I'd been speaking with Leran, Aeolmar had spoken to his men. They denied any knowledge of demons, and despite their drunkenness Aeolmar believed them. Not only did we have the answer to our question, we also knew that we remained unwelcome, and neither of us wanted to endure another moment of Tingu's false hospitality.

After we assembled our belongings we got the horses. The stable master was most distrustful, and sent a boy to fetch Leran. We shrugged, since if Leran came to us it would save us the trouble of finding him, and readied the horses. I was grumbling something about country elves and bad manners when Aeolmar caught my hand. I turned and saw Leran watching us. He and Aeolmar again took the measure of the other, this time with respect.

"She is your woman?" Leran asked.

"Yes. Latera is my mate."

"You're fortunate to have a woman such as her." Leran rubbed the back of his neck, and I saw that he was wearing the Sala. I interpreted that as a good sign.

"I'm not going to pretend that I enjoyed having you here, or that I'll be saddened by your departure," Leran began. "I will say that Latera's words have restored some of my faith in Parthalan, and for that I am grateful. You can tell Asherah that Tingu remains loyal to her Lady."

The two men exchanged a formal farewell, and Aeolmar and I departed. While I was happy to have helped Leran achieve a measure of peace, I didn't enjoy his company or his ways, and I hoped to never visit Tingu again.

CHAPTER FORTY-ONE

After leaving Tingu, Aeolmar and Latera travelled to the land of Sengra, and then to Urth'nn; just like Rael and Tingu, neither region had seen a demon for well over a century. As they rode out of Urth'nn and toward Thurnda, Latera noted Aeolmar's troubled expression. "Beautiful man, what are you thinking?"

"I'm thinking that this journey is a distraction."

"What are we being distracted from?"

"Don't you find it odd that we saw great numbers of demons coming from this very direction, yet those who live here haven't seen hide nor hair of them? I think whoever's behind the recent increase in demonic activity—any perhaps the appearance of these beasts, too—managed to draw us north."

"Why would someone do that?" Latera asked. "More importantly, who?"

"The why I can answer readily: to remove us from Teg'urnan and leave the queen with less protection. As to who would bother with this charade, I imagine that Asgeloth is ultimately behind it, but not directly. One of his minions is at work." Latera urged her horse closer and reached for Aeolmar's hand, ignoring how hers trembled.

"Do you think we've put the queen in danger?" Latera asked.

"We have not done so," he said, squeezing her fingers, "but I fear we may have inadvertently followed their plan."

"Should we return to the palace, instead of going on to Thurnda?"

"We will go on to Thurnda," Aeolmar said, with more confidence than Latera felt. "They're expecting us, and offending the Lady of Thurnda would not be wise. Once we're there I'll send a message to Teg'urnan. If we're needed at home, Finlay will let us know." Aeolmar's shoulders relaxed, though Latera still gripped his hand.

"Beloved, you're safe with me."

"I know," she replied. "I worry for the others, without us there to help them."

They rode on, and Aeolmar told stories of his last journey north with Innetha. They all involved her annoying him, and a few ended with him refusing to speak to her for days after an argument. When he began yet another tale, Latera interrupted him.

"You don't have to distract me. I'm accustomed to danger."

"I don't want you to be frightened."

"I'm not. Soon, we'll have word from Finlay, and if someone has led us all this way maybe we'll come across them and defeat them here, far from the palace. And I have you, First Hunter," Latera added. "I won't be afraid of anything as long as you're with me."

***

The final region Latera and Aeolmar visited was Thurnda, the largest and wealthiest of the elfin kingdoms. It was ruled by Sibeal, the Lady of Thurnda, and her son, Senan. Latera found it odd that Thurnda was a wealthier land than Tingu, but Aeolmar explained that many trade routes crossed through Thurnda, and that most merchants avoided Tingu altogether. She wondered if Leran had run the tradesmen out of his lands.

Yet again a meal was held in Aeolmar and Latera's honor, though this one was a small affair with only Sibeal and Senan joining them. Latera enjoyed the intimate dinner, since she had the chance to get to know her hosts. She was also grateful because she had nothing formal to wear.

"Beloved, I do regret what happened to your dress," Aeolmar said, when she grumbled about the gown he'd destroyed in Rael.

"You do not," she said. "You enjoyed every moment."

He raised his wine cup to hide his smile. "What if I hire a seamstress to make you a hundred pretty purple dresses? You can keep one to wear, and the rest..." He raised an eyebrow. She laughed.

"I counter your most generous offer with a request for one lovely dress, that will remain intact for at least a year."

"I will consider that counteroffer."

After the meal Aeolmar and Latera were shown to their rooms. As soon as the *saffira* were gone, they tumbled onto the sumptuous bed. They hadn't been there nearly long enough when they heard a frantic pounding.

"Someone knocks on our door, beloved," Latera said.

"Ignore it," he said against her neck. The pounding continued, but Aeolmar's interest only shifted from Latera's neck to her shoulder. When the pounding was accompanied by shouts he leapt from the bed and stalked toward the door.

"Be kind, beloved," Latera called after him. "No one would disturb us without good reason."

"We'll see about that," he growled, and threw open the door with such force it struck the wall.

"M-My lord," the *saffira* said, averting her eyes from his bare chest.

"What?" he demanded. When she cowered he added, "Forgive me for yelling, but I must know what this is about."

"We're being attacked!"

Aeolmar's back straightened, his hand moving to where his sword normally rested at his side. "Give us a moment to get our weapons," he said, and the *saffira* ran down the corridor. Aeolmar turned around, and saw Latera already dressed and strapping on her blades.

"You like that we're being attacked?" she asked, noting his smile.

"It's feels good to go out to battle," he replied, buckling on his sword belt. "Exhilarating, even."

"What if this is the very trap you suspected?"

"If it is we have the advantage, since they don't know we suspect them," he replied. "Fear not, beloved. I'll destroy anything that tries to ensnare you."

The hunters found Senan standing just inside the castle gates, thunderous sounds shaking the ground. "Earthquake?" Aeolmar asked.

"They have some kind of catapult," Senan replied. "They've been lobbing boulders at the wall." Senan leaned close, and whispered, "We've seen them, and they are demon."

"They must have been here for some time if they managed to build a catapult," Latera said. Senan glared at one of his captains, who grumbled about lazy watchmen.

"Do you know how many are out there?" Aeolmar asked.

"Ten at last count. Since you have the greater experience against demons, I give you full command of my men," Senan proclaimed, giving Aeolmar an elfin salute.

"We won't need them," Aeolmar stated.

"There are only ten," Latera added. "Let your men sit this one out."

Senan looked from Aeolmar and then to Latera as if they'd lost what little sense they had. "Surely just the two of you cannot prevail against so many," he cried.

Aeolmar studied the elf for a moment. "We've never met, and you must receive very little news from Parthalan in this area, so I'll forgive you your ignorance. This time."

With that Aeolmar and Latera walked toward the gates, leaving Senan to gawk after them. Aeolmar issued a few orders to the guards, telling them to bar the gates and stay as far back as possible. They climbed to the walkway atop the castle wall, and saw that two groups of demons had erected ladders on each side of the gate. The fortification was only twice Aeolmar's height, and the demons would be on them in a moment.

Aeolmar pulled Latera against him as a boulder sailed through the air. He braced himself for the impact, and they stayed upright as the boulder hit and the walls trembled. Once the shaking dissipated, Aeolmar silently indicated he would take the group on the left, while Latera dealt with the one on the right. Then he kissed her, as passionately as he had in bed a short time before.

"Stay safe, beloved," Aeolmar whispered, holding Latera's face close to his.

"You, too," Latera murmured. Aeolmar kissed her forehead, then he flashed a grin as he stepped off the wall. Latera heard the sounds of fighting below, and moved toward the other group of demons.

Latera peeked over the edge at two demons crawling up the wall, and smiled ruefully; Aeolmar had sent her after the smaller amount of foes. She sighed, knowing that his protective nature would never change, and shoved the ladder forward. The demons squealed as they fell, then she leapt down and plunged her sword into the demon pinned by the ladder, and decapitated the other.

This is too easy. Latera looked toward Aeolmar, saw he needed no assistance, and ran toward the catapult.

She inspected the mound of boulders the demons had assembled, the catapult resting at its crest. It was a crude wooden device, hastily

lashed together with old, frayed ropes. Latera tested the joints, recalling the large siege engines stationed about Gannera castle, when she
heard a nearby branch snap. She looked up and saw a demon the size
of Mersgoth staring at her as if she was his dinner.

Latera darted behind the mound and ran straight into two lesser
demons. She stabbed one as the other leapt onto her back, its claws
tangling in her hair. She slammed her back against the rocks, stunning
the creature but not enough to release his grip. She reached back and
pulled the demon off of her, and threw it forward. Before her eyes the
larger demon caught the lesser in his jaws, and tore in in two.

Latera scrambled up the boulders and shouted for fire. The demon
bellowed as the flames ignited on his arms, singing his crude shirt,
but he didn't slow. She readied herself to jump when a massive blade
cleaved the demon's head from his body. Latera dropped her swords,
and leapt into Aeolmar's arms.

"Are you hurt?" she asked.

He shook his head. "A scratch, nothing more."

"How many?"

"Four at first, then eight more. You?"

"These three, and two at the wall."

"I mean are you hurt?"

"Oh. No, I'm fine. I thought Thurnda was never attacked."

"It isn't."

Aeolmar and Latera set about burning the bodies and the pathetic
catapult; as he moved a demon onto the blaze she saw long gashes on
his forearm. Latera grabbed his arm and ran her hands across his skin.

"I'm not burnt," Aeolmar said, taking her hands in his. "None of
their blood got on my skin."

"I don't want you to suffer like I did," Latera said, pressing her face
against his chest.

Aeolmar kissed the top of her head. "Let's report back to Senan," he said. They did, and after scouting the area returned to the castle.

Senan went white upon learning that there were seventeen demons outside his walls, one of them a *mordeth*. His fear was replaced with awe when Aeolmar confirmed that all were dead.

"Thurnda is in your debt, First Hunter, and yours, Latera," he said solemnly. "We haven't seen a demon in over three hundred winters, and had you not been here I don't know how we would have fared. I thank Nexa that you were here."

Aeolmar inclined his head to Senan. "We're merely hunters in service to the queen, doing what we were trained to do."

"Nevertheless, you have our gratitude," Senan said. "Tell me your needs, and I'll have them seen to at once." Senan spied Aeolmar's arm and added, "I'll send for healers, as well."

"I will tend the First Hunter," Latera said.

Aeolmar quirked a brow, but only said, "By your leave, we'll return to our rooms."

Senan nodded and they returned to their chamber. Aeolmar sat before the fire and pulled off his torn and bloody jerkin. When Latera knelt beside him and began cleaning his wounds, he asked, "Personally tending me?"

"You let no healers touch me," she replied. "Consider the favor returned."

Aeolmar would have teased her further, but there was a knock at the door. Latera opened it, and a small legion of *saffira* bearing bandages, salves, even food and drink marched into their chamber.

"Senan is determined to show his gratitude," Latera said.

Aeolmar grabbed Latera's elbow. "Get rid of them."

"You don't want any food?"

"I want you."

Face flushed, Latera announced, "Thank you, but our First Hunter is weary. Please, allow him his rest." The assorted *saffira* filed out, and as soon as the door shut behind them Aeolmar scooped up Latera and walked toward the bed. "What if there are more demons?"

"I don't care if there are a thousand demons outside the walls," he said. "I need you now." Aeolmar dropped her on her on the bed, and took her with the force of the sea striking a cliff.

Afterward, Latera asked, "Are you always like this after a battle?"

"Battle?" Aeolmar asked, his dark blue eyes glinting. "This was only a skirmish. If we face a battle together you'll need to run from me."

"Why would I run? I belong in my warrior's arms."

"Latera, I love watching you fight. You're beautiful as you swing your sword. You make my blood sing for you."

Latera laid her head on his chest. "Tell me of past battles you've fought." He did, and as they drifted off to sleep Latera imagined she was there with him, fighting at his side.

Chapter Forty-Two

Latera Speaks

*S*ibeal insisted on holding a feast to celebrate our victory against the demons the prior evening; those were her words, not Aeolmar's and mine. She would hear none of our protests, so we ceased complaining and helped where we could. After all, who doesn't enjoy a celebration? And I understood this one would have cake.

I joined Sibeal in her chambers while we readied ourselves, and since I had nothing to wear she presented me with a gift of the most splendid gown. It was rich burgundy velvet, with the bodice and sleeves embroidered in gold, and it was lined in matching gold silk. The sleeves came to delicate points over my wrists, a style that was reserved for royalty in Gannera.

"It's exquisite," I said, tracing the delicate golden threads with my fingertip. "But I cannot accept this. It's too much."

"Nonsense," Sibeal said. "You can, and you will. Thurnda is in your debt, and not only because you defeated the demons. I'm sure you've been in the elflands long enough to learn that our men would prefer we remained 'round the hearth."

I remembered how Leran had referred to me as Aeolmar's woman, and how his men were shocked that Aeolmar let his mate hunt demons. As if I needed Aeolmar to let me do anything. "You'd think having a warrior queen would be education enough."

"I was never much of a warrior, certainly not like Asherah was, and still is. Or like you." Sibeal moved to the window, and watched the bustle of the courtyard below. "Thurnda is the birthplace of the greatest elfin queen of all, she who slew Ehkron, Asgeloth's sire. She tracked him from this land all the way to the mortal realm." My ears pricked up when she mentioned the mortal realm, but I tamped down my many questions. I'd learned long ago that most just assumed I was a faerie, albeit a very small faerie. I had no idea how elves felt about humans, and wasn't of a mind to learn just then.

"How did she track the mordeth-gall between worlds?" I asked.

"She followed him through the underworld." I shuddered; no matter how much I wanted to see my family again, I was not going to wander amongst soul eaters and dark gods to reach to Gannera.

Sibeal glanced at me, and said, "You remind me of her, with your red curls and swift blades."

"Thank you," I said. Sibeal studied my face for a moment before turning back to the window. "What became of her?"

"She died of her wounds in the mortal realm, and never saw Thurnda again." Sibeal gazed at the sky, it was plain that she still felt the loss of this queen, much as Leran still felt the loss of his father. She sighed, and returned her gaze to me. "That's enough recollection for one day. Now let's see to getting you properly outfitted as my guest of honor."

I donned the gown, and Sibeal's saffira placed my feet in gold silk slippers as they arranged my hair. They twisted my curls into elaborate knots, securing them with small golden pins around the crown of my head, and they used brushes and creams on the length of it until my hair rippled down my back.

Grooming complete, I scrutinized my reflection in Sibeal's mirror, tugging at the tight bodice that showed a great deal more of my breast than my usual clothes did. I turned from side to side, straightening my back and clasping my hands before me just as my mother would have done.

"You have the regal bearing of a queen," Sibeal said.

"My mother is a queen. She loved nothing more than dressing up me, and my sisters."

"That explains everything."

The saffira-nell advised us that all was ready in the hall and we departed for the celebration, my feet hardly skimming the floor in my dainty slippers. Sibeal walked ahead of me, her head high atop her graceful neck. Her blue gown was lovely against her pale hair and skin, and if I didn't know better I would have thought she was a young woman, no older than my mother, but I knew that Sibeal had fought with Asherah at the Battle for Teg'urnan. The only aspect of her form that betrayed her age was her white hair, coiled at the nape of her neck and secured with silver combs.

We entered the hall and sat at the women's hearth. Aeolmar was standing clear across the room with Senan. Aeolmar had also received a gift of clothing, which made me wonder what these elves had thought about the clothes we'd arrived in. The last garment I'd been given was a dress from Elma, on the day I'd turned up in her stable. Surely Aeolmar and I hadn't been that bedraggled and travel worn.

For all my suspicions, Aeolmar wore his new clothes well. His tunic was deep blue edged with black embroidery, paired with black trousers and boots. I wondered how the small and slender elves could have found a garment large enough for his broad shoulders, unless it had been sewn earlier that day. I imagined Aeolmar being fit by a seamstress, wrapped in fabric with pins sticking everywhere, and almost laughed out loud.

From the moment I entered the hall I felt Aeolmar's gaze upon me. I smiled at him as I took my place next to Sibeal, and ended up sitting with my back to him. Even though I couldn't see him, I knew his gaze hadn't wandered.

"I must say, the First Hunter has caused quite a stir," Sibeal said. "The unattached girls have been speaking of him and nothing else since he arrived, but he's enchanted by the very sight of you." I glanced over *my shoulder, and Aeolmar inclined his head toward me. A murmur erupted from the assembled ladies, grumbling that their quarry was spoken for.*

"He has that effect wherever he goes," I said. "Everyone is either enamored with him, or deathly afraid."

"And which are you, my dear?" Sibeal asked.

"The former. He's my mate."

"It's good to see a hunter so attached. I've never known of any of Asherah's hunters to do anything that resembled pleasure. Mostly they just kill, and eventually get killed themselves."

"None are ever released by Asherah?"

"Oh, yes," she replied, "but the more common release is their death."

After that revelation, Sibeal pursed her lips and turned toward her ladies. While she composed herself, I looked around the hall. Musicians were playing a lilting tune and a few couples were dancing. In Teg'urnan dancing was a formal procedure, with everyone turning this way and that in perfect synchronicity, while in Rael dancing had been more of a group affair. In Thurnda, however, dancers paired off and gazed into each other's eyes while swaying to the gentle notes.

I wondered if Aeolmar would dance with me. We'd always found excuses to leave these sorts of events in the past, but the peaceful expression on the dancers' faces, their arms draped across their partners' shoulders and hips, made me want to join them.

My gaze moved on about the hall. I was struck by the number of families in attendance, and the vast amount of children. Most of the residents of Teg'urnan were solitary, and other that the queen and Finlay, and myself and Aeolmar, I only knew a handful of mated pairs.

"There certainly are a lot of children here," I said.

"Of course," Sibeal said. "Are there many little ones running about Teg'urnan?" I realized that I'd never seen a child in the palace; in fact, I was the only one referred to as "little one". When I shared these facts with

Sibeal, she sighed and patted my hand. "It has ever been that way with Asherah, duty to her people before herself, and all follow her example. It's not all her, though. Everyone knows how rare a faerie birth is to begin with, not like we elves."

I'd never considered that faerie children were rare to the point of being unusual; due to their lack of presence in my life, I'd hardly considered faerie children at all. Aeolmar had mentioned that he was from a large family, and I wondered how his mother could have managed so many children while others had so few.

"Nevertheless, you should enjoy your time with Aeolmar while you have it," Sibeal continued. "Things have a way of changing in Asherah's court, suddenly and not always for the better."

"I do enjoy my life with Aeolmar." I leaned close to Sibeal, and whispered, "He wishes to be bound to me."

She smiled. "If you bind yourself to him, you'll know a companionship and joy unlike any other."

I returned her smile, eagerly anticipating my binding with Aeolmar. I wanted nothing more than to live my life with him, whether it was as hunters in Teg'urnan or a tiny cottage by the sea. My mind wandered to our upcoming ceremony as I examined the delicate gold embroidery on my sleeve. "I don't think I've ever worn a garment so fine," I said. "Maybe I'll wear this when I'm bound."

Sibeal's brows knit together. "You cannot..." she began, and I could not imagine how my words had perplexed her so. I needed something to wear for our binding, and in Gannera a lady always wore her finest dress when she was married. Wouldn't a faerie woman do the same?

"Don't you know the custom?" she whispered at last.

"I do," I said weakly. I'd always equated a binding with a human wedding, when in truth I didn't know if that was the case. I really only knew that the bond was eternal, and nothing of the details. As I wrestled

with these thoughts my head drooped forward, and Sibeal asked if I was all right.

"Yes," I replied, raising my head. "Forgive me, I'm still a bit tired from yesterday." Sibeal accepted my explanation, and our conversation turned to lighter topics. I didn't hear a word she said as I nodded and agreed, so concerned I was over this binding ritual. I loved Aeolmar, nothing would ever change that, but the fact that I'd agreed to something I didn't fully understand made my stomach writhe.

After we'd been served, and I'd picked at my food for a time, I excused myself and crossed the hall to Aeolmar's side. Senan, who'd been telling a tale complete with flailing arms and wild gestures, bowed when he saw me, and offered to freshen my wine.

"No, thank you," I said. "I came to ask my beloved to dance." Aeolmar, who'd looked positively bored while Senan told his fantastic story, smiled.

"Dance, eh?" He took my hand and leading me to the center of the hall. He held me close as we swayed among the rest, and the world fell away around us.

"I worried you'd refuse me." I said.

"You know I can deny you nothing." Aeolmar tucked a stray curl behind my ear, stroking my neck in the process. "You're breaking Senan's heart," he continued. "He was just informing me of how magnificent you are."

"And how did you respond?"

"I agreed with him on all counts."

I laid my cheek against Aeolmar's chest as he led me around the floor. Images of weddings in Gannera still swirled in my mind's eye, but I pushed them aside. I still didn't know if I was anything other than mortal, and I didn't want to question Aeolmar about a binding when I didn't even know if I could be bound. Then I saw a group of children playing in a corner, and a pang in my heart made it clear that I needed answers, even if the answers were bad.

"Have you noticed all of the children here tonight?"

Aeolmar glanced around the hall. "I have now."

"Why do faeries have fewer children than elves?"

"Why would you think that?"

"Sibeal told me. I need to know if that's true."

He snorted. "At the risk of offending our gracious host, she's mistaken."
Undaunted, I continued my inquiry.

"Why can't I wear this when we're bound?" I asked, indicating my
velvet gown.

"There's a ritual garment you'll wear, as will I," he answered, his
brow furrowed.

"What does it look like?" I demanded. When he merely stared at me,
I pressed, "Why have I never seen a binding?"

He stopped moving, the dancers around us craning their necks to see
what was happening with us. "You mean you don't know?"

"How would I? I'm human, not faerie," I said. Aeolmar placed his
palm on the back of my neck and drew me close.

"These are things to be discussed privately, not in the center of a hall."

"Then take me somewhere private."

Wordlessly he turned and led me away. I could feel Senan's eyes
burning a hole in my back while Sibeal gave me another of her knowing
smiles; I could only imagine what was going through their minds.

We walked out into the clear, cold night, and found ourselves in a
small courtyard. It had snowed earlier in the day, and everything was
blanketed in a layer of sparkling white. We found a sheltered bench,
and Aeolmar bade me to sit beside him. "Ask me whatever you'd like,"
he said.

I figured I should begin with my most pressing concern. "What is a
binding?"

"It's when our very essence is bound together. It can only be performed
on two immortals, and only if both hearts are willing. After we're bound

nothing will be able to part us; I'll always know where you are, in body and spirit, as you'll know me." He glided his knuckles over my cheek, and I knew he felt that he'd fully answered me. Gods, I felt like screaming.

"But what is it? What happens during it?"

"It's a temple ritual, performed in the old language—"

"What old language?" I interrupted.

For a moment he just stared at me. "The original language of the fae, the language of the gods. It's called ahm'ri, *" he explained. "It hasn't been commonly spoken for generations, but it's still used for magic. You use it yourself, when you call fire."*

"I do?" When Finlay taught me to call fire he'd given me a few words to say, but he never mentioned they were part of an ancient tongue. "What does it mean?"

"'Fire, come to me'. And when you extinguish it, you say 'fire, be gone'."

My head drooped; I'd been speaking a magical language for four winters and never even knew it. Gods, no matter how I tried to avoid magic it worked its way into my life, more insidious than any demon. "When you work other magic, like charming doors, are you also speaking this language?"

"Yes," Aeolmar replied. "Latera, I thought you knew this."

"That's the problem," I said, leaping to my feet. "Everyone assumes I know all of these customs, but I don't. I hear half-truths and rumors and don't know what to believe. I wasn't born here, and I certainly didn't have faerie parents to explain this world to me." Pain clouded Aeolmar's face, and I regretted my outburst. "Mar, I'm sorry, I didn't mean it that way."

Aeolmar's smile was more of a grimace, but his words were soft. "I know you didn't... and you're right. I do take for granted that you know what I know, and you're right about my parents, especially my mother. She had a wonderful sense for magic. She could see it moving through the air like a living thing, and could weave spells for almost anything she desired." He pulled me into his arms. "I'm sorry, for assuming so much." I laid my head on his shoulder and played with the edge of his tunic.

"Tell me about a binding. What does it look like?"

"I don't know, as I've never seen one. Most only see their own binding," he said. "I can tell you that it will take place in the temple, upon the altar. We'll speak vows in the old language that will unite us, making us one in two bodies."

"Will you teach me this language?"

"Yes. I'll teach you anything you want to learn, and if I can't teach you I'll find someone who can."

"Do you still want me now that you know how ignorant I am of your ways?" I asked, feeling more like his burden than his mate.

"Our ways," he corrected, "and I want you more with every passing moment." He brushed his lips against my jaw, slowly working his way to my neck.

"Do you know why there are so many more children here in Thurnda, than there are in Teg'urnan?" Aeolmar lifted his head, and became my instructor once again.

"It's the inherent nature of each race. The children of elves are a need of the body, whereas faerie children are a need of the soul." I stared at him, a silent reminder that I knew nothing about these "inherent natures". "Elves are of the earth, and their children spring forth like seeds from fertile soil. Those who are fae are of the sky, of the suns and the moon. You know the tale of Olluhm claiming Cydia?"

"I do," I affirmed.

"Then you know how we came to be." How faeries came to be, that is. I held my tongue, and let him continue. "While elves and faerie are both immortal races, elfin immortality resides in the enduring nature of the earth and stone, whereas we are as eternal as the dance of the elder sun and the moon. For a faerie child to be created two souls must truly want

that child to be born; the magic that unites mates as they are bound is the same force that creates the child. While you will often find elves whose parents were not bound, you'll rarely find a faerie child born of such a union, unless the woman knows the proper magic to ensure a birth."

"But I will bear your child if I'm bound to you?"

"The likelihood is increased with a binding, but our children do take a long time to come. Sibeal was right about that."

"How many siblings did you have?"

"Six."

"And your mother was as adept as you with magic...." My words trailed off, unwilling to ask if he and his siblings were born of love or other sources. Aeolmar heard what I'd left unsaid, and answered me anyway.

"She was much more adept than I, and I have no doubt she would have known the ways to increase her children in that way... But my parents were devoted to each other. Mama would race out to the fields at midday to bring Father fresh water to drink, and bread warm from her oven. Father would joke that if she'd only let him alone, he could finish twice as much work and we wouldn't be so poor." He was silent for a moment. "I never asked if we were born of magic or love, but I imagine it was a blending of the two. I remember Mama saying that she'd dreamt of each of us before we were born. that could have been a spell."

"You're so happy when you talk about your family." A cloud crossed Aeolmar's face, so I changed the subject. "You know, I don't even know how old you are."

"Older than you. I'm not nearly as old as Asherah, but I am much older than you."

"How long have you been a hunter?" I pressed. "I know the Battle of Esguth was over one hundred winters past—"

"It was one hundred and fifty-seven winters ago," he interjected. "I'd been a hunter for ten winters when it happened, to answer your next question."

"And, what was your age when you became a hunter?"

"Age doesn't matter. We're long lived, and in time we cease to realize how old we are. Once a child reaches adulthood, around their hundredth winter, they're seen as grown, nothing more or less."

"One hundred winters to be an adult?" I was stunned. "I've only reached twenty winters. You don't see me as young and foolish?"

"I do see you as young, but never foolish. I see you as my beautiful girl, she who gave me back my life. I was dead after my family died. Nothing made me happy. I couldn't be happy, not while they were cold." Aeolmar wrapped his arms tight around me. "I only lived again the day I met you."

"Then I wish I'd been born sooner." I shifted against him; the buttons on his tunic were biting into my flesh, but his arms were like steel. "I suppose this makes me older than you."

"I fail to see your reasoning."

"If you only lived again the day you met me, you're not yet five," I said brightly. Aeolmar moved me to his lap and off those infernal buttons, his brows halfway up his forehead. "I'm your elder," I proclaimed. He smiled, which was all I'd wanted, only to frown when he saw the imprint his buttons had made on my skin. He bent to kiss the red marks as I continued, "You'll need to mind me from now on."

"As you've always minded me?" he countered. "If our children are as stubborn as you, I don't know how I'll cope."

"Will our children be children for one hundred winters?" It seemed there was no end to my questions that evening. "If they're only half faerie?"

"I don't know," he replied. "We can only learn by having one. Why are you so interested in children? Do you want one so badly?" I cast my

gaze downward; I didn't want to speak my fears out loud, but I owed him nothing if not my honesty.

"Can humans and faeries even have children? And if we do, will I die before they're grown?"

"There are many of mixed races in Parthalan. Before the Great War, those of pure blood were targets. Of all the hunters only the queen and I have pure faerie blood. But then, that's only what we've been told; who knows if one or both of us have an odd relative a few generations back." I frowned, and asked something that had been on my mind for some time.

"Is Harek part troll?"

Aeolmar burst into laughter; great, bellowing peals of laughter that I hadn't thought him capable of. He laughed until tears rolled down his cheeks while I sat dumbfounded.

"I have no idea," he panted, "and I know many trolls who would take offense at your suggestion." He became serious again, but his eyes retained their happy glow. "Beloved, you're not wholly human, I'm certain of it. Even if I'm wrong once we're bound you'll share my life, my soul, even my immortality. You'll see our children grown." He smoothed back my hair. "Nothing will take you from me, not even death. I swear it."

"May I ask you something else?"

"Would you like to know why the stars are in the sky and not the sea, or why flowers don't sprout from bare rock?" he countered. "When I said I'd teach you everything, I didn't know you wanted to learn it all tonight." I smiled at his scolding, and promised only one more question and he could teach me the rest tomorrow.

"Your parents." I hesitated, but only for a moment. "What were their names?"

"Caol'nir and Alluria."

"Did they know the queen?"

"You promised, one question," he said, but answered anyway. "They remembered the days before Asherah, but I don't see how a farmer and *baker from far in the west would have known the queen. She never once came to our village, and I don't remember them ever talking about Teg'urnan."*

"So if we have a son, he may be named Caol'nir," I said. "That wasn't a question!"

"He may be, yes," Aeolmar agreed. "You'd do that?"

"I'll do anything for my mate." I laid my head on his shoulder, my mind churning from all I'd learned. He kissed my temple, but startled when I touched his neck.

"You're shivering," he said, as he chafed my hands. We returned to the warmth of the castle, avoiding the hall. As we made our way to our rooms, Aeolmar whispered something to a nearby saffira. *I asked what that was all about but he refused to tell me, and I refused to be dragged into yet another one of his guessing games.*

Once we were inside our chamber I began unfastening my gown, but Aeolmar stayed me. Before I could ask why, there was a knock at the door and two saffira entered, one bearing a tray of food and the other a jug of wine. When he assured them we would need nothing further, they bowed and left. He took my hand and we sat before the food, Aeolmar settling me on his knee.

"Why did you send for all this?"

"You want to learn more of our ways, and I'm teaching you. Another of our customs is that a bound pair will feed each other. Close your eyes." I did, and he held something cold against my lips. I bit into the soft flesh of a melon, the sweet juice running down my chin.

"How will I learn your language if my mouth is full of food?"

"You know more of it that you realize. Teg'urnan is 'stone palace'; Alia is our word for 'sky'; Finlay means 'stalwart'." He gave me a knowing glance as he continued, "Caol'nir means 'warrior's fire', and Alluria is 'servant of the gods'." I thought they were odd names for a farmer and a baker, but lovely nonetheless.

"And your name, First Hunter?"

"'Bird of prey on the wind'. Mama saw a hawk overhead one morning; later that day she bore me. It's a silly name."

"I love your name," I said, feeding him a bite of melon. "Do all faerie names have meaning in the old language?"

"Most, but not all. Enna means only Enna."

"If we have a daughter, maybe we'll name her Enna. Although, you've gone and named my horse Enna, so I suppose we'll have to pick another name."

"Maybe we'll name her Latera," he suggested, but I shook my head.

"No, I want a faerie name for our child. I'm to be bound to a fae man, and I need to follow his ways." Aeolmar beamed at me, and plucked the pins from my hair. As my curls fell about my shoulders I asked my final question of the night.

"I can't wear my pretty dress at our binding?"

"No, you may not. And I'd prefer you not wearing it, even now," he murmured, his fingers finding the buttons.

"You will not ruin this one like you did the last! If you keep destroying my clothes I'll refuse to bear you any children!" His nimble fingers had the buttons unfastened in an instant, and not a thread was out of place. His hands slid underneath the fabric, and squeezed my shoulders.

"Maybe I can convince you to always wear dresses, just so I can remove them," he said, his breath soft on my neck.

"As I said, I'll do anything for my mate." With that, I stood and let the gown fall around my feet. As I led him to bed he spoke to me in the old language, the first time I'd ever heard so much of it at once. As the unfamiliar sounds tumbled from Aeolmar's lips, I understood that he said he loved me.

Chapter Forty-Three

Two days went by, during which Aeolmar and Latera enjoyed all that Thurnda had to offer. On the morning of the third day they visited the Northern Contingent. The outpost was less than a day's ride from Thurnda's castle, and Aeolmar wanted to speak with the contingent's commander, Elkin.

"How long has Elkin been a hunter?" Latera asked.

"Longer than I have," Aeolmar replied. "In fact, we knew each other as boys."

"Really? Perhaps he'll divulge a few of your secrets."

Aeolmar snorted. "Not if he knows what's good for him."

The contingent was situated on the edge of a great plain with the imposing Northern Ridge, a mountain range that the elves called the World's Spine, at its back. The central structure was a stone tower, similar to Tingu's keep. A small clearing, surrounded by a few outbuildings, was in front of the tower.

"Elkin," Aeolmar bellowed from the clearing. "Get your arse out here!"

After a small flurry of activity, Elkin himself exited the keep. "Gods, man, you could have warned us you were coming," Elkin said, striding toward the First Hunter. "Last I checked, messengers were cheap and plentiful."

Aeolmar glared at Elkin, but only for a moment. "It's good to see you."

"And you. Are you going to introduce me to this beauty you've dragged here with you?" Elkin asked, his gaze alighting on Latera.

"This is Latera," Aeolmar said. "She's my mate."

"Hello," Latera said with a wave.

Elkin's eyes went wide, then he laughed and clapped Aeolmar on the back. "About time you found some happiness, my friend. Let's relax for a spell before we discuss whatever grim news you've brought me."

"What makes you assume it's grim?" Aeolmar asked.

"The First Hunter doesn't journey all the way to the Northern Ridge to reminisce about old times," Elkin replied. "The ills of the world can wait while we have a drink or three."

After the horses had been seen to, Elkin called for ale and the hunters gathered in the keep's common room. Aeolmar noticed that the hunters clustered around Latera, and at first he thought they were asking for news of Teg'urnan. He listened closely, and realized they were questioning her place as a huntress.

"We hear you only put in two winters at a border," one said. "How'd you get off so easily?"

"Are you really a hunter? You're so small."

"So how'd you end up with Aeolmar?"

"Do you have any relevant questions?" Latera snapped. "I'm not here to defend myself."

Aeolmar stepped to Latera's side. "Drop your inquiries. Latera is an excellent huntress, easily the queen's equal." The hunters offered their apologies, but Aeolmar was done with them. "Elkin, may we speak privately?"

"Of course," Elkin replied. He led them to the farthest corner of the common room. After they'd tapped another cask and refilled their mugs, Aeolmar revealed the purpose of their visit.

"Three days ago, Thurnda was attacked," Aeolmar began, and he told Elkin of everything that had transpired over the past moons, from the increase in demon activity near Teg'urnan, to the poisoned blood burns, and finally to the *mordeth* outside Thurnda's gates. Elkin was well into his fourth mug of ale by the end.

"Poisoned blood burns," Elkin said, shaking his head. "I've never heard of demons using any sort of poison, through blood or any other means."

"It was awful," Latera said. "I hope you never learn what it's like."

"And these beasts... You've dispatched some of them?" Elkin asked Latera.

"I've killed four," she replied. "When we first saw them at the border, we ran. I only engaged the first because it attacked another hunter."

"How many hunters have managed to kill these beasts?"

"Only one other to my knowledge," Aeolmar answered, "another huntress at the Eastern Border. While Alia is skilled, she is no Demon-killer," he added, squeezing Latera's hand.

"You're Demon-killer?" Elkin asked, eyes widening when Latera nodded. "No wonder the First Hunter took you as a mate. I bet you can teach him a thing or two," he said with a smile that made her bristle.

Elkin sat back for a moment, steepling his fingers under his chin. "I don't like that Thurnda was attacked. In all my time here that region has been peaceful. I'd hate to abandon this post to help defend the elves."

"Yes, it would be terrible to unleash your vermin on the demons," Latera muttered. Elkin set down his mug and scowled at the huntress. Latera scowled back, then she rose and left the room.

"Your mate is... Is feisty a word that won't make you kill me?" Elkin asked.

"The problem here is your hunters," Aeolmar said as he stood. "They seem to have forgotten that women are warriors too."

Elkin's shoulders drooped. "I could blame you," he said. "The ones who get sent here wouldn't even do at Brynne's."

"I'll see what I can do about that," Aeolmar said. "I can't have the second best hunter in Parthalan surrounded by such louts."

"Second best, eh?" Elkin asked. "Go, speak to your mate. I'll inform my hunters of the grievous affront they've committed. With any luck we'll all be friends by supper."

***

Latera wasn't interested in eating with such narrow-minded men, and truth be told neither was Aeolmar. She and Aeolmar decided to depart, and Latera had Myrnnhe and Enna saddled as quickly as if she was two people. While she made a final adjustment to Enna's tack, she heard footsteps behind her. "Mar," she called over her shoulder, "Can you hand me the black saddlebag?"

"Mar?"

Latera turned around, and saw Elkin standing beside Aeolmar. Elkin raised an eyebrow, but Aeolmar ignored him and retrieved the saddlebag and brought it to Latera. Realizing that he wouldn't get a response, Elkin shrugged and addressed Latera.

"I came to persuade you to stay until morning, but I see you're already set to leave," he said. "You won't get far before nightfall."

"Then we will camp," Latera said. "We'll be safe."

"I have no doubt that the First Hunter and Demon-killer will be well." Elkin frowned, and added, "My men don't speak for me. The fact that Asherah named you a huntress is everything about you I need to know."

"Thank you," Latera said. "When next I'm here, I'd like to spar with your men. I suspect after I beat them a few times they'll change their attitudes."

Elkin laughed. "I can't wait. Until then, I'll extend our patrols to Thurnda. If the elves need assistance, the Northern Contingent will be there." Aeolmar thanked Elkin, and stated that he would be advised of any further attacks in Thurnda. With that, Aeolmar and Latera said farewell to the Northern Commander.

***

The ride back from the Northern Contingent was without incident, and shortly after sunfall Aeolmar and Latera camped for the night. In the dead of night Latera woke with Aeolmar's hand clamped over her mouth. Her eyes and ears strained against the darkness, and she heard the telltale sounds of demons scratching in the trees.

Latera untangled herself from Aeolmar, then she crept toward Enna and placed her palm flat between her nostrils; after a moment she did the same to Myrnnhe. The horses knew the command well, and wouldn't move or make a sound, not until Latera signaled all was well.

Leaves rustled overhead, and Latera flattened herself against a tree. She saw two demons in the branches above her, eyeing the horses. "Terrible beasts," she muttered. "No one hurts my horse."

She looked at Aeolmar and pointed upward, then she swung herself up behind the vermin. They squealed as she cut them, their bodies landing on the grass below with a dull thud. Latera jumped down, and studied the corpses.

"They're quite small," she said, "whelps, even."

"The mother is never far from her young. We're leaving now," Aeolmar said.

They burnt the bodies and set out for Thurnda, pushing the horses and themselves to the brink of exhaustion. They arrived at the castle as the elder sun rose, and immediately sought out Senan.

"What is happening?" Senan demanded. "We've been left alone for hundreds of years. Why are demons attacking us now? Nothing about Thurnda has changed. There's nothing here they want."

"I believe demons followed us here from Teg'urnan," Aeolmar replied, "and I deeply regret that they followed us to your door. I've spoken with the Northern Contingent, and they will extend patrols to Thurnda." Senan nodded, but Aeolmar wasn't finished.

"Winter is almost upon us, and that's always the worst season for demons. If you're in agreement, Latera and I will remain here until the spring thaw and teach your men to fight as hunters. Until they're ready, she and I can handle any further attacks." Aeolmar spoke to Senan but his gaze rested on Latera; they hadn't discussed remaining in Thurnda until spring. Latera squeezed his fingers, a reminder that she'd follow him anywhere.

Senan's anguished expression became one of gratitude. "To host the First Hunter and his best huntress until spring is quite an honor," he said, bowing his head. "As I said before, you have full command of my men, and anything either of you require will be yours. Thurnda is truly in your debt."

Aeolmar sent a message to Teg'urnan detailing the events of the past few days and their extended stay in Thurnda, along with his concerns that they had been led into a trap. In twenty-two days Ae-olmar received the queen's reply. Asherah affirmed her agreement of Aeolmar's suspicions that the demons followed him, and her support of his and Latera's plan. For the next few moons, Aeolmar and Latera were Thurndians.

CHAPTER FORTY-FOUR

Aeolmar and Latera wasted no time before they began training the elves. They organized Senan's men as if they were *nuvi*, and transformed their training field into an elfin version of the *sola*. Before long the elves were performing the same maneuvers Latera had learned four winters ago. The elves were taught how to catch demons unawares, and the best ways to dispatch ones of various sizes; they were also instructed how to care for the inevitable gashes and bites they would suffer, as well as how to treat blood burns. The only technique Aeolmar and Latera declined to teach the elves was how to call fire. That was a skill reserved for the queen's hunters.

Their mornings were filled with such tactical pursuits; Aeolmar would begin each day stalking before his assembled trainees while he yelled out orders, his fearsome manner inspiring respect and admiration among the ranks. Latera inspired an entirely different set of emotions from the soldiers: confusion, and awe. That was apparent on the first day, when Aeolmar and Latera demonstrated maneuvers before them. The elves questioned why the First Hunter would choose someone so small to assist him, and a woman at that.

"I've chosen Latera because she's the only one here with skill comparable to mine," Aeolmar declared. "Would anyone care to challenge her?" When his words were met with silence, he turned back to Latera and they resumed the demonstration. Afterward, as they stood panting, he repeated his challenge.

"You ask us to fight against a woman. It's not fair. To the woman!"

"Step forward," Aeolmar ordered. The elf strode to the front of the ranks. "Your name?" Aeolmar demanded.

"Brucka, my lord."

"You now have the honor of sparring with Latera," Aeolmar said, as Brucka scowled. "Latera, show Brucka what's fair."

Latera smiled, and waited for the elf to make the first move. Brucka stared from the tiny huntress to the First Hunter. Aeolmar's frown told the warrior that disobeying was not an option, so Brucka drew his sword and halfheartedly swung at Latera. She parried and struck back, the swiftness of her attach putting him off balance. Brucka stumbled, and dropped his weapon at Latera's feet.

"Surely you can do better than that," she said, handing him his sword. The other warriors laughed, and Brucka glared first at them, then at Latera. He snatched the sword from her hand and swung at her almost immediately. Latera stepped aside and as Brucka moved past her, she slapped his back with the flat of her sword. For his third attempt Brucka barreled toward Latera, his sword extended.

The soldiers gasped and shouted, for surely Brucka would impale her and Aeolmar just stood there, making no move to halt Brucka or rescue his mate. The huntress did not move or flinch until the last moment, when she ducked under Brucka's sword. He was unable to slow himself and fell forward, landing in the dust at Aeolmar's feet. Latera kicked away his weapon, and set her foot on his back while her blade rested alongside his throat.

"Would you like to try again?" she asked as more laughter erupted from the ranks. They fell silent under Aeolmar's glare.

"The lesson you're being taught is that the size of your foe is irrelevant," he said. "Most demons are small, much smaller than Latera, yet they're no less lethal. Overconfidence is your deadliest enemy."

"I didn't mean to shame you," Latera said, stepping back from Brucka. "You almost had me the third time." Brucka got to his feet, face red and nostrils flaring. He opened his mouth, looked at Aeolmar, and without a word h reclaimed his sword and returned to his place in the ranks.

Later that day, Sibeal asked Latera, "Did you really disarm Brucka?"

"I did," Latera admitted. "I fear I've made myself an enemy."

"You've done nothing of the sort," Sibeal said. "He's been telling anyone who will listen about his fiery faerie huntress, she who thrice disarmed him without breaking a sweat."

"His huntress?" Aeolmar demanded.

"Besting Brucka even once is quite a feat," Sibeal continued, ignoring Aeolmar's outburst. "He's one of the most respected warriors in Thurnda. I daresay you've made a friend, rather than an enemy."

Latera looked up at Aeolmar and smiled. "See that?"

Aeolmar wrapped his arm around her shoulders. "My Demon-killer, an inspiration to elves and fae alike."

***

Aeolmar ensured that training sessions always ended by midday, and once the warriors dispersed the makeshift *sola* was overrun with second legion, this one comprised of the castle's children. All of the children loved Aeolmar, and it was plain that he adored them in return. He indulged their every whim, from carving them tiny, blunt swords to organizing them into contingents. He even helped them build a fort in the rear of the field, and assigned them guard shifts with instructions to report on everything they saw.

One day Latera found Aeolmar and the children not at the fort but resting under a tree, the First Hunter telling stories of past battles. The children sat as close to Aeolmar as possible, and if they all could have fit on his lap he would have let them. Latera sat behind the little ones, and realized Aeolmar was telling the story of the death of Mersgoth.

"Was Mersgoth really bigger than you?" asked a girl perched on his knee.

"Yes," Aeolmar replied, "much bigger. If you don't believe me, ask Latera. She's the one who cut off his arm." The children's wide eyes turned to Latera.

"Really?" asked a boy. "Were you scared?"

"I was, but only because I didn't want the demon to hurt Aeolmar," Latera replied, rumpling his hair. "But then Aeolmar killed it, and all was well afterward."

"I couldn't have done it without my mate. She defended me, and kept me safe when I was hurt," Aeolmar said.

"And he has kept me safe ever since," Latera added.

"Was she your mate back then?" the girl asked.

"That's a tale for another day," Aeolmar said as set the girl on her feet. "Run along now. There will be more stories tomorrow." He smiled as the children wandered away, playing at mock battles and swinging their swords at invisible demons.

"They worship you," Latera said as they walked back to their rooms. "You're a hero to them, inspiring them to be more than they thought they could be."

"They're quite taken with you as well," he said, draping his arm around her shoulders. "Their favorite tales are of the Demon-killer."

"Perhaps one day you can tell these stories to your own children," she said. His only response was to kiss the top of her head, and they walked the rest of the way in silence. Once they entered their room

Aeolmar pulled Latera into his arms, telling her stories he hoped to one day tell their children.

Chapter Forty-Five

S pring arrived all too quickly, and as the ground thawed Aeolmar and Latera prepared for their return to Teg'urnan. No demons had been sighted since their trek from the Northern Contingent back to Thurnda, and both wondered if the trap they had been so certain about only existed in their minds.

Not only was the lack of foes forcing their return, Thurnda's army had been trained as well as Parthalan's hunters, a fact Brucka demonstrated whenever possible. Aeolmar was impressed at how quickly the elves learned fae fighting tactics, and remarked that he might recruit a few elves for the *sola*. Senan laughed heartily at that, and claimed that elves had been warriors since the dawn of time, unlike the fae who only became warriors out of necessity.

The hunters thought they had witnessed the extent of Sibeal's generosity, only to be stunned by the amount of gifts she insisted they bring back to Teg'urnan. Her largesse included gems mined in Thurnda's own mountains, and casks of elfin brandy, which Aeolmar claimed wouldn't get far past Bron's watchful eye. She also included bolt after bolt of fine fabric, mostly because Latera had shared how Aeolmar had destroyed her favorite gown. Her final gift was a pack horse and cart, for there was no way their own horses could have carried them and the Lady of Thurnda's gifts all the way to the palace.

Latera and Aeolmar's journey back to Teg'urnan took twelve bittersweet days. They spent the last night at an inn that was hardly occupied, thanks to the season. The innkeeper, who had the same twinkling eyes and friendly demeanor as Ingvarr, granted the First Hunter and his mate the greatest hospitality, and the two remained before the main hearth long after he'd retired.

"I'm sorry to see this journey end," Aeolmar said, once the inn had fallen silent. "This time with you has made me determined to stop Asgeloth, and petition Asherah to release us."

"Finlay will make a good First Hunter," Latera said. "Tonight, I want to dream of our small house by the sea."

The next day at high noon Aeolmar and Latera rode through the dark iron gates of Teg'urnan. They were met by the Second Hunter, who greeted them as if they'd been gone much longer than two seasons. He ushered them into Asherah's presence, her dark eyes sparkling as they relayed the events of their journey. She was pleased to learn of the elves continued loyalty, and was especially pleased to hear of Leran. Asherah said she hoped his father's memory would remain strong in Tingu for many generations to come.

As they described the unusual attacks in Thurnda, Finlay's face darkened. He pushed a map across the table, which was covered with his careful notations. "I've noticed a disturbing trend," he said. "Wherever our Demon-killer travels, the demons do follow. First, there was the large increase in the east, along with the appearance of the beasts. Latera leaves, and the attacks subside while the beasts all but vanish."

"They also subsided due to the season," Latera said, but Finlay held up his hand.

"There's more," he said. "You returned to Teg'urnan, only to come across six demons and a beast right outside the gate. No demon had approached the palace in many winters, and none have come that close during my entire time here." Asherah and Aeolmar both nodded.

Finlay continued, "You also saw the demons and beasts coming from the north. I agree with Aeolmar in that they were meant to fool you into leaving Teg'urnan. No demons have been seen up north for over three hundred winters, yet they attacked twice when you arrived there. And since you departed none have been seen near the palace, and the east remains quiet."

"Have demons been sighted anywhere else?" Aeolmar asked.

"No," Finlay replied. "They follow Latera like moths toward a flame."

Latera looked at Aeolmar, silently asking if he agreed with Finlay's assessment. To her horror, he nodded. "Why would they want me?" Latera asked.

"We don't know," Asherah replied. "Someone has put a price on your head, and we need to find out why."

Latera looked from the queen to Aeolmar, her face bloodless. Finlay reached across the table and squeezed her forearm.

"Don't worry," he said. "We can counter anything they use against us. We've considered hiding you somewhere to watch them chase their tails, or using a decoy to flush them out." Latera nodded, and Aeolmar grasped her hand.

"Beloved, there is nothing a demon can do that we can't undo," he said. "You may be their prize, but I won't let them have you."

Latera smiled at her mate, then she said to the queen, "When I find out who is responsible for this, I'll kill them."

"Of that, I have no doubt," Asherah said as she rolled up the map with her slender hands. "Now, on to more pleasant matters. I will have someone here in the morning who can determine your bloodline."

The queen and Finlay beamed, Aeolmar returning their smiles while Latera's gut clenched. *What if Aeolmar was wrong? What if I'm only a human, and I can't be bound?*

"Thank you, my queen," Latera said at last, not wanting to appear ungrateful or worse, that she didn't want to be bound to Aeolmar.

"It is my pleasure," Asherah said.

Aeolmar and Latera remained with the queen and Finlay for the better part of the day, sharing a meal while they heard all about what had happened at Teg'urnan in their absence. Asherah dismissed them shortly before the elder sun set.

"I cannot believe I'll really know," Latera said when they were in the corridor. "Will you still love me if you're wrong, and I'm only a mortal girl?"

"I've told you time and again, I don't care what the result is," Aeolmar replied. "I've also told you that I'm not wrong. You're not wholly mortal, my beloved, and you can be bound. You will be bound, and I'll never let you go."

Latera leaned against him. "Let's go to the hall, and find the rest of the hunters."

"I've something to show you first," Aeolmar said. "It's in my tower room."

"But, we haven't seen the others in so long."

"It will only take a moment. Afterward we can do whatever you'd like."

Once they were inside his rooms Latera sat on the steps that led to the bed, watching as Aeolmar rummaged in a dark corner until he found a small wooden box. He sat next to Latera and placed it on her lap. She lifted the lid, and inside was a necklace made up of an opalescent blue teardrop on a fine silver chain.

"It's beautiful," she said.

"It belonged to my mother," Aeolmar said as he fastened the clasp at the back of her neck. "My father gave it to her the day they were bound."

"Mar, I couldn't."

"Yes, you can," he said. "It belongs on you, not packed away in an old box."

"I'll never remove it," she said. "You honor me with her memory."

Aeolmar kissed the nape of her neck, and asked, "Would you still like to go to the hall?"

Latera said, "Tonight, I would rather remain as we have been, just you and I."

They lay awake that night, Aeolmar stroking Latera's back, her head on his chest as she listened to his heart. As the sky lightened with the coming dawn Aeolmar stirred, and broke the silence.

"I love you completely," he murmured. "I love everything about you; your flaming hair, your eyes like the sky at midday, your big, beautiful heart. You are my soul."

Latera shifted so he could see her smile. "I cannot imagine being happier than I am right now. I cannot wait to be bound to you."

"Do humans have mates?"

"Yes, but they're called husband and wife."

"Which would you be?"

"Wife."

Aeolmar pulled her up the length of his body until her face was directly over his. "My wife," he said, smoothing back her hair. "My wife."

Chapter Forty-Six

Latera speaks

*T*he next morning Aeolmar and I rose long after second dawn, and broke our fast in the hall with the hunters. Our first act was presenting Innetha with the gifts from Micon, which included a necklace so laden with gems it could have funded Asherah's entire household for at least a moon. Innetha's face reddened as we laughed, Luth loudest of all. She flung the jewelry at him, and proclaimed that while Micon was a fool at least he knew how to treat a woman.

Once Innetha had calmed down, we told everyone about our journey; well, Aeolmar told them. All I could think about was binding myself to Aeolmar, and every time our eyes met he flashed me his special half smile, letting me know he felt the same. Alia noticed something happening between the two of us, and begged me to share our secret with her. I promised that all would be revealed by nightfall.

Innetha, who had overseen the sola in Aeolmar's absence, asked us if we would attend the training class later in the day. She was preparing the nuvi for the upcoming Trial by Combat, and wanted a demonstration from each hunter.

"Must I let Aeolmar win?" I asked.

"I'd prefer it if you didn't," Innetha replied. "We do want the demonstrations to be accurate."

"Latera will not best me on this or any day," Aeolmar proclaimed.

"Not like she hasn't done it before," Bron commented. While Aeolmar and Bron traded barbs, I rose to refill my tea. Innetha followed me.

"*At midday I'm to bring a seer to the queen who will reveal your heritage. Now why ever would you want to know that, princess?" Innetha asked.*

"*Your face tells me you already know," I said, and she nodded. I leaned close and asked, "Am I a fool for wanting this?"*

"*You should do what your heart tells you. And maybe once the other hunters see how happy the two of you are, they will be more willing to become bound themselves." Innetha's gaze travelled to Luth, laughing at something his brother said.*

"*You would bind yourself to Luth?" I asked. "Have you told him?"*

"*Not Luth, but someone you met in the north," she replied. "Let's see how things work out with you, first. Make me proud, princess." She grinned, and left for the sola.*

After we'd eaten Aeolmar and I retreated to my chambers, and soaked in my bath until we absolutely had to emerge. We donned our leather gear, since after we saw the queen we were expected in the sola. Aeolmar drew me to him, tracing the chain around my neck.

"*Your time as an unbound woman grows short," he said. "We can be bound today, if you wish."*

"*We can?" I asked, remembering the grand weddings in Gannera that took months or years of work. "There aren't preparations to be made?"*

"*They are simple, and made by others. Would you prefer a different day?"*

"*No. Today is perfect."*

It was close to noon when we entered the queen's receiving chamber. Asherah, Finlay, Innetha, Luth, and Harek, along with two con'dehr, were already there, as well as a small woman in a gray cloak who I assumed was the seer. I had no idea why Harek was there, although the Prelate did enjoy placing himself as close as possible to the center of affairs, whether they involved him or not. I ignored him, since even Harek couldn't dampen my happiness. As we approached the small gathering, the queen's gaze settled on my necklace.

"Latera, where did you get that?" she asked.

"Aeolmar gave it to me," I replied, my hand moving to my throat. "Isn't it lovely?" She nodded, and asked Aeolmar the same question.

"It was my mother's," he replied.

"It's... lovely," Asherah said. "Do you know where she got it?"

"We should begin," the seer croaked. I was surprised that she interrupted the queen, but Asherah motioned for us to continue.

"Ready, princess?" Innetha asked.

"Yes," I proclaimed. "What do I need to do?"

The seer pushed a small bowl toward me; it was carved from a single piece of bone and painted with unfamiliar symbols. "I require a few drops of your blood."

I pricked my palm with my dagger, then I set the blade on the table as my blood dripped into the bowl. When the seer proclaimed she had enough Harek handed me a cloth to blot the wound; the cloth smelled sweet, like meadow hay.

"Thank you," I said. Aeolmar took my hand in both of his and we watched in rapt attention as the seer added various powders to my blood, stirring the mixture faster and faster.

"Remember," Aeolmar said, "I love you, beautiful girl. Nothing that happens today, or any day, will change that."

The seer stirred her bowl of blood and powder so fast the table shook, and my dagger clattered to the floor. I released Aeolmar's hand, and bent to retrieve it.

"Latera," Innetha shouted. "Behind you!"

I looked up and saw the room moving away from me. Behind me was a vortex, as swirling and angry as the one that had taken me from my home all those winters ago.

"Aeolmar," I shrieked.

"Latera! Beloved!" Aeolmar lunged toward me, but I was out of reach. How was he so far away? I'd been right beside him.

Panicked, I looked toward the others. They, too, were out of my reach. Gods, not again.

My feet weren't on solid ground and I was falling, falling away from Parthalan, from Aeolmar. The others were running about and shouting, but I only watched Aeolmar. I yelled his name, but the winds were so loud I couldn't hear myself over the din.

Again, I was gone.

CHAPTER FORTY-SEVEN

Aeolmar's arms closed on empty air. Right before his eyes, Latera had disappeared.

He stared at the space where his mate had been standing only a moment before as they waited for the seer to reveal if she was human, or something else. To Aeolmar the test was a waste of time; he had known that Latera was more than mortal when he first laid eyes on her. Still, she had wanted to know, and Aeolmar saw nothing wrong with granting his beloved a little peace of mind.

Now, his beloved was gone.

Aeolmar turned toward the seer and drew his sword in one fluid motion. "Where is she?" he demanded, the blade level with her throat.

"I've no notion," the seer replied. "I'm a woman of charms and herbs. I do not possess such magics!"

"You lie," Aeolmar said. "Return her now, or I'll kill you where you sit."

The seer blanched, but remained silent. Aeolmar moved to strike, but Asherah stayed him.

"Aeolmar, she has a point," Asherah said. "A vortex is a tool of an experienced sorcerer, not a hedgewitch."

"My lady is wise," the seer said.

"I did not say I thought you innocent," Asherah snapped. "The facts are this: you arrived. You took my huntress's blood. My huntress is now gone." Asherah leaned across the table, pushing the seer's spell-crafting implements aside. "You will tell me who you're accompliced to. Immediately."

"My lady, I am no one's accomplice," the seer cried. "I am naught but a simple woman, who came here at your request."

Asherah eyed the seer, and said over her shoulder, "Bring me a sack." Luth stepped forward with the item. "Put her things into the sack. Then, put her in the dungeon. We'll see if a few days of rats and damp will loosen her tongue."

Luth swept the herbs and bowls into the sack while two *con'dehr* grabbed the seer's arms and hauled her to her feet.

"See her to the dungeon, Luth," Asherah ordered. "I want a hunter's eyes on her at all times."

Luth nodded, and followed the *con'dehr* and the prisoner. Aeolmar surveyed the remaining occupants of the room: Asherah, Finlay, Harek, and Innetha.

"I will find her," he vowed.

Asherah nodded. "We will. Harek, alert the guards. Have the gates sealed, and order the *con'dehr* to search the palace. If they find anything—*anything*—out of the ordinary, alert me at once. And send for my sorcerers." Asherah spoke to her Prelate without looking at him, her gaze fixed on the First Hunter.

"It will be done," Harek said, then he left the room.

"Aeolmar, sit," Asherah said once Harek was gone. "You're shaking like a leaf."

"No."

"Aeolmar—"

"Latera's gone, and you want me to sit?" he demanded, his arms flailing wildly. "All you can do is tell me to sit?" Finlay stepped between Aeolmar and Asherah, drawing his mate away from Aeolmar's sword. Aeolmar dropped the weapon, the metal clanging against the stone floor, and covered his face with his hands.

"I can think of many things to tell you," Asherah began. "Once the seer has stewed a bit, we will question her again. My sorcerers will know who has the power to raise such a vortex. Perhaps they can even reverse it."

"I don't know where she is," Aeolmar said. "She could be in the underworld, surrounded by demons."

"If she is, then demons will truly learn fear," Asherah said.

"Didn't Latera arrive in Parthalan by way of a vortex?" Innetha asked.

"She did," Aeolmar confirmed. "She did! When she was ten winters old, she appeared in a cottage outside of Brennus." He looked at Finlay, who nodded.

"Four days west," his second confirmed. "Three, if we ride hard."

"We ride hard," Aeolmar repeated. He didn't know if Brennus would offer any clues as to Latera's whereabouts, or to who had taken her, but it was something. It was a start. As they discussed who would travel with them, Luth reentered the room.

"The seer," Luth said, his face bloodless. "She's gone. Just like Latera, she disappeared."

Chapter Forty-Eight

Latera Speaks

*T*he roaring winds faded as I landed on something solid, my arms shielding my face. Beneath me was a gray stone floor. I didn't know where I was, but I hoped I was still in Teg'urnan. My fingertips grazed the tiles; they were rough and gritty, lacking the flawlessly smooth polish of the palace's stones.

Not Teg'urnan, then. A vortex had claimed me yet again. I closed my eyes, and tried not to weep.

I became aware of others crowded about me. I recalled the last time a vortex had taken me and brought me to the hag's cottage. Of how the cloaked people had taunted a frightened child.

This time, I will be in control.

I felt my back, relieved that my swords had made the journey with me, then I stood and faced my kidnappers. The small crowd shrank back as they exchanged nervous whispers. As the group eyes me, I realized that they weren't fae, or even elfin. Olluhm's Balls, I was surrounded by humans.

How had they traveled to Parthalan, and how they had managed to create the vortex? I also wondered why they were all so small; I was at eye level with some, and taller than at least half of them. In Parthalan I was usually the smallest person in a room.

I took a step forward, and they shrank back. Good. I wanted them afraid of me. "What is this place?" I demanded. "Why have you brought me here?" The humans parted, and a man approached me.

"We were attempting to locate my daughter," he said. "The spell retrieved you instead."

I stared at him, taking in his pale blue eyes and curly golden hair. He looked exactly the same as he had the last day I'd seen him, as if time hadn't touched him.

How could that be? I'd been gone longer than I'd lived under his roof. "Father?"

King Harold's eyes narrowed. "Why did you call me that?"

"It's me, Latera," I cried. Weren't parents supposed to know their children as well as they knew themselves? Better than they knew themselves?

"How do you know my daughter's name?" he demanded.

"I am your daughter! You named me!"

"My daughter is ten summers old," he said. "You're grown, and you look nothing like her."

"She looks exactly like my mother," said a woman's voice. Queen Ladyslava stepped forward, ignoring the king's order to stay back. "We've been searching for you," she said, her eyes wet. "What horrible things must have happened to you?" My heart swelled, and untold layers of despair fell away at her words. To know that they really had searched for me, just as Aeolmar had always believed...

"Am I in Gannera?" I asked.

"Yes," she replied, "we've brought you home." She tried embracing me, but I grabbed her hands.

"You must send me back," I implored. "I cannot be here, not now! There are things I need to do, to finish..." I remembered Aeolmar's face as I was falling away from him, the terror in his eyes when he couldn't catch me.

"We've only just gotten you back, why would we send you away?" asked the queen. "And you've only been gone a short while, what could you possible need to finish?" She frowned, since my appearance was more than enough to disprove her.

"How long have I been gone?" I asked, glaring at the assembled sorcerers. I suspected trickery wrought by those in league with Asgeloth and his deva'shi, further evidence of the demonic trap Aeolmar and Finlay suspected.

King Harold followed my gaze, and I remembered his opinion that magic handlers were little more than charlatans, lying to appease the distraught and earn a few coins. "Four days my daughter has been gone," he said. "That is how I know you're not my child."

"Then return me," I spat. "I reside in Parthalan now, under Asherah's gracious rule."

The king's nostrils flared, and his guards moved between him and me, brandishing swords. As if I couldn't dispatch the lot of them bare-handed. Amid all of that a man wearing a brown cassock approached the king and uttered a string of excited whispers.

"How can you be sure?" Harold growled. The smaller man blanched, rambling on as he gestured wildly.

"Address us all," the queen commanded.

"M-My lady," he began, "it's known that Asherah is the faerie queen. The villages in the hills count her as a goddess, and they bake cakes in her image. They erect a large pole in the spring, and—" The king's scowl warned the little man against digressing to the religious practices of the hillfolk. He continued, "Time in Faerie does not pass like time in the mortal realm. It can be faster, or slower, or move in a spiral..." and he chattered on about how time is not a straight line but more like a wrinkled piece of fabric, with some points touching and others far, far apart.

"And your point?" demanded the king.

The man flushed and wrung his hands. "My point is that while she was only gone a short time from here, it may have been a much longer time there."

The assemblage resumed staring at me, as if I might perform a trick or suddenly turn into a toad. The king leaned closer and scrutinized me. "She looks nothing like my daughter," he repeated.

"She has my mother's red hair and blue eyes," the queen said. My hair had been red and my eyes blue as a child, not that the king cared to remember. A memory rose to the surface of my mind, bursting like a soap bubble.

"Your mother... Elvasla?" I asked, my voice catching on the name I hadn't spoken in over a decade.

"Yes," the queen said as her eyes lit up. "What else do you remember?"

The king watched me with a cold stare. The conjurers kept insisting that I must be his daughter, since everyone knows that magic cannot be fooled, and other nonsense used to sway the soft-minded. He silenced them with a glare, then he spun on his heel and left. Ladyslava offered a weak smile.

"You must be tired," the queen said, and I nodded. "We all must rest, and consider this situation." The queen turned to leave, and I fell into step beside her. We'd only reached the hall's exit before my father returned, looking no less irritated, and declared whether I was his daughter or not I needed to be put somewhere for the night. I resented being treated like a wayward piece of furniture, but I did want to be alone with my thoughts. I wondered how my mother had so easily convinced herself that I was who I claimed to be, for if the situations were reversed I'd be as suspicious as the king.

Orders were issued and rooms were prepared for me, and the queen said that she would personally see me to the chambers. As we stepped into the corridor guards flanked me, as if they thought I'd try to run or worse, was an impostor. They eyed my swords and dagger, and part of me wished they'd attempt to relieve me of the blades.

Ahead of us in the corridor, I saw two of the castle's nursemaids walking with three small girls. One of the nurses saw the queen and pointed her out to the children.

"Look, the queen," she whispered to her charges, for don't all little girls want to see the queen? Then the smallest child wrested herself free of her nurse and ran toward me. I recognized her at once, kneeling down to catch her as she threw herself into my arms.

"Tera," she cried, and I buried my face in Sasha's golden curls. In her garbled baby talk she told me how she saw me get swept into the wind, and had worried I was gone forever.

"I'm not hurt," I said, hugging her tightly, "not at all." My other sisters, Elia and Jannei joined us. They were just as excited as Sasha but much more inquisitive.

"Why are you so big?" Jannei asked as she looked me over.

"Your clothes are funny," added a giggling Elia. I pulled them into my arms and squashed them against me.

"I've so much to tell you," I said. "There's been an adventure." Their eyes widened and they clamored for stories, but I hushed them. "Not now. I'm tired and need to rest, but I promise I'll tell you everything." I scooted Elia and Jannei toward their nurse, but Sasha wouldn't leave me. She wailed in my arms, having decided that if she let go of me I'd leave her again. Once I'd calmed her to pouting rather than bawling, I asked the queen, "She's so tired. May I hold her until she's asleep?"

"Of course you may," she replied. "She's your sister."

It felt natural to hold Sasha on my hip, and my heart ached as I remembered Aeolmar surrounded by the children of Thurnda. Everything about me fascinated Sasha; first she played with my hair, then she ran her fingers across the tip of my ear, checking the other to make sure it was pointed as well. Finally, she became enamored with my pendant.

"You're very patient," the queen observed. "Do you have children?" She frowned and looked at the floor. "I cannot believe I just asked my ten summers old daughter if she has children."

I smiled. "We're of an age now, Mother."

"Well?" she pressed. "Do you... have them?"

"No. I don't."

By the time we reached my temporary chamber's door, Sasha had fallen asleep in my arms. I handed her off to my mother and stepped inside the chambers; the queen moved to follow but I begged solitude. She smiled stiffly, and advised that she would check on me in a short while.

The apartment turned out to be a three room suite. I gazed at the spacious floor plan and fine furniture; I'd have rather spent time in the nursery with my sisters. A saffira*—no, humans had servants—a servant told me that my belongings had been relocated to these rooms. I opened the heavy armoire and found the clothes and toys of a small girl. The servants must have gathered the possessions of ten summer's old Latera, as per orders. I shut the doors, deciding to send them back to the nursery. Elia could use them, then Jannei, and, if they survived, on to little Sasha.*

A large chest was next to the armoire. I ran my hands across its deeply carved lid, then I opened it and was greeted by the inviting smells of old wood and leather and incense. Inside I found thick woolen blankets and soft sheets, and a cloak long enough for me. I spread a blue blanket across the bed, which was already brimming with quilts and pillows. I remembered how my childhood bed had had a canopy, which I hated. This one, thankfully, did not.

I looked around the rooms, interested to see what else I'd find. There was a low dresser comprised of the same dark, heavy wood as the other pieces. I stared at the large furniture for a moment, for I'd never realized how different the room of a human is to that of a faerie. In Teg'urnan there were no such large, oppressive things cluttering the palace, but these humans seemed to enjoy filling up every bit of space with something or other. As soon as the thought formed in my mind I felt shame. These humans were the family that I'd missed so terribly.

I opened the dresser's many drawers. The bottom three were empty, but the top drawer held a comb and a small mirror. I left the dresser and entered what was meant to be a library, as evidenced by the empty shelves lining the walls. The only other furniture in the room was a small table with two chairs pushed into the corner.

Next to the hearth was a chest that contained candles, a lantern and flints, and a small kettle. I rummaged further and discovered a tin of tea and two dainty cups; for a moment I couldn't imagine what the cups were for, having forgotten than humans drink their tea from these objects instead of bowls. I set the kettle on its stand in front of the hearth as I placed the tin and cups on the table. I would send a saffira for water, and a proper bowl, and maybe some bread...

"No!"

I dropped the tin onto the table and ran from the room, threw myself onto the bed and sobbed. Even if this was where I was born, I wanted to go back to my real home, and my rooms in the palace, and my soft, warm bed, and to my life that I loved, my mate that I loved... I wept as I thought of Aeolmar, how he had tried to grab hold of me, how the loss of me would hurt him so. I wrapped myself in the blue blanket and cried until I slept.

***

The bed shifted under another's weight. I reached out to where Aeolmar should be, but found only emptiness. I opened my eyes, and saw my mother seated at the foot of the bed.

"I hope I didn't wake you," she said. "I worried I'd never see you again but here you are, my little girl returned. Well, not so little anymore."

"You didn't wake me. I wasn't truly asleep." I sat up and pushed back my hair; Aeolmar hadn't braided it that morning, claiming he was tired of my hair being wound in knots. Gods, could my heart break further? "Have the sorcerers gone?"

"Yes. The king sent them away." When I merely nodded, she continued, "Latera, you must understand that I only used the sorcerers out of desperation. I had no idea what had happened, where you had gone or who took you..." She turned away, and a tear rolled down her cheek. "Sasha was so upset. She cried and cried, and kept telling us that the pond taking you. I wouldn't have believed it, but the guard saw what happened. He said a whirlwind took you."

"Yes. The whirlwind was created by a sorcerer in Parthalan. Faerie." I paused, remembering Aeolmar's stricken face as I fell away from him. "In Parthalan, they called it a vortex. A similar event returned me."

"Then we shall enact safeguards so these evil ones cannot kidnap another child of ours!"

"I wouldn't bother," I said, almost offhandedly. "The spell is difficult, and few are powerful enough to create such a thing. In the eleven winters I spent in Parthalan I never knew of another who was taken as I was."

"Eleven... winters?" she asked. That's right, humans count summers to mark the passage of time. "How is that possible? And why do you look like one of them? Did they do something to you?"

"The longer I remained, the more I became like them," I answered. "My ears were the first to change, while I was still very young. Asherah always said she'd never known a mortal so affected."

"Asherah, this queen you met... she was your friend?" she asked.

"She was more than a friend to me," I replied. "She gave me a place in her court, and trained me herself. The queen was very kind to me."

"What was she training you for? Something courtly?" My mother assumed that I'd been trained in music, or languages, or any one of the more refined pursuits of royalty. I knew she wouldn't like my response, but I wouldn't lie and spare her pain. I hadn't been spared any.

"I am a huntress in the court of Asherah the Ruthless," I replied.

"Oh?" Her tone made it clear that she thought hunting was far beneath her daughter. "There are a few women here who hunt small game, birds and the like, but it's more of a man's calling. What were you after? Deer, perhaps?"

"Why would one hunt a deer? For a ritual?"

"For food, of course."

I gasped as my mother frowned, for no Parthian would ever harm a deer... and silently berated myself. She didn't know the customs of Parthalan. "The faerie god once walked Parthalan as a stag. We revere them as a representation of him among us."

She took my hand, and said, "I'm sorry. I didn't know. You might not remember, but we don't have that custom here. However, we are a tolerant and respectful court, so venison will be banned from the kitchen."

The queen beamed at me, but my thoughts were only about Aeolmar. Mar, Mar, are you looking for me? Do you miss me? Is your heart torn from your chest like mine? I hoped—no, I knew—he would find me. I also knew that Asherah needed me to fight in the coming war, against Asgeloth and his deva'shi, *and all my mother wanted to do was stop eating venison, as if that would help anything!*

I tamped down my outrage, and smiled at the woman I hardly remembered. Mother was being so kind, and trying so hard to help me, yet all I could think of was how Asherah knew me so much better than this stranger. "Thank you, but there is no reason for everyone to follow my ways."

In an instant, her gaze went from a mother's kindness to the firm resolve of a monarch. "Yes, there is. You are first born, heir to the kingdom. If abstaining from venison is your will, so be it."

A memory tugged at the back of my mind; my mother carried more royal blood than my father, even though her family had been exiled from their homeland long ago. When the royal family of Tarac came to Gannera seeking asylum Lady Ladyslava had marched through the castle gates with her head held high, expecting everyone to treat her like honored royalty, not the homeless outcast she had become. She'd been all of twelve summers old. I wondered if she now saw in me the chance she never had to claim the throne as first born. Only, I didn't want the throne.

I sighed again; it was not the time to tell the queen I was rejecting my position heir. "As you wish, Mother."

She smiled. "You haven't said what you were hunting."

I wished I could lie to her. "Demons."

Her hand flew to her mouth. "You could have been killed!"

"Asherah herself is a huntress," I said. "She led her legion against a horde of demons when she seized the throne of Parthalan. It's the highest honor to follow in the footsteps of the queen." I glanced at my mother. Her hands were clenched so tightly her knuckles were white. "I'll tell you more another time."

She nodded, and changed the subject. "Do you have everything you need?" she asked. She opened the armoire, saw the small dresses and frowned. "I'll have some clothing delivered, and a seamstress will be here in the morning. I'll also have your dinner sent up, as I can imagine you're not prepared to face the court so soon after your return." I wondered if there was a stag roasting at that very moment. "I'll give you some time to collect your thoughts this evening, and return in the morning. And, darling, I'm so glad you're home."

***

Shortly after Mother departed, there was a knock at my door. I opened it and found several young girls standing in the corridor, their arms laden with supplies.

"Good day, my lady," the tallest one began. "We have garments and other essentials for you."

"Of course." I stepped aside. "Please, enter."

They filed into my chamber, and I got a look at what each carried. One girl carried two jeweled pitchers into the sitting room, while another followed with a covered platter. A third girl had a basket of soaps looped over her arm, and she carried a plain clay pitcher, which she brought into the other room; hm. That room must be for washing.

The girl who'd spoken earlier, who was a bit older and the leader of the small group—their saffira-nell, *so to speak—spread her armload of clothing out on the bed. And what horrible clothing it was. The entire lot consisted of filmy gowns in pale colors, suitable for princesses to wear while receiving guests and perfecting their embroidery.*

I didn't receive guests, and the only sharp metal objects I liked were my swords.

"Is there anything else you require, my lady?" the girl asked, doing a bad job of hiding her smile.

I looked at the clothing on the bed, then down at my own attire. My riding leathers clearly amused her. "Are there any shoes, or just gowns?"

"Yes, shoes!" She ran to the corridor and returned with a small chest. "There are several pairs in here. The queen didn't know what you'd like, so we brought many colors for you."

"Thank you," I said. "What are you called?"

"Wren."

"Will a seamstress attend me tomorrow?"

Wren nodded. "I'll accompany her myself to ensure she is acceptable."
I couldn't bring myself to tell Wren I didn't care for these frilly gowns
and wanted something different, something that would make me look
less like a princess and more like a huntress. I wondered if this seamstress
would craft me some leggings and tunics.

"Thank you, Wren," I said. Wren grinned, then she gestured to the
other girls. They went to the armoire and gathered up the children's
clothes, curtsied, and left me, alone again.

I locked the door behind them, then I stripped off my clothes and
spread them on the bed, and took stock of what, besides myself, was from
Parthalan. There was a vest, leggings, gauntlets, belt and boots, all made
of thick tan leather, each item worn and soft; a linen blouse the color
of clouds, and my smallclothes; my hunter's gauntlet; my dagger and
swords, along with their sheaths and belts; and the small pouch that hung
from my belt. I poured out the contents of the pouch, which amounted to
some gold coins, a thin leather strap to tie off my hair, and the bloody
cloth from earlier that day.

I did not remove the pendant Aeolmar had given me the night before.
That wasn't leaving my throat unless Aeolmar removed it himself.

I folded my leathers and placed them in the armoire, and deposited
the contents of my pouch into one of the dresser drawers. I even kept the
bloody cloth, so reticent I was to part with anything from Parthalan.
I entered the washing room, and was pleasantly surprised to see that
the girls had drawn me a bath. The clay jug held scented oil, which I
poured into the bath. I sank into the water, shut my eyes and followed
my memory to happier times.

I was in Thurnda, and a thick layer of snow blanketed the training
field. I watched Aeolmar lead the morning's maneuvers, his voice echoing off the stone walls as he shouted commands, pushing the elves until

sweat ran from their brows. Aeolmar saw me and held up his hand, signaling the end of training.

The elves dispersed and my beloved came to me. He lifted me in his arms and carried me outside the castle walls and across a snowy field, more snow that I'd ever seen, more snow than I thought existed. It was over Aeolmar's knees, but he strode purposefully, him not saying and me not asking about our destination. The snow melted away and we were in a green meadow, then he climbed the Hill of Torim, and as he laid me before the twisted old oak he promised he'd come for me...

I coughed and splashed; I'd fallen asleep in the bath. The water had gone cold, so I dried myself and braided my hair for the night, the first time in seasons I'd braided it myself. I examined the clothing Wren brought and donned a simple white dress, the least awful of the bunch, and blue silk slippers.

My stomach reminded me I hadn't eaten since first dawn. I lifted the dome from the platter and discovered an assortment of bread, fruit and cheese. I tore a portion from the loaf and investigated the pitchers; one contained water, the other wine. I poured myself a glass of wine and sat before the hearth, and as the fire sprang forth I was glad that faerie magic worked in the mortal realm.

I took a long draught of wine and stared into the flames, too numb to weep, too numb to do anything but form a plan. For too long I'd relied upon Aeolmar in all things, and while I knew he would search for me he had no idea of where I was; he certainly wouldn't suspect I was in Gannera. I had to find a way back to Parthalan, and I had to do it myself.

Gods help me.

Chapter Forty-Nine

Aeolmar speaks

*M*yrnnhe galloped down the one road in Brennus, which led directly to the village inn; it seemed so long since I was last in this clearing, waiting for Latera to say goodbye to the innkeepers before she left with me for Teg'urnan. I brought Myrnnhe to a halt, then I dismounted and rubbed his nose.

"You did well," I told him. "Thank you, for bringing here me so quickly."

I heard hoof beats behind me, which meant that Alia and Bron's horses had done well, too. I'd meant to come to Brennus alone, but Asherah had insisted I take at least two hunters with me. It was sound advice, since for all we knew Latera was being held behind an army.

If that's true, I'll kill every soldier that stands between her and me.

While Bron saw to the horses, I entered the inn. I found Ingvarr standing behind the polished bar, tapping a keg. "First Hunter," he said, so loudly I wondered who he was warning. "How may I assist you, my lord?"

"Latera," I said, "have you seen her?"

"Not since she left with you, oh, three winters past."

"More like five." It irritated me that Ingvarr didn't know how long it had been since Latera had left Brennus, but then she'd just been his stable girl, not his beloved. "Do you know where she came from?"

"The mortal realm, or so she claimed."

I clenched my fist. "I mean, once she was in Parthalan, how did she make her way here? Where was she, before she was in Brennus?"

Ingvarr, having successfully tapped the keg, wiped his hands and grabbed a mug. Alia and Bron joined me at the bar, so he grabbed two more.

"I don't rightly know," Ingvarr said as he filled the mugs. "She was a wild thing at first, nothing like the princess she claimed to be. I found her hiding in my stable, full of stories about portals and people in cloaks chasing her."

"Latera always said they were gray," Alia said. "The cloaks, that is. When she came through the portal she was lying on a dirt floor, surrounded by people in gray cloaks."

"I fear you three know more about her journey here than I ever did." Ingvarr shoved the mugs toward us. "Here, on the house. I know how dusty that road gets."

Alia and Bron accepted their ale, but I hadn't finished my inquiry. "Do you know what direction she came from?" I pressed. "Any detail would help."

Ingvarr leaned toward me. "Left you, did she?"

I struck the bar with my fist and walked away before I struck Ingvarr. "I meant no disrespect," he began, but I held up my hand.

"She didn't leave," I said. "She was taken."

My throat closed up and my eyes ached, and the last thing I could bear was explaining yet again how I'd broken my promise to Latera. How I hadn't kept her safe. Alia gave Ingvarr the details of Latera's abduction while I crossed the room and stared out the small window. If I only had a clue as to how she'd gotten here...

"She was taken?"

I turned and saw Elma, Ingvarr's mate, standing in the kitchen's doorway, wringing her hands.

"Yes," I said. "Right before my eyes, and the eyes of the queen, she was taken."

Elma's eyes widened. "Magic, then?"

"Yes."

"Latera always hated magic, hated the mere mention of it." Elma glanced toward Ingvarr, then she gestured for me to follow her. "Come with me. Perhaps what I have can help you find her."

Elma led me through the kitchen and upstairs to a storage room. Most of the room was covered in dust and cobwebs, but one corner was freshly scrubbed. Elma went to that corner, pulled a chest away from the wall, and opened it.

"This is everything Latera had with her when she arrived," Elma said.

I reached into the chest and picked up a sheaf of pages. It was a child's rhymer. "Why didn't she take these things to Teg'urnan?"

"She said she never wanted to see any of it again," Elma replied. "But I knew she didn't mean that so much as she missed her family, so I kept everything safe for her."

I looked through the chest. In addition to the rhymer there was a doll, a girl's dress and underpinnings, and a bracelet so small I could have worn it on my thumb. "I don't think I ever appreciated how young she was when this happened," I said, holding a tiny shoe on my palm.

"Oh, she was a wee thing," Elma said, "but you'd never know it. She was full of fire, right from the start."

I smiled, the first time in days. "She still is."

Elma laid her hand on my arm. "Love her, you do?"

"She's my mate."

Elma nodded. "It was plain how you loved her, even all those winter's ago."

"Did she ever tell you how she got here?" I asked. "What direction she came from, anything?"

"Oh, yes," Elma replied. *"She told me everything, and I remember it all."*

Blessed Cydia. *"Elma, will you tell me everything she told you?"*

"Aye, anything to help find our girl."

***

Elma told me everything she remembered, and while it was a great deal of new information it didn't point me in the direction of Latera's abductor's. Latera had been right about her six-day trek through the woods, since she had arrived the night of the full moon, and was found in Brennus just as it began waning. Based on Latera's descriptions, Elma assumed the cottage she'd arrived in was northward.

"I'm sorry I don't have more details for you," Elma apologized.

"You have given me much more information than I had before," I replied. *"Thank you, for helping me find her."*

I moved to place the bracelet back in the trunk, but Elma stayed my hand. "Give it to her, when you find her. Tell her it's from me."

I slipped the bracelet inside my jerkin. "I will do that."

We descended from the loft to the inn, and I found Alia and Bron sitting at a corner table while Ingvarr busied himself with his other patrons. Before I could tell them what I'd learned, Innetha burst into the room.

"The Southern Contingent," she panted. *She was soaked in sweat, and her legs trembled. I caught her as she fell, and eased her onto a chair.*

"The Southern Contingent what?" I demanded.

"They're dead," she replied. *"All of them. Asgeloth."*

I squeezed my eyes shut and clenched my fists. My duty was to my mate first, but I was still the First Hunter. If Asgeloth had attacked the Southern Contingent, it was my responsibility to hold him accountable.

My hand moved to my jerkin, felt the tiny lump created by her bracelet. I shouldn't waste time on demons when Latera remained missing... But, Asherah and the rest of the hunters needed me. I could not let the mordeth-gall *decimate us, nor would Latera want me to search for her when I could be destroying demons. As Asherah had said, if Latera was in the underworld then demons would truly learn fear.

When I find whomever took Latera from me, that person will learn fear, as well.

I stood, and said over my shoulder, "Alia, Bron! Back to Teg'urnan."

Chapter Fifty

Latera Speaks

I leaned back and rubbed my forehead. My head was pounding, my eyes were gritty, and I was so mad I could spit. "And this is how you retrieved me?"

"Yes, my lady," replied Nermell, while the other sorcerers' heads bobbed in agreement. It had taken me five days to convince the king that I was his daughter, and another three for him to let me meet with the sorcerers in order to learn how they found me. After all, what if this happened again? What if someone else created a vortex and tried taking one of my sisters? I'd asked all these questions and more, and at last he relented.

My reward, after eight days of careful negotiation with the king, and three days of hearing each spell, where it originated, why they chose it, and so forth, was the certain knowledge that these supposed magic handlers had not handled any magic.

Spread before me was an assortment of scrolls, sketches of otherworldly beasts, and countless tomes of spells. In the center of the table were the objects that had fueled this glorious spell: a comb, a doll, and a pair of sandals I'd worn to shreds. Since I'd used these items often as a child my essence lingered on them, or so the sorcerers claimed, and that essence is how they found me across the veil.

Too bad the child they were searching for had grown into a woman.

I'd read the spell many times over, desperate to find a word or phrase that I'd overlooked, but that wasn't the case. It was a simple locator spell, *intended to be used with the aid of a map to find one's location, not bring them bodily from one place to another. Variations of this spell were often used in Parthalan, usually by messengers to find their intended recipient. I was amazed that these sorcerers, either in their arrogance or stupidity, thought they'd accomplished anything.*

"Tell me," I began, "how astonished were you when this worked?"

"I had the utmost confidence," cried Nermell, then his face wilted under my gaze.

"You base your claim on a locator spell, yet there's no charmed map in this heap of tricks. Any charlatan knows you need a charmed map for the spell to reveal your target's location." Nermell's face reddened as he babbled an explanation. "Enough," I said, rising from the table. "I know, even if you don't, that you're all fools."

I left them in stunned silence, unable to fathom where or how my parents had found such incompetents. With what little I knew of magic I'd known those spells were useless, and the fact that they'd so duped my family made my blood boil. I strode down the hallway to the king's reception hall, but a royal sentinel barred me from entering.

"State your business," he demanded.

"I wish to speak with my father the king."

"The king is busy."

"He will make time for me.

"Move along," he ordered, now placing his hand on his sword.

The next moment saw the sentinel's face against the wall and his own weapon at his throat. "Do not try my patience again," I growled in his ear.

I released the sentinel and entered the hall. Before King Harold could question why I was carrying a bare sword the sentinel clamored into the hall, yelling that I was a spy who had tricked his weapon from him.

"Your guard doesn't seem to know which end is sharper, so I relieved him if it," I said, then I laid the sword at my father's feet. The sentinels eyed me as if I was a demon. I lifted my chin, and didn't correct them.

"Latera," Father said, shaking his head. "Is anything ever easy with you?"

I tossed a final glare at the sentinels, enjoying how they flinched. "May I speak with you privately?" I asked.

Harold nodded to the assemblage, and they filed out of the room. Once we were alone he gestured for me to sit; instead, I paced before the dais. "What is so urgent you feel the need to attack the guards rather than merely stating your business?"

"Your sorcerers are blithering idiots," I replied. "Something or someone else brought me here."

"They couldn't conjure a puddle in a rainstorm, but your mother will not be so swayed," he said. "I'm grateful for whatever force returned you, and I agree it was no doing of theirs."

"Don't you want to know how this happened? Why I'm here again?"

"No. All I wanted was my little girl to come back to me." He smiled weakly; he'd wanted me returned as the child I was, not the grown woman I'd become. I returned his smile, and didn't argue when he said he was sending the sorcerers away.

What I needed to do was to speak with competent sorcerers, not that gaggle of fools. I left the hall knowing the king wouldn't allow me to send for magic handlers, regardless of my reasons, and that when—and if—any sorcerers were summoned again, I'd need to speak with them without his knowledge. That could take weeks or even seasons, and I couldn't wait that long. I also knew that my mother was the one who usually sent for sorcerers and the like, so I went to her apartments to learn when the next batch of magic handlers would arrive.

While I walked to my mother's chambers I thought about my second abduction. Nothing had seemed amiss in the queen's chamber, though I had thought it odd when the seer asked for a bit of blood. Still, I'd bled into the seer's bowl as asked, but how could that have sent me to another realm? My blood should have held me fast, not pushed me away. The bowl had been covered in tiny carved symbols, and I wished I'd taken a closer look.

Really, I'd known nothing about the seer, and I worried that my blind faith led to my current plight. I should have questioned her, made her explain the ritual, but I'd let my heart lead my head. I reached further into my memory, and stopped dead in the corridor.

The hag. The hag in the gray cloak, in the cottage all those winters ago.

My mind spun as I remembered the decrepit creature, hunched over and laughing at the frightened child that had been me.

Relle. The man had called the hag Relle.

Could that have been her, sitting right next to Asherah? I couldn't remember anything about Relle other than her gray cloak. I thought about the cottage, the heaps of herbs that had littered the benches, and went to my chamber. Once inside I retrieved the small cloth that Harek had given me to stanch the cut on my palm.

I unfolded the cloth, and saw the bloodstain and herbs that had been crushed into the fabric. I smelled the sweet fragrance, and remembered the smoky, rotted smell of the cottage. Are these herbs part of a spell? My mind traveled down a separate path, a path that wondered why Harek had handed me the cloth in the first place.

The Prelate had never shown me any sort of courtesy in the past; in fact, he'd constantly belittled me. He'd never even said a word to me if he could avoid it. I paced, wondering if his dislike of me was so strong he'd seek to banish me from Teg'urnan, permanently.

I replaced the cloth, carefully preserving the crushed herbs within. I didn't want to leap to conclusions, and I had no evidence that Harek was anything other than an unfriendly man who had performed one decent act. I also couldn't blame my situation on the seer, since stirring a few powders into a bowl of blood could not create a vortex; at least, I didn't think it could. I resumed my journey to my mother's chambers and left those concerns behind, if only for a moment.

I found the queen sitting with her ladies around a table that was buried under stacks of parchments, not unlike the usual state of Asherah's map table. I sat next to Mother, and after we exchanged pleasantries the ladies were sent for refreshments. As she asked about my day I picked up one of the sheets, and saw that it was a record Alberon's royal family.

"What's all this?" I glanced at the table, and realized that every parchment detailed a different family. "Are you organizing an event?"

"In a way," she replied. "Your father wants to know which families have a son near to your age. I hadn't thought I'd be dealing with these matters so soon."

Near my age... "Why is Father assembling lists of men?"

"Of course," Mother replied. "Won't a spring wedding be wonderful?"

"You cannot," I said. "I already have a mate, in Parthalan."

"You have a husband?" she inquired. "You haven't mentioned him."

"The day I was brought back was the morning we were to be bound. Married," I corrected, using the human term. "I didn't get the chance to be his wife." A tear fell onto my lap, and as I wiped my cheek she put her arms around me; gods, I'd forgotten how good it feels to be comforted by your mother.

"I'm so sorry," she said. "Perhaps we can bring him here, and you'll be together again."

"Perhaps I can find a way back to him."

Mother drew back as if she'd been burnt. "You've been here a handfuls of days and already you want to leave!"

"I'm needed in Parthalan! A war's coming! The queen needs me, Aeolmar needs me—"

"We need you!"

"And I need Aeolmar," I finished. "He's my mate, my beloved, and I cannot let him face the coming days without me! I don't want to face them without him!" I leapt to my feet and resumed pacing; gods, I'd paced more since my return to Gannera than I had in my entire life. My belly rumbled, reminding me I hadn't eaten since the day prior, and I rubbed my midsection. When I turned toward my mother, she eyed my hand.

"Did you lie with him?" she asked.

"What kind of a question is that?"

"Answer me!"

"Yes!"

"When was the last time?"

"Mother, I will not—"

"I need to know if you could be with child!"

I fell silent, wondering if it could be true. Aeolmar and I hadn't been bound, but he'd said that occasionally faerie a birth would result from an unbound pair. The chance was small, but it was still a chance, wasn't it? For the first time since I'd returned to Gannera, I felt something other than hopelessness and despair.

"The morning I came back," I whispered. "We rose and ate with the others, then returned to my chambers for a bath... Is it really possible?"

"Of course it is, and from the look on your face you'd welcome such news." Her eyes softened, and she beckoned me to sit beside her. "Tell me about your Aeolmar. I feel I should know more of him than just his name."

I stayed with my mother for the rest of the afternoon. I told her how Aeolmar and I met, and calmed her when she learned I'd been a stable girl. She raised an eyebrow when I described how handsome he was, and remarked that I was quite smitten with him. I replied that I wasn't smitten but loved him completely, as he loved me, and being separated from him was worse than I could ever describe. From the wistful expression she bore, I don't think my mother shared such affection with the king.

When I returned to my apartments I carefully set myself in the middle of my bed and willed myself to relax. That was the only advice I knew about children, that a woman with child needed to remain calm so she wouldn't agitate her baby.

Wren checked on me when I wasn't at the evening meal. I told Wren of Mother's suspicions and she sprang into action, and sent for a tea that would help me sleep. Once she returned she lectured me on the need for rest, and told me I'd need to eat well and regularly for the health of the child. She brought me a basket of apples, which she knew were my favorite, along with some dark bread and ordered me to eat. After I'd taken a few bites she sat with me, and we talked long into the night about the baby, with Wren as excited as I.

For the next moon I was so happy I floated above the floor, having convinced myself that Mother was right. I knew Father would help me return to Parthalan, for he couldn't keep my child from her father. Every night I dreamed of my baby, gazing up at me with Aeolmar's eyes.

I petitioned the queen for my own servant, to which she agreed. Her happiness dimmed when I declared that I only wanted Wren; my mother tried to sway me, and gave examples of older women who had much more experience and could better assist a princess in her daily life. I responded that my needs were simple, and that Wren and I had already become close. Mother eventually relented, and Wren's elation when she learned of her new assignment was unmatched, save for my joy about my child.

Time moved on, and the happiness I'd felt during that first moon had become anguish by the third, when it was clear that my womb was still. I felt barren, hollow to my core. I hid in my chambers, mourning the child that had never been, the baby that had only lived in my dreams. Wren finally got the nerve to enter my rooms unbidden, and found sitting at the library's window, staring westward.

"What are you looking at?" she asked, and started making a fresh pot of tea. She reached for the kindling, but I called a fire to the hearth and she yelped. When I'd first shown Wren that I could call fire she'd nearly fainted, and I tried to be conscientious of her when using the spell. I apologized but she waved it away, saying she would just have to get used to things bursting into flames. I turned back to the window, my eyes searching for a sign, a glimmer of hope...anything, anything at all.

"When I was at the border, Aeolmar remained west," I said. "I looked westward every night, and though I didn't know it he watched the east. I like to think he's looking east, even now." Once the tea was ready Wren sat next to me; she'd put my tea in a bowl, just as it was prepared in Parthalan.

"Is he westward now?"

"I wish I knew." I hung my head, despair washing over me. "What if I can't return to him? Dear goddess, is this my fate, forever separated from my beloved?" Wren sat quietly, until something caught her eye.

"Look at that magnificent bird," she said.

"What?" I followed her eyes; there was a great bird flying in from the west, its brown feathers gleaming in the sunlight.

"I think it's a hawk," she said.

"It's a bird of prey on the wind," I said, my eyes wet. The goddess had heard my plea, and answered me. I would be with Aeolmar again.

Chapter Fifty-One

Latera Speaks

At Wren's insistence, and with her invaluable help, I ventured outside my rooms again. We started with short walks, and once I'd gotten into the habit of spending time away from my bed I went to Mother's chambers, and told her that her suspicions were unfounded: I was not carrying Aeolmar's baby. She was relieved by my childless state. I remained despondent.

Days passed, I lost count of how many, and Father requested I join him at his midday meal. I did, and found him seated before a splendid buffet with my mother and a man I'd never met.

"Latera," Father said, rising to his feet, "this is Prince Gannok, first born of the Highlands." I inclined my head and stood behind my seat. It was a faerie custom, not human, to wait for the queen—or in this case, king—to be seated before oneself, but I was a faerie huntress. I nodded to my mother, who wouldn't meet my gaze. Father launched into a speech about how the Highlands and Gannera had been allies for many generations, and of how allies such needed to reinforce those bonds to ensure their continued strength. When Father began recounting Gannok's lineage, I held up my hand.

"My lord, why are you telling me all of this?"

Father took my elbow and led me away from the table. "You are twenty-two now, long past when you should be betrothed. Gannok is of a good family, and an appropriate match."

My hand flew to the teardrop at my throat. "I have a mate in Parthalan. You'd have your daughter betray the one she is sworn to under your own roof?"

"He is not here with you—"

"Because you snatched me from his arms and your incompetent sorcerers can't return me," I yelled, not caring if the prince or the whole kingdom heard. I would not betray Aeolmar, and if Father didn't agree he could have me banished, for all I cared.

He surprised me by smiling. "Latera, please. I only want what's best for you. Gannok has come a long way, and he's hungry. Can you just sit with him, and be pleasant for a time? The final choice on any betrothal will be yours, you have my word."

I looked at the table, and my belly rumbled. "Eating, nothing more."

"Of course," Father said. I sat, then he and my mother made their apologies and left me alone with the prince. Cowards.

I observed Prince Gannok from the corner of my eye; his eyes were a dull gray, his hair a meaningless blond, and his skin was sallow. His face and arms were soft, as if he'd spent his life cosseted by nurses, never once venturing outside for a ride or a hunt or anything that required the slightest exertion. In short, he was hideous. I wondered if tales of a damaged princess had spread far and wide, and he was all my father could find for me.

"You're name is lovely, Lady Latera," Gannok said, piling his plate with sweets he clearly didn't need.

"I'm also called Demon-killer," I said, reaching for an apple. "Did the king tell you I'm a huntress? I'm considered among the deadliest in Parthalan." I sliced the apple into sections with my dagger, and ate them right from the blade.

"Is Parthalan far from here?" he asked.

"Yes." I replied, then the only sound was of me chewing. There weren't any apples in Parthalan, at least none I'd ever come across, and apples were one of my few joys in Gannera.

"That is a very nice necklace," Gannok said.

"Thank you. It belonged to my mate's mother."

"The king says your husband is irrelevant since you weren't married before the crown," Gannok said around the food he shoveled in his mouth. I slammed my palms onto the table, hard enough to make the platters jump and the goblets fall to their sides.

"Speak of my mate again, and I'll kill you," I growled. The color drained from Gannok's face, and I wondered if he would faint. I turned on my heel and stalked away.

I burst into my apartments and paced back and forth, so furious I could hardly breathe. Wren, who had been dozing in my sitting room, joined me.

"What happened?" she asked.

"My father seeks to marry me off."

"But you have Aeolmar!"

"The king claims he doesn't matter." I sat on the bed, supporting my aching head in my hands. "The truth is, he doesn't care. I embarrass him, and he wants to be rid of me. You should see the prince he dredged up, lazy and dull-witted." I fell back on the mattress, and Wren flopped down beside me. "All I learned from those sorcerers was that they didn't bring me here. Something else is at work, but I don't know what." I rubbed my eyes. "I wish I'd let Aeolmar teach me more about magic."

"Was he good with magic?" Wren asked.

I smiled. "Aeolmar was very good with magic. He could call fire, and cast glamours, and charm doors so only certain people could enter."

"Better than a lock."

"Yes, much better than a lock. He could work many other spells... He had a sense about magic and how it behaved. Everyone in his family did."

"Maybe you just need to learn about magic yourself, instead of relying on someone else to help you."

"How could I learn such things, and who would teach me?"

Wren frowned. "I don't know, but it would seem to me if Aeolmar's entire family can learn about magic, you can do it, too."

"They're fae, creatures of magic. I'm trapped here among humans, who know little of anything faerie." I thought of the outlying lands, where there were magical beings that might be willing to help me. I knew of a few elf tribes in the north...

"Then we're approaching this the wrong way," Wren declared. "We're staring at the vast forest, and we're trying to clear it in one fell stroke. We need to look at the individual trees, and chop them down one at a time."

"What are you saying?"

"Well, if you want to return to Parthalan, don't you need to know where it is before you figure out how to get there?"

I rose and went to the window, gazing toward the west. It had never occurred to me to learn where Parthalan was in relation to Gannera. The single sun shone down on me, and I wondered if it could be the elder sun. I saw other aspects of Gannera that were identical to Parthalan—the birds, the trees and grass, not to mention our language—and realized that just because I had traveled between realms by magic didn't mean that was the only way. Maybe I was closer to Parthalan than I'd dared to hope. A memory surfaced, and I faced Wren.

"When I returned I mentioned Asherah, and one of the scribes said there was a temple dedicated to her. I must speak with that scribe."

"That was probably Quill," Wren said. "He studies the old gods and odd bits of lore. We can probably find him in the scriptorium."

I threw on my cloak, pulling my hood low over my ears, and followed Wren to the bowels of the castle. The scribe's chamber was dark, with stacks of books and scrolls blocking the meager candlelight. I went from one worktable to the next until I found the one I sought.

Quill was a small, balding man clad in a coarse brown robe, thoroughly engrossed in his work. I sat across from him and lowered my hood.

"Are you Quill?" I asked.

"Yes, yes," he muttered, then he looked up. "Lady Latera," he gasped, "Forgive me, I didn't realize it was you."

"I take no offense. You were there, the day I returned?" He nodded. "You spoke of a temple dedicated to Asherah. Can you tell me where to find it?"

"Yes, my lady." Quill darted behind a stack of precariously balanced parchments, fumbling through the layers until he found what he was after. He returned to the table, unrolling the map and explaining that the temple was less than a day from the castle.

"Have you been to this temple?" I asked.

"Oh, yes," he replied. "It's a replica of Asherah's own palace, and it's quite beautiful. Her priestesses maintain it." I wondered how Asherah would react to mortal worshipping her as a goddess. She'd probably find the whole situation a bit foolish.

"Do you know their customs?"

"The priestesses are rarely seen outside the temple grounds. Very few have ever seen their rituals." He leaned forward, and asked, "Have you really seen her? The Asherah?"

"She's one of my dearest friends," I replied. "In Parthalan she's not a goddess but a queen, generous and gracious and adored by her people."

Quill bowed his head. "To speak to one as you, who has travelled so far, is an honor. You give me hope that my life's work hasn't been for naught." I withdrew a coin from my pouch and slid it across the table toward him.

"Thank you, for helping me," I said, rolling up the map. "When I next see Asherah, I will tell her of your good heart."

He didn't look at the coin before sliding it back to me. "My lady, I will take no payment from you."

"Take a closer look at the coin," I said, nudging it toward him; he did, and his eyes went wide. "It was struck to commemorate the five hundredth year of Asherah's reign."

"My lady, I cannot accept this. It's priceless!"

"I have others. But I would ask another favor of you. Will you check your tomes for information of others who have traveled between Gannera and Parthalan?"

Quill agreed, and Wren and I left as he flipped through his pages. We went to Mother's rooms, where I informed her that I would visit this temple. Mother regarded us through narrowed eyes, her gaze settling on Wren.

"Leave us," she commanded.

"Wren stays," I said. "She'll make this journey with me."

"I won't speak of private matters before a commoner," Mother said.

"I'll do as the queen wishes," Wren said, and left us. Once the door shut behind her I turned toward my mother.

"Why do you hate her?" I demanded. She ignored my question, and asked one her own.

"What do you intend to accomplish at this temple? To leave us again?"

"I mean to communicate with those who sheltered and cared for your daughter for many winters," I retorted. Mother recoiled; it wasn't her fault I'd lived without her for so long. "I have a place in Asherah's court, and I have a mate. They need to know that I'm alive." Mother sighed, and sank back in her chair.

"This is about Gannok, isn't it?" she asked. "I held your father off for as long as I could, but when you confessed you weren't with child he decided you must be betrothed."

"You told the king I was with child?"

"I told him it was a possibility. I know, I shouldn't have said such a thing, but it gave you a few fortnights without suitors. Forgive me?"

"Of course you're forgiven—but you could have warned me, and told me to put a pillow in my dress." We laughed together. "You know I'll go to this temple, regardless of what you or the king have to say about it. I promise to be back by nightfall of the second day. Can you keep Father distracted until then?"

"Will you be safe?"

"Surrounded by humans? Absolutely."

***

The next morning, Wren and I readied ourselves in the dark hour before dawn. We went to the stables, and I impressed Wren when I saddled the horses myself; it seemed there were no women stable hands in Gannera, just like there were no women warriors. And the list of reasons to return to Parthalan grew ever longer. Wren impressed me in her own way when she convinced the lone groom to forget he saw us.

Wren asked me many things while we travelled. Mostly, she asked questions about Parthalan she didn't dare to ask while in Gannera castle, and I told her everything. She gasped when I told her about the vortex that took me and the cottage I'd woken in, and smiled all through the stories of Queen Asherah's training lessons. I told her about the sola, my time at the border, and the many beasts and demons I'd faced. When *we stopped to water the horses, she asked if I could teach her how to call fire.*

"I've never taught anyone about magic before, so I don't know how this will turn out," I warned. I remembered how Finlay had taught me, and hoped I'd do him justice.

"Close your eyes," I instructed. "Hold your hands together, as if you're scooping water. Good. Now, clear your mind, pretend it is an empty room. Calm, all you feel is calm." I waited for a few moments, and said, "Now repeat, nir si'lan."

"Nir si'lan." Wren cracked an eyelid, and saw fire licking between her fingers. "It doesn't burn," she said, leaning close to the flames.

"You cannot be burned by a fire you created." I held a twig over her palm, and watched it ignite. "But it burns nonetheless. Now, say nir si'la."

She did, and the fire extinguished itself. "In time, and with much practice, you'll be able to call fire with a moment's notice." I waved my hand over the sticks we'd assembled, and a crackling blaze burst forth. I went on, telling her how each hunter used fire differently, from Finlay's fireballs to Aeolmar's walls of flame.

"You miss him a great deal, don't you?" Wren asked. I'd fallen silent, wandering among my memories.

"Yes. I'd give anything to be with Aeolmar again."

She patted my hand. "Don't worry, we'll get you back to him."

We arrived at the temple by midafternoon. While it wasn't nearly as large as Teg'urnan the temple was made of smooth gray stone, and had spires that corresponded to the palace's six towers. A short fence encircled it, an imitation of the palace wall, complete with a stag and doe leaping toward each other over the gate. Three women robed in white stood in front of the entrance.

I dismounted and approached the women. "I seek an audience with those who follow Asherah."

The central priestess stepped forward, her hands clasped above her heart. "I am Alyon, High Priestess of Asherah the Deliverer," she proclaimed.

"I am Latera, huntress in the court of Queen Asherah. This is my companion, Wren." I lowered my hood, and their eyes widened when they saw my ears and eyes.

"I've come to you for help," I continued. "I've been kidnapped from Asherah's palace, and I must return to Parthalan." Three sets of eyes settled on my pendant.

"Where did you come by that jewel?" Alyon asked.

"It was given to me by Asherah's First Hunter."

Alyon ushered Wren and I inside the temple and led us to an altar, above which was a blue stone identical to my pendant. "This is called the Goddess's Tear, for the day Asherah became queen was a day of great sadness," said Alyon. I stared at the jewel, but before I could ask where it came from, I caught Alyon studying my features. "Have you truly come from Faerie?" she asked.

"I have," I replied, extending my arm to reveal my hunter's gauntlet, and the royal Parthian seal.

"How may we help you, traveler?" asked Alyon.

"Do you know how to move from this realm to Asherah's?"

"We have not done so, but it can be done," replied Alyon. "In all the nine realms, the earth is the same, only separated by a veil of magic. To travel betwixt the realms you must pierce that veil."

"Is the knowledge of this veil contained here?"

"It is not, for we are sworn to remain in the temple."

"Please, I must return to Asherah," I implored. "She is besieged by demons, by the mordeth-gall himself."

Alyon's eyes narrowed. "Demons also travel between realms, but they use the underworld as their roadway." She glanced at her sisters and continued, "Your coming has been foretold, and we will offer what assistance we can."

The priestess guided me to a dark inner chamber. The word "nyshanti" was inscribed over the arched entryway; I wondered what that word meant, or if it was someone's name. The room was empty save for a pool in the center of the floor.

"This is our oracle. If there is aught you may do to help Asherah, it shall be revealed here," Alyon said, then she left me alone in the blackness.

I stared into the dark water until my legs went numb and I forgot where I was. After a time the surface stirred, and I saw a great battle. Aeolmar was in the thick of it, fighting back to back with Asherah. They were fighting for their lives, soaked in demon's blood, and Asgeloth roared up behind them.

The water rippled as the scene dissipated; I'd reached out to warn them about the mordeth-gall. I sat on my heels and rubbed my face, wondering how that vision was supposed to get me home to Parthalan.

"On your honor, will you do all you can for Asherah?"

I looked up and saw a faerie woman, as beautiful as the queen herself, with brown eyes and golden hair that fell in heavy waves about her shoulders. As my eyes adjusted I realized she was transparent; the oracle had deemed me worthy of her time. "Yes," I replied. "You also wish to help the queen?"

"I have watched over her for many years, as she once watched over me." She turned to the scrying pool. "There is a traitor near the queen."

"Who?" I cried.

"The traitor is marked by Asgeloth. He is the one closest to her, not in her heart, but in body."

"Is the traitor the deva'shi?" I asked

"Asherah has been lied to by the traitor," she replied. "The deva'shi will stop Asgeloth."

"If I determine who this traitor is, and he is as close as you say, how will Asherah know to believe me?"

"Give her the name Hillel. Then tell her I would die for her again, over and over until the end of time. Tell her my love is everlasting."

I bowed my head. "Thank you, oracle. I will give Asherah your message."

"Your way home lays with he who brought you here, not the traitor but his brother. You will know him as he is also marked by the mordeth-gall. *Learn of the* deva'shi. *You are the key."*

The oracle faded from view, and I considered what she'd told me. If the traitor had lied to Asherah about the deva'shi, that made the traitor Harek, since he had uncovered the information several winters ago.

As hateful as he was, I couldn't imagine Harek betraying Asherah. He'd been with her since the beginning, and his loyalty had never been in question. I remembered the cloth he handed me, packed with herbs that smelled like the hag's cottage, and wondered again why he'd needed to be present for my meeting with the seer. Then I remembered the oracle's words: the one closest to Asherah, not in her heart, but in body. Harek was the closest rank to the queen, and he always stood on her left, closer than Aeolmar or any other.

The traitor is marked by Asgeloth. *I'd never noticed any sort of a mark upon Harek, but then I'd only ever seen his face and hands. Thank Cydia I'd never seen anything more. I recalled a lesson in the sola, about how* mordeths *marked their slaves by burning a handprint into their flesh. Might the Prelate bear one?*

My mind churned, recalling what Finlay had said about demons following me across Parthalan and then on to Thurnda. Harek had known when I went to the border, and when I returned to the palace. He'd also driven Aeolmar mad with his endless questions about our journey north. Aeolmar had mentioned how odd he found Harek's behavior, but he hadn't suspected him of treason.

The question remained, why would Harek so desperately want me removed from Parthalan? And did this mean he had a brother who had transported me to Gannera?

I left the oracle's chamber and informed the priestesses and Wren of what I'd learned, but not my suspicions. The priestesses were familiar with the legend of the deva'shi, *who was said to be the descendent of a great elfin queen. I mentioned Sibeal's tales of the warrior that had killed Asgeloth's sire, and Alyon confirmed that they were one in the same.*

"Her name was Elvasla," Alyon began. "She and her mate tracked Ehkron from Faerie to the mortal realm by way of the underworld. She prevailed in battle and slew Ehkron, but suffered such terrible wounds that she died moments after him. While they still clung to life she dipped her finger in her own blood and touched his brow, then marked her forehead with his.

"'We are bound by blood,' Elvasla said as the demon king died. 'My line will destroy yours. My descendants will bring forth the deva'shi *and your evil will be gone from the world of my home, and the world of my children.' As the curse left her lips, death took her."*

Elvasla.

My grandmother, my mother's mother, was called Elvasla.

My mind spun, but I pushed those thoughts aside. Alyon continued, and told me that I needed to discover what became of Elvasla's line to find the deva'shi. *As for returning to Parthalan, I needed to find the one that brought me here and determine how he had pierced the veil, for that was the only way for me to return, save the underworld. I would gladly cross the plains of hell if it meant returning to Parthalan. I asked Alyon what* deva'shi *meant, and was stunned by her answer.*

"It's an elfin word, meaning 'killer of demons,'" replied the priestess. I blanched and Wren's eyes went wide. This was a coincidence; it had to be coincidence, for I was not prepared to think of it as anything but. I

was not an elf. I was human. My grandmother merely shared a name with a legendary elfin queen. That was all.

The priestesses offered Wren and me a room for the evening, and we gladly accepted. As I lay amidst the stiff cushions, I knew the moment I began to dream. Normally my dreams involved fond memories, but this dream was different from the moment I shut my eyes.

Aeolmar stood on his balcony, staring east. I watched him for a time, remembering his soft hair and softer skin, before I dared touch his hand.

"I'm here, beloved."

Aeolmar looked at his hand, and then at me. I slid my arms around his waist, and as he gathered me close he felt so solid, so real, that even within my dream I wondered how that could be.

"I thought you were lost to me," he said. "Beloved, I'm trying to find you."

"I'm trying to find my way back."

"Where are you?"

"Gannera."

His shoulders tensed. "How can I get to you?"

"I don't know." I knotted my fingers in his hair, rubbed my cheek against his throat, and breathed in his scent, desperate to experience as much of him as possible. "I'm with people who are trying to help me."

"I need you so much. So much has happened."

"I know." I took his hand and led him down the narrow stairs to bed, but he hesitated.

"You won't be here when I wake," he whispered.

"Then let's make the most of tonight." Aeolmar climbed into bed and wrapped his arms around me. I tried warning him about the traitor, but Aeolmar murmured of how he missed me, how he was trying so hard to find me. I hushed him, and decided to tell him in the morning.

Afterward, Aeolmar fell asleep while I struggled to stay awake. I couldn't tear my gaze from him, my beautiful warrior, and fought tears while I prayed and prayed for the suns not to rise. I leaned down to kiss his cheek...

I woke with a start, and saw Alyon sitting beside me.

"That was a gift from the oracle," the priestess told me. "She allowed you be with the one you love most."

"Did he feel it to?"

She nodded. "It was more than a dream."

"I'm forever grateful to you, and your oracle," I said. "I cannot express what a precious gift she's given me. If there is ever anything I can do, for you or your temple, you have but to ask." Alyon's eyes were somber, and her words spoken with conviction.

"My only request is that you follow the oracle's words and raise the deva'shi. Asherah must not fall."

Chapter Fifty-Two

Aeolmar sat straight up in his bedroll, panting. *By all the living gods, was that a dream or a curse?*

Aeolmar pulled on his clothes and stormed out of his tent toward the river. The hunters, save the queen and Finlay, were camped along its bank, a short respite as they, and Harek and his soldiers, tracked the demons rampaging across Parthalan. Asherah had wanted to join them, but with both the Prelate and First Hunter away from the palace someone needed to stay behind and manage things. As for Finlay, there was no way Aeolmar would separate a bound pair. Not after what had befallen Latera.

Latera...

Aeolmar dropped to his knees before the water. Had he angered the gods? Was that dream some kind of torture, that he may imagine his beloved but not be with her?

No, torture it was not. Nor did he feel it had been a dream, at least not in the truest sense. His hands had the recent memory of her skin, his ears recalled her breath quickening beneath him, her heart pounding when she cried out his name. Whatever else it had been, last night was not a punishment.

A gift, then. But from whom?

"Aeolmar." Innetha knelt beside him. "Gods, you're sweating as if you've run leagues," she said. Aeolmar looked down; the shirt he'd put on a few moments ago was soaked through.

He ran a hand through his hair. "I... I had a dream," he began, then he told her of his nighttime vision. Innetha listened closely.

"This is good," she said when he'd finished. "For this to happen, Latera must be alive and well."

"You think so?"

"I do. How was her form? Was she injured in any way?"

Aeolmar recalled her bright eyes, her soft laugh. "She was perfect."

Innetha nodded. "Then your princess found a way to contact you. Our Demon-killer may be far from us, but she wants to return." Innetha looked over her shoulder at Harek's tent, and scowled. "If only we could get away from these fools long enough to help her."

"Agreed," Aeolmar said. "I grow weary of chasing Asgeloth's tail."

"If Harek's spies are as skilled as he claims, why do we always arrive days after the battle?" Innetha demanded. "The man's a fool. An ass and a fool."

"I'm surprised you haven't murdered him yet."

"Don't think I haven't considered it." Innetha stood, and offered Aeolmar her hand. "I'm going to wake Elkin. Will you be all right?"

"Elkin?" Aeolmar accepted her hand, though she pulled him up with more force than necessary. "Are you finally back with him?"

"We'll see," Innetha replied with a wink. "If you have another vision, I'd like to know. Perhaps there will be a clue as to how we can help Latera."

"Perhaps."

Aeolmar reentered his tent and sat on the rumpled bedroll, knees up and his head in his hands. Since there was still time before first dawn, he yanked off his boots and lay on his back. As he stared at the ceiling, his hand caught on long filaments in the blanket. He assumed them to be strands of his own hair, but they felt...different.

A puff of fire bloomed on his palm, and Aeolmar examined the hairs. They were long, and curly, and red. Latera's hair. Quickly he gathered the hairs and plaited them into a tiny rope.

"Beloved," he said as he tucked the hairs against his heart, "I will find you."

Chapter Fifty-Three

Latera and Wren returned to Gannera Castle the next day. Latera quickly changed her clothes from that of a huntress to a princess, and smiled at the king as she entered the dining hall for the midday meal. Her mood soured when she saw Gannok seated at the king's left.

"Why is he still here?" Latera asked her mother.

"He's our guest," Ladyslava replied. "We expected him to stay for some time. It's not out of the ordinary."

Latera turned her attention to her food, playing the part of the docile princess. Then Gannok spoke and ruined everything.

"Another fine meal, King Harold," Gannok said, "made all the finer by Latera's presence." Latera bristled, but she held her tongue. Gannok beckoned to one of the servers, and asked, "Might you be able to bring out some venison? I believe the rich meat would do Lady Latera some good."

Latera's head snapped up. "Please," whispered Ladyslava, "just let it go." Latera nodded, and laughed when the server informed Gannok that venison was not served in Gannera.

When the meal ended, everyone retired to the seats around the hearth to enjoy some music and the bards' tales. Latera closed her eyes and imagined that she was back in Thurnda, dancing with Aeolmar. When another touched her hand, she smiled.

"Latera, may I speak with you?"

Latera opened her eyes, and saw that Gannok was the one touching her. She rose and fled to the courtyard, pacing along the garden paths.

"How dare he speak to me," she muttered, "how dare he touch me." The day was bright and warm, and she remained outdoors for a time, enjoying her solitude. When she returned to the hall, a servant informed her that the king wished to speak with her.

"You wanted to see me?" Latera asked, when she arrived at her father's chamber.

"We must discuss your treatment of our guest," he began. "The prince is quite taken with you. He mentioned your spirited nature, and claims you speak to him as no other dares to."

"That's because I have no interest in him," Latera said

"He thinks you're shy around men."

Latera snorted. "I have a mate. What's left to be shy about?"

Harold frowned, but he continued, "Gannok believes he'll win you over in time."

"My lord. Father. I've told you, I have a mate—a husband—in Parthalan. I won't betray him, not even for you," Latera said, arms crossed and chin lifted.

"I don't know how much you know about matters of diplomacy," Harold began, "but the Highlands would be a strong ally to Gannera, and marriage is the best way to create that alliance. I need to think of my people and what is best for them, above what is best for my family."

Latera's hands fell to her sides. "You would send me away? All the way to the Highlands?"

"It is custom for the first born to remain with their land, but as you're both the eldest you'll go with your husband."

"I was given your word that I would make the final decision on any betrothal," Latera reminded him. "I say no."

"I will not accept such insolence, not from my own daughter," Harold said.

"My mate once called me insolent," Latera retorted. "You'd like Aeolmar. He is the First Hunter of Parthalan, outranked only by Queen Asherah and her Prelate. He has an admirable sense of honor and loyalty. Aeolmar would never expect a woman to betray her husband over something as foolish as politics."

Harold sat, and rubbed his eyes. "Latera, I don't know what to do with you," he said at length. "I don't want to send you away, but what choice do I have? Negotiations between Gannera and the Highlands have been ongoing for many years. You or one of your sisters would have married one of their sons eventually." Latera sat beside him.

"Father, I'm not trying to be difficult. Truly, I'm not. If you could only understand the many nights I couldn't sleep, wishing I could hear your voice...hoping you'd come for me." Her voice trailed off, then she lifted her chin and met her father's eyes. "I won't marry Gannok, or any other prince you find. I won't betray Aeolmar, not for you, or Gannera, or any other reason." Having said all she could, Latera stood and walked toward the door.

"Sit," Harold commanded. Latera halted, but remained standing. "I'm grateful I instilled a sense of honor in you," he began. "However, daughter or not, I will not tolerate defiance. Prince Gannok will remain here for the next two seasons. You will be pleasant to him, and you will get to know him. This is your duty to your family and your kingdom. Our conversation has ended."

Latera bowed her head, and left without another word. *Two seasons. I have two seasons to find a way out of this nightmare.*

***

The next morning, Latera told Wren about her conversation with the king.

"But King Harold is known for his fair and just hand," Wren said. "To order you to marry another is the most unkind act I've ever heard of."

"Agreed." Latera stood, and grabbed her cloak. "Let's visit Quill. Perhaps he's found something useful."

Before either could move, there was a knock at Latera's door. Wren opened it and found Gannok standing in the corridor.

"I bid you good morning, my lady," he greeted. "Would you give me the pleasure of accompanying me at my first meal?"

"My apologies, but Wren and I always walk together in the morning," Latera replied. "I'd ask you along but we discuss womanly matters, nothing that would interest a prince," Latera added. Gannok frowned, and Latera remembered her father's words; if Gannok told the king she was avoiding him, her situation would take a turn for the worse. Luckily, Wren came to her rescue.

"My lady," Wren began, "if it would please you, I can arrange for you and the prince to share your midday meal in the garden."

"Why, that would be lovely," Gannok said. "Shall we plan for noon?"

"Noon it is," Latera mumbled.

"Until then, my lady," Gannok said, and Wren closed the door. Latera sagged against the wall, rubbing her eyes.

"I'm sorry I suggested lunch without asking first," Wren said, but Latera waved it away.

"Worry not," Latera said. "My only plan was to jump out the window. Lunch is much more practical."

"You're not cross, then?"

"How could I be cross with my only friend?" Latera countered. "And the garden is perfect. With any luck we'll have rain."

Unencumbered by the prince, Latera and Wren walked to the scriptorium and found Quill. He'd located several accounts of traveling between the mortal realm and Parthalan, but none detailed how the journey was accomplished. Latera relayed what had happened at Asherah's temple, and the oracle's words. Quill was familiar with the story of Elvasla and the *deva'shi*, and said that there was information on both within the scriptorium. They left Quill among the scrolls, searching for the information.

After Latera and Wren left the scribe's chamber, the younger girl hurried off to prepare for the garden lunch. Latera wandered the corridors, and before long she found herself standing in front of the royal library.

She pushed open the doors, remembering how imposing the endless shelves of books had been when she was small. Now she found them comforting, and as she ran her hand across the spines her thoughts returned to Teg'urnan's archive. It was stocked with books on every subject one could hope to learn, even magic. Perhaps, even books on how to move from one realm to another.

Perhaps, Gannera's library was just as well stocked.

Why didn't I think of this before? Latera scanned the shelves, and recalled that one needed a writ from the king to be granted full access. She resumed her pacing, and formed a plan.

After a time she looked to the window and saw the sun nearly overhead, and shrugged. After all, she had no desire to eat with Gannok, so being a little late was perfectly acceptable. As Latera stepped out to the garden she saw that Wren had set up a table and two chairs near the arbor, and that Gannok was already waiting for her. She also saw her sisters playing nearby.

Latera inclined her head to the prince as she sat and their table, and laughed when all three of her sisters jumped on top of her.

"You don't mind if they stay, do you?" Latera asked. "We've always been so close, and I missed them terribly while I was gone."

"Of course not," Gannok replied, though his tone was strained. "How long were the four of you apart?"

"More than ten winters," Latera replied.

"Liar," shouted Elia. "You were gone four days."

"Young lady," Gannok began, but Latera spoke over him.

"Now Elia, I've told you I was in Parthalan for twelve winters," Latera said, "but you're right, I was only gone from you for those four short days. You've always had the best memory of us all," she added, hugging her sister. The prince appeared baffled, and Latera realized that his mind was as flabby as the rest of him. She wondered if she could trick him into leaving Gannera altogether.

Their meal continued in this manner, and while the prince remained polite it was clear that he didn't care for children. Gannok ate quickly and then excused himself, and Latera hoped their luncheon had dampened his desire to find a wife in Gannera. Once he was gone, and the girls had gone inside for their naps, Latera asked Wren if she had planned the episode.

"The royal nursemaid cared for me when I was small," Wren replied. "I just asked her where the children would be at noon, and planned the meal around it."

"When you were small?" Latera asked, ruffling Wren's hair. "You're small now."

Wren giggled, and they both smiled. "I feel we're so alike," Latera said. "I don't think I could bear this place without you."

***

Shortly before supper Latera waited in the corridor the king would pass through on his way to the great hall. She'd spent the afternoon rehearsing what she would say, and his probable responses. Her gut churned at the thought of lying to her father; however, he had gone back on his word about a possible betrothal. If he was willing to lie to her, Latera thought it only just that she return the favor.

Latera stepped to the side when she heard the royal retinue approach, hiding her hands into the folds of her skirts. To help her cause she'd worn a shimmering pink gown covered in white lace. It was worse than all the other gowns combined, but it made her look like the princess her father wanted her to be. For her ruse to succeed, Latera needed to play the obedient daughter who'd seen the error of her ways.

"Hello, Latera," King Harold said, when he saw her. "Are you on your way to supper?"

"Father, may I have a word with you before dinner?" she asked.

"Of course," he said, and sent the rest on their way.

"I've been thinking about our conversation," she began, "and you were correct. I have a duty to Gannera, and my birthright. Can you ever forgive me?" Latera averted her gaze, marveling he didn't hear her racing pulse.

"Of course I forgive you," Harold replied. When Latera looked up she saw his wide, almost fatherly smile. "You were away in that strange land far too long, and needed a reminder of our ways."

Latera returned his smile; he'd said exactly what she'd hoped. "May I trouble you for a favor, one that I believe will help me better remember our customs?"

"Name it, daughter."

"May I have a royal pass to the library? If I can read about Gannera's history I'll reconnect with my true heritage, and thus be able to serve my kingdom as I should." Harold frowned, and Latera worried she'd asked too much.

"Forgive me," she said. "I've overstepped. I see that now." Latera bowed her head and turned away, but Harold caught her elbow.

"There is nothing to forgive," he said. "Researching our history is an excellent idea. I will have the pass prepared at once."

"Thank you, Father. I'll make you proud of me yet."

***

The pass was delivered to Latera the next morning. She and Wren went to the library and were met by the keeper, Sarfek, a stocky man with a genial smile. Latera sensed that he wasn't originally from Gannera, but didn't question his heritage. She didn't want to leave clues about what she truly sought among the archives.

Sarfek led them to the section that held books about Gannera's history, and implored them to call for him should they need assistance. Once he'd disappeared behind the stacks, Latera sent Wren off to search for books about magic. Latera pretended to read three volumes of history before Wren returned, lugging two thick tomes.

"These were the only ones in a language I could understand," Wren explained.

"What other language could they possibly be in?" Latera wondered, since Gannera and the surrounding lands all spoke *feh'lah*, which was the common language of their ancestors." When Wren shrugged, Latera went to the keeper's desk.

"Might I trouble you for a parchment and quill?" Latera asked, and Sarfek dutifully produced them. Latera scribbled a few words in *ahm'ri* and showed them to Wren.

"Yes, that's how the words looked," she confirmed. Sarfek looked over Latera's shoulder.

"Ah, *ahm'ri*," he said, "Few have an interest in the old tongue."

"Would you show me some of the volumes written in this language?" Latera asked. The keeper brought them to the farthest corner of the library, which was as dark and dank as the scriptorium. Latera regarded the shelves and shelves of books, then she removed and opened the thinnest volume, only to be confronted by words whose meaning she could not guess.

"The words are lovely, are they not?" Latera murmured, gliding her hand over the page. "I wish I could understand them."

"A moment, my lady." With that, Sarfek disappeared, and returned a moment later with two volumes.

"Begin with these, my lady," he said. "These books contain the same tales, but one is in *ahm'ri*, the other in *feh'lah*."

"You have my sincere gratitude," Latera said. "May I bring these, and the volume on history, back to my rooms?"

"Of course, my lady."

***

Wren and Latera spent the next season practicing their new language. When they were alone they only spoke *ahm'ri*, to the point that when they encountered one speaking *feh'lah* it took them a moment to comprehend.

After a few fortnights of their studies, Ladyslava demanded to know what Latera and Wren were doing. Latera showed her the royal pass and the volumes of Ganneran history, though she kept the texts in *ahm'ri* hidden. Ladyslava smiled when Latera mentioned the kind-hearted keeper, and shared that Sarfek had served her family in Tarac before they were exiled. Once Ladyslava arrived in Gannera, Sarfek appeared and offered his services, and had maintained the library ever since.

When Latera felt that she'd mastered speaking *ahm'ri*, she returned those first two books and asked for more. The keeper acquiesced, and showed her to a quiet corner for her studies. Latera settled herself at a table and Sarfek brought out fragrant cups of tea.

"Thank you," Latera said. She fumbled with the handle; she just couldn't train her fingers around those dainty loops. Latera noticed that Sarfek also had difficulty.

"Where *ahm'ri* is spoken, they drink tea from bowls," he said. "I find it much more civilized."

"Have you been to these lands, master keeper?"

"Oh, yes. In the north there are areas that still follow the old ways."

Latera's heart fell, and she returned her attention to the book before her. It was a text on Parthian history, and the rulers before Asherah. She made sure to bring it back to her rooms, since she was far more interested in Parthalan's history than Gannera's.

Chapter Fifty-Four

At times Latera thought Gannok would never go home, but the two seasons of his stay finally came to an end, and grand feast was to be prepared in honor of the prince. Instead of helping with the preparations, Latera and Wren spent the day in the library; if Latera had it her way she would have remained in the library until Gannok left the castle once and for all, but she could endure one more night with him.

"One more night, then I will never see him again," Latera muttered as she turned a page.

"What was that?" Wren asked.

"Just talking to myself," Latera replied. "Let's say goodbye to Sarfek, and then we can get ready for this night of boredom." As they bid good day to the keeper, Quill burst through the doorway.

"My lady," Quill shouted. "I've finally found what you've been searching for." He babbled on, which Latera knew only happened when he'd found something noteworthy. Wren slipped away while Latera waited for Quill to take a breath and compose himself, then she asked him what exactly he had discovered.

"I've found mention of your *deva'shi*," he said. "It's written in an ancient text, and the language is archaic, but it has everything you need. I've set it aside in the scriptorium for you."

"I cannot see it now," she said. "I must attend this banquet, but I'll meet you as soon as I can slip away."

"I will be waiting for you," Quill said, and he left the library.

Latera flopped down onto the nearest chair. "How does he not drop from exhaustion?" she muttered. Sarfek appeared at her side with a bowl of tea.

"Many thanks," she said, as she accepted the bowl. "Master keeper, do you know of a thing called *deva'shi*?"

"I'm afraid not, my lady," he replied. "If it's not within these walls, then I know nothing of it." Latera took in the vast expanse of shelves, and smiled at him over the edge of the bowl.

"Then you have a great deal of knowledge, indeed." She sipped her tea. "The tea is strong today."

"Yes, I brewed it that way," he said. "That feast will last until the small hours of the night, and you'll need your stamina. I can brew another batch if it's not to your liking."

"It's fine." Latera took another sip. "Thank you. You're very kind to me"

"I'm merely an old man performing my duties."

"No, you're more than that. Much more."

****

Later that evening, Latera stepped into the hall clad in a dark purple gown in honor of the one Aeolmar had destroyed in Rael, and observed the carefully regulated customs that surrounded a human banquet. She normally found such formalities absurd, but that night she was grateful for every detail, for it meant that as an unmarried woman she could only interact with her female relations, thus keeping her far from Gannok.

Once the dinner ended the restrictions were lessened, and several men asked Latera to dance. She politely declined each and every one of them. Eventually, Ladyslava had enough of Latera's behavior and led her to a quiet corner.

"You haven't participated in a single dance," Ladyslava said as they sat. "This does not please the king."

"He's not pleased with anything I do."

"Maybe you could dance with one or two people," Ladyslava suggested.

"I've only ever danced with one man, kissed one man…loved one man," Latera said. "I'm not looking to add to those numbers. Any of those numbers." Ladyslava dropped her gaze, and clenched her hands in her lap. "Mother, surely you know how I feel."

"Of course I do. I was fifteen when I married the king."

"Was he the king when you were married?"

"He was newly crowned. As you know, when my family was exiled all of our allies turned us away, but Gannera took us in. Since I have more royal blood than your father we were betrothed, to lend more credibility to Harold's children. To you," she added.

Latera felt that she finally understood her mother's indulgent smiles when she spoke of Aeolmar; her parents' marriage was one of convenience, not love. Before Latera could ask if her mother had grown to love her husband, Wren entered the hall. Latera waved her over, but Ladyslava grabbed her hand.

"You spend too much time with that girl," she hissed. "I'll find someone more appropriate to attend you."

"Why do you hate her so?" Latera countered, then she saw that Wren was shaking. Latera led her to the courtyard, and asked what had happened.

"Quill is dead," she cried, bursting into tears. She threw herself into Latera's arms, wailing against her shoulder. "There's a knife in his back, stuck through to the table. His eyes are still open…"

"Have you told anyone else?" Latera asked.

"No," she sniffed.

"Come. Let's speak to the queen," Latera said. They reentered the hall, and found Ladyslava.

"I must speak with you," Latera whispered, "alone."

"We cannot leave," she whispered. "Harold will be furious with us."

"This is bigger than the king, bigger than Gannera." Latera turned to leave and the room moved with her. She grabbed the back of a chair as Wren rushed to her side.

"What's wrong?" the queen demanded.

"I haven't eaten today, I'm just a little weak," Latera replied, knowing full well that it wasn't hunger that affected her. "May we go to your rooms?"

"Yes, may the gods help us all," Ladyslava muttered. Latera got herself out of the hall without collapsing, and once inside the queen's chambers she sank into the nearest chair. Ladyslava puttered about, saying that she would send for food and drink, when Latera spoke.

"The scribe, Quill, is dead," Latera said, then Wren told the queen what she had seen.

"Why were you seeking Quill?" Ladyslava asked.

"He was researching something called the *deva'shi*." Ladyslava flinched at the word. "You've heard of it?"

"I have."

Of all things Latera had expected to learn in Gannera, that her mother had knowledge of a legendary demon champion was not one of them. "Well, what is it? Who is it? Where does it come from?"

Ladyslava went to a cabinet and retrieved a book. "Everything you need to know is here. Please, don't hate me."

Latera stared at her mother, then she opened the book.

It was the story of Elvasla.

Elvasla and her mate, Tarac, had driven Ehkron from their homeland of Thurnda, and tracked the demon through the underworld to the mortal realm. Elvasla rallied the northern elves against the *mordeth-gall*, and slew Ehkron on the battlefield, but her own death came a moment later. After his mate's death, Tarac ruled the land with his and Elvasla's children, and gave the region his name. On the last page of the tome was a family tree, which confirmed that the royal family of Tarac was directly descended from Elvasla and Tarac. A scribe's lovely hand had detailed the family history, right down to Ladyslava.

Latera closed the book, her thoughts whirling. "Are you an elf?"

"Nearly full-blooded," Ladyslava replied. "Your father is, too. In times past all royalty was descended from the ancient elf tribes, but only us northerners have pure elf blood. That's why lineage is so important in a royal match."

"Why are elves always in the north?" Latera wondered.

"It's not the north that attracts us, but the mountains," Ladyslava replied. "Our race is of the earth and stone, and we find comfort in such places."

"But your ears and eyes..." Latera's voice trailed off, for Ladyslava's small eyes and round ears made her look as human as any Ganneran.

"The mortal realm dampens the characteristics of magic. While you were in Parthalan, your true nature was revealed."

Aeolmar always knew I wasn't completely human, which is why he was so confident when he offered me his immortality...

"Am I immortal?" Latera asked.

"In Parthalan you are," Ladyslava replied. "In the mortal realm, no one really knows. We tend to be killed, rather than die of old age."

Latera leaned her head against the back of the chair. Aeolmar had been, right, she could—no, she will—be bound to him. *If I ever manage to find my way across this accursed veil, that is.*

"Does the king know about Elvasla?"

"He knows of the legend, but I doubt he suspects the truth of the matter. When my family was exiled it was because Asgeloth had returned. My mother had the look of Elvasla, and she rode out to face him. After he killed her the people of Tarac revolted, and we were cast out."

"What do you mean, the look of Elvasla?" Latera asked. Ladyslava opened the book to a portrait of the elfin queen. Elvasla had striking sky blue eyes, pale skin, and red curls that tumbled over her shoulders like a waterfall. Latera may as well have looked into a mirror. Below the portrait was the word *deva'shi*.

"*Deva'shi*," Latera said. "It's an elfin word."

Ladyslava nodded. "Yes. It means killer of demons."

"They call me Demon-killer," Latera said. "When I was sixteen, Aeolmar and I were attacked by three demons. I'd never so much as touched a sword, yet I took his and killed them as easily as if I'd trained for years. Since that day, I've been called Demon-killer."

"That's the blood of Elvasla. She is strong within you. The legend says it will be a first born of her line to defeat Asgeloth."

"Was your mother first born?"

"No, but she had red hair and blue eyes. When Asgeloth attacked she was convinced that she was the *deva'shi*, and rode out to her death."

In that moment, everything Latera had learned came together. She understood the oracle's words, the priestesses' veiled clues, the strange demon attacks that had followed her across Parthalan... She understood everything, and it all centered on one truth.

"I am the *deva'shi*," Latera proclaimed. "I am what Asgeloth fears."

"I shouldn't have told you," Ladyslava said.

"You should have told me long ago," Latera said. "Why didn't you?"

"You'd like to know why I didn't want my daughter engaging the demon king in battle? I wanted to spare you, and spare myself the pain of another I loved being killed!" Her voice choked on the last, and she covered her face with her hands. Latera rose to embrace her, and fell to the floor instead.

Chapter Fifty-Five

Latera speaks

*I*t was Midwinter Day, and the ball commemorating Asherah's ascension to the throne was underway. I loved the formal affairs, with the beautiful dresses and wonderful music. For the celebration I'd chosen a gown of deep green with gold embroidery, and emerald-encrusted gold slippers. I stood on the balcony high above the rest, and watched the dancers spin and twirl like petals on the wind.

While I enjoyed watching the festivities, I only danced if Asherah requested it, and she hadn't done so in many winters. Despite my pointed ears and eyes, everyone knew I was only a mortal girl. Others whispered behind my back, wondering what right I had to be in the court of the Faerie Queen. Even after the many years I'd served Parthalan, I remained an outcast.

I heard footsteps behind me. I turned around and saw Aeolmar, the First Hunter, step onto the balcony. He was wearing a black silk tunic with blue embroidery that matched his eyes, black trousers, and black boots. His long chestnut hair was pulled back, and his skin glowed in the candlelight. As always, he was beautiful.

"Why are you hiding up here?" he asked.

"I'm not hiding!" I hadn't meant to snap at him, but he was confused rather than offended. "The others stare at me, and I don't like it."

"They stare because when you're in a room, it's foolish to look elsewhere," he said, and my face heated. "Or, it's possible that your reputation as Latera Demon-killer has spread far and wide, and they're *frightened of stepping on your toes." I laughed, for surely he was as kind as he was handsome. "You don't want to dance? Don't you enjoy it?"*

I stared at my sparkling slippers. "I'm content to watch from above."

Aeolmar bowed, and extended his hand. "Then do me the honor of dancing with me here, away from the others." When I didn't move, he added. "Please. I promise I won't stare."

I accepted his hand, and Aeolmar led me in a graceful circuit of the balcony. In the past men had only asked me to dance to gain Asherah's favor, but that wasn't the case tonight since Aeolmar far outranked me. For the first time a man wanted to dance with me, plain Latera.

When the music paused Aeolmar did not release me. A new song began, and he again led me in our private dance. We spun and twirled, only stopping when the musicians put down their instruments at the end of the evening.

Aeolmar gathered me close and murmured, "Thank you, beautiful girl." He bowed and left me, alone again on the balcony.

I watched until he disappeared beyond the edge of the torchlight, then I followed him into the darkness. The corridor held many twists and turns, unlike any I'd ever before seen in Teg'urnan. After a time, I saw a golden glow ahead. I stepped into the scribe's chamber, and screamed.

There was a body on the table, a sword thrust into its back. I couldn't see the victim's face, but their long brown hair was matted with blood. I reached out to the lifeless form...

***

My fever dream broke, jerking me back to reality. I lay still for a moment, trying to slow my breathing, and realized that this poison was different than what I'd gotten by way of the blood burn. The burn's poison had plunged me into the deep sleep of the dead, whereas this concoction dragged me in and out of nightmares.

Gods. I never thought I'd prefer a blood burn.

When my breathing calmed I opened my eyes, but the fever had left my vision blurry. I barely made out a figure sitting next to my bed. Assuming I'd been brought to the healer's ward and my beloved watched over me, I smiled. My gaze focused on the far wall, which wasn't the smooth gray of Teg'urnan but a polished brown.

Didn't the ward's cots have curtains? *My eyes adjusted further, and while the seated figure remained blurry, I saw the figure's blond hair.*

"Alia?" *I asked.*

"It's me, Gannok." *He moved closer, and I smelled his sour breath.* "I'm so glad you're awake."

My senses snapped to life, and I felt his clammy hand holding mine. I snatched my hand away, and thrust it under the bedclothes. I scanned the room, and learned to my utter, nauseating horror that I was alone with Gannok.

"How long have you been here?" *I demanded.*

"You've been ill for many days. I was so worried," *he said, reaching out as if to stroke my cheek. I grabbed his wrist and glared at him, and used my anger's heat to clear my mind.*

"You have no right to touch me," *I said.* "Get out."

"I will have the right, that and more," *he said.* "If you hadn't taken ill, I would have announced our betrothal at the feast. While I've agreed to wait until you're well, make no mistake, Lady Latera, you will be my wife." *He made no move to leave, so I squeezed his wrist until I felt his bones grind. I wondered if I could make him weep.*

"My mate will kill you if you touch me, if I don't kill you first." *The blood rose in my face as my hatred of Gannok welled up, threatening to overflow.* "Leave."

I dropped his wrist as if it was a taint, and jerked my chin toward the door. Thank the gods Wren burst into the room, her arms laden with herbs and teas and other things for the ill. She announced that she needed privacy to care for me, and shooed the prince from my chamber.

"I'm so sorry, I didn't want you to wake up with that buffoon at your bedside," she said. "I only left for a moment. He's been here every day, talking to you, babbling on about how you'll be a wonderful wife..."

"I don't know if he's foolish or wicked," I said, slumping back against the pillows. "How long have I been ill?"

"Four days," she replied. "No one knew what was wrong."

"Poison." I rubbed my eyes; whomever wanted the deva'shi removed from Parthalan also didn't want me alive in Gannera. "I've been poisoned before. I remember the feeling well."

"But who would have done such a thing?" asked Wren.

"Whoever murdered Quill, I imagine." I regarded Wren's innocent face, and asked her something horrible. "Do you remember anything? About his body, or the room?"

Her lower lip quivered, but she answered anyway. "I remember the knife in his back. I tried turning him over but it was all the way through, holding him to the table. I looked around for whatever he'd wanted to show you, but everything was so bloody..." her voice trailed off, and I squeezed her hand.

"Whoever did it probably took what Quill found," I said. "Let's go to the scriptorium, see what we can learn."

"Absolutely not," Wren said. "You're as pale as death."

"I am a huntress—"

"You'll be a dead huntress if you don't build up your strength first."

I set my feet on the floor, determined to go the scriptorium with or without Wren. I stood, and promptly fell to back to the bed.

"There, there," Wren said as she helped me sit up. "Let's get some soup in you."

Wren sent for the soup, and after it arrived we sat before the hearth and ate. The warmth of both the fire and broth made me feel much better than I was ever going to admit. When we finished our meal I read aloud from the volume on Parthian history. Wren took over when the words got too blurry for me, and her delight at reading about past kings and queens began lightening my foul mood. After a time, she reached a section about Asherah.

"Is this your queen?" Wren asked.

"Yes, that's Asherah the Ruthless."

"Ruthless, is she? We'll see about that."

Wren read on, and I closed my eyes and imagined a young Asherah and Torim as they overthrew the old king. Wren got to a passage concerning Harek, which made mention of his brother dying a few centuries after the Battle for Teg'urnan.

"Read that again," I cried, startling poor Wren. She did, and my mind raced back to the oracle's words: Your way home lays with he who brought you here, not the traitor but his brother. You will know him as he is also marked by the *mordeth-gall*. Learn of the *deva'shi*. You are the key.

I'd already determined that Harek was the traitor, but who could his brother be? Was he here, in Gannera? I looked down at the bowl of tea in my hands, and the last piece fell into place.

"Do they name Harek's brother?" I asked.

Wren scanned the pages. "Sarfek. He was a sorcerer called Sarfek." The book slipped from Wren's grasp. "You don't think...oh, gods."

"We must go to the queen," I said. This time, Wren did not object.

We went to my mother's chambers as quickly as my wobbly legs would carry me, and told her everything we learned, from the oracle's words to my suspicions of Sarfek. I insisted that his tea was the vehicle for my poison, and my mother revealed that the healers had already suspected poison as the reason for my collapse.

"*Bear in mind,*" *Mother continued,* "*that while I do believe you, we have no proof to bring before the king.*"

"*There must be evidence within Sarfek's rooms,*" *I said.* "*The oracle said that the traitor would be marked by Asgeloth. Maybe Sarfek has also been marked.*" *I remembered that my mother's family had been dealing with demons in the mortal realm for almost as long as Parthalan had.* "*What is the penalty for such a mark?*"

"*Death by beheading,*" *Mother said.*

I walked to the window, and looked west. "*Does Sarfek ever leave the castle?*"

"*Why would he, he is the keeper,*" *Mother began, when Wren stepped forward. Mother glared at her, but I motioned for her to speak.*

"*He regularly leaves to collect the tax ledgers from the surrounding lords,*" *she offered.* "*It's his responsibility to keep them organized in the library.*"

"*Can you find out when he will leave again?*" *I asked. Wren nodded, and after she left I faced my mother.* "*Forgive me, but I must know what she's done to warrant such hatred.*"

Mother sighed. "*She's the king's daughter.*"

I lost what was left of my balance and landed on the window seat. "*Wren is my sister?*"

"*Half-sister,*" *Mother clarified.* "*Her mother was a scullion the king took a fancy too. He was crowned before Wren was born, but he's never denied that she's his; if you see the two of them together it's plain how alike they are. Harold claims he never loved her mother, but who knows.*"

"*What became of her mother?*"

"*She hung herself on my wedding day, and Wren has lived with the servants ever since.*"

"*Then Wren is first born and the king's heir, not me?*"

"The heir is first born of the king and his wife, which Wren is not. You're still the heir." She smiled weakly. *"Would you try to pass her on to Gannok?"*

"I like her too much for that. Does Wren know?"

"I don't know. I suspect she views Harold as nothing more than a kind old man who's good to his servants."

Wren returned and informed us that Sarfek was due to collect the ledgers in three sennights. I nodded, too stunned by this most recent revelation to offer anything more. I hoped no other surprises were awaiting me.

Mother advised the king that I remained ill, and would stay in my chambers with only Wren attending me. My plan was to give Sarfek the impression that his poison had done me in, and had the added benefit of keeping Gannok away from me. Hopefully the prince would give up on finding a wife, and go home.

Twenty-one endless days passed before Sarfek left to collect his ledgers. Wren and I watched his departure from the queen's balcony. After he was out of sight, we entered his rooms. The keeper was so arrogant he hadn't even locked his door.

The keeper's chamber looked much like the scribe's room, with many scrolls and books stacked in precarious heaps. Wren poked through a chest near the door, and found a tin of tea. She pried it open and an acrid stench wafted out; there was the poison he'd given me. We continued our search, yet found nothing but patched clothes and moldy parchments.

Eventually, we came across a cabinet hidden under mounds of blankets. It was locked, the only lock in a room that hadn't even had a locked door. Since lock picking wasn't a skill Wren or I were familiar with, I called fire and burned away the wood around the metal clasp. The interior held a single volume bound in pale leather; as my fingers brushed the covering, I saw the face of the one whose skin had been stolen.

Gods, the binding was human flesh. Hiding my revulsion from Wren, I opened the book and was confronted by horrible yet familiar characters.

"How many languages are there?" Wren asked, being that these symbols weren't ahm'ri. *"Do you know what it says?"*

"Yes. This is written in the demon tongue."

We left the chamber, having found more than enough evidence of Sarfek's true nature. While we walked to the queen's chamber, I flipped through the flesh-bound pages and found the spell to create beasts. Disgusted, I turned to another page, and halted. Staring up at me was the spell to move between realms. I'd found my way home.

The spell said that a talisman was used to pierce the veil, coupled with a certain herb with an odd, unfamiliar name. I was still puzzling out the name of the herb when we reached the queen's chamber.

"We must go to Harold," Mother said, after learning what we'd discovered, and she sent one of her attendants on to set up an audience with the king. While we waited I determined that the herb I needed was called grass-of-the-plain, a name I hadn't heard in Gannera or Parthalan. As we traversed the short distance to the king's chamber I listed all the plants I knew, saying their names first in feh'lah *and then* ahm'ri, *hoping that the name just translated oddly. It didn't.*

We found the king seated behind his immense desk. When he saw his wife and his two most troublesome daughters standing before him he demanded to know what was happening. I'd forgotten about my feigned illness; if his dark expression was any indicator, his next words would cast me from his sight, permanently. So, I spoke first.

"The keeper, Sarfek, is a traitor," I began. "He is in league with Asgeloth, and he is the one who twice moved me between realms." I placed the book of demon spells before Father. He eyed the strange covering, but didn't touch it.

"You present a book as proof of these allegations?" he asked. I turned to the spell for piercing the veil.

"Have you seen these symbols before?" I demanded. He remained silent, his brow furrowed. Undaunted, I continued, "This is the demon tongue, the language of the mordeth-gall. Why would an innocent man in service to the king hide a demonic spellbook in his chambers?" Father glared at me, then Wren stepped forward with the tea tin.

"My lord, he also poisoned Latera," she said. "She was not ill these past days, but sick with poison. We found this in his room." Wren set the tin next to the tome, and backed away.

"I believe Sarfek has been marked by Asgeloth," I said. "Sarfek is the one who moved me to Parthalan, and then back to Gannera, and we have the tea which proves it is he who poisoned me. It's Asgeloth's plan to kill me, and Elia, Jannei, and Sasha."

"What?" he roared, rising so fast his chair toppled over. "Why would the mordeth-gall be interested in my children?"

"We're the descendants of Elvasla," I began, when Mother touched my elbow.

"I will explain," she said, and she led the king to his private rooms. They remained inside for some time, their voices rising and falling as they fought, reconciled, and fought again. When they finally emerged their faces were red, and Mother was wiping away tears. Wren and I rose, and waited for the king's decision.

"I will have Sarfek apprehended," he stated, "and brought back for questioning. If he is so marked, he will die."

"He cannot be killed before I learn what the talisman is," I said. "And this herb, this grass-of-the-plain. I need it to return to Parthalan."

"You really believe you are this deva'shi?" he asked.

"I am the Demon-killer," I proclaimed, "and I have sworn an oath to defend Parthalan. I will fulfill my duty." I raised my chin and met his gaze. I would not be denied the opportunity to make good on my oaths, both to myself and the oracle. Asherah must not fall.

His gaze softened, and he became the kind father of my memories. "You make me wish I hadn't instilled such a sense honor in you," he said, then he took my mother's hand. "Come, Laddy, let's inform the sentinels that we've a rogue librarian to catch." With that, they left to raise the guard.

While my parents went to the royal guard, Wren and I walked to the pond where this had all begun thirteen summers ago. The sun was warm on my face, and the spell to pierce the veil was ringing in my ears. The day had exhausted both Wren and I, and we stretched out in the tall grass. I studied Wren's features, her pale blue eyes and golden curls, and asked the question.

"Do you know who your father is?"

"Yes," she replied. "I also know that my mother died because the king didn't want her, just like he doesn't want me." I put my arms around her, squeezing her with all my might.

"It wasn't that he didn't want you, or your mother," I said. "These royal matters are very complicated. Look at how he's trying to marry me off, all because of an agreement he made before I was ever born." I wondered if Father had wanted a life with Wren's mother, but his own father forbade it. "Would you like me to speak to him?" She shook her head, her voice lost to sobs.

After a time her shoulders relaxed, and we returned to naming every plant we knew. We called out fanciful names in both feh'lah *and* ahm'ri, *our laughter dancing across the pond.*

The sun dipped low in the sky, and Wren and I were grateful for the calm night. I recited the words of the veil spell aloud in both languages; I would not speak the demon tongue unless there were no other options, and even then I'd find a way around it. As I stretched the weariness from my limbs, I saw the shimmer of magic at my belt.

It was my dagger.

"The dagger is the talisman," I yelled loud enough to startle a dozing Wren. It made perfect sense; when I'd arrived in the hag's cottage, the dagger was next to me on the floor, and it was in my hand when I was taken from Asherah's chamber. I went over the wording of the spell in my mind; the talisman could be in either realm, either to pull the intended victim through, or to slice open the veil.

I felt like an utter fool. My way home had been at my side all along.

"Are you sure?" Wren asked. I nodded, and as we got to our feet the scent of the crushed meadow hay wafted up to my nose. It smelled so familiar, but I brushed it off as a memory from my youth—then I stopped, since I was standing where I'd first been taken.

I grabbed a handful of grass and ran to my chamber, Wren following close behind. I burst through the door and opened the top drawer, and retrieved the cloth Harek had given me over a year ago. Precious bits of herbs were folded within, and I placed them next to the fresh grass. My heart sang for they were identical, save that one was newly picked, and the other dry and crumbling.

Meadow hay. Grass-of-the-plain was meadow hay.

***

After all the time that had passed since my return to Gannera, the few days while we waited for Sarfek's capture felt longer yet. At noon on the third day guards marched Sarfek, bound in chains, into the castle and forced him to his knees before the royal seat.

"I've learned that you are marked by evil, master keeper," said the king, voice echoing through the hall. I waited for his response, hidden behind the throne with my swords drawn.

"I'm but an old man," Sarfek protested. "I've harmed no one."

The king nodded, and a guard ripped open Sarfek's tunic and exposed his chest. The assemblage gasped as Asgeloth's mark was revealed. It was burned into Sarfek's flesh above his heart, a handprint with a man's fingers and a cloven palm.

"For your association with the demon lord, and for the kidnapping and poisoning of my daughter, I condemn you to death," the king declared. Sarfek laughed, then his metal chains fell away as if they were gossamer. The guards leapt upon him but Sarfek's laugh became a roar as he cut them down, sorcerer's fire dancing upon his fingertips.

"You think you can hold me?" he shouted, the stench of burning flesh thick. "I walk between worlds. Your chains cannot bind me!" A guard crept up behind him, but Sarfek spun around and grabbed his throat. "No mortal can harm me," he bellowed, as the color drained from the guard's face.

I leapt from the dais, bounding over the fallen guards as I aimed my swords. Sarfek tossed the guard aside and reached for me, but I thrust my sword into his neck. His body toppled over, and I remembered the old tales, gruesome ones that said a sorcerer wasn't truly dead until his head left his body. I raised my other sword, and took care of it.

"And now you're done," I said. I'd thought it would be difficult to kill him, but for all his magic Sarfek was just a man, and as vulnerable as any man was to sharpened steel.

I stood and looked upon the keeper's body; the mark of the demon had confirmed all my suspicions about him and the Prelate. My gut clenched, for every moment that Asherah remained unaware of Harek's treachery put her a moment closer to death.

I ripped a cloak from a guard's body and wrapped it around Sarfek's head. Wren handed me a satchel containing the tomes of demon spells, and Elvasla's legend. To it, I added the head.

"*I must go to Parthalan,*" *I said to my parents. "I'll return once Asgeloth has fallen." I took Wren's hand and turned to leave, but the king grabbed my elbow.*

"*What if he doesn't fall?*" *he demanded.*

"*I won't fail,*" *I replied, holding his gaze as a warrior would. "I can't." He embraced me, only releasing me to go to my mother's arms. When I broke free, Wren and I left the chaos of the castle and ran to the meadow.*

We reached the pond, and stopped near the water's edge where I'd first been taken. The spellbook explained that once the veil had been pierced a tear would always remain in that location, thus making travel between realms easier. Since I'd never attempted anything like this before, I needed all the help I could get. I grabbed handfuls of meadow hay, then I threw my arms around my sister.

"*I will return,*" *I promised. Wren nodded around her tears, and stepped back. I wound the meadow hay around my wrist and turned to the water, and recited the spell. I felt the dagger shimmer, the magic heating it until it burnt me.*

For the third time, I was gone.

Chapter Fifty-Six

Latera's third journey between worlds was much calmer than the first two. Instead being tossed about by cruel winds and hearing blood-curdling shrieks from the darkness, she floated as if on a cloud. When gray shapes formed in the mist she visualized Teg'urnan, and willed herself toward the palace. The shapes became the Hill of Torim, so Latera concentrated on the oak at its crest. When she could see the oak's gnarled branches, she stepped forward and fell.

And fell.

She hit the ground and rolled to her side, gasping for breath. Latera rubbed her eyes, and looked at the ancient tree. She touched the bark, grateful and so elated o be home she feared she would weep, and thanked the oak for being her guidepost. Then she looked toward Teg'urnan, and her happiness turned to dread. Every hunter and soldier in Parthalan was battling the largest demon horde she had ever seen. Worse, Asherah's forces were losing ground.

Latera leapt to her feet, and staggered as pain bloomed across her right foot. She bent to examine her foot but the noise of battle distracted her. She closed her mind to the dull ache, and ran headlong into the fray.

At the battle's edge Latera saw the Prelate astride a horse. *Gods, he's a fool as well as a traitor. Any* nuvi *will tell you that a horse is the worst liability against a demon.*

Harek saw Latera, and yelled something that was lost to the din of battle. Five demons appeared before Latera. She drew her sword and slashed at them, moving on before she knew if they lived or perished. She had to find Aeolmar, and nothing would stand in her way. Then, she fell again.

Latera was both annoyed and embarrassed, being that she'd stumbled into Lura, Kemen's lovemate from the Eastern contingent. "Come on," Latera said, "I'll help you up." When Lura said nothing Latera assumed she was sulking, then Latera touched her cold hand.

I didn't knock her down; I tripped over her body. She and Lura and never been friends; in fact, Latera could hardly stand the border huntress. Still, Latera mumbled a prayer over Lura before she scrambled to her feet.

Where are the hunters? Latera searched the conflict, and heard great bellowing war cry. She turned and saw Bron bury his axe in a beast's skull, oblivious to the demon that crept up behind him.

Latera ran toward them, and used the beast's body to vault over Bron and plunge her sword into the demon that was rearing to strike. She braced herself for another hard landing, only to be caught in Bron's massive arms.

"Little one," he rumbled, "where have you been?"

"Struggling to return," she replied. "Where's Aeolmar?" Bron frowned, and set her on her feet.

"You cannot approach him. No one can. He was already half crazed with losing you, and this war has made him truly mad."

"I need him," Latera cried. When Bron wouldn't look at her, she grabbed his shirt. "If he's crazed, he will remain so until he is with me, you know that well. Help me find him." Bron sighed, then he clambered atop the beast's corpse, scanning the plain. After a moment he jumped down and pointed toward his left.

"There. Be cautious, little one," Bron warned.

Latera nodded, and said, "Stay clear of the Prelate, and the *con'dehr*." Bron grunted, and Latera ran toward her mate.

Latera darted through the fight, evading rather than engaging despite how badly she wanted to fight. She cursed her small stature, hardly able to see around the bodies choking the field. Furious, she killed the demon in front of her just so she could see around his stinking hide, and almost dropped her swords.

Aeolmar was only a few paces in front of her.

***

Aeolmar stalked across the battlefield, gore and mud and Cydia knew what else soaking his jerkin and boots. Lesser demons scattered before him, and he was content to ignore them. Aeolmar had no interest in lessers. His quarry was the *mordeth-gall* himself.

Aeolmar sensed someone approaching him from behind, and without looking turned and struck with a great arching swing. He heard the clang of steel, and realized he'd been blocked. He turned, and saw that his blade had been caught by two smaller ones.

"I'd take your helm, if you were wearing one."

Aeolmar's gaze dipped lower, and he saw the red curls and crystal blue eyes of his mate. "Are you real?" he asked, lowering his sword. He out reached to her, but held back. If this was another dream sent only to taunt him, he truly would go mad.

Latera took his hand and pressed it to her cheek. He grasped a stray curl, feeling it between his thumb and forefinger.

Gods.

She's real.

She's real she's real she's real

Aeolmar dropped to his knees and wrapped his arms around Latera's waist.

"Beloved, I'm here," Latera said.

Aeolmar pulled her to her knees, his gaze moving over her eyes, lips, cheeks. Latera's brow pinched and she wiped his cheek, her fingers coming away bloody.

"Are you hurt?" she asked.

He glanced at her fingers. It wasn't his blood, so Aeolmar leaned forward and caught Latera's mouth with his. She tasted just the same, warm and sweet and his, and Aeolmar let go of his doubts. His mate was returned to him.

He moved so they were sitting against a boulder, out of view of other demons and fae alike. The battle raged on, but having Latera in his arms was more important to him than all of Parthalan.

"Where were you?" he asked. "No, that's not what I want to say. I love you. You are my beloved." He shook his head. "I was mad with fear I'd never be able to tell you I love you again."

Latera brought his face to hers. "Beloved, I'm sorry it's taken me so long to return to you," she said against his lips. "Only my love for you kept me alive this year."

"A year?" he repeated. "It's been little more than a season."

Latera's brow wrinkled. "I was in Gannera well over four seasons. I was taken by the same man who kidnapped me when I was ten."

"I'll kill him," Aeolmar declared.

"I already have. Aeolmar, beloved, I have so many things to tell you about this war and what's really happening here, but what I must tell you first is selfish, and only for us." Latera grasped his hand and held it against her breast. "You were right."

"Right about what?"

"About how you knew I wasn't entirely mortal, about how you saw magic on me, about everything." Latera smiled, and grasped his hands. "I'm an elf."

He smiled. "Elf or not, you're my Latera."

"Always, my Aeolmar."

"I was dead while you were gone. Now you've returned to me, and I have a soul again." Aeolmar loosened his hands from hers, and gathered her close. "What's in here?" he asked, feeling the odd-shaped lumps in her satchel.

"A severed head and two books."

"Whose head?"

Latera grabbed his chin. "There is a traitor close to Asherah!"

"Who?" Aeolmar demanded.

"Harek," Latera hissed, "he's in with Asgeloth."

"I knew I hated him for a reason." Latera moved to rise, but Aeolmar held her fast.

"Another moment, then we'll find the queen. I can't let go of you just yet." Latera smiled, then she tugged open his collar and laid her cheek against his skin.

"Beloved, I've missed you so," Latera said. Aeolmar dragged her flat against his chest, her arms and legs curled around him. He buried his face in her hair, his tears wetting her curls. The last he wept was the day Latera told him she was going to the Eastern Border; now, he wept over her return.

After an entirely too short interlude, Aeolmar stood and helped Latera to her feet. Latera limped heavily, and he grabbed her.

"You're hurt," he said.

"I'm fine. I can walk, and run if I have to." Aeolmar tried lifting her, but she pushed him away. "You will not carry me through a battle, you'll get both of us killed!" He would have argued, but he realized something about her speech.

"You're speaking *ahm'ri*!"

"I had to learn it to find my way back."

"Beautiful girl, you've amazed me once again."

"It was nothing." She shifted her weight, and Aeolmar tried lifting her. "Mar, I can walk. I'm going to walk, and that's final."

"You will not leave my sight."

"Never again."

When they stepped onto the field, they saw the demons retreating. "Odd," Aeolmar said. "Why would they fall back when they had the upper hand?"

"Harek saw me," Latera muttered. "I imagined I spoiled his plans."

Aeolmar placed his hand on Latera's back, guiding her through the carnage. "Good. Let's spoil them further."

As they crossed the field hunters and *nuvi* alike stared at Latera. Neither she nor Aeolmar offered an explanation for her return as they sought the queen. They found Asherah issuing orders before Teg'urnan's gates. Asherah fell silent as Latera limped forward and grabbed her hands.

"My lady," Latera began, "I must speak with you, alone. There is a traitor!"

"Latera?" Asherah removed her helm and peered into Latera's face. "Where have you been?"

"I will explain everything."

"All right." The queen nodded and looked toward Finlay; he was never far from his mate. "I'm trusting you on this."

"I know. Thank you." Latera would have said more, but Finlay ran to her and wrapped his arms around her, lifting her off her feet.

"Sweetheart," he said. "No more disappearing acts."

"I'm sorry, I didn't mean for any of this." Her voice caught in her throat, and Finlay set her on her feet. Asherah glanced between them, then frowned at the battle.

"Finlay, we must retreat for a moment,' she said. "You have command. Instruct the soldiers to deal with what's left of the enemy, and meet us inside." The Second Hunter nodded as Asherah turned away, beckoning Aeolmar and Latera to follow her.

"Wait," Latera said, her hand on Finlay's arm. "Lura...she's gone."

Finlay frowned. "Where?"

"Toward the Hill of Torim, near the royal road."

Finlay nodded. "I'll get her."

Latera followed Aeolmar and Asherah, the pain in her foot causing her to lag far behind. Aeolmar glanced over his shoulder as Latera stumbled. Without a word he turned and scooped her into his arms. She didn't protest being carried, which explained better than words how much pain she was really in.

They entered in Asherah's private room, and Aeolmar set Latera on her feet, only to steady her when she wobbled. He settled her on a chair as the queen stood waiting.

"You have my ear, huntress," Asherah said. "Who is this traitor? Is it a hunter?"

"It's Harek," Latera replied. "He's working with Asgeloth."

Asherah's gaze went cold, and she turned to Aeolmar. "Has she gone mad? Or is she herself the traitor?"

"Latera is not—"Aeolmar began.

"Mar." Latera squeezed Aeolmar's hand, then she addressed the queen. "It was Harek's brother, Sarfek, who moved me between realms."

"Sarfek is dead," Asherah said. "He's been dead for centuries."

"He's been dead less than a day." Latera pulled Sarfek's head from her satchel, and set it on top of Asherah's maps and charts. Asherah's face went as pale as her hair, and she reached toward the head.

"You've been lied to," Latera continued. "We've all been lied to, and not only about Sarfek. The *deva'shi* is not a champion for demons, but against them. It's the descendant of Elvasla, who was my ancestor. I am the *deva'shi*."

"You're descended from Elvasla who slew Ehkron," Asherah said, her eyes narrowed. "Why haven't you told me this before?"

"I didn't know. When I was taken I was sent back to the mortal realm, and there I learned the truth." Latera removed the blood-spattered books from her satchel, and opened one to the painting of Elvasla. "This is Elvasla, she who cursed Ehkron's line with her last breath."

Asherah glared at the image. "Even any of if this is true, how dare you call my Prelate a traitor? Have you any real proof, or just these stories?" Aeolmar again moved to defend Latera, and again Latera held him back.

"Harek bears Asgeloth's mark, as Sarfek did," Latera said. "I saw Sarfek's with my own eyes, a demon's handprint burnt over his heart." The queen removed her gloves, and threw them onto the table.

"How did you learn of such things in the mortal realm, while we in Parthalan were not aware?"

"Someone is watching over you, and told me much of what I now tell you."

"No one watches over me," the queen seethed, "certainly no human."

"I was told to tell you the name Hillel," Latera said. The queen sat heavily, and covered her face with her hands.

"How do you know that name?" Asherah asked. "No one living knows that name."

"There is a temple dedicated to you in Gannera, and I spoke with the oracle. She said it was the one name that would make you believe me."

"How did this oracle appear to you?"

"A faerie woman, with golden hair and brown eyes," Latera replied. "She looked a great deal like you."

"She was golden like the sun, and I as pale as the stars," Asherah murmured.

"Who?" Aeolmar demanded.

"Torim," Asherah replied, raising her head. "Your oracle must be my Torim, she whom I loved more than my life. Did she tell you who Hillel was?"

"No," Latera replied, "that wasn't for me to know."

"This oracle was in a temple?" Asherah asked, and Latera described the temple of Asherah the Deliverer, and of the priestesses who offered her guidance on the sole condition that she not let the queen fall. Lastly, Latera told her of the scrying pool, the terrible vision she had, and everything the oracle had said.

"She still loves you," Latera concluded. "She said she would die for you again, over and over until the end of time."

Asherah smiled. "Torim always was selfless to a fault." She raised her dark eyes to Latera's. "Forgive me, for not believing you."

"It's a hard thing to believe," Latera replied. "There is nothing to forgive."

Asherah stood, beckoning Aeolmar and Latera toward her receiving room. "Come. We must deal with this traitor."

In the receiving room they found not only the palace hunters, but those assigned to the outlying contingents and the *nuvi* assembled inside. An excited murmur erupted when they saw Latera. She nodded an acknowledgment, and sat beside Alia.

"Where in the nine realms have you been?" Alia demanded. "And how are you back here?"

"After," Latera whispered, "let the queen speak."

"My hunters," Asherah began, "there is a traitor in our midst." Whispers erupted in the chamber, and Asherah silenced them with a glare. "We believe it is the Prelate." Silence settled over the room, and Aeolmar sent Elkin to fetch Harek. After Elkin left, Aeolmar set Sarfek's head upon the table, his dead eyes staring at the hunters. When the Prelate entered the chamber and saw Sarfek's head, the color drained from his face.

"What trickery is this?" Harek growled. "What has befallen my brother?"

"I thought Sarfek died long ago," Asherah said. "You yourself informed me of such, crying on the floor as you recounted how sorcerers ambushed him in the west. Yet Latera took his head this very morning." Harek cast his gaze about the chamber, and found Latera.

"You killed my brother, you treacherous whore?" Harek lunged at Latera, his hands poised to throttle her, but Bron and Luth grabbed him by the arms. Aeolmar flung aside Harek's armored breastplate and ripped open his tunic, revealing the mark of the *mordeth-gall* above his heart. Hunter and *nuvi* alike leapt to their feet, calling out curses at the evil marking.

"Harek, why have you done this?" Asherah demanded. "Why have you betrayed your own people?"

"You made us weak," Harek said, then he turned his glare to Latera. "I will deliver you to the *mordeth-gall* myself for what you've done." Aeolmar grabbed Harek by his neck.

"Don't give me another reason to kill you," Aeolmar said. "Take him to a cell."

"The guards won't imprison the Prelate without the direct word of the queen," said Luth.

Asherah stepped forward and yanked the Prelate's ring from Harek's finger and handed it to Aeolmar. "First Hunter, you are now my Prelate as well. Take whomever you need with you, but imprison him. Question all of his captains, all the soldiers if you find it necessary, and imprison all of the *con'dehr*. Every last one of them is guilty, until I say otherwise."

Aeolmar looked at the ring in his hand, then at Latera. "Go, I'll be fine," Latera said.

"Innetha, Elkin," Aeolmar said, and the two hunters followed as Harek was removed. Finlay stepped up as well, but Aeolmar barred him.

"Stay with the queen," Aeolmar said to his second, "she needs you more than I." Asherah was already retreating to her chambers; after a nervous glance about the room Finlay followed. Aeolmar kissed Latera's forehead. "I'll be with you as soon as I'm able," he promised, then he and his hunters dragged away their burden.

Chapter Fifty-Seven

Latera Speaks

After Asherah dismissed the rest of the hunters, Alia helped me to my chamber, all the while asking me question after question. "I would tell you more," I said, being that I'd only given her the barest replies, "I'm just so...so..."

"Exhausted?" Alia supplied. "Overwhelmed? Injured?"

I grimaced. "Yes, all of those." We reached my door, which swung open for me. Apparently these door charms have long memories.

"Will you need help inside?" Alia asked.

"My foot's not all that bad," I said, leaning on the wall. "Thank you, for getting me here."

"It's what friends do." With that, Alia left and I hobbled inside my chamber.

As the door closed, I gazed around my chamber and finally let myself believe I was home. Everything was just as I remembered, with the doors to my balcony wide open, my bed piled high with cushions and furs; even the hanging lanterns were lit. As inviting as the balcony and bed were, what I truly desired was in the rear of the chamber. A bath.

No one had disconnected the plumbing during my absence, and before long hot water was pouring into the basin. I shed my gear and entered the bone-meltingly hot water, and stood under the spout, letting the water rinse away more than the dust of battle.

Thanks to the too-hot water my skin flushed bright pink, so I pulled myself out of the bath and sat on the edge. I held my sore foot underneath the hot water as I combed out my hair. I was grappling with a particularly stubborn knot when my door opened. Knowing it could be only one, I looked up and saw Aeolmar striding toward me.

"What happened with—" I began, but he kissed me silent.

"I only want to talk about you right now." Aeolmar caressed my cheek, then gave me a rueful smile. Before I could ask, he grabbed a sponge and dabbed at my face. "I'm a bit dirty," he said, indicating his filthy hands.

"I wouldn't care if you were covered in mud." I clutched his hand, and gaped at the amount of dirt that smeared onto my fingers. "Get in the bath, dirty man."

Aeolmar smiled that half smile of his, and it had just the same effect on me it always had. "All right."

He set about removing his gear. As the heavy leather fell to the floor I saw dried blood caked on him, and hoped most of it wasn't his. Aeolmar tossed the Prelate's ring onto the floor with the discarded garments, then he got into the water. He stood under the spout as I had, but I didn't like him standing clear across the basin.

"Let me wash you," I said, and he moved so I could reach him. I grabbed a fresh sponge, and cleaned the dirt from his face and neck. Once that was done I washed his hair, drawing the long strands through my fingers, loving the feel of my hands in his hair. When his hair was clean and rinsed, I turned him until his back faced me. Along with many layers of dirt, I found a gash that spanned his shoulder blades.

"This is not from today," I stated, gingerly touching the edge of the swollen wound. "Did you even have this cleaned?" I held out his arm, lathering each finger individually, working my way past his elbow and toward his shoulder. I washed him slowly, reacquainting myself with every muscle and sinew, and his wonderfully smooth skin. When I moved to his other arm, I asked, "Well? Are you going to answer me?"

"Without you, I just didn't care," he replied. I leaned forward and massaged his chest clean.

"I'll get you a healer tomorrow," I said, against his ear. "I'll order you to one if I have to."

Aeolmar turned around, and gave me his best attempt at a stern face. "You can't order me. You have no authority."

"I'll order you as your mate," I said, looking down into his beautiful blue eyes. He put his hand on my neck and drew me to him.

"My mate," he said, and his lips met mine. I pressed my forehead to his and smiled.

"My mate," I repeated, kissing him again. Aeolmar's other hand stroked my leg, then found its way around my hip and to the small of my back. He held me for a moment, his forehead pressed against mine. Then he pulled me off the edge and slid me down onto him.

I yelped and he hesitated for a moment, but only one. He held me under my hips as he climbed out of the water and laid me on the stone floor, and jerked one of the rugs under my back. Tears stung my eyes; so many nights I'd refused to let sleep claim me, despondent that I'd never see Aeolmar again, much less make love to him. I cried out as he pushed me off the cliff, his own leap coming a moment after. He rolled onto his back, keeping me against him as we floated back to the floor.

"Did I hurt you?" he asked, wiping my tears away.

"I was certain I'd never see you again," I said, lacing my fingers with his, "and I'm so happy I was wrong." I closed my eyes and my other hand tangled in his hair. I drifted off to sleep, startling awake when he shifted against the floor. Remembering his injury I sat up, pulling him along with me.

"Beloved, let me tend your wound." I stood, having forgotten about my own injury, and gasped in pain. Aeolmar scooped me up and deposited me on the bench. He touched a few points on my foot, his brow pinching when I flinched.

"It's your ankle that's broken, not your foot," he said.

"Oh, good," I said, thinking that one broken ankle bone was preferable to many broken foot bones.

"Beloved, this is a far more serious injury." He located some bandages, and set about binding my ankle. "You must have been in a great deal of pain. How were you able to run, and fight?"

"I had to reach you," I replied, for that was the only reason.

"I can't have you hurting yourself, not for me or anything. If you're ever hurt again, send someone and I'll come for you in an instant." Once he finished with my ankle, he dutifully turned around and I salved and bandaged the wound on his back; I must remember that threats of a healer can transform the fearsome First Hunter into a meek kitten. When I'd done all I could for the gash he brought me to bed, and tucked the furs around me.

"I don't need all these," I said. "I only need you." Aeolmar smiled and climbed under the furs. He nestled himself against me, tracing the silver chain at my throat.

"You still wear it," he said.

"I haven't removed it since you put it on me." I looked at his eyes, rimmed in red and swollen from lack of rest. "When was the last time you slept?"

"Sleep was impossible," he said. "Every time I shut my eyes I saw you being dragged away from me. Except for one dream..."

"When I was with you," I finished. "It wasn't a dream, but a gift from the oracle. From Torim."

"It's the greatest gift I've ever received," he said, stroking my shoulder. He tightened his arms around me, and I heard his weary bones creak. I glided my fingers across his neck, watching his eyes struggle to stay open.

"Rest now, beloved. I'm here, and I know their secrets. They can't take me from you again," I promised.

"I'll sleep later," he murmured. "For now, I just want to look at you." Aeolmar caressed my cheek and neck, his eyes never leaving mine until *he bent to kiss me. "I don't know if I want to start kissing your face and work my way to your toes, or the other way 'round." He brushed his lips over my eyes, my cheeks, but paused when he felt tears.*

I hid my face against his neck, and said, "When I was first taken, I hoped I was carrying your child. I thought that you would be drawn to her and find us. I dreamed of her, with eyes like yours... I held her in my dreams, and she seemed so real." He stroked my back, then moved down my body and kissed my belly.

"Our child will come," he said. "Did you name the little one?"

"Mara."

"Little bird of prey." Aeolmar's eyes overflowed with a father's pride. "A perfect name." I thought he would find me foolish for naming her; I hadn't even shared her name with Wren. He stroked my hair and murmured of what he would teach Mara once she was with us, of the stories he would tell her about the stars, how he would protect her.

I wrapped my arms around him, and laid my head on his chest. "The most wonderful sound I've ever heard, in this realm or the mortal, is the beating of your heart."

Chapter Fifty-Eight

Despite the valiant fight he waged against fatigue, Aeolmar's eyes soon closed. After a time, someone knocked on their door. Latera threw on a shift and limped her way to the entrance, and found Innetha waiting in the corridor.

"I'm here to report to Aeolmar," Innetha said.

"He's sleeping," Latera said, beckoning her inside. "Would you like me to wake him?"

"No, no, he's slept little enough of late," Innetha said, then she proffered a length of wood. "I brought you a cane, for your ankle."

"Thank you," Latera said. "How did you know it was my ankle?"

Innetha smiled tightly. "I know something of wounds."

"I do appreciate this." Latera put weight on the cane, pleased with how it helped her lead Innetha toward the seating area. "Have all of the *con'dehr* been spoken to?"

"They have." Innetha listed the names of those questioned, and detailed who had outright admitting to being in league with Harek, and who was imprisoned based on suspicion. As she spoke, Latera realized that Innetha was giving her the report intended for Aeolmar.

"The only good thing to come of this mess is that very few appear to be part of the conspiracy," Innetha continued. "And, those who are involved are all *con'dehr*. It seems that Harek's minions were loyal to the *mordeth-gall*, not Asherah. The others were shocked." Innetha exhaled heavily, and met Latera's gaze. "We're all shocked. Harek is a hateful man, but no one suspected this. This has wounded Asherah deeply."

"What happened to the seer?" Latera asked. "Was she imprisoned?"

"After the vortex took you, she said she was innocent but Asherah didn't believe her. As she was being led to the dungeon, she disappeared into thin air. I wouldn't have believed it, but Luth witnessed everything."

Latera nodded. "What will be done next?"

"That's for Asherah and Aeolmar to decide." Innetha studied Latera's face. "Harek and his brother were the ones who sent you away, weren't they?"

Latera nodded, and explained how Sarfek had abducted her as a child, only to send her back to Gannera when Harek couldn't kill her. She went on, and told Innetha about her elfin heritage, the oracle in Asherah's temple, and how Sarfek had conspired toward her grandmother's death at Asgeloth's hand. Innetha was silent for a time after the tale concluded.

"You saw Torim?" Innetha asked.

"Yes. She's as beautiful as the queen."

Innetha's doe eyes were thoughtful as she continued. "To think that she has watched over Asherah for all of these centuries. Perhaps it was good that you were sent back to Gannera, otherwise we might not have known about this treachery until it was too late."

Latera said, "I agree, but I wish I'd found my way back sooner. Gannera's not my home any longer. Parthalan is."

"I'm glad to hear that, princess, for we need you here. It seems you're our savior, little *deva'shi*."

"May the gods help us all," Latera said. Innetha stood, casting a glance toward the bed curtains that shielded the First Hunter from view.

"I'll have food sent for you," Innetha said as she walked toward the door. "The queen will want to see both of you when he wakes." Latera hobbled alongside her, but when they reached the door Innetha embraced her.

"Don't get taken again."

"I won't."

Innetha left without another word, and Latera limped back to bed. She slid under the blankets, and found Aeolmar's eyes wide open.

"How long have you been awake?" she asked.

"Since you got up," he replied. "Innetha is correct; no one would have ever suspected this of Harek." He rolled onto his back and rubbed his eyes. "I heard what you said, about wishing you found your way sooner. You need to know that I was looking for you. We all looked for you."

"Mar, I haven't doubted that for a moment," Latera said. "I was so worried you'd never find me..."

"I'll always find you," Aeolmar said, kissing her forehead. "I would have found you long ago if not for this blasted siege."

"The siege," Latera said, "how did it begin?"

He rubbed his eyes again. "After you were taken, those skirmishes that followed you from one end of Parthalan to the other erupted into full attacks. The demons were as clever as they were cruel. We would ride to the west, and the next attack would be to the east, and so forth. We spent more time riding in circles than engaging the enemy." He uttered a small, mirthless laugh. "Harek led all of those missions, and I, acting as his second, never once saw his true plan."

"There was no way for you to know," Latera said. "Harek knew that no one would suspect him. I didn't suspect Sarfek until I learned that Harek had a brother, and if Torim hadn't told me that the traitor's brother is the one who transported me, I might never have put the pieces together." Aeolmar blew out a breath, and continued recounting what had happened while she was away.

"As we blindly followed the traitor across all of Parthalan, the demons eventually led us to the High Desert. While we were there, we received word that the palace had been attacked by Asgeloth himself. We returned to find the plain thick with demons. That was yesterday, and so we fought until you appeared." Aeolmar moved onto his back, and draped an arm over his eyes.

"I've never needed you more than I did this past season, not only for your love, but for you cunning and skill on the battlefield. If you'd been with me, we would have seen the treachery before us, and we could have stopped it."

"They removed me to distract you, and keep me in a world where Asgeloth wasn't." She fell silent for a moment. "The way Harek spoke of me, always belittling my ability. I never realized I was the one person that scared him."

"Do you regret it? Coming here from Brennus?" Aeolmar asked. "I brought you into all of this. You would have been safe if I'd just let you alone." Latera grabbed his chin, and forced him to look at her.

"I regret nothing. Don't ever think that way, not even for a moment." Latera laid her head on his shoulder. "I will kill him."

Aeolmar glanced at the woman in his arms. "Harek? I'm sure Asherah will take his head."

"No. Asgeloth. It's my destiny to kill him."

"I don't like it," Aeolmar said at length. "How do we know that this bloodline of yours is true, and not more trickery?"

"My mother told me that we're descended from Elvasla and Tarac. Sibeal told me much of the same legend in Thurnda. My grandmother, who was named for Elvasla, was told she was the *deva'shi* by Harek's brother. She met Asgeloth in battle, but he killed her. It's my mother's belief that Sarfek wanted to destroy Elvasla's line so I wouldn't be born. But I was, and I'm still here. There must be a reason." Latera regarded him for a moment. "Do you know the elfin language?"

"No one speaks elfin any longer, not even elves," Aeolmar replied. "Have you learned that language as well?"

"*Deva'shi* is elfin for 'killer of demons'," Latera replied. "Have you never wondered how a girl who'd never touched a sword could so easily kill two demons while the First Hinter slept? Or not be killed by a *mordeth*? You claim I'm your equal in swordplay, yet you have what, two hundred winters of experience, while I have only six? Mar, there must be a reason. I-I can't believe all of this is just chance." Aeolmar held her gaze for long moments before he pulled Latera against his chest.

"I don't think it's chance. I've never thought that," he said. "But, before we do anything else we must speak with the queen, and question Harek in order to learn what he knows of Asgeloth's plans."

"He will not talk."

"He will talk to me," Aeolmar said coldly. "And when I'm done with him, he will welcome death."

***

After the food Innetha promised arrived, and Aeolmar and Latera stared at it for some time, they went to meet with Asherah. It wasn't long before Aeolmar and Asherah were arguing about who should interrogate Harek.

"Just let me do this, Asherah," Aeolmar said.

"He betrayed Parthalan," Asherah hissed, "and betrayed me. He's been betraying m all along! Give me one reason why you should do that which is mine by rights?"

"He'll try to sway you, and likely succeed."

"He will not!"

"You always say that you remember when Harek was good," Aeolmar spoke over her. "I harbor no such misconceptions."

Asherah stood with her fists and jaw clenched. "You speak to me as you would a weak-minded sot."

"No, I speak to you as my gracious and noble queen whose heart is big enough to encompass all of Parthalan," Aeolmar replied. "One who can see good in everyone, even when there is no good to be had." Asherah looked toward Latera, hoping for support. She didn't get any.

"Asherah, just let Mar handle this," Latera said. "You know he means well, and his noble heart will turn sour otherwise." Aeolmar scowled at his mate, but Asherah relented.

"Very well," Asherah said.

Aeolmar stood. "I'll go immediately." He strode toward the door, but stopped when Asherah and Latera followed him. "No. Both of you, stay here."

"Mar," Latera implored, but he shook his head.

"No," he said, then he turned on his heel and left.

"His noble heart will be the death of him," Asherah muttered.

"I fear you're right," Latera agreed.

They returned to the receiving chamber, and where Finlay, Elkin, and Innetha waited for them; it seemed that Aeolmar had forbidden several people entry to the dungeon. Asherah sat next to Finlay and laid her head on his shoulder, and Finlay wrapped his arms around his mate. Innetha and Elkin were similarly close, which Latera thought was odd for a woman whose arrangement was with another. Latera, bereft of her mate, wanted to pace about the room, but her throbbing ankle prevented that.

The shadows grew long before Aeolmar returned. He sat next to Latera, and said nothing for a time. "I would have rather spent time with Mersgoth than him," he said, at last.

Asherah cleared her throat. "What did you learn?"

"At first, nothing," Aeolmar began. "Then he began raving of how peace made us soft, of how we needed battles to keep the soldiers fit." Aeolmar laughed mirthlessly. "He said that his *con'dehr* didn't want to be farmers or poets; they wanted to fight. Wasn't their true purpose to guard the temple?"

"It was, once," Asherah confirmed. "What did he reveal about Asgeloth?"

"Harek claimed he wouldn't have let demons overrun Parthalan," Aeolmar replied. "He would have installed one with royal blood on the throne."

"What, after Asherah's death?" Finlay demanded.

"Yes," Aeolmar replied, "after Asherah's death." He regarded the queen with solemn eyes. "I won't continue if you don't wish it."

"Go on," Asherah said.

"Harek believed that putting another on the throne would have pitched Parthalan into two wars, a civil war and war against the demons. And, war was what he wanted."

Asherah closed her eyes, her fingers laced tightly with Finlay's. "Sarfek's role?" she prompted.

"Sarfek's role was to end Latera's family," Aeolmar said. "He convinced Latera's grandmother she was the *deva'shi*, and engineered her death at Asgeloth's hand. He expected the Taracian royal family would be executed in the subsequent revolt, but when they were taken in by Gannera, Sarfek installed himself in the court. Then he sent you to Parthalan." Aeolmar's mouth quirked into a smile, and he caressed Latera's cheek. "They'd thought you dead those winters you were in

Brennus. Imagine Harek's surprise when he found you right here in Teg'urnan."

"We *deva'shi's* are hard to kill," Latera quipped.

"How am I to be disposed of?" Asherah demanded.

"Harek was to convince you that the *mordeth-gall* only wanted a portion of Parthalan, and he was to get you on the plain before the palace, alone," Aeolmar replied. "He thought he could convince you to negotiate with the demon lord."

"And that's how I was to die," Asherah said. "Was he tortured?"

"Yes."

"Does he live?"

"Yes."

"He will be executed at first dawn."

With that declaration Asherah left the room, the Second Hunter by her side. After they were gone, Aeolmar recounted what else occurred in the cell.

"I had his brother's head put in the cell," he continued. "Harek claimed Sarfek was speaking to him, begging him not to talk for fear of Asgeloth's punishments in the underworld."

"Madness," Elkin muttered. "Likely, another deception."

Aeolmar looked at his friend. "I heard him, too."

The four of them sat in silence, pondering how a severed heard might offer warnings from beyond. Then, Latera touched Aeolmar's hand.

"What were their plans for me?" Latera asked.

"I wanted to keep you away from that," Aeolmar replied.

"Aeolmar, just tell her," Innetha said. When Aeolmar glared at her, Innetha rose to leave. "Keeping secrets from your mate will only lead to strife." Elkin also rose, but first offered a few words.

"Latera is strong. She'd have to be to put up with the likes of you," Elkin said. "Anything that traitor said, you can tell her. She can handle it." Elkin clapped Aeolmar on the shoulder and followed Innetha.

"Innetha, wait."

Innetha paused, and glanced over her shoulder. "Yes?"

"Harek confessed to many things." Aeolmar stood and approached the huntress. "Remember the battle against the dark fae, when Finlay was hit with the spear and nearly died? The *con'dehr* struck the blow, on Harek's orders. They did the same to—"

"To Olwynn," Innetha finished. "My Olwynn."

"I'm sorry," Aeolmar said. "I wish Olwynn hadn't perished. I would bring him back, if I could." Aeolmar looked toward the queen's closed door. "I would bring them all back."

"All?" Latera repeated. "Who else did Harek kill?"

Aeolmar bowed his head. "Lormac."

Latera gasped. "Mar, you have to tell Asherah."

"I will." He nodded to Innetha and Elkin, then he returned to his place beside his mate. Once they were alone, Latera rested her head on Aeolmar's shoulder.

"We should throw him to the wolves," Latera said. "Starving, mad wolves, who will rip him to pieces."

"Agreed."

"Are you going to tell me what he said about me?" Latera asked. When Aeolmar remained silent, she continued, "How am I to defend myself if I don't know what my fate might be?"

Aeolmar took a deep breath, and met her eyes. "Asgeloth won't kill you; he wants you chained to his throne, mother for a new line of demons." He paused for a moment. "I nearly killed Harek when he said that. I could have. Asherah would have assumed his death happened in the course of interrogation. But he'd already told me everything he was allowed to know. Killing him would have been murder, and…" Aeolmar shook his head. "And, Harek is a murderer, and I am nothing like him."

"No, you're not." Latera gazed at the man that loved her. "Beloved, I've been on this journey too long and come too far to end it in chains. I earned the name Demon-killer long ago, long before I knew of my heritage or Harek's treason. Asgeloth will fall before me."

Chapter Fifty-Nine

The next morning, the Queen of Parthalan and the First Hunter stood before the palace gates on a newly-erected wooden platform. Asherah wore her crown, a silver circlet set with blue stones, and a white gown embroidered with blue gems that glinted in the early light. She was unarmed, unlike Aeolmar, who was dressed for battle and wore his sword at his side.

Latera stood at the base of the platform, with Finlay and Innetha flanking her. Like the queen, Latera wore a dress rather than her usual leather gear but for a far more practical reason: her ankle had swollen so much that she couldn't stuff it into her boots, nor could she pull any of her leggings over it. She leaned heavily on her cane and on Finlay, and hoped she wouldn't slip and fall in front of every resident of Teg'urnan.

The legion was assembled in the square, with the *con'dehr* kneeling before them in chains. Harek was hauled forward, his tunic ripped open so everyone present could see the mark of the *mordeth-gall*. Sarfek's head was carried behind him on a pike. The grisly trophy was stuck into the ground next to the dais as the guards dragged Harek up the steps, and dropped him at the queen's feet.

"What say you, traitor?" Aeolmar demanded, his voice booming across the square. Harek spat towards Aeolmar's feet.

"I only answer to the queen," Harek barked.

"You lost that right when you plotted against Asherah and all of Parthalan," Aeolmar shouted. "What say you?"

"Do you expect me to cower before her like a dog? She who has made Parthalan weak? You'll regret not delivering her to Asgeloth! You'll all regret it!"

The crowd shouted when Harek spoke the *mordeth-gall's* name, begging for his death. Asherah snatched Aeolmar's sword from its scabbard and in one stride she was before Harek. He pleaded with the queen, but she ignored him and grabbed his matted hair, exposing his neck before she beheaded him in two swift strokes.

Asherah raised Harek's head above her, not flinching as his blood flowed down her arm and soaked her gown. The crowd cheered and called out her name, pledging themselves again to this usurper of the throne. Asherah flung Harek's head into the dirt and looked toward Aeolmar; he barked an order, and the *con'dehr's* heads fell as one.

Asherah kept her gaze forward as she ascended Teg'urnan's steps. When she reached the massive doors she turned and held Aeolmar's bloody sword aloft, the crowd working itself into a frenzy. She gazed at her people, her Parthians, then she dropped the sword and entered the palace, leaving the throngs to celebrate the traitors' deaths without her.

***

Asherah walked to her chambers alone, her head held high and gaze forward. She didn't remember anyone approaching her, but then she might have just ignored them. In truth, she didn't care.

Harek was dead.

She'd killed him.

She'd kill him again if she could.

She stepped inside her rooms and undressed, leaving a trail of bloody garments that led toward her bathing chamber. Attia had thought to prepare a bath, and also had the good sense to grant Asherah her privacy. Asherah stopped before the bathing chamber's mirror and stared at her reflection.

I followed him—believed in him—for almost my entire life. How did I not see his treachery? How did I not know?

Asherah moved closer to the mirror, touched her forehead to the cool glass.

Lormac, I wish you were here to guide me...

Innetha found Asherah huddled against the tub, her body streaked with tears and blood. She shed her own clothing and got herself and the queen into the bath, and helped her wash.

"Thank you," Asherah said once her sobs lessened.

"This isn't the first time I've bathed you." Innetha's voice cracked, and she covered her face with her hands.

"What is it?" Asherah asked.

"Aeolmar... He told me what Harek said. About Olwynn." Innetha ground the heel of her hand against her eyes. "Harek had Olwynn killed, just like your Lormac."

Asherah felt the world fall out from under her. Aeolmar had told her hardly anything he'd gleaned from Harek, much less those the Prelate had killed over the years. She remembered Lormac's wound, how he'd been run through from behind. The sort of killing strike only a coward would use.

"When did Aeolmar tell you this?" Asherah asked.

"Yesterday, after you declared Harek would die." Innetha brushed Asherah's hair from her face. "Did he not tell you?"

"I didn't see Aeolmar after I left you, not until this morning. I... I didn't know."

Innetha drew the queen against her stroking her hair. "I'm so sorry, love."

"Gods," Asherah wailed, "I wish I hadn't killed Harek yet, so I could still make him suffer."

Chapter Sixty

"I don't understand why Asherah didn't say anything," Latera said. She and Aeolmar were sitting in the queen's enchanted garden, waiting for Asherah to finish her bath. They'd been waiting for quite a while. "Surely, the people could have benefited from a word or two from their queen."

"Asherah didn't say anything when she beheaded the old king, either," Aeolmar said. "She claimed he wasn't worth the breath she'd have used. I imagine she feels the same about Harek."

"You saw the old king's death?"

"I did not, but I've heard the story my entire life. What if I had been there? Do you think I'm an old man? You know my kind lives long," he teased.

"I don't think you're old," Latera replied. "I was merely impressed by your historical knowledge. And don't be so pretentious. My kind lives long, as well."

Aeolmar laughed; after a moment Latera did as well, both of them doing their best to leave behind the morning's terrible business. The day was warm, and the elder sun high was overhead as the child sun struggled to catch him. Aeolmar sat with his back against a tree, and Latera lay on the grass, her head in his lap and her ankle propped up on a cushion she'd filched from the queen's sitting room.

Latera breathed in the sweet air, and smiled. "I've only been back for two days, yet my memory of the mortal realm is already fading."

"Will you be happy here, away from your home?"

"Yes. Parthalan is my home. I don't belong in Gannera, not any longer. Almost everyone there hated me."

"I don't believe you," Aeolmar said, as he smoothed back her hair. "I think word of your beauty spread far and quickly, and you had dozens of suitors."

"Well, there was one."

Aeolmar's eyes widened, his mouth a slash across his face. Latera closed her eyes and turned her face into the breeze. At length he said, "You were gone for a very long time, uncertain if you'd return. I'd understand if you sought comfort with another."

Latera opened her eyes and saw the hurt in his, and felt a pang of guilt. "I've only ever found comfort with you," she said. "My one suitor was a stupid prince that my father tried to marry me off to, claiming that it was good for Gannera for the first born to marry the first born of the Highlands. And there was the added benefit of my father being rid of me. He found it embarrassing to have a daughter who was ten summers old one day, and a grown woman the next."

"Humans...mar-ree...instead of binding?"

"Yes. There's a celebration called a wedding and it's held in a grand hall. Many gifts are exchanged, and the feast lasts for days. Both families attend and pledge their loyalty to each other, and then the wife is sent off to live with her husband, wherever that may be."

"But they don't love each other?"

"It's not the purpose of marriage. I don't even know if my parent's love each other. My mother was betrothed to my father when she was very young, much younger than I was when I met you. He had to wait years for her to come of age."

"Your suitor didn't profess to love you?" he pressed.

Latera quirked an eyebrow, but continued, "While I was sick with poison he sat at my bedside, telling me about the wonderful life he'd give me in the Highlands... but he never mentioned love. I was delirious, and hardly realized he was there. When my fever broke I told him to get out before I killed him."

"You were poisoned?" Aeolmar glided his thumb across her cheek.

"Yes. I've so much to tell you about my time in Gannera." Latera recounted how Sarfek had befriended her, only to give her tea laced with poison; and of Quill, how he'd only wanted to help and been murdered. Lastly, she told him of Wren, her older sister that she'd never known, and how she was her only friend in Gannera.

"If Sarfek wasn't dead I'd kill him myself," Aeolmar said bitterly. "When you were taken I tried to catch you, but I was too slow. I'm so sorry I failed you, beloved."

"You didn't fail. There was nothing you could have done. The spell was cast and I had the dagger on me; there was no stopping my journey. I don't know if you could have followed." Latera closed her eyes, trying not to think about Aeolmar lost in the vortex.

"Will you still bind yourself to me?"

"Of course I will."

"Bind yourself to me today. Right now."

Latera's eyelids fluttered open. "Today?"

"Our bindings are different than how humans mar-ree," Aeolmar continued. "Your custom is a public display. Ours is private, between two mates and no one else. Unlike humans, we've no need for the whole realm's approval when we take a mate." When Latera remained silent, Aeolmar shifted their position so she was sitting upright against his legs. "Beloved, I don't mean to poke fun at your home's customs."

"I know you mean no harm. But what if one of us doesn't survive the days ahead? Ask me again once the enemy has fallen."

"No," Aeolmar said. "What if I die before I have the chance to be bound to you? I've lived a long time, but I've never loved another."

Aeolmar kissed her, then pressed his forehead to hers. "I will never love another. I'm yours, for as long as you'll have me."

Latera watched the emotions play over Aeolmar's features, his words ringing in her ears: *What if I die before I have the chance to be bound to you?* She'd felt a similar pain when they'd been separated, knew it all too well.

"Yes, today I'll bind myself to you."

Aeolmar pulled her tight against him. "So, how long will you want me?"

"Forever," she said against his neck. "Forever." He laughed, and Latera laughed with him. "You're the most feared man in Parthalan. Demons run from you. Yet here you are, laughing in a garden."

"My mood has much to do with the beautiful girl in my arms."

"Does it?" Latera asked, and he kissed her in reply. "Should we tell the queen?"

"No," he replied. "It's only for us to know."

Aeolmar kept Latera in his arms as he stood, then strode into the queen's chambers to advise Attia that he needed to attend to an important matter. The *saffira-nell* bowed her head and he set off down the corridor, still carrying Latera.

"Mar, I can walk," she protested. "Let me down!" Aeolmar laughed as she squirmed, moving swiftly until he reached the temple doors.

"We're here, beloved," he said.

Latera looked up, and noted that they stood before the eastern door, which was made of solid silver, and set with a red disc to represent the goddess as the moon.

"You must enter first and wait for me," he said.

"I don't know what to do," Latera whispered. She'd never been inside the Great Temple, and hadn't learned anything more about bindings since that snowy night in Thurnda.

"Atreynha will help you," Aeolmar whispered back.

"Atreynha?"

"The High Priestess," he replied. "She will assist you. Now go, and I'll be with you in a moment." Aeolmar kissed Latera's forehead and nudged her toward the doors. Having no other options, she stepped inside.

Latera gasped at the interior of the temple. The walls and floor were the same smooth gray stone as the rest of the palace, but these tiles glistened as if they'd been sprinkled with crushed gems. The ceiling was so far above she could hardly see it in the darkness. Arched windows set high in the walls sent rays of sunlight dancing across the floor. In the center was a large, high platform with steps on all sides.

A woman appeared at Latera's elbow. She introduced herself as Atreynha, the High Priestess, and Latera her to a small chamber. Atreynha laid out a flowing blue robe and white veil, and said she would help Latera with the garments.

"But you don't know why I'm here," Latera said.

"You're here for a binding. It's the only reason to enter from the east," Atreynha replied.

After Latera donned the robe, Atreynha unbound her hair and pinned the veil in place, then she placed a silver band on each of Latera's arms; one was set with amber, and the other with a moonstone. Then Atreynha offered her arm, and helped Latera across the temple and to the top of the platform. Atreynha arranged Latera on the raised altar stone, then she turned to leave.

"You won't stay?" Latera asked, clutching Atreynha's arm.

Atreynha smiled, skin crinkling around the corners of her eyes. "You will know what to do."

With that, Atreynha disappeared down the stairs. Latera looked around the altar. Behind her were the figures of the stag and doe, rearing toward each other. There were short pillars with flat tops at each corner of the altar, with shining copper caps set atop them. Latera's gaze moved upward, and saw that the ceiling was covered in familiar patterns; she squinted, and realized that they were constellations. Latera considered the contrast of the sky represented above, and she on a stone slab covered in flowers.

She heard the gentle rustle of fabric, and saw Aeolmar approaching her from the east. He was wearing a black robe, cinched at the waist with a golden belt, and armbands set with red stones. His path was lit by sunlight, and as he ascended the steps, Latera understood the ritual.

Aeolmar was clothed as Olluhm, the elder sun, and Latera was Cydia, the moon goddess he'd spied napping in a meadow. When Aeolmar reached Latera he lifted the veil from her brow, just as the sun's rays burn away the morning fog. Latera thought of the morning greeting to the elder sun, the daily affirmation of the god and goddess creating life. And here they were, representing the eternal pair.

Latera faced Aeolmar, and he took her hands his. Aeolmar spoke so softly Latera could hardly hear him, and then she surprised herself by answering him. They spoke their vows as the light grew brighter and brighter, until Latera was certain they would be consumed by it.

They remained on the altar stone until the light faded, and darkness surrounded them once more. Aeolmar gathered Latera in his arms and carried her down the back of the platform, toward the west. Atreynha appeared at their side and guided them to a low table set with silver bowls of water and platters of small, sticky cakes made of oats and honey. Aeolmar sank down to the cushions with Latera in his arms, and they fed each other the little cakes and washed their fingers in the bowls of water. Somehow the honey got in their hair, and they laughed as they untangled themselves.

"I hadn't thought it possible for you to be more beautiful, and yet you are," Aeolmar murmured, caressing Latera's cheek.

"How long can we remain here?" Latera asked as she fed him another cake.

"Some remain in seclusion for weeks after a binding," he replied. "I don't believe we'll have that luxury." With that Aeolmar rose and crossed the room to where their clothes lay neatly folded, and set Latera on her feet.

"Will you ever allow me to walk again?" she asked.

"I'd heal you if I could," he replied. "But I can't, so I'll content myself with carrying you."

They dressed slowly, neither wanting their quiet time in the temple to end. The High Priestess returned, and Aeolmar whispered something in her ear. She darted from the room, and returned in an instant with a simple wooden cane.

"Thank you," Latera said. Atreynha smiled, and disappeared from the room. Latera turned to Aeolmar, who shrugged.

"You said that humans give gifts when they mar-ree. Consider this your gift from me."

"I hope it's the first of many," Latera said, testing her weight on the cane. Aeolmar helped her up and they left the temple through the west entrance, and walked toward the queen's chambers. When they arrived, Attia informed them that Asherah desired to be alone with her thoughts for the time being. Aeolmar nodded at the *saffira-nell*, and they left for their own rooms.

Finlay encountered them in the great hall, and launched into a report about the state of the legion, news that had flowed in from the outlying villages, and everything else that would have previously been told to Harek. When Finlay paused, Aeolmar advised him that he had an urgent matter to attend to, and that the Second Hunter would need to oversee the obligations of the First for a time.

"How long will this task be?" Finlay asked.

"A long time," Aeolmar replied, gazing at Latera, "many days." He turned back to Finlay, and leaned close to his second. "Attia said that Asherah has withdrawn into her chambers. Delegate my obligations to whomever you wish, but I'm ordering you to your mate." Finlay nodded, and set off to be with his beloved.

Aeolmar resumed walking, and Latera followed as fast as her injured ankle would allow. When they entered their chamber, Aeolmar dragged the cushions down from the raised bed so Latera wouldn't have to navigate the steps. Latera helped him set them up on the floor in front of the hearth, and then she lost herself in her mate's arms.

It was three days and nights before anyone dared to knock on Latera's door; it was a lone *saffira*, inquiring if Latera might need anything. Aeolmar asked her to bring food and wine, and said nothing more. They later learned that during those three days when neither the queen nor the First Hunter were seen, the palace teemed with rumors that they were drawing up plans for a great battle. After Aeolmar's request, the rumors claimed that Latera had been gravely injured and was on her deathbed.

Only when Innetha was crossing the courtyard the morning of the fifth day, and saw Aeolmar and Latera standing on their balcony, did anyone suspect otherwise. She saw the First Hunter's arms wrapped around Latera while they greeted the child sun as only a bound pair would do. Innetha quelled as many rumors as she could, and diverted all tasks away from Aeolmar to keep them undisturbed.

Their seclusion totaled eight glorious days. During that time, Aeolmar told Latera many stories of his youth, and his family. He spoke of the time he returned home to find his family slaughtered by demons, and how he'd learned that the one responsible was Mersgoth. When Mersgoth had dealt him the leg wound on that day near Brennus, he'd thought that the demon had succeeded in wiping out his entire family, but when Aeolmar saw that Latera had gravely injured the demon he finally had the strength to kill him.

"That was when I knew I never wanted to be parted from the beautiful girl I found in a stable," he finished.

Latera snuggled against him. "Even then I didn't fear you," she said. "Everyone was telling me stories about the scary First Hunter, your ferocity both in and out of battle, but they never swayed me."

"What, did you think I was more kitten than warrior?" Aeolmar asked.

"Stop," Latera said, then she kissed his neck. She knew he liked that. "I mean that I saw beneath the stories, that you're kind and fair, and that you cared for your hunters more than you care for yourself." Latera laced her fingers with his, and kissed his knuckles. "I've never regretted the day I followed you out of Brennus on a borrowed horse. I'd follow you anywhere."

"Anywhere?"

"Yes, anywhere."

Aeolmar rolled her beneath him, and kissed her shoulder. "I know where I'd like to take you."

On the seventh day just before first dawn, Latera asked Aeolmar why they greeted the child sun differently now that they were bound.

"Fae births are rare, but much more likely right after a binding," Aeolmar replied. "The prayers are meant to reaffirm our desire for a child to follow our binding, just as the younger sun follows the elder." Aeolmar frowned. "If you don't want a child so soon, we can stop."

Latera touched her fingers to his lips. "I'd like nothing more," she said, drawing him out to the balcony. Aeolmar wrapped his arms around her, and they greeted the elder and then the younger sun together.

Chapter Sixty-One

Shortly after second dawn on the ninth day, Aeolmar and Latera were roused by a knock at their door. Latera nudged Aeolmar out of bed, and he found the Second Hunter standing in the corridor.

"You look well," Finlay said as he stepped inside. "Being a bound man must suit you." Before Aeolmar could reply, they saw Latera hobble toward them. Aeolmar was at her side in an instant, but she shooed him away.

"You'll only make it worse," Aeolmar warned.

"You cannot carry me everywhere, it's not practical," Latera said. "I can get about, it's fine."

Aeolmar let her walk to the chairs, then he pulled her onto his lap. Latera sighed, knowing that resistance was futile. Besides, she liked sitting on Aeolmar's lap. "Have you news?" she asked Finlay.

"Of a sort," Finlay replied. "There's nothing to tell of demons. We haven't had any sightings for a sennight. I'm afraid the lack of information is making me nervous."

"Agreed," Aeolmar said. "It's unlikely that such a large offensive would be launched only to end so abruptly."

"Asherah wants to see both of you today," Finlay continued. "I'm sorry to interrupt your seclusion, but she feels she's given you all the time we can spare."

"She's been most generous," Aeolmar said. "I'd expected you to come knocking days ago."

"After how you helped Sher and I when we were bound?" Finlay asked. "If it were up to me, I'd board up your door and forget your names."

"Were you and Asherah secluded?" Latera asked.

"A moon, we had," Finlay replied. Aeolmar snorted, and Finlay glared at him.

"What's that all about?" Latera asked.

"We announced that the queen and I were travelling south, alone," explained Aeolmar, "and that Finlay was traveling west. Asherah and Finlay spent their time holed up somewhere while I was alone by the sea, waiting for them to emerge."

"As I've always said, you're the kindest, most wonderful man I've ever known," Latera said, stroking his cheek.

"You wouldn't feel that way if you'd heard the way he complained on the journey home," Finlay said. Aeolmar scowled, but didn't argue. The mates readied themselves, and in a short time they were in the queen's receiving chamber. Asherah began by discussing the recent siege of Teg'urnan.

"I'm glad they retreated, I just don't understand why," the queen said.

"According to Harek, Asgeloth was waiting for word from him before launching his final attack against Teg'urnan," Aeolmar said.

Asherah frowned at the map before her. "That makes me wonder where the beast is hiding."

"Wasn't Harek always going south?" Latera asked. "Perhaps that's where the *mordeth-gall* is."

"Only the *con'dehr* accompanied him on those journeys," Finlay said.

"You're right," Asherah murmured, then she called for the scrolls that recorded the *con'dehr's* confessions. Latera watched as the queen and Finlay noted maps, establishing Asgeloth's location.

"We cannot go to him," Latera said. "He'll be too strong. We need to bring him here, to unfamiliar ground. Asgeloth has never set foot or hoof or whatever he has before Teg'urnan."

"He doesn't know that Harek's dead," said Asherah. "We could ambush him."

"We will," Latera declared. "He's waiting for word from Harek that his plan is in place. Once he has the signal he will advance, expecting to find you weak and defenseless, but he'll find me instead." Aeolmar grabbed Latera's shoulders.

"No," he said. "No, no, no! You will not engage Asgeloth!"

"I must," she said. "It's the only way."

"I will find another way," he ground out.

"We have time to plan," Asherah said, eyeing them. "My guess is that he's four days to the south; in the time it will take to get a signal to the *mordeth-gall* and for him to advance, we'll have at least eight or nine days to prepare, perhaps longer." Aeolmar nodded, his gaze still fixed on Latera.

"There is also the matter of Kemen," Finlay said.

"What of him?" Latera asked.

"He's in the dungeon," Finlay replied. "He was questioned along with the *con'dehr*."

"Why was he questioned?" Latera asked. "And why is a hunter in the dungeon?"

"Harek approached Kemen shortly before the two of you went north, and swayed him to the *mordeth-gall's* cause. The demons you encountered in Thurnda were all Kemen's doing."

"Why would he do that?" Latera demanded.

"Because Harek promised him he could have you in the end," Finlay replied.

Latera's mouth dropped open. "I never would have gone to him, not for any reason. Kemen is too smart to fall for such a foolish plan."

Finlay shrugged. "Men in love are often fools."

"Why wasn't he executed with the rest?" Aeolmar demanded.

"He's not *con'dehr*," Asherah said. "I didn't want one of the hunters associated with that filth."

"Perhaps he can be redeemed," Latera said. "Kemen will bring word to Asgeloth. He can find the demon camp."

"He'll likely run," Aeolmar said.

"If he does, we've lost nothing but a traitor under our roof," Latera said. "My queen, do I have your leave?"

"Let him redeem his soul by committing one decent act. If he doesn't agree, he can continue rotting in his cell," Asherah proclaimed.

The queen didn't join Aeolmar, Finlay and Latera as they walked to the dungeon. Kemen was in the farthest cell, so deep in the bowels of the palace there was little light and the air was stale. When they reached his door Finlay set their torch in a bracket, and held out the key to the Kemen's cell.

"Which of us will speak to him?" he asked.

"I will," Latera said.

"Finlay and I will be right behind you," Aeolmar said. "Call if you need us, and we'll be there."

"I know," Latera said, then she unlocked the door.

Latera opened the door and saw Kemen crouching against the opposite wall. The torchlight blinded him, and he shielded his eyes.

"Get up."

Kemen got to his feet, bumping his head against the low ceiling. As her vision adjusted, Latera saw that the cell was little more than a dirt hole, the floor covered in moldy straw.

"Latera?" he asked, but she held up a hand.

"You will go to Asgeloth and give him a message," Latera said. "You will tell him that many hunters are dead, and Asherah's defenses are weak. You will tell him that the *con'dehr* are on the side of the *mordeth-gall*, and that I remain in Gannera, unable to aid the queen."

"I don't know how to find the demon."

"We will give you a map."

"If I go to him, he'll kill me. This is a suicide mission."

"If you refuse, you will remain in this cell. If the queen's in a foul mood, maybe executed."

Kemen pushed the lank hair back from his eyes. "If I do this, will you forgive me?"

"Yes."

Kemen raised his head, and mustered what dignity he still possessed. "Then give me that map."

***

Alia and Latera stood in the watchtower as Kemen was escorted to the gates, flanked by four guards. He was led before Aeolmar, Finlay and Elkin, given the map and a few brief instructions. As Kemen put his foot in the stirrup he looked toward the watchtower, then Aeolmar grabbed his arm and growled in his ear. Kemen nodded and mounted up, and cast a final glance at Teg'urnan before he rode south.

As soon as Kemen was in his saddle Aeolmar was at Latera's side. As he helped her down the steps, she asked what he said to Kemen.

"I told him that while you have forgiven him I have not, and that he remains unwelcome here." Latera fumbled her cane and almost fell.

Aeolmar caught her, and demanded, "What's wrong?"

"I'm fine," Latera said. "I just can't believe Kemen would betray us." Aeolmar frowned, but before he could say anything further Finlay spoke.

"The queen wishes to meet with all the hunters once the elder sun rests," he advised.

"Very well," Aeolmar said. He and Latera went to their chamber and sat in their favorite spot, on the rug before the hearth.

"You'll face Asgeloth no matter what I say," Aeolmar said.

"Yes."

"You will not face him alone," he vowed.

"I know," she said, "I have you."

***

Aeolmar and Latera spent the day in their chamber discussing, planning, and arguing about ambushing Asgeloth. By the time the elder sun set, they had a plan.

They went to the queen's receiving chamber, which was crowded with every hunter and *nuvi* in Parthalan. The tables had been moved out and replaced with the long benches from the great hall, and Asherah stood at the front of the room like an instructor surveying her students. Aeolmar took his seat at the queen's right, with Latera beside him.

Aeolmar and Latera advised the queen of their plan, and once they gained her approval he explained it to the hunters: Latera would meet Asgeloth on the plain before Teg'urnan, disguised as Asherah. When the obvious issue was raised, that Latera looked nothing like the queen, she had a quick answer.

"I'll wear the royal armor," Latera said. "If I'm wearing the helm he won't know the difference."

"You're two heads shorter than the queen, surely he'll notice that," Bron said.

"Not two heads," Latera grumbled, while Asherah said, "Asgeloth has never seen me in close proximity. He has no idea of my stature." Asherah turned to Aeolmar, and asked, "What of the legion?"

"We'll conceal them behind the northern wall, and surround the demons once Asgeloth is down. However," Aeolmar added, "the question remains as to who will lead the legion."

"I've named you Prelate, you will lead them," Asherah said.

"My queen, I love you and would lay down my life for you, but I cannot be both First Hunter and Prelate," Aeolmar said. "I'm a hunter, not a soldier."

"Is that the only reason?" she asked, her eyes narrowing.

"You know I won't leave Latera before the demon alone," he replied.

"She won't be alone—" began Innetha.

"I'll be there," he snapped.

"In Gannera, the king leads the soldiers," Latera offered.

"Latera, there hasn't been a king in centuries, and I'm a hunter, like Aeolmar," Asherah said.

"You could take a king," Innetha said, and several interested murmurs rose from the hunters. The queen silenced them all with a look. Alia alone braved the royal glare, and rose to her feet.

"Forgive me," Alia began, "I mean no disrespect, but we all see how you and the Second Hunter avoid each other's eyes, and those of us who have watched him look upon you know why." Many heads turned toward Finlay, whose gaze remained downward.

"Only Harek thought that taking a companion was a sign of weakness," Aeolmar said, "and by convincing you of such he made you all the weaker. To stand with you mate beside you gives you more strength than any legion could muster." The queen looked from Aeolmar's face to his hands, noting that he held both of Latera's in his.

"Finlay," Asherah said.

He raised his gaze to hers, and summer blue met shining black. "My queen?"

"You're already my mate. Will you consent to be my king?"

Finlay strode forward and took Asherah's hand, and kissed her fingers. "I'll do anything you ask of me, beloved," Finlay replied, and the hunters cheered. He glanced over his shoulder at the room, then gave Asherah a wry grin. She smiled and threw her arms around his neck. The cheering subsided and the conversation turned to how Finlay would be crowned, for there hadn't been a king for so long no one remembered the ceremony.

"We're ignoring the obvious," Brynne yelled. "Your foolish plan calls for sending Latera out alone, yet she can barely walk!"

"I fought in the last battle, and I'll fight in the next," Latera said. She turned to Aeolmar for support, but his gaze rested on Innetha, as did Asherah and Finlay's.

"Are you going to order me?" Innetha asked.

"You know I can't," Aeolmar replied. Latera asked what Innetha couldn't be ordered to do, then Innetha knelt before her. She took Latera's injured foot onto her lap, and removed her sandal and then the bandage.

"What's happening here?" Latera asked.

"Hush," Aeolmar said. "Patience."

Innetha prodded Latera's ankle, and said, "This is a nasty, nasty break, princess. The bone is split into many pieces." She resumed her careful examination, and Latera felt magic moving throughout her body, pooling in her belly like liquid fire. Moments stretched long between them, then Innetha raised her eyes to Latera's, and Latera knew all that Innetha was. Latera knew that she was cursed.

And, that cursed woman had healed Latera's injury by absorbing it into her own body. Latera smoothed the hair back from Innetha's sweaty brow, grateful for her cherished, doe-eyed friend.

"You alone have made me able to fulfill my destiny. Thank you, dear one," Latera said. Innetha released her ankle and slumped forward, then Elkin was beside her. He gathered Innetha in his arms and brought her back to the bench.

Latera replaced her sandal and tested her ankle, smiling at Aeolmar when she could bear weight upon it. He returned her smile with a grin of his own, then he turned to his hunters.

"Tomorrow, we will crown our king, and we will celebrate," Aeolmar proclaimed. "The day after, we will prepare to fight."

***

The next morning, King Finlay and Queen Asherah were crowned upon the palace steps by the High Priestess, for they were now the living representatives of the god and goddess, the wolf and the she-wolf of Parthalan. The day was nothing if not jubilant, and all remarked of how their queen had never looked happier, and how the new king already had a regal bearing about him.

A great feast followed the crowning, and as the royal pair sat before their subjects, smiling and feeding each other small bites of food, Latera remarked to Aeolmar that the celebration was similar to a human marriage.

"Would you like a feast to celebrate our binding?" Aeolmar asked, drawing her close. "Say the words, beloved, and I'll make it happen."

"I don't need a feast," Latera replied, winding her arms around his neck. "I have you, and you're more than enough."

Chapter Sixty-Two

The morning after Finlay's crowning, everyone resumed preparations for their offensive against Asgeloth. Asherah, Finlay, Aeolmar, and Latera were in the midst of drawing up plans when Attia entered the room.

"An army's arrived," Attia announced.

"Army?" Asherah repeated. "Who's army?"

"Yours, really," Attia replied, then she stepped aside as Senan and Brucka joined them.

"Lady of Tingu," Senan greeted. "We're here to help defend against Parthalan against the *mordeth-gall*."

Asherah blinked, then looked at Aeolmar. "My lady, this is Senan of Thurnda," Aeolmar introduced. "And his second, Brucka."

"Sibeal's boy," Asherah said, as she stepped forward and took Senan's hands. "I haven't seen you since you were no higher than my knee."

The tips of Senan's ears went pink. "Yes, it has been some time. I hope you'll accept our services. My warriors have been trained by the First Hunter himself."

"And your Demon-killer," Brucka added, giving Latera a rueful smile. "I fear for anything that gets in her way."

"Senan, you make me proud," Asherah said. "I only wish you'd arrived yesterday."

"Was there an attack?" Senan asked.

"No, not at all," Asherah replied, drawing Finlay to her side. "This is my mate, Finlay. Yesterday he was crowned King of Parthalan." Senan and Brucka both dropped to their knees, to Finlay's embarrassment and Asherah's delight.

"Sit with us," Finlay said, once they'd gotten to their feet. They apprised Senan and Brucka of their plans, including that Latera was descended from Elvasla.

"Have you heard of the legend?" Latera asked.

"Heard of it? I know it as well as my own name." Senan grinned at Latera, and said, "Elvasla was my mother's sister. It was the Lady of Thurnda what tracked Ehkron to the mortal realm. It would seem that you and I are cousins," he added.

"Cousins," Latera said. "I like that."

***

Once preparations for the coming battle were as complete as they could be, scouts were sent out to watch for Asgeloth's advance. Asherah proclaimed that all dealings of war would cease until there was word from the scouts, and that all everyone should spend the few days that remained with those they held dear. The king and queen took their own advice and sequestered themselves in their chambers, with strict orders that they were only to be disturbed if the *mordeth-gall* himself was before the gates.

Aeolmar and Latera left Teg'urnan and rode west, past the carnage still evident on the plain, not slowing until the palace was no longer visible. They found a clearing bordered by a stream, and followed the water until it emptied into a pool. They swam in the cold water, then they stretched out on the shore and imagined what their lives would be like once Asgeloth was gone.

"You still need to bring me to the sea," Latera reminded him.

"I will," Aeolmar promised. "Maybe our children will be born there."

"I can still see Mara," Latera said. "Can you see her, too?"

"I see Mara, and many others." He went on, and detailed how he would build her that cottage, and named an absurd amount of children. Aeolmar swore he would take their family far from anything that would harm them, and that their lives would be filled with endless perfect days.

Latera propped herself up on her elbows, letting her damp curls fall onto Aeolmar's chest. "This dream of ours; it's only a dream, isn't it?" she asked.

Aeolmar pulled her close. "I don't want it to be."

"We can't leave Asherah. She needs us."

"Perhaps, in time, we can."

***

Aeolmar and Latera returned to Teg'urnan as the elder sun set. When the sentries caught sight of them, Innetha rode out and advised that another army had arrived, and their leader was refusing to speak with anyone but the First Hunter.

"Another army," Latera said. "Where are all these warriors coming from?"

"Yes, Innetha, what army is this?" Aeolmar asked.

Innetha rolled her eyes. "Only the army one led by the most impossible, most difficult man in existence," she replied.

"You're joking," Aeolmar said.

"Have I ever joked with you?"

"Who are we talking about?" Latera demanded. She got her answer soon enough. As they followed Innetha to the palace square they found the legion of Tingu, led by Leran himself.

"Tingu is loyal to Asherah," Leran said. "She needs us, and we are here."

"No one has ever doubted your loyalty," Aeolmar said. "Have you spoken with Asherah yet?"

"I've not," Leran replied. "I was informed that the queen is not to be disturbed."

"She won't mind if you disturb her," Aeolmar said. With that, they left Innetha to find accommodations for Tingu's warriors, and Aeolmar and Latera explained their grand plan to Leran. He shook his head and asked Aeolmar how such a scheme could possibly be effective against the *mordeth-gall*.

"My mate is the *deva'shi*," Aeolmar replied, with that prideful gaze that still warmed Latera's cheeks.

Leran halted, and regarded Latera as one would look over a horse. After a moment, he nodded. "As I said before, you're fortunate to have a mate such as Latera."

***

Nine days after Kemen had gone south to deliver his message to Asgeloth, the hunters of Parthalan again assembled in the royal receiving chamber. This time, they were joined by Senan, Brucka, and Leran. The queen and king stated that the scouts had returned that morning, and that Asgeloth's force would reach Teg'urnan by noon tomorrow.

What followed was a flurry of activity as plans were finalized, weapons were checked, and farewells said. When all had been said and done Aeolmar and Latera retreated to his tower room a few hours before first dawn. They made love fiercely, both fearful it may be the last time.

"No matter what happens tomorrow," Latera began, "never will another be in my heart. If I die, I'll wait for you at the gates of the underworld."

Aeolmar buried his face in her hair. "You won't fail. I won't let you."

Latera looked toward the window, and saw the lightening sky. "It's almost first dawn."

Aeolmar slipped out of bed and went to the balcony, reappearing a moment later. The set of his shoulders told Latera everything she needed to know: the demons were in view. "So soon," she said. "I wish we had another day, another hour, even."

Aeolmar pulled her into his arms. "That's where we differ, beautiful girl. I want to kill these beasts quickly, and spend the rest of my days and hours loving you."

Latera smiled. "All right, we'll do it your way."

By the time Latera and Aeolmar reached the ground floor, the alarm was raised. They went to the queen's chambers, where the mates were issuing commands. Once the legion was in position, Latera and Aeolmar were alone with Asherah and Finlay.

"Asherah, have you a brush?" Aeolmar asked.

"Of course," Asherah murmured, retrieving the item from her inner chambers. Once the brush was in hand Aeolmar sat behind Latera and dragged it through her hair.

"I don't want your curls getting singed," he said as he wove her hair into a braid. After he tied off the end, Latera leaned against him, trying to absorb whatever strength he could spare. She pressed her face to his throat, inhaling the masculine, musky smell of him that drove her mad with longing, and prayed yet again that the next morning would find her waking up in his arms.

Finlay startled her with his hand on her shoulder. "It's time, sweetheart," he said. "We'll help you with the armor."

They strapped the queen's armor onto Latera, then they exited the palace. When they reached the grand stairs Finlay kissed the queen with such tenderness it stunned the onlookers. As they praised Asherah for her choice in a king, Finlay joined the legion.

"I believe taking a king was one of the wiser things I've done," Asherah said, watching him walk away.

"I agree," Latera said, rubbing her armored belly. The smell of the tallow smeared across the armor was turning her stomach, and she was glad she hadn't eaten.

The hunters and *nuvi* were assembled just outside the gates, each wearing a mask of courage, some better than others. Aeolmar and Elkin issued a few last-minute orders, then the queen said a few words. Once Asherah finished, Brynne pointed at Latera's weaponry.

"Your swords are too short," Brynne stated. "The blades won't reach his heart."

Elkin and looked at her swords. "She's right," he said. "If Asgeloth is larger than Esguth or Mersgoth you won't have a long enough reach." Elkin called for another sword, but Aeolmar drew his own, and handed it to Latera.

"Are you sure?" Latera asked.

"It was made for killing demons," Aeolmar said, taking both of hers to replace it.

"Those short swords will compromise your reach," Brynne began.

"Brynne," Elkin said. "He'll manage."

Surya and Padashen descended from the watchtower, and announced that the demons were cresting the last rise. The hunters took their positions in front of the palace wall, with Brynne and Elkin flanking the gate. Aeolmar and Latera stared out over the plain, mesmerized by the dust cloud kicked up by the demons bearing down on Teg'urnan. Latera turned to Aeolmar and kissed him as passionately as if they were alone, not caring that fifty-odd hunters were watching.

"I'll be right here," Aeolmar promised. "The moment I think you need me, I'll be at your side."

Latera pulled off her glove and stroked his cheek, then she found the leather cord he kept at his belt and tied back his hair. "I don't want you singed, either."

Aeolmar rained kisses onto Latera's face as he told her he loved her, and again as he made her repeat the entire plan. When he was satisfied with her response, he placed a final kiss on her forehead, and set the helm upon Latera's head. With that, the *deva'shi* strode twenty paces from the gate, and waited.

Elvasla's blood legacy sang in Latera's veins, clad in the armor of the she-wolf as she waited for the *mordeth-gall* to arrive. Her wait was short, and the approaching horde transformed from one writhing mass into hundreds of misshapen forms. Latera was no stranger to the varied forms demons took, but the beasts before her were unlike any she'd ever seen. Some ran on two legs, others on four or even five; some had horns, some had claws, some had both. A gargantuan figure loomed above the throng, and she knew it was Asgeloth.

The *mordeth-gall* was easily twice Latera's height, and many times her weight. His skin was a dark, dirty red, and he had the face of a bull, with teeth jutting up from his mouth and curved horns upon his brow. His back and legs were covered in matted black fur, and he had hooves where feet should have been.

The demon lord swaggered as he approached Teg'urnan. The rest of the force hung back, letting Asgeloth mark the queen as his kill. He stopped less than two paces before Latera, the fetid stench of him nearly overpowering her. Asgeloth surveyed the wall from one end to the other, pleased that she appeared to be alone.

"We finally meet, Asherah," he rumbled. "What do you think of your loyal Prelate now?"

"I think he died like the traitor he was, as did his brother," Latera proclaimed, pointing toward the wall. The *mordeth-gall* followed her outstretched hand and saw Harek and Sarfek's heads mounted on pikes, their eyes having been torn out by raptors. Asgeloth leaned toward her, so close she could feel his hot breath.

"And yet you still came to treat with me. Have you a death wish, queen?"

"I'm not Asherah." Latera removed her helm and stared at the monster. "I am the *deva'shi*, and I am your death!"

Asgeloth roared, his arm lashing out.

Latera darted to the side, as pain exploded in her shoulder.

She hit the dirt, her head swimming from the impact, from his disgusting odor, but mostly from the fear that she was mistaken. She feared wasn't the *deva'shi*. Asgeloth was about to kill her.

Aeolmar shouted his first command, and the hunters were visible again. It had taken Aeolmar three days to teach his concealment glamour to the rest, and in the end those that became adept were spaced between those who were less confident. They shook off the spell and stepped away from the wall, but if Asgeloth was troubled by their sudden appearance he didn't show it.

"They can't help you," Asgeloth said. Aeolmar shouted more orders. The ground shook and a line of fire erupted around the *mordeth-gall* and Latera, cutting the beast off from his demons. Finlay hadn't disposed of all of the explosive powder Harek had brought into the palace, and his first act as king had been to lay a course of the explosive outside Teg'urnan's walls.

Asgeloth roared and lunged toward Latera. She rolled away and scrambled upright, wildly swinging her sword. She wasn't familiar with Aeolmar's heavy weapon and her blow was well short of him. She swung again and the tip grazed Asgeloth's chest, hardly scoring his thick hide. He laughed as he bore down on her, and Latera fell flat on her back before the *mordeth-gall*.

"Pathetic girl," Asgeloth bellowed. "You are the best they have to offer? You are the legendary warrior? I'll grind your bones to bits while your hunters watch."

His laugh shook the foundations of Latera's soul, and she believed him. She believed that she was nothing but a tiny half-human, arrogant enough to think she could best the most evil being ever to walk this or any world. She was a poor excuse for the she-wolf; she was nothing but a girl.

Asgeloth lunged again, catching the edge of Latera's armor and flinging her head over heels. As her face struck the dirt she thought her only hope was taking Asgeloth with her in death, as Elvasla had taken Ehkron. Latera glanced toward Aeolmar, far more distraught by the thought of him witnessing her demise than of death itself.

Once the calm that only comes when one has accepted the inevitable settled over Latera, she felt a lick of fire in her belly. She stilled her mind, letting the sensation fill her, and as the tiny flame expanded she knew she had more than herself to live for.

And she was going to live.

Latera stood, holding her position as Asgeloth charged. Then she raised her head and gave him a wicked grin.

"*Nir si'lan!*"

The tallow smeared across Latera's armor burst into flames and the demon stumbled back, his face creased with terror. Asgeloth turned to run, but the wall of flames cut off his escape. The *mordeth-gall* let out another blood-curdling roar as he charged toward Latera, but she held her ground, and thrust her sword forward and up, into his torso. Asgeloth's ribs cracked when the hilt struck his chest, and black blood soaked the ground at Latera's feet.

The stench of blood coupled with the burnt tallow overtook Latera, and her stomach heaved over the *mordeth-gall's* corpse. Then Aeolmar was at her side, ripping away the hot armor with no regard for his own flesh, and holding her while she retched. Latera saw the legion advance from behind the wall, and heard the sounds of battle in the distance.

"Your sword," Latera rasped, "it might be broken."

"I can get another sword," Aeolmar said, as he stroked her cheek, "I can't get another you."

Latera retched again, her stomach heaving as if it would leap from her throat. Aeolmar held her until it passed. "I need to get you away from the battle," he said.

Latera nodded, then the world swam and her vision went dark. She felt Aeolmar place something against her lips, and tasted cool water as she slipped from consciousness.

When Latera's eyes next opened, she was lying flat on her back in the watchtower. Aeolmar's sword was lying next to her, cleaned of all traces of the *mordeth-gall*, the hilt resting beside her head. She sat up, fighting the urge to retch again, and saw the queen crouched beside her.

"What happened?" Latera asked.

"You defeated him," Asherah replied, her eyes shining. "You fulfilled your destiny, *deva'shi*. The demon lord is dead." She helped Latera to her feet, and they looked out across the plain.

"We're routing them, even now," Asherah said. "Parthalan will not fall on this day." Latera scanned the battle and found Aeolmar wielding her swords; his eyes met hers for a moment and he grinned, then he struck down another foe.

"Shouldn't we join them?" Latera asked.

"You've done more than your share," Asherah replied. "As for me, I've been forbidden from the battle, by both your mate and my own." Asherah smiled as she mentioned Finlay, and Latera leaned her head against the queen's shoulder.

"It's a beautiful thing to be bound, isn't it?" Latera asked.

"Yes, it is," Asherah agreed.

Chapter Sixty-Three

The demons were defeated soon after Asgeloth fell, and the hunters spent the night burning corpses. Asgeloth's bones would not reduce to ash, and a company of soldiers was assigned to gather his remains, take them out of sight of the palace and bury them in the deepest hole they could manage. The black smoke that rose from the battlefield aggravated Latera's throat until she could hardly breathe, and irritated her stomach so she couldn't eat. The greasy stench hung low over the field, and Latera's sole relief was sitting on the balcony in Aeolmar's tower room, breathing the only clean air she could find.

Latera remained in the tower for two days before she felt well enough to venture into palace, though Aeolmar would have preferred keeping her sequestered for another moon.

"Truly, I'm fine," Latera repeated. "Come, the queen is waiting." Aeolmar frowned, but let her walk to the stairs. When Latera looked down to the floors below she felt a new wave of dizziness. "Um, Mar...will you carry me?"

Instead of helping her down the stairs, Aeolmar hauled Latera back into the room. "What are you doing?" she demanded.

"Never, not once in six winters have you ever asked me to carry you," Aeolmar said. "You walked on a broken ankle rather than let me carry you. What's really wrong?"

"I'm just a little bothered by the height," Latera insisted. "Please."

Aeolmar's frown deepened, but he relented. As they made their way down the stairs, he said, "Swoon again, and I'll tie you to bed."

"I do not swoon. I kill demons."

"Yes, and then you swoon."

Aeolmar and Latera went to the great hall, where all the hunters and soldiers waited to hear the king and queen speak. Aeolmar took his place at the queen's right, but as Latera came into view a great whooping cheer erupted from the elves, with the companies of Tingu and Thurnda clapping each other on the back and telling anyone who would listen that an elf woman had saved them all.

Once Senan and Leran quieted down their soldiers, Asherah addressed the crowd, first naming those who had not survived. Latera remembered Lura's cold hand and shuddered, and wished her soul a speedy journey to the gods. Asherah and Finlay led the assemblage in a quiet prayer honoring those who had fallen, and thanked the gods for seeing Parthalan to victory.

The queen's voice resonated throughout the hall as she declared that the *con'dehr* would not be reformed, and that Finlay would lead the legion. Asherah then stated that Harek had perpetuated a myth that soldiers were more deserving of respect than hunters. The queen disagreed, proclaiming that the hunters had considerable skill and the king and queen were themselves hunters. Further, she proclaimed that Leran and Senan's men had fought admirable and bravely.

"Therefore," Asherah concluded, "all soldiers will now be trained by hunters, for we already share the same bravery and devotion to Parthalan, and now we will share the same skills!"

Another great cheer roared through the hall, Aeolmar handed Finlay the Prelate's ring. "I want nothing of his against my skin," Aeolmar said.

The king set the ring on a metal plate as he and the queen called fire, and melted the ring into a shimmering pool of gold. Finlay took the plate of liquid metal and poured it over the hearth, and nothing of the former Prelate's treason remained in Teg'urnan.

Afterward, Latera and Aeolmar got their horses and rode across the plain. Aeolmar was overseeing the repairs to the area, and ensuring that the evidence of battle was swiftly hauled away. As they walked among those laboring, they paused to advise Aeolmar of their progress, always bowing their heads and addressing him by his title. They also referred to Latera as First Huntress.

"Why are they calling me that?" Latera asked.

"They know who you are, my Demon-killer," he replied, "and they know that they're alive today because of you." Latera gazed across the plain and took in the adoring faces, the mothers who thanked her for keeping their children safe, and smiled.

"I'm glad to have helped."

After Aeolmar had issued a few orders, and offered much encouragement, they returned to Teg'urnan. When Latera dismounted she felt a new wave of dizziness, that one much stronger than the last, and clutched Enna's mane. She touched her belly and a smile crept across lips, and she considered how she should tell her mate something very important. Since he loved teasing her that was the route she chose.

"Beloved, will you come to Gannera with me?" Latera asked as they walked toward the palace, Aeolmar's arm around her shoulders.

"You want to return so quickly?"

"I promised my family I would. They need to know I survived."

Aeolmar kissed her forehead. "Then of course we will go."

"We should leave as soon as we can."

"I know you miss them, but we should wait. There's much to be done following our victory." Aeolmar detailed training regimens, changes to be made in the *sola*, and so forth. Latera grabbed his hand and put it on her belly; his brow pinched as he wondered why she'd done such a thing, but they continued walking.

"I think we should go now, before I'm too heavy to travel."

Aeolmar stopped, his puzzled expression turning to joy when he understood her wide grin. He dropped to his knees and rained kisses onto Latera's belly.

"Aeolmar," Latera hissed. "Get up! People are staring!"

"Let them. When did you know?"

"When I stood before Asgeloth. I felt her, as if she was helping me defeat him." Latera remembered Elvasla's curse upon Ehkron: *My line will destroy yours. My descendants will bring forth the* deva'shi *and your evil will be gone from the world of my home, and the world of my children.* Latera now understood the crux of the curse; more than one of Elvasla's descendants were needed. Latera's baby had helped her defeat the *mordeth-gall.*

Aeolmar stood and gathered Latera in his arms. "I never thought we'd be blessed with a child so soon."

"A wise man once told me that the children of elves spring forth like seeds from fertile ground. I am, after all, an elf." Latera grinned, and Aeolmar lifted her up and spun her around until she complained that the dizziness returned. Aeolmar he set her down and glowered, the set of his jaw belying the happiness in his eyes.

"I forbid you to hunt while you carry my child," he said. "I cannot have you running around and getting yourself and the baby hurt. And we'll discuss how often you ride Enna."

"You've forbidden me to do many things these past winters," Latera rebuked, not liking that he'd brought her horse into this. "What makes you think I'll start obeying you now?"

"Maybe motherhood will dampen your stubborn streak," he replied. "We can leave for Gannera whenever you're ready. Let's go to Asherah and Finlay, and share our happy news."

"May we keep the child to ourselves for a time?" Latera asked. "I like being the one with a secret, for once."

"Yes, beloved, whatever you wish."

***

They found the king and queen in their chambers, and advised them of their wish to travel to Gannera. Latera had worried that Asherah wouldn't approve of their leaving, but her concerns were unfounded.

"Of course you may go," Asherah said. "Neither of you need seek my approval for anything, not after what you've done for Parthalan."

"Thank you," Latera murmured.

"We'll need to pierce the veil again," Aeolmar said. He placed the spellbook Latera brought from Gannera on Asherah's map table. "Have a look at the spell with me?"

Asherah sat, and flipped through the pages. "In all my time, I've never seen the like," she said, running her fingers across the rough characters. "This book may yet be useful against our foes. Well, what foes still remain," she added. "Do you mind if I keep this here, to study?"

"You may as well." Latera replied. "Mar won't let me touch it."

"He's quite protective," Asherah said, smiling at Aeolmar.

"He is right," said Finlay, his stern voice making Asherah lift her fingers from the page. "Once this travelling spell—or whatever you want to call it—has been worked out I'll have one of the scholars research it. I don't want you touching this evil, either." They stared at each other for long moments, since Asherah was not in the habit of following orders. But Finlay was her mate, and her king, and it was his duty to keep her from harm. At last, Asherah inclined her head toward him, a smile tugging at the corners of her mouth.

"As you wish, my lord."

While Asherah and Aeolmar studied the book, Finlay and Latera sat in the royal garden, both glad to be away from the relic. Finlay's eyes were firmly fixed on the back of Asherah's head while she and Aeolmar read and re-read the spell, his jaw set and brow furrowed.

"She'll be fine," Latera said. "Aeolmar won't let anything hurt her. You know that."

"Are you trusting Asherah to keep Aeolmar safe?" Finlay nodded toward Latera's hands, clenched and white-knuckled in her lap.

Latera straightened her fingers. "Yes, I suppose I am."

In the end, Aeolmar and Asherah determined that while the spells were transcribed in the demon tongue they weren't demonic, and that the book itself was nothing more than a few spells wrapped in a repulsive binding. Aeolmar stripped the wrappings from Latera's dagger's hilt and scrutinized the symbols carved on it, and learned that with it one could simply step from one world to the next.

"When I returned from Gannera I fell from nothing, and landed on the Hill of Torim," Latera said. "It's how I broke my ankle."

"That won't happen again," Aeolmar assured her. "We'll travel the proper way."

"What of the time difference?" Latera pressed.

"Now that we'll be casting the spell as it was meant to be worked, everything should be fine," Aeolmar said.

Latera scowled. "You're lucky I worked the spell as well as I did."

Aeolmar kissed her hair. "You're right. I am."

***

The next day, Aeolmar and Latera stood atop the Hill of Torim, Aeolmar holding a satchel and both with meadow hay wound around their wrists. Latera grasped Aeolmar's hand as he sliced the dagger through the veil, and in the space of one step they were beside the pond in Gannera.

"This is where it began," Latera whispered. "I was in this very spot when Sarfek first took me."

Aeolmar looked about the courtyard, and said, "I'm eager to learn about Gannera. It's much more similar to Parthalan that I'd…"

Latera followed his gaze, which rested on the lone sun overhead. "How can there be no child sun?" Aeolmar asked.

Laughing, Latera pulled him toward the castle. "I can't wait until you see the moon."

They approached the sentinels, and asked to be announced to King Harold. When they reached the hall's entrance, Aeolmar noted how one sentinel blanched.

"Oh, I once took that one's sword," Latera explained. "Ever since, he's thought me evil." Aeolmar looked down at the sentinel and strode past him into the hall, Latera in tow.

King Harold leapt to his feet and rushed forward as Aeolmar stepped in front of Latera. "It's all right," Latera said, then her father embraced her.

"This day is blessed, for now I know my daughter is a hero," Harold whispered as he held Latera. He sent for the queen and the princesses, then turned to Aeolmar.

"Father," Latera began, "this is my mate—my husband—Aeolmar, First Hunter of Parthalan."

"An honor," Aeolmar said, inclining his head. "You have my pledge that I'll care for Latera all my days, ever putting her happiness above my own."

"All I want for her is the same," Harold replied.

"Tell me, how do negotiations fare with the Highlands?" Aeolmar asked.

"Mar," Latera hissed, but her father merely sighed.

"Not well, I'm afraid," Harold replied. Before he continued the rest of Latera's family entered the hall. Her mother embraced her so tightly she worried for the baby, and her sisters flung themselves onto her legs.

"This is my mother, Queen Ladyslava," Latera said to Aeolmar, and he bowed his head and kissed the queen's hand. Latera pried the girls off her to introduce them, but Aeolmar held up a hand and crouched down to their level.

"Let me guess. You are Jannei," he said as she giggled, "you are Elia," who was amazed that he had deduced her identity, "which means that you are Sasha!" he finished, sweeping the little one into his arms amidst a chorus of laughter. Before long, the girls were draped all over him, Sasha's arms around his neck while Elia and Jannei fought for his lap.

"The guards, even your father, seem frightened of Aeolmar, yet your sisters adore him," remarked Ladyslava.

"It's that way wherever we go; people are either enamored with him or deathly afraid," Latera said, then she spied Wren standing—or rather, hiding—at the back of the hall.

"Why are you hiding?" Latera asked.

"I didn't want to interrupt," Wren replied, her eyes downward.

"You're my sister, there is no interruption." Latera hugged her tightly, then led her to Aeolmar. He stood and bowed his head, greeting her with the same respect he had shown the queen.

"Latera has told me of you. It means a great deal to me that you helped her, for I was lost without her," Aeolmar said, as Wren blushed and looked at her feet.

The queen then proclaimed that Aeolmar and Latera had travelled far and needed rest, and they were shown to the apartments Latera had occupied during her year of exile. Aeolmar discovered one oddity after another; the bulky furniture with many drawers mystified him, along with the separate rooms. In Teg'urnan, rooms had few furnishings and were large and open, allowing air and light to flow freely, whereas the multitude of items in these human-designed rooms created many dark corners. This led to his careful evaluation of the small windows, and he declared that humans must enjoy darkness more than the light.

When Aeolmar learned that the hearth was in a separate room from the bed he was convinced that humans must be mad, for did you not need warmth while you slept? Latera reminded him that castles were constructed differently in Gannera, with tiny windows and small rooms easy to keep warm, and that the fire was merely a pleasantry. He continued to explore the rooms, and eventually opened the armoire. He laughed as he touched the filmy gowns within, hardly believing that his mate would wear such things.

"That is what princesses wear, my love," Latera said, as she selected an awful yellow creation. "They have to be lacy, and itchy, and fit for nothing more than sitting quietly and looking pretty."

"Then we should bring them all back to Teg'urnan," he said, wrapping his arms around her, "for you're to do nothing but be beautiful until the child comes."

Despite Aeolmar's many requests for the yellow dress, Latera wore her burgundy velvet gown to the evening meal. When Ladyslava complimented her dress, Latera shared that it was a gift from the first Elvasla's own sister.

Latera insisted that Wren sit beside her; after all, she was the king's daughter too. When they took their seats at the grand table Aeolmar stared at the cutlery, having never seen so many implements in his life.

"You expect me to eat with these tiny devices?" he demanded, eying the many forks.

"Maybe now you'll appreciate all I had to learn in your world," Latera replied, demonstrating their purposes on a piece of bread.

During the meal, they learned that Sasha was as in love with Aeolmar as Latera was. She sat on his lap for the entire evening with her arms twined around his neck, and outright refused to leave him. Her nurses, thoroughly embarrassed by her behavior, tried to pry her away, but Aeolmar insisted that he didn't mind, and that she could stay with him as long as she wanted.

"She reminds me of Enna," Aeolmar said, once they'd shooed the nurses away.

"Did Enna pull your hair too?" Latera asked, swatting Sasha's hand away.

"That, she did."

Latera divided her time between reassuring Wren of her position at the table, and telling Sasha to leave Aeolmar's hair alone. When the platters of meat were passed she hoped the food would distract them both, but as Aeolmar took his portion the smell of it made her grab his hand.

"The meat is stag," Latera said. "They eat them here."

"Do they also eat wolves?" Aeolmar demanded. Ladyslava glanced over, mortified, and ordered the platter back to the kitchens, but not before Sasha detected that her hero was upset.

"No venison?" she asked, and described how it was her favorite, and he should try it because she knew he would love it too, all in her garbled baby talk. Aeolmar looked down at her tiny face, smeared with meat juices, and smiled.

"Since you love it so you may have the entire piece, and I'll eat something else," he said, and she tore the meat to bits, gobbling it as if she hadn't eaten in days. Latera piled Aeolmar's plate with other foods unique to Gannera, apples and hearty dark bread. After he'd eaten his fill, he admitted that not all human food was horrible.

The feast had been intended to last long into the night, but Latera was exhausted and made her apologies shortly after dinner. Aeolmar claimed their child sapped her strength, needing to share her mother's to grow. As they readied themselves for bed Aeolmar remarked that humans even sleep strangely, since he'd never before seen a pillow stuffed with down or sheets atop a mattress.

"But there are blankets, which are the same," Latera said, climbing onto the bed, "and nice thick coverlets, which are the same...and me, who you're quite used to." She knelt in the center of the bed and smiled. "I promise, it's not so bad."

Aeolmar eyed the wooden frame as if it may collapse, and sat next to Latera. "I suppose it's soft enough," he muttered, then he grabbed a pillow. "What is the purpose of these tiny cushions? For your feet?"

"Head, actually."

He snorted. "That will likely lead to a stiff neck, come morning."

"Is there anything you like about the mortal realm?"

"I like you, very much," Aeolmar replied, drawing the combs from Latera's hair. "I'm sure this strange bed will be fine, so long as I'm sharing it with you."

Latera woke before dawn in her human bed, surrounded brown stone walls. She bolted upright, convinced that her return to Parthalan was another cruel fever dream. Aeolmar's eyes snapped open at the sudden movement.

"What's wrong?" he demanded. "Is it the baby?"

"A dream, nothing more," Latera said, wrapping her arms around him. "Nothing is wrong, as long as you're with me."

The next morning Aeolmar and Latera visited the temple of Asherah. After a long and heated debate about her capabilities, Latera let a groom saddle the horses, then they set out at an infuriatingly slow pace.

"Women with child have been riding horses since the dawn of time," Latera said. "A gentle trot has never harmed a baby in the past."

Aeolmar laughed. "If you think I'm overprotective now, wait until the baby's here."

As before, the three priestesses waited outside the temple's entrance. Once Aeolmar and Latera were inside the temple, Alyon led them before the altar. Aeolmar dropped to his knees, pulling Latera down beside him.

"The ancient altar—the one that was destroyed during the Battle for Teg'urnan—was said to have looked like this," Aeolmar murmured. "How is it possible that this is here, so far from Parthalan?"

"Asherah's first priestess, our mother, was once a priestess in Teg'urnan. She brought us the Goddess's Tear, and built the altar you see before you," Alyon replied. Latera touched Aeolmar's hand, and indicated the pendant at her throat.

"How is it that you gave me a Goddess's Tear?" she asked.

"I never knew it had a name," he replied. "I only knew that my father gave it to my mother. She wore it every day. On her deathbed, she told me I was to give it to my mate."

"Rise," Alyon said, "there is more for you to see."

The priestess led them to a vaulted room full of scrolls and tomes, much like Quill's chamber but bursting with light instead of mired in darkness. She stopped before a large relief sculpture, a representation of Asherah on the steps of Teg'urnan. Latera asked Alyon what it meant, but Aeolmar answered.

"It's the Day of Sadness," he said. "When Asherah took the throne it should have been a day of jubilation, since our kind was free again. But Asherah couldn't be happy, for she lost almost everyone who was dear to her; Torim had given her life for Asherah, and then her mate was cut down during the battle. As the people cheered, Asherah fled to the temple and wept." Alyon stepped to the relief and indicated two shining points in Asherah's hand.

"She wept over the destroyed altar, for all that Torim made her promise not to mourn her," Alyon related. "A priestess caught Asherah's tears, so heavy with sadness they became jewels in her hand. Rahlle brought a Tear to this very spot, along with our mother." Alyon led them to a scroll that looked older than time itself, and indicated a passage. It was written in *ahm'ri*, the language so archaic Aeolmar had a difficult time reading it. Nialla stepped forward to translate.

"This scroll tells of the rise of the *deva'shi*," she said. "We have studied it for many, many years, to be sure we would know you once you came to us."

"And how did you know me?" Latera asked, for she hadn't known herself.

"It is written that the mate of the *deva'shi* will place a Tear around her neck, and when it was reunited with the second Tear her destiny would be revealed. When you stood before us, wearing the Tear, we knew you had finally come to us."

Latera looked from the scroll to Aeolmar. "I..."

He laced his fingers with hers. "I know."

They remained with the priestesses that night, telling them of how Asgeloth had been defeated, and that Asherah had taken a king. At length they approached the oracle's chamber.

"What does that word mean?" Latera asked, pointing above the doorway.

"*Nyshanti* means dawn," Aeolmar replied. "There was a goddess called Nyshanti. She was the beloved of the Deliverer, but she's gone now."

"Where did she go?"

Aeolmar shrugged. "That, I do not know."

Aeolmar and Latera knelt before the pool she told him of the vision she'd had, and how Torim had saved all of Parthalan, just as she had almost a millennia ago. The pool was dark on that day, and Asherah's dear friend offered no words of guidance.

The next morning Aeolmar and Latera returned to Gannera castle, and stayed for two days before they returned to Parthalan. Much of their time was spent in the gardens, where Aeolmar and Latera spoke with her parents while Wren chased after the girls. Ladyslava still hadn't accepted Wren as part of her family, but she no longer scowled at the girl. Latera supposed that was progress.

On the morning of the third day the royal family, and Wren, followed Aeolmar and Latera to the pond, where they all picked tufts of meadow hay. The younger girls wailed over Aeolmar leaving, far more concerned with his departure than Latera's.

Latera embraced her parents, and then her younger sisters, promising that they'd return soon. Lastly, she said farewell to Wren, the one she'd miss the most. Wren hugged Latera tightly, tears falling onto her neck.

"Take me with you," Wren begged.

"But this is your home," Latera said. "You've never even seen Parthalan. You don't know if you'd like it there."

"I have nothing here, no family, no real life," she said, staring up at her with wide, pleading eyes. "Please, sister, you're all I have."

"Wren, the king and the girls are your family," Latera said. "You're not alone."

She shook her head. "They're not," she said, her voice little more than a whisper. "It's not their fault, and I don't blame them, but they're not." Latera turned to the king.

"May Wren come with Aeolmar and me to Parthalan?" she asked. Harold regarded his eldest daughter with kind eyes.

"I've failed you as a father," he admitted. "If you think you'll be happier in Parthalan, go with my blessing." Wren smiled, and Harold embraced her for the first since she was a baby. He whispered that he'd always loved her, and swore that there would always be a place for her in his household. Wren nodded to the king, her father, and took her place next to Aeolmar and Latera.

"Hold on to me," Latera said, wrapping her arm around Wren's shoulders, then she grasped Aeolmar's hand and he cut into the veil, and the three of them stepped onto the Hill of Torim. They returned to Teg'urnan and introduced Wren first to Asherah and Finlay, and then to the rest of the hunters. At the end of her first day in Teg'urnan, Wren remarked that she went from no family to one that could fill a palace in the space of a sunrise.

"Parthalan is so wonderful," Wren said. "I never thought I could be this happy."

Latera laced her fingers with Aeolmar's, and smiled. "I know exactly what you mean."

Chapter Sixty-Four

Latera speaks

*A*eolmar and I kept news of the baby to ourselves for as long as we could, not even sharing our happy secret with Alia or Wren. It was fun, being the one with a secret for once.

I'd assumed my belly would remain flat for at least a few fortnights, but soon after our return from Gannera I woke to find a small but discernable bump. With a hint of sadness I abandoned my leather gear for loose tunics, wondering how I'd find clothes to fit my ever-growing form. Aeolmar again suggested that I shouldn't ride Enna, and again I disagreed; after all, Enna was the finest horse in all of Parthalan and would never throw a rider. Still, I walked her more often than we rode, and assuaged my guilt by filling her with enough treats for two horses.

I remember well one day when I'd returned from walking Enna, and happened upon our new king in the corridor. Royalty hadn't changed Finlay one bit; he still did everything himself and reported to the First Hunter on all matters, with Aeolmar reminding him that the king should be the one hearing the reports.

"My lord," I greeted, only because Finlay hated the title as much as Aeolmar always had. He responded by trying to ruffle my hair, and as I evaded him my tunic stretched tight across my body.

"Is there something you want to tell me?" Finlay asked. I said that I had no messages from Aeolmar but everything seemed well within the sola, when Finlay placed his hand on my belly. "You can't hide these things forever, sweetheart."

"I'm hiding nothing. I'm enjoying having this knowledge to myself for a time, something you should be familiar with," I said, and his smile grew into a grin. He patted my belly, and offered me a quiet congratulation.

"You should tell the queen," Finlay advised, since Asherah hated to be the last to know things.

"I've already told the king, he can tell her himself," I said, as I continued on my way. "And make one of your own, so my daughter has someone to play with," I called over my shoulder.

Finlay did indeed tell the queen, along with everyone else in Teg'urnan. Our chamber was soon overrun with people congratulating us, offering advice, and generally just seeing what was going on. Asherah shared that no hunter had ever had a child while they remained with her, and she could hardly remember the last time there were any children in Teg'urnan. Mallia, the matriarch of the healers, also paid us a visit, thrilled to show off her midwifery skills. She continued to visit me every few days, always reciting lists of what I should and shouldn't do, could and couldn't eat, and so forth. After one of her longer visits, Alia looked at me and rolled her eyes.

"She wants you to be nothing but a great lump in your bed for how many more moons?" Alia asked. "How can you bear this?"

"It's not as bad as all that," I said, resting my hand on my belly. Then I felt a flutter; Mara had moved.

Mallia had told me that I'd feel her moving about soon, but I didn't think she'd be so strong, or the sensation so amazing. I gasped at the tiny kicks, which made Aeolmar rush to my side and demand to know what was happening. I put his hand on my belly and asked her to do it again; our little one obliged and kicked with all her might. My mate was as amazed as I, and he proclaimed that Mara may be a huntress like her mother. I turned back to Alia, who wore her own stunned expression, and told her that all of Mallia's restrictions were well worth it just to know that my child was safe.

From that day forward, the hunters treated me as if I was made of glass. They leapt to get things for me, and were constantly asking if I was too warm, too cold, thirsty, hungry... until they almost drove me mad. Bron was fascinated with my growing belly, and often speculated that it would become larger than his. Only Innetha treated me as a something other than an invalid, her sarcasm a welcome respite from all the well-wishers.

Aeolmar was a perfect, overprotective, loving father-to-be. He saw to it that nothing rough touched my skin, nor did any harsh sounds find my ears—except for the sounds of him arguing with Alia and Wren. Each of them insisted they knew what was best for the baby and me. Wren, because had spent a vast amount of time in the royal nursery, while Alia claimed that caring for her siblings had taught her everything there was to know about children. Aeolmar overruled them both, proclaiming that since Mara was his child his word was final. Each fight ended up with him banishing one or both of them from our chamber, bellowing that they were upsetting me. Of course, they were all friends again by the next day.

On the day Mara came, I was pacing back and forth in the southern tower. Aeolmar was up in his old rooms, and I desperately wanted him to come down. I'd just spoken with Mallia, who assured me that my baby would soon be born, and I wanted him to assign away all of his obligations and stay close to me. The matriarch also said that elfin births were quick, so quick she doubted she would have time to reach me if my labors began in my chambers, and wanted me to relocate myself to the healer's ward. When I refused, she had the unmitigated gall to say that she would speak with the queen regarding the matter. After I left the ward, I immediately went to the southern tower, since I needed to get to Aeolmar before she did.

So there I was, glaring up the stairs as I willed him to descend. I considered yelling for him, but that would bring people running from all directions, and I'd certainly be confined with the healers after that. Impatience got the better of me and I started up the stairs, another activity Aeolmar had forbidden. I stopped twice to catch my breath, and hoped that the trip back down would be much more pleasant.

When I entered his chamber Aeolmar rushed to me, reprimanding me for climbing so many stairs on my own. He went on, saying that I could have sent a saffira to fetch him and he would have come immediately. Well, I hadn't thought of that, had I? Aeolmar and I sat on the steps that led to the bed, and he asked what was so urgent that I couldn't wait to tell him.

"I've come from the healers; they want me to begin my lying in soon," I replied, squirming against him. While Mallia had done her usual poking and prodding my back had begun aching, which I thought was my baby's way of saying she'd had enough of these examinations. "She wants me to go to the ward, but I told her I'd rather remain in our chamber." I looked up through my lashes, and gave them a flutter for good measure.

"I'll see to it that our chamber is prepared," Aeolmar said, smoothing my hair. "After you've had a moment to rest, I'll send for Mallia and have her assemble whatever my two loves need."

I loved how he would do anything for me and our baby. I was about to tell him that Mallia had already informed me of what was needed, when a wave of pain unlike anything I'd ever experienced struck me like lightning. I grabbed Aeolmar, clenching his arm so tightly I bruised him.

"Mara's coming," I said, once the pain had passed. Aeolmar rose to bring me to the healer's ward, but another pain struck me and I pulled him back to bed. He held me until it subsided, saying that it was pain for a good reason, soothing me like the baby about to be born.

"I will—" he began as a third pain hit me, and I cried out. "Latera, I'll get someone."

"She's coming now," I panted. "There isn't time!" Mallia had stressed that elfin births were fast, and as swift as he was I didn't think he could return in time.

"You'll need a healer," Aeolmar said. "I don't want anything to happen to you, either of you."

"Aeolmar, we only need you."

And so Mara was born into her father's arms; when she opened her eyes for the first time she saw Aeolmar smiling at her. My baby's cry broke the air in Teg'urnan, and I knew I was where I belonged.

***

The story continues in...
Golem
The Chronicles of Parthalan, Book Four
Available here

.

Keep scrolling for a sneak peek!
Join my mailing list here (and get a free ebook): newsletter signup
If you loved reading about Latera and Aeolmar, please leave a review.
Thank you!

***

Golem, Chapter One
Asherah speaks...

I am the worst ruler Parthalan has ever known.

For nearly a millennia I'd counted as my closest friend and advisor a man who had only used me. Harek, my former Prelate, and his brother, Sarfek, had sought power, were prepared to grab it by any means necessary, and I was nothing more than their witless, willing pawn. They used me as soundly as Sahlgren had used all of us imprisoned in those *dojas*, though the king's betrayal had been a different sort.

Sahlgren hadn't known me. Harek's betrayal, that had been personal.

A good ruler never would have allowed such treachery. A good ruler would have seen Harek and Sarfek for what they were, and a good ruler would have dealt with them long before they made a pact with the *mordeth-gall*.

Lormac would not have allowed such traitors to stand so close to his throne.

Lormac...

Lormac is not here, and—gods!—how I miss him still. I will never be the sort of ruler he was, not if I reign for another thousand years.

When Latera had returned from the mortal realm bearing Sarfek's freshly severed head, every fear I'd ever had was dragged out into the harsh light of day. I'd never felt so unsure, unsafe...unfit. Then I'd severed Harek's head myself on the steps of Teg'urnan, much as I had taken Sahlgren's head so long ago. Again, the people cheered; again, I was drenched in a traitor's blood. Before, it was the blood of he who would have traded us all for his own ends. The second time, it was the blood of one I'd thought was my friend.

After Harek's execution I hid in my chambers for nigh on a sennight, not that I'd meant to. I'd only intended to wash away the blood and gore and then return to my people, but as the bathwater swirled pink my carefully arranged emotions crashed about me, shattering like a fine crystal vase flung against the wall. So I crawled into my bed and hid, wailing away like a child. You would think that after Harek's death—my Prelate's death, he who was guilty of the vilest acts of treason—I would have settled somewhat, but in truth I felt like an utter fool. A sham. Nothing more than a pathetic former slave masquerading as queen, with neither the right nor the ability to lead Parthalan. Gods. I could hardly manage to lead myself around Teg'urnan without incident.

And so I remained, until Finlay coaxed me out of my bed, and then my chamber, and eventually back to the daily rigors of life.

Finlay, Finlay. My man from the desert. If it hadn't been for him I truly would have gone mad in those days after Harek's execution. Finlay convinced me that it wasn't my fault I'd been duped, that both Harek and Sarfek were thoroughly adept in their evilness and I was naught but an innocent. Then Alia told the whole of Teg'urnan that the man who shared the queen's bed was also her bound mate, and against my better judgment I made Finlay my king. That remains the best decision I've ever made.

With my mate-king and my First Hunter to lean upon, the burden of ruling wasn't so taxing anymore. I could breathe again, for with both Finlay and Aeolmar as my staunch supporters I felt that nothing bad could happen. They were there to protect me from myself.

Once all the land knew that the Virgin Queen was virgin no more, talk turned to the inevitable royal child. I demurred, ignored, and outright resisted such talk; then Aeolmar's daughter was born. Mara was a beautiful babe, just like her parents and yet so clearly herself, and her big blue eyes and gurgling laugh swayed my heart a bit. Not much, but a bit. Then Finlay held Mara for the first time, and his summer blue eyes shone like they never had before.

"Would you like one of your own?" I'd asked after an evening spent with Aeolmar, Latera, and a newly-walking Mara.

"A hell beast like that one?" he joked. During the short visit Mara had knocked over several chairs, a table, and while we righted the furniture she ate one of my maps. Ate it like it was a piece of cheese, not a priceless vellum depicting the ancient boundary of Ysr. "I don't know if Teg'urnan could stand it."

"Me, either," I'd agreed, and we left it for a time. Then he started making comments, and after a time I stopped ignoring them, the end result being that when I celebrated my thousandth winter as queen I was heavy with child. We named our son Finlay Torim, his first name honoring his father for if it wasn't for the prodding of my mate I never would have attempted to bring another being into this world. Even if I did, I never would have made a wreck like me responsible for his well-being.

My child's second name honored my first love, she who died for me, and then saved me again from beyond the veil. Gods, even those in the afterlife understood that I could barely manage.

Always seeking to do me one better, our First Huntress bore her second daughter on the same day I bore Finlay. Latera had always made motherhood seem effortless; whereas I'd been clumsy as an ox and twice as large while I'd carried my son, Latera remained the petite, graceful being she'd always been. She'd even borne her children with no one present save Aeolmar, unlike me who had been fussed over by an army of healers doing all manner of undignified things to me.

It wasn't just that Latera excelled at motherhood. The little elf had accomplished everything she'd ever set out to do with hardly a bead of sweat upon her brow. She'd killed the mordeth-gall, found and eliminated those responsible for kidnapping her from the mortal world, and reduced the fortress around Aeolmar's heart to so much rubble. I didn't know which of her feats I was most jealous of.

Before you could blink Latera was heavy with her third babe, though she didn't breeze through that event as she had with the rest.

The birth had been difficult for our life-bearer, and Aeolmar had been beside himself with worry. We all were, really; if Latera didn't survive, I feared for Aeolmar's sanity. I feared for my own sanity, were Aeolmar's stalwart shoulder taken from me.

I reached for my tea, bitter and hot, and drank deeply. It made my eyes heavy and soft, my limbs warm and liquid. I lay back against the cushions, and hoped I'd find myself in my usual calm, darkened dreamscape. It was nice there, no hard decisions or past regrets. Soft. Warm. Nice.

Gods. I hope my son grows quickly, for Parthalan may need him soon.

***

Continue the story here.

About The Author

Jennifer Allis Provost is a native New Englander who lives in a sprawling colonial along with her beautiful and precocious twins, a dog that thinks she's a kangaroo, a parrot, a junkyard cat, and a wonderful husband who never forgets to buy ice cream. As a child, she read anything and everything she could get her hands on, including a set of encyclopedias, but fantasy was always her favorite. She spends her days drinking vast amounts of coffee, arguing with her computer, and avoiding any and all domestic behavior.

Find Jenn on the web here: http://authorjenniferallisprovost.com/

For up to the minute sale notifications, follow her on Bookbub here: - https://www.bookbub.com/profile/jennifer-allis-provost

For exclusive content, follow her on Patreon: https://www.patreon.com/jenniferallisprovost/

Friend her on Facebook: http://www.facebook.com/jennallis

Follow her on Twitter: @parthalan

Happy reading!

Also By Jennifer Allis Provost

The Chronicles of Parthalan, a six volume epic fantasy (and one short story collection)

Heir to the Sun

The Virgin Queen

Rise of the Deva'shi

Pieces of Parthalan: Six All-New Stories From The Land Of Parthalan

Golem

Elfsong

Sunfall

The Copper Legacy, a four book urban fantasy:

Copper Girl

Copper Ravens

Copper Veins

Copper Princess

A duology based in the Copper world:

Redemption

Salvation

Poison Garden, an urban fantasy filled with seers, witches, and one seriously hot detective:

Belladonna

Oleander

Bleeding Hearts

Thornapple

Gallowglass, an urban fantasy set in Scotland and New York:

Gallowglass

Walker

Homecoming

Winter's Queen, an urban fantasy set in Scotland and Elphame:

Touch of Frost

Giant's Daughter

Elphame's Queen

Changes, a contemporary romance:

Changing Teams

Changing Scenes

Changing Fate

Changing Dates